'Vividly passionate, ... reminiscent of ... ...lish' **Daisy Buchanan**

...ansporting narrative that's as much about per-
...ge and parenthood as it is about sexual identity'
library

...od – an intense and unflinching exposé of desire
Elizabeth Buchan

writer of enormous intelligence and sensitivity.
...onate with so many women who feel lost in the
...' **Mary Loudon**

...kind of slow burn and ever-mounting tension. A
...ophisticated novel that pulls a big emotional punch.
...ommended' **Louisa Treger**

...poses unwavering questions about choice and honesty,
...how sacrifice can impair an entire existence and that
...will return, always' **Catherine McNamara**

...enjoyable. Packs in a huge number of life choices
...changes in a very elegant way' **Ella Berthoud, The**
...herapist

...e are points of menace, danger and excitement – it's
...ng that like a fine perfume, Costello manages to hit all of
...different notes' **Donna Freed, Radio Gorgeous**

...orious gift ... a cracking good story' **Georgina Godwin,**
...ocle Radio

'It's great to see a diverse character base reflected through themes of female desire, queer love, the role ageing plays in identity and the importance of friendship and human connection' **Emily Jarman, Boogaloo Radio**

'Vivid storytelling from an accomplished writer that will transport you to France' **Trip Fiction**

The author's portrayal of Paris and the French way of life really won me over. The sounds, the smells, the people are exquisite and quite perfect. This is a novel of passion lived and then lost. Candidly, painfully beautiful in places' **Anne Cater, Random Things through my Letterbox**

'Scent is a classy and intriguing story – the ideal book for Francophiles and readers who like to delve deep into the relationships that we make throughout our lives' **Nicola Smith, NB Magazine**

'Filled with olfactory observations and passion, the book is a sensual treat' **GScene**

'This was a highly enjoyable novel' **The Bumbling Blogger**

'A beautifully written book with delicate depictions of character, place, and time. I was enchanted by it. An intense story of love lost and love wanted. Clémentine is so believable'
Jon Wilkins, Everybody's Reading

'This is fiction that lifts the lid on love and relationships with a deft sense of description and place – as close as you might get to France this year' **Living Magazine**

Also by Isabel Costello

Paris Mon Amour

SCENT

Isabel Costello

MUSWELL
PRESS

First published by Muswell Press in 2021
This edition published 2022

Typeset in Bembo by M Rules
Copyright © Isabel Costello 2021

Isabel Costello has asserted her right to be identified as the author of this
work in accordance with under the Copyright, Designs and Patents Act, 1988

Printed and bound by CPI Group (UK) Ltd, Croydon CR0 4YY

A CIP catalogue record for this book is available from the British Library

ISBN: 9781739966027
eISBN 9781916207776

Muswell Press
London N6 5HQ
www.muswell-press.co.uk

For Kristin

Car le plus lourd fardeau, c'est d'exister sans vivre.

For the greatest burden is to exist without living.

Victor Hugo

Chapter 1

At times like this, I take comfort in the fact I've never loved Édouard. I knew it all along, but have never been one to dwell on uncomfortable truths. Frankly, I don't know what I've been thinking for most of our time together. More than half my life. My husband chose me like an item on display, fresh but far from innocent. In fairness, I was willing. I'd seen where love could lead and I never wanted to go there again.

When today's magazine interview comes out, thousands of people will see inside our home and my perfume shop. They'll look at my clothes, the pictures on our walls, maybe squint at the spines of our books. They'll think they know about my life, and they'll be wrong.

I keep fiddling with my hair, debating whether to wear it up or down for the photos. For once Édouard is looking at me. Before I can even attempt to decode his expression, he says, 'You know, in your line of work certain things could be seen as an investment.' Our eyes meet and part in the mirror but I don't release my grip; if anything, it tightens. Without intending to, I've been pulling my hair so hard that my face has lost most of its lines, my eyes wide and bright against the unfamiliar smoothness of my skin. It takes years off, just like that. If Édouard had never found me beautiful we wouldn't be here, but what can you do?

Not what he was suggesting, that much I know.

His tone offends me more than anything: studiously uncritical, bordering on sympathetic, as if he thinks I'm seeking his blessing. And so fucking euphemistic – if we're talking about taking a knife to my face, he should have the balls to say so.

I don't react but the laser-like quality of the moment lets me see myself, the two of us, as never before. It's been ten years since I looked like that, five since Édouard and I stopped touching beyond the minimum expected by friends and relatives. Which is to say, five years since my husband stopped touching me. I'm not looking for a consolation prize, but I am looking for something. More than this.

With an exaggerated gesture, I let my hair fall with a rush of relief as the blood returns to my cheeks. Édouard starts to make encouraging noises but it's like trying to blow up a tyre he's just slashed. He can think I'm doing this interview for him, if he wants. I've never made much effort with publicity and wouldn't be now if Delphine hadn't been so persistent, mentioning the idea every time our paths crossed. It's all the same to me that she's just married a powerful man Édouard wants in his corner with a crisis looming, but I am impressed by her determination to be her own woman, the only way to embark on marriage to a man with big ambitions. It took me a while to figure that out, but the way they look at each other tells me they have more than time on their side. Every day in Paris carries proof that love exists, in the air, on the streets and behind closed doors. Just not mine.

I feel the lack of it so badly I almost cry out.

&

Édouard can't be held entirely responsible for my flat mood and poor performance, my self-conscious smiles for the camera. Delphine is frustrated and mystified – this is my passion, after all. She shares her husband's business acumen, persevering with questions to which I give no convincing replies. I suppose it is surprising that I only have one shop, haven't sought to expand Arôme de Clémentine or to capitalise on the success of my perfumes in awards and beauty columns. She asks why I don't make a virtue of my Provençal heritage and all I can say is that enough brands are working that angle without me joining in – not that I would register on my competitors' radar. Despite being trained by a professional nose, I have no official credentials, no diploma or corporate CV.

That would have made a charming anecdote: *A year with my aunt in Grasse.*

But it's not memories of beautiful landscapes and intoxicating scents that suddenly assault me; it's the events that led to being disowned by my wreck of a mother, to refusing food and lying in a darkened room for so long that Tante Yvette had to flood it with patchouli to get me out.

'Tell me something personal about yourself, something surprising,' Delphine asks, unaware how close she's already come to both.

I am forty-six and the mother of two grown-up children. That's not a story.

I'm married to a man who found me on a perfume counter in a department store on boulevard Haussmann. That's not a story I can tell.

My job has saved me over and over but only words can rescue me now. Delphine looks hopeful. 'Perfume is a way of expressing emotion,' I blurt out. Sometimes it feels like the only way.

'*Le parfum, c'est l'émotion,*' she paraphrases, all smiles. 'That would make the perfect title for the piece. Hold it!' She raises her hand. The photographer's packing his kit away but she asks for a last shot, the only one with no direction or warning the shutter was about to fire. It would either be the best or the worst of the lot.

'No, you can't use that line. It's really banal and unoriginal.' If I'd known she wanted clichés, we could have been done an hour ago.

'*Pas du tout!* It's touching, intriguing. It hints at everything you're not saying.'

But I'll tell my story sooner or later. Perhaps before I know how it ends.

Chapter 2

Four months later

It's said that nobody knows what goes on in a marriage except for the people in it, but even then, not always. Now it was just Édouard and me, it felt as if there must have been some mistake for us to still be together. In truth, there had been many. I found myself speculating about how our marriage had lasted, the way nosy acquaintances might and probably did, and in the absence of answers I moved quickly onto how and when it would end. What the rest of my life would be like if I were to spend it *alone* alone.

Whenever my friend Martha asked, 'What is it you actually want?' I treated it like an outlandish or rhetorical question. My desires were muffled voices in a corridor, too distant to make out. I hadn't dared to try. I was lucky to have my children, my health, a job I loved. A very comfortable life, for which some luxuries had to be sacrificed. That's only fair. I'm never going to be one of those women who think they can have it all.

Darkness and daylight were fighting over the morning sky.

5

At the end of the month, the clocks would change to winter-time, the days get even shorter, but still it would just be me and Édouard until one of us died or simply couldn't stand it any longer. I was tired of waiting for it to be him.

I was in a dark place, and a silent one. Our apartment had never been home to the dense, oppressive quiet that filled every room since Bastien left. It tormented me to think how I used to moan about the racket from whatever he was watching on YouTube: extreme mountain biking in Utah, weird conspiracy theories, rap hits with the misogynistic lyrics I can't stand and he claims not to notice.

When other mothers equated their sense of loss when the kids had gone with bereavement, I used to think they were being dramatic or a little too keen to emphasise their devotion. That is, until it happened to me. Some days everything feels like grief. In reality Bastien was alive and well, and still in Paris, but that was slim comfort given the circumstances of his departure.

Édouard was very late leaving for work. Normally he was gone before I got up and the time before I set off to open the shop used to be my favourite part of the day, until all inspiration deserted me: a relaxed breakfast followed by some playful experimenting with ingredients at the long table that doubles as my workbench. Édouard came in, greeting me from the far end of the kitchen – no need to keep up appearances when we were alone – and adopted his 'top of the agenda' expression. The way we spoke to each other reminded me of the 1960s businessman and his secretary, à la *Mad Men*: diary co-ordination, hot coffee and cold civility. The difference was that Édouard didn't want to screw me, but the feeling was mutual.

A siren started blaring in the street below and Édouard opened the big glass doors, the volume briefly doubling until it faded as the police car rounded the corner onto boulevard Raspail. 'Nothing to see,' he said, pausing to take in the view anyway. We chose this place because of its unusual balcony running the entire width of our corner apartment, separate spans for the large kitchen – (*heart of the home*, if it had one), the living room and the *chambre parentale* where Édouard slept alone. I'd been ignoring his occasional comments about moving for years, knowing it would never happen unless I took on the project. For all its advantages, this property no longer corresponded to Édouard's vision of what he'd made of himself. The first time he mentioned wanting higher ceilings I laughed out loud.

The balcony had always been my territory and I wouldn't surrender it lightly. The Virginia creeper woven into the railings was currently at its blazing best, scarlet tendrils admired by passers-by and customers of the café opposite. Like my work, that plant had been a cause of inordinate satisfaction over the years, the kind that makes other things bearable. Whenever I wanted to sample a new ingredient or blend, it was a ritual to bring it out here. Liking it was not essential, but if it didn't excite me, make me long to use it, that was fatal. No doubt there was purer air in Paris, but six floors up we were safe from the taint of exhaust fumes and dustbins.

I kept scrutinising Édouard as though I'd missed the vital detail that would make us make sense. He looked tired and seemed to be inhaling the espresso he'd made, although his smell detection was so poor you could light a bonfire and he'd barely notice. He was still handsome, dark-blond hair now greying at the temples, those cheekbones giving him a look of breeding he doesn't possess. Not that I can talk. We are both country people but whereas Édouard hails from generations of landowners in the Jura, his family farming pedigree sheep, I'm a genuine *plouc* from what used to be a rural backwater down south, now a paradise foreigners flock to, with price tags to match.

Lately I suspected that Édouard was getting style tips from another woman. His deep pink shirt was a gorgeous colour, but he was neither masculine nor feminine enough to carry it off. More than a touch of irony there, given his objections to Bastien's fashion sense.

'You haven't forgotten it's Gabrielle's birthday party tonight?'

Édouard groaned. 'Tell me it's not.'

I shrugged, unable to oblige and not particularly inclined, given all the functions he dragged me to when it would look bad to go alone. He happily attended any number of work dinners and receptions, but social events require painful effort of a man who lives to do business. I dreaded the events we attended as a couple far more than the evenings he didn't come home or dashed in and out. I did not break the unspoken code of no questions. Since our daughter Apolline had also left home for good, I'd taken to sleeping in her old room. It wasn't the noise of Édouard's late night returns that bothered me, but the smell of sex and cheap perfume, the same one worn by two different women he'd frequented over the years. It's beyond most people, but I couldn't just smell *it*, I could smell *them*.

'Well, today is Gabrielle's actual birthday.' It hadn't been mentioned, but everyone knew it was her fiftieth. Édouard had a cheek complaining – she's the wife of his colleague, not mine. But I like Gabrielle. She's charming, intellectual, high-powered, lots of things I'm not. She's always been very kind to me.

'You have to admire her for putting a brave face on it,' Édouard said. 'What is it, a dinner?'

'No, a *cocktail*,' I handed him the invitation and he relaxed, knowing he wouldn't be stuck next to the same boring people all evening, although with this kind of party there's always too much to drink and not enough canapés (and if there were, a woman can't be seen to gorge). This formula spells danger for me. Words had been spoken, and I doubted very much that it was just within our walls.

'Do we know who's going to be there? Kerglaven still isn't returning my calls.' Keeping his cool mattered to Édouard but the anxiety in his voice was palpable. Normally one to thrive on a challenge, this time he was facing a problem that wouldn't go away. Just over fifty, when he felt respect was his due, it was the last thing he was going to get unless he found a way to turn things around, and fast. People like Kerglaven made a killing out of corporate cock-ups. There's a term for it: *disaster management* or *crisis resolution*, something like that. It wouldn't surprise me if he was biding his time to extract a higher fee, but I kept that theory to myself.

'And after I did that interview with his wife!'

Édouard was too busy agreeing to pick up on my sarcasm. My phone beeped and I ignored it. 'I don't know if the Kerglavens are going,' I told him. For a number of reasons, I really hoped not. It was tempting not to turn up, to hide in the little room at the back of my shop or go for a long aimless walk along the banks of the Seine, a favourite escape from obligations I'd rather avoid. Of late this included coming home from work. At least mine was the kind of misery that keeps you fit.

It was so rare for Édouard to try to read me that I found it unnerving. His face contorted with the shape of words he couldn't say. Maybe he was feeling guilty about the mouthful he gave me last week for *drinking and dancing at a party*, leaving in tears, with an audience far more mortifying for him than for me. At the time I didn't give a shit what anyone thought.

'Clémentine, I realise—' He faltered immediately and I felt

9

my whole body stiffen with trepidation. We didn't do this – talk. The complaint women often make about men was just as true of me. I said too little, too late, the wrong thing. I was only beginning to realise the cost of not speaking my mind more often. Doing something starts with saying something, if only to yourself. *What do you want, Clémentine?*

We exchanged desperate looks. God, I felt sorry for us.

'It can't be easy for you – for any mother – when the children leave.'

But it's never just the kids leaving; it's what's left. Our attention diverted to the sound of a key in the lock. We both knew it wasn't Esmeralda's day. The door slamming was a giveaway. 'I couldn't wait any longer – I'm desperate for a piss.'

When Bastien walked in, drying his hands on his jeans, he and his father came face to face for the first time in nearly two months. It was as if the air around us had been stretched and released with an almighty snap. At least Bastien wasn't wearing eyeliner this early in the day. They both turned to me, glaring, and I threw my hands up. When have I ever known what to do about it? By the time Bastien had kissed me hello, Édouard had slipped out without a word.

'Why was he still here?'

'*Chéri*, your father lives here. He can come and go as he pleases.' This raised a vicious little snort, which I did not appreciate. It's never comfortable to realise your children have any awareness of your private life, and it's worse when they're grown up and think they understand.

'But I messaged to say I was coming round. My class was cancelled.'

'We were in the middle of a conversation.' I ignored Bastien's sardonic eyebrow raise. 'What was I supposed to do, order him out? You two need to bury the hatchet. You made

10

the right decision moving out, but that should help you see things differently.'

'It was the *only* decision.'

And I've decided not to do the *I miss you so much* routine, limiting myself to two one-line messages a week, and those usually go unanswered. Bastien had never witnessed my sadness over him leaving, unless he was watching me return to the car after the last box had been unloaded, and I doubt that. As Martha kept reminding me, in many places it's the norm for children to move out for college. But this was Paris, and we were us, and that was no consolation.

And now I finally had my son in front of me, we were talking about Édouard, *putain*.

'Surely it should be easier if you only see each other now and then?' I had to tread carefully, given the encounter that had just taken place. 'Is this how you want it between you for the rest of your life?'

With the balcony doors still open, we heard the sickening impact of metal on metal, followed by a man and a woman hurling insults at each other. What a start to the day. At the same time, I envied these strangers the overtness of their rage, their ability to let it all out.

'Do you talk to him about this?' Bastien never referred to Édouard as his father if he could avoid it. 'Or is it just me you expect to *behave like an adult?*'

They say that when you long for change, it's best to start with something small and achievable. I couldn't think of anything small.

But I'd had enough of being their referee. That would have to do.

Chapter 3

Édouard was not in a party mood. He took off the too-bright shirt while still in the hallway, announcing that he wouldn't be wearing it again. I could imagine what might have been said – his deputy, Corentin, was after his job at only thirty-five. It was a shame that Édouard hadn't noticed the peak of his career until he saw it from the far side. I heard the worry every time he spoke of another contemporary being eased into a consultancy role. Two years on a fat retainer doing next to nothing before the real doing nothing and being nobody kicked in.

We made it to the Delacombes' home overlooking the Arènes de Lutèce, where the original Parisians used to tear each other apart. Gabrielle was radiant, which we all told her, and didn't look fifty, which we didn't. The 'no gifts' request had resulted in the usual pile of artfully wrapped packages with coiled ribbon or simple straw bows.

Jacques and Gabrielle's elegant double salon was already so crowded that it was hard to hear. The combination of velvet curtains, central heating and overdressed bodies made for an uncomfortable temperature. Before I could turn to

Édouard to comment – there was a certain complicity in the fact neither of us wanted to be here – he left me standing by myself with a fixed smile. A fug of warring fragrances splashed on newly shaven jaws, dabbed on wrists and sprayed over décolletages, not to mention those who'd forgotten the deodorant, was triggering one of my protest headaches.

So many people I knew, and not one of them knew me.

Just as I decided nobody would care if I left, a smiling woman accosted me, saying we'd met before. I had only a vague recollection but it was soon apparent that the conversation required no more than the occasional smile or nod. Thanks to this chatty soul, I was no longer conspicuous but free to have a drink – that would help – and a good look over her shoulder. It would be the height of bad manners if she noticed, but there wasn't much chance of that.

The guests were an attractive bunch. Mostly in their forties and fifties but wearing their increasing awareness of mortality lightly, they were happy to have made it or to have attached themselves to someone who had. Eased by family connections, the burden of expectation had passed to a new generation, showing the promise that comes with a safety net attached. It's not that they weren't good people; as with any gathering, most probably were and a few definitely weren't. It was still my instinct to say *they*. Édouard and I had parachuted into this circle but our children were born inside it. When I was young I used to look on affluent Parisians as a different species, and in a way not much had changed. When Martha wasn't on the quest for my deepest desires there was something else she liked to come out with: *Be careful what you wish for.*

Did I have an opinion on the relative merits of the Pyrenees and the Alps for a Christmas skiing trip? I did not. 'You should talk to my husband,' I said, flinging a hand in the direction of practically everyone present. 'He loves skiing, although as he grew up near the Swiss border he's bound to say the Alps.' Realising that topic was a non-starter, the woman – could it be Nathalie? There are so many Nathalies – gave me a warm smile. Seeing her take a deep breath and resolve to try again made me want to hug her in solidarity but after the looks several guests gave me when I arrived, someone else could provide the entertainment tonight.

'Aren't they an adorable couple?' she said of our hosts, and they did seem very happy together. Jacques proposed a toast to Gabrielle, a senior curator at the Louvre, although he made it sound as if she'd done nothing but look divine, cook extraordinary dinners and raise their son and two daughters, all of them present, exquisite and desperate to avoid talking to their parents' friends. Being well brought up, they concealed this when I eventually disentangled myself from Nathalie (I was right) after the speeches. The elder daughter was in the same year as Apolline at high school but they hadn't kept in touch. Giving an update felt like the one moment I belonged. 'She did a three-month internship with a law firm in Sydney and now she's travelling with her boyfriend. They're on their way to Brisbane.'

'Is he Australian?' asked Mireille, the youngest.

'No, Apolline and Mathieu met at law school here. We got to know him well.'

Our children have always been opposites. With Apolline, moving out was less of an issue than when she moved back in to complete her master's. This entailed bumping into her lover walking around in his underwear. The reminder that they *were* the only lovers in the household. The fact that Bastien couldn't stop ogling his sister's boyfriend.

'And your son?' the eldest Delacombe enquired. He was at least twenty-five and didn't know Bastien, and yet the facetious note was unmistakeable. Before I could reply, some-one ambushed me from behind, grabbing me so hard around the waist that I nearly dropped my glass.

'There you are, my darling Clementine!' Several guests exchanged disapproving glances, but I had never been so pleased to see Martha. Around us everyone returned to their gossip, spared from having to listen to her. For someone whose French was grammatically close to perfect, her accent was painful. We got to huddle together in our own little zone. I had studied English but couldn't speak it very well until I met her. We liked to joke that I've *gotten pretty good*.

'Thank God you made it. Couldn't you have let me know you were coming? I've spent the whole day on edge.'

'Oh, Clemen-tyne!' She really does pronounce it like the song. 'You spend your life on edge. Have another of these and relax.' Accepting the second glass that was supposed to be my limit half an hour into a long evening wasn't a great idea but Édouard was too far away to notice, leaning against a baby grand piano. Even at this distance I could see the laughter at an anecdote didn't reach his eyes.

'Édouard was hoping to bump into Olivier Kerglaven, but there's no sign of them. I haven't seen Delphine since we did the interview, but that can't last for ever.'

'That was months ago. Is it ever coming out?

I would have been delighted if it had been rejected or put on hold. 'She texted me yesterday to say the December issue will be on sale next week. I'd forgotten they come out so far in advance.' I clutched my face and my hand came away with lipstick on it.

'Come on, you can't have messed it up that badly. Think what your rivals would do for the exposure!'

There was a lull in the conversation next to us. An extremely good-looking man was smiling at me, letting his eyes linger. If he was hoping for a response in kind, he'd be disappointed. His incredible resemblance to Ludo sent a chill through my body and I took advantage of some movement in the crowd to turn away; not Ludo as he looked in our twenties, but how he might look now. Either way, he was the last person I wanted to see and anyone who reminded me of him a close second. I tried to calm myself with the certainty that it wasn't him – this man was not as tall – but the possibility that we could ever meet again had simply never occurred to me and that in itself felt unbelievable. My *personal and surprising* story didn't belong on the pages of any magazine. There was me, Ludo, and the girl we'd both loved. I didn't know what had happened to any of us.

Martha tugged my sleeve. 'Don't you think? Are you even listening?'

'Of course, you're right.'

'Damn right I'm right! You deserve a lucky break.' This is what I love about Martha: her belief that the world works like that. The opposite of my mother's *Everyone is out to get you*. Growing up with that in my ears it wasn't surprising that I was constantly reprimanded at school for being in my own little world. Or that I've never known where to look for love.

'Thanks, Martha. Sorry, I'm not myself this evening. I'd better go before I do something I'll regret.'

Martha didn't try to dissuade me, after the last time. She'd decided our sexy neighbour was eyeing her up. 'That article is going to change everything,' she said, making off in his direction. 'Just you wait and see.'

Chapter 4

Provence, 1992

We knew now that there would be no compensation for Maman's broken arm, no sick pay from the agency. They said it was her own fault for slipping on a wet floor and if I hadn't stepped in, she'd have lost the job altogether. 'All those years doing rich people's dirty work and that's the thanks I get.' The thanks she got was having the work and being paid, but I knew better than to point that out. Her accident was the only reason I'd come home for the summer, but the job wasn't all bad. I loved the winding roads and feeling the heat in my bones despite the rush of wind across the car with the windows open. Next to me in a leather satchel were the day's keys, labelled only with numbers, which I had memorised to keep my brain alive. As a child, I'd spent hours in some of these places, drawing, reading and writing stories while Maman dusted and mopped and tutted. I wasn't allowed in the swimming pools, but sometimes I dangled my feet in and hardly ever got caught.

As the houses were set in large gardens or the middle of

nowhere there was even less chance of getting caught now, but the possibility gave me a thrill. The thought of my reward sustained me from the moment I decided on my dip of the day, depending which pools were clean and uncovered and whether I felt like swimming or lounging around to cool off. I had to remember a towel but rarely bothered with a bikini top, lying back with a Coke watching the beads of water on my top half evaporate in the sun. Eyes shut, I imagined someone else's hands sweeping over my skin.

That morning I'd stopped for petrol on the main road and was looking at a map to locate a new place on my circuit. On realising the extra driving was going to add half an hour to my day I gave the nearest tyre a feeble kick and winced at the pain in my toe.

'Lost so close to home?' Ludovic Bellechasse sounded just as I'd have imagined and looked even better – I'd only ever seen him at a distance. *Keep away from that lot* had been a surprisingly easy order to follow, considering the people in question were our neighbours. As if the Bellechasses with their fancy winery would want anything to do with the single mother and her brat scraping by next door.

But Ludo introduced himself as if we had no history and I did the same. I could hold my own with the people I'd been brought up to despise, but with the Bellechasses it was personal, a longstanding grudge over the purchase of some land from my grandfather. To me it sounded like he'd been a fool for not negotiating a better price, but according to my mother he'd been had by wealthy opportunists out to exploit an honest *paysan*. Sometimes, growing up, I'd wondered if there was more to it, but it could be that with her tendency to harbour grudges Maman had blown the whole thing out of proportion.

'Never seen you driving,' Ludo said.

'I got my licence this year. I'm at uni in Marseille but I got a job in a hotel bar to pay for it.' My babbling came across as *Aren't I clever?* and *Poor me, I'm so broke*, but Ludo nodded approvingly. I looked at him, knowing it might be my only chance, and tried to ignore the churning of my stomach and the tremor in my legs. Ludo must have been used to having this effect on women, but he wasn't living up to his reputation as a player. The reason was obvious. He didn't fancy me and that was just as well.

'Strange, don't you think, that we've never got to know each other?'

Not really, considering he was several years older than me and the bad feeling between our families, unless it was purely on my mother's side. When I didn't answer, Ludo tilted his head to catch my eye and said I looked sad. Funny thing is, it made me feel better. 'You know, just because our parents don't get on, it doesn't mean . . .'

So he did know.

'It's not passed down the generations,' I interrupted, unsure if that sounded deep, amusing or just ridiculous. 'Not like your estate.'

Ludo laughed. 'I understand if you don't think so, but there are drawbacks, especially as the only son. It's just as well I am interested in wine, because I don't have much choice.'

A car had pulled up behind Ludo's pickup and the driver was getting impatient. We rushed in to pay, and as I stood next to him at the cash desk, his sweat hit my nostrils along with the sweet mustiness of ripening grapes that I'd grown up with. Underneath it was the hot, complicated smell of skin and breath and hair. I'd had lovers, if you could call them that, and had recently broken up with my college boyfriend. But I'd never felt physical attraction like this and it depressed me that it had to be for him.

The motorist had moved to another pump. Ludo put a hand on my arm, seeing my hurry to get away. 'And you, who are free to decide, what are you doing this summer?'

He would pity me. I could be making better money at my hotel job, and what's more, keeping it for myself. But when I explained about my mother's injury and the holiday homes, he said it sounded interesting.

This pissed me off.

I guess he hadn't scrubbed a lot of floors or cleaned so many windows his elbow still hurt the next morning, although he did have workman's hands, not the smooth, pale ones that look like they belong to a woman.

To call it boring would show a lack of imagination, and that was one problem I didn't have. 'It gets lonely,' I said. That's all.

Chapter 5

I swiped my sunglasses off the hall table, indulging a new obsession with the mood-enhancing power of good weather and my resolution to register the slightest thing that was beautiful or uplifting. Lately I'd been wearing dark glasses of a different kind, and the relief of feeling even passably okay, the slightest sign that this bad patch wouldn't last for ever, was overwhelming.

A brown-and-white dog and a little girl were hiding from her *maman* in the old wooden park-keeper's cabin inside the nearest gate to the Jardin du Luxembourg. Visible from our apartment, it was the green backdrop to our family life. I remembered pretending to search all over, wondering out loud, 'Where can they be?', the children's muffled giggles. The little girl raised her finger to her lips and I copied, smiling first at her and, as I continued on my way, at the young mother, who was pregnant. She would look back on this one day.

Less endearing was the narrow escape from having my feet doused by a street-cleaning truck, which veered at me on a corner. It wasn't hard to guess what the bright green brushes had been blasting off the pavement. I approached my shop from the opposite side of the street. It had taken this long to be convinced by the radical makeover I'd rushed into for the magazine shoot, the designer relishing my bizarre instruction that it shouldn't look like a shop window. The result was stark and exposing, with oversized perfume bottles suspended in mid-air. Passers-by could see in, I could see out, and the space seemed much lighter and larger. This industry makes everything too complicated, given that what we're selling is, in a way, so basic. Pleasure, transformation, desire. Wants dressed as needs, memories softened by illusion, fantasy made possibility. People want to feel different, to be transported. I get that. I always have.

'*Voici, madame,*' said the postman, handing me the mail without stopping the trolley. By the time I made it into the shop I was trembling and sweating. Delphine had said next week, but here it was, Marion Cotillard on the cover, my name next to her ear:

INTERVIEW EXCLUSIVE
Clémentine Dujardin
Le parfum, c'est l'émotion

It took several deep breaths to keep myself from throwing up. The magazine spent the next half hour face down on the counter as I paced around, forgetting to open the shop, then worrying about business being slow. Delphine texted to ask what I thought of her biggest commission so far. I left the door locked and made coffee, drinking it in the kitchen alcove because I don't like the aroma loose in my workshop or out front.

The caffeine did nothing for the shakes but it powered me up to slit the packaging delicately along one end and let the magazine slide out. The double-page spread was stunning and Delphine's write-up beyond anything I could have hoped for. She described the *niche brand* I'd built from nothing with the *skill and vision of a fragrance maestra*.

Tears slid down my face. Unexpected joy at the outcome. Unexpected joy that I could feel it. Delphine presented my lack of expansion as a conscious decision to *keep things on an intimate scale (although all products are available to order online)*. I couldn't have put it better if I did know anything about PR.

Martha was going to love her *told you so* moment.

I looked good in the only close-up, taken in front of my newest fragrance, which is to say the latest to make it out of development. Behind every marketable perfume is a trail of the blends it took to get there. I honed my skills for ten years with my aunt's guidance before my first commissions, fifteen before opening the shop. The true masters of perfumery were forever pushing the boundaries of wearable scent, synthetic molecules capable of reproducing the smell of almost anything, but my customers don't want to walk around Paris or their hometowns in a cloud of penicillin mould or wet cement.

Still glowing with pride in my *sophisticated and elusive* creations and *intuitive approach*, I registered why the last-minute photograph was so flattering. It wasn't the great job done by my hairdresser or the magazine's make-up artist, nor was it my genuine smile of relief that the ordeal was almost over. The image had been airbrushed, obliterating sun damage around my eyes, softening the lines between my nose and mouth. It made me look vastly more attractive and not much like myself. If I'd known my morale boost wasn't going to last five minutes, I'd have made more of it. Since Édouard's comment on the morning of the interview, I kept seeing what he saw. It was shallow to care, but my distress went deeper than appearances. Beyond reason, to lost time.

By the time I turned to the final page, separated from the rest towards the back of the magazine, there could be no more pleasure in it. There was a well-composed picture of me on our balcony, looking down the street to the Luxembourg with my arm diagonal to the railing. 'Good photography is all about angles,' the photographer said. The back of my head was a good angle.

I slapped it down, telling myself again that none of this mattered, that the piece was about my perfumery, a world where there are no words or mirrors. I can summon scent the way musicians can hear notes they read on a stave. Closing my eyes, my head filled with sweet, cheerful mimosa, a match for the day outside, if nothing else.

It was only on returning to the counter that I read to the very end, where Delphine's attention turned to *the beautiful home in the 6th arrondissement*, which I share with my husband. This would have been fine if she hadn't proceeded to identify him as head of the food company that had recently *made the news*. I looked at it in disbelief. She hadn't drawn any connection between our occupations, because there was none. When I started Arôme de Clémentine, Édouard was adamant that our business lives be kept separate, since he doesn't see mine as a serious occupation. He wouldn't be happy to have the link publicised in this way and although it would never occur to him, nor was I. Just as well I'd already sent a grateful reply to Delphine because she wouldn't get one now. At least she hadn't gone into the petitions, the protesters and their masks outside the packaging plant. It's not my business that stinks.

By the time I opened up it was almost noon. Trying to do everything myself allowed such shambolic practices – it wasn't like running a store catering to daily needs. I only saw my regular customers once or twice a year. As the *artisan parfumeur*, I couldn't prowl around staring out of the window when it was quiet or lurk in the doorway with my phone like some bored shop girl watching the clock. It was impossible to concentrate on paperwork and I'd learned not to bring my blending work out front. It made a mess and distracted from the products on sale. On more than one occasion a customer had taken a liking to something I was working on and been reluctant to leave without it; the area is popular with wealthy foreign visitors with premium-brand shopping bags, rope and ribbon handles lining their forearms like rainbow bracelets. People accustomed to getting what they want.

I couldn't delay recruiting a new assistant any longer. There, an easily achievable change – I did think of one in the end.

It started out as an average afternoon, the handful of customers finding something they liked without much input from me. Later, in walked the highlight of my day, or so I thought: an old lady I hadn't expected to see again.

'Weren't you moving to be nearer your son?'

'You have a good memory,' she said, without meeting my eye. 'I changed my mind because my daughter-in-law wasn't in favour. Didn't want to cause problems between them.' She managed a smile, saying she needed a pick-me-up and had run out of her favourite perfume. It's one of the first I came up with, deceptively old-fashioned with gardenia at the heart, shaken up with a twist of cardamom and a sharp, almost metallic shot of oakmoss. It's a good sign when customers' expressions keep changing, when the scent is far more complex than the first impression suggests. It was something to make a woman at least twenty years older than me blush as she inhaled, eyes closed. 'I've missed this,' she said. 'It makes me forget I'm not young any more!' We agreed on how the years race by, and how hard it is to believe we are where we are.

Or who we are, in my case.

Decades had passed, but since the magazine interview and that close encounter at the party, everything seemed to rake up the best and worst year of my life. I thought of another customer, who'd turned to Buddhism and traditional Chinese medicine after her own year from hell: first widowed, now devastated by disease. Perfume was one of her remaining indulgences. She told me every cell in the human body is replaced over a seven-year cycle. I asked how, then, we are still the same person we started out as. Some things are hard-wired into patterns.

Memories.

Curses.

Sometimes I couldn't believe that was ever me, my flawless young body sandwiched with theirs in a crush of breasts, cock and toned limbs, so consumed by pleasure and sensation that at first it didn't matter who was doing what. Other times it's as though that version of me has never grown up, never left home. Wanting it both ways can leave you with nothing.

My '*Cherche vendeuse*' notice had only been in the window an hour when a stunning young woman came in and peeled it off the glass. Handing it to me, she said, 'You're looking for help,' as if claiming something that belonged to her.

'Oh, yes. Would you like to leave your CV?'

She frowned. 'It says ask inside for details. So I'm asking.' She looked pointedly around the empty shop. I couldn't claim to be rushed off my feet.

'Sorry, I wasn't expecting anyone so soon. I only just put the card up.' The woman looked at me as if I were a bit dim. An interested person is no more or less likely to walk past whether it's just gone up or been there weeks. 'So, *do* you have a CV?'

I had to stop myself laughing when, ignoring a silver

handbag the size of a briefcase, she patted herself down, especially as everything she was wearing was skin-tight. Although if I had a body like that, I couldn't keep my hands off myself either.

'I wasn't expecting to find a job this afternoon.'

I had no idea if she was mocking me. Her manner was startling but so was everything about her. Her short black hair had streaks of purple and the platinum shade in vogue with women too young for real grey hair. Her gaze was so unnerving that I found myself staring at her perfect breasts, presumably the intention, given that her black top was practically transparent. The effect was surprisingly classy and almost impossible to ignore.

She'd be great for Jean-Paul Gaultier or one of the hipper brands, but she wasn't who I'd imagined for Arôme de Clémentine. I simply didn't have the energy to deal with her or how ancient she made me feel. 'I'm afraid I have to close early today.'

'No problem,' she said, with a killer smile that was wasted on me. I wasn't in the mood to be won over. On the way out, my would-be assistant paused in the doorway, running a finger over the opening hours on the glass.

'Out of interest, what's that fragrance you're wearing?' I asked, half expecting her to say, 'Oestrogen.'

'*Héliotrope noir*,' she said. 'Look it up.'

Chapter 6

In view of the day's meagre takings, it was welcome news that I needed to increase production of a fragrance that was taking off in Japan as an outrageously expensive import. Careful to keep it flat, I returned the magazine to its sleeve. Best to get this over with; Édouard had more important things on his mind, but it would be worse if he heard about it from someone else. I had nothing to apologise for – his name had not come up in my conversation with Delphine – it would simply be a case of listening to him rant.

If he was home at all.

We'd arrived at a strange situation where I kept the fridge stocked and if he appeared, I cooked dinner and if not, or if he breezed in and out, I made do with bread and tapenade or some cheese. A handful of salad. As much wine as I pleased, although that wasn't when I needed it.

It was more and more like an incompatible flat-share.

Soon after Martha and I met, she told me my marriage wasn't sustainable. I could chart the course of my reactions, beginning with indignation that someone I hardly knew had the audacity to say that. I let it pass, thinking maybe

Americans were accustomed to such frank observations. I'm not everyone's cup of tea, but Martha liked me, and it's partly due to her honesty that I've always liked her. More than anyone I know, Martha is consistent in any situation. I admitted things weren't great once we got to know each other. I said it was difficult to explain, and although much has changed, nothing's changed about that. The older you get, the harder it is to admit you don't know what you're doing with your one short life.

It's the twenty-first century. I knew I had a choice. Many think it's as simple as *why stay when you could leave?*

If only it had ever felt that simple. If I'd put my son first, I would have got out long ago. Even as a little boy, Bastien knew who he was; he's always been better at that than we have. But he's not my only child, and that's why I'd never been able to write us off completely.

Of all the great lines turned trite with overuse, it was Kierkegaard who offered me the best advice with 'Life can only be understood backwards, but must be lived forwards', not that I had ever succeeded in doing this. It was hard to say where I'd been all those years: terrified to look back, never fully present, unable to contemplate the future. I used my children as a cushion between me and their father, a sweetener (Apolline) and a distraction (Bastien). Much as I hated them, the constant bust-ups between Édouard and Bastien served as a buffer. There came a point when I no longer protested against Martha's pronouncements on my marriage, and a point when it no longer needed saying.

All of this had led to now.

I stopped on rue Bonaparte and retraced my steps past the shop towards the river without any real notion of where I was going, disconnected from my surroundings. My spatial awareness shot, I misjudged the height of a kerb and came close to turning my ankle, taking the weight off just as the tendon started to scream. When I need a talking-to, I repeat things I've paid professionals to tell me, right down to addressing myself by name. Not out loud. I'm not that strange.

You have as much right to exist as anyone else, Clémentine. As much right to feel what you feel.

Being human is not a first-world problem.

I walked for hours, counting off the bridges, past the Gare d'Austerlitz, all the way to the Bibliothèque Nationale, and back. My feet rubbed and swelled. It clouded over and got dark. I forgot if it was supposed to be a punishment or a remedy.

Finally I returned home to find Édouard rifling through the fridge. 'What's for dinner?' he asked, without looking up. We may not do endearments, but we did usually say hello.

'How was your day?' I said.

The vulnerability in his eyes startled me. This was a deviation from the script and Édouard shook his head grimly, as if to remind me. By silent agreement, his problems were not mine and mine were not his. That's not how it should be; it's the way it was. With us, the moments a couple might hug, comfort or confide in each other were notable for their absence.

Still, clearly there was no way I could heap anything else on him tonight.

'I'm about to cook. It won't take long.' He mumbled something and went to take a shower. The evening was chilly, but I opened the balcony doors for the sounds of the neighbour-hood. I picked up the jacket he'd draped over a chair – that wasn't like him either – and saw something silver in the breast pocket. Without thinking, I pulled out a business card, as tacky as most things containing the word *exclusive* are. On the back, in Édouard's writing: 'Ludmilla 21h00', and today's date. It was past eight already.

And I'd been feeling sorry for him.

First I threw it on the floor. Then I put it back where I found it. I'm not stupid: I knew there were other women. My clothes still lived in the master bedroom even if I didn't, and Édouard flinched if ever he caught sight of me topless or half dressed – me, the mother of his children. Even if it was for stress relief, he was going to want sex from somewhere. But for an attractive and successful man to pay for it – or worse, to choose to – depressed me deeply when really, what difference did it make? We were every kind of broken, Édouard and I. Together, separately, each of us in our own right. Perhaps we would be even if we'd never met, but not like this.

I considered walking out once and for all, without bothering to shut the door. This was not a marriage; it was an endurance test.

It was a total sham.

Naturally I didn't do that. After all this time, it would be crazy to act in haste. I owed it to myself to think this through.

Having made no progress with the promised meal, I put the kettle on for pasta and opened the magazine to my feature, leaving it where it couldn't be missed. But when he returned, it was with one arm in a different jacket and an eye on his watch.

'Aren't we having dinner?'

'It's too late. I'll grab something.' His eyes dropped to the table and back up, too late to pretend he hadn't seen it.

'Oh yes, look what arrived today.' Like it or not, he was going to acknowledge that I was good for something. He picked up the magazine, looked at the photo and at me, doubtless noting the flattering tweaks, and gave a nod of approval. He skim-read the first two paragraphs at most.

31

'Bravo!' he said, as if addressing a junior employee. 'You must be pleased.' He slapped it shut and handed it to me. Over in less than a minute.

I rushed onto the balcony, my lungs clutching at the cold air as I watched him walk off into the night, shocked to realise I wanted a fight; about the interview, our son's reluctance to set foot in his own home, even about the way things were with us. If I'd breached protocol to ask about his plans, he'd have fobbed me off with some fictitious business rendezvous, unless I had the courage to say, *I know where you're going.*

I used to be so much braver than this.

Long after Édouard had disappeared, I stood staring down the empty street. Not for the first time, I wondered what all this was doing to me. What twenty-five years of it had done. Édouard detested histrionics. He disapproved of displays of emotion, loss of control. But I wasn't angry with him, not really. I was absolutely fucking furious with myself.

Chapter 7

The next morning, as I steered round the potholes in the track leading to the road, I had visions of Ludo waiting for me in the gap between the trees. Everyone needed something to dream about, especially me. Moving away to study was supposed to be my big escape, and look how far that had got me, my days hunched over books and essays, and working in the evenings to make ends meet. Some students had studios, some lived with their parents in nice flats in town or villas with pools, not so different to the ones that kept my mother – and now me – in work. Considering how she resented the job, it was strange that she didn't understand me wanting more from life than cleaning slimy hair out of plugholes. She blamed my aunt for filling my head with pretensions and took anything I aspired to as a personal slight.

Although it was the only known fact about me, Maman and I both struggled to believe that I was her daughter, and at times we both wished I wasn't. I couldn't help feeling that way and she couldn't help telling me.

33

I'd stopped to make fresh coffee after she appeared in the kitchen looking terrible. The day started better for both of us when hers began at lunchtime. Her temper I was used to, but a lack of sleep wasn't helping. The plaster cast went past her elbow, her shoulders knotted with the weight. Maman didn't thank me as I handed her the cup, but then she hadn't thanked me for standing in for her. She was one of the year-rounders and with her attitude I was surprised she'd kept the job this long.

It was mid-afternoon before I got to think about pool time after devising an itinerary that ended at the new place, where I went straight to the garden. The owners didn't want anything as ordinary as a perfect turquoise pool like every-one else's – theirs was modelled on some pond at Versailles. Maman was sneering when she told me, but I liked the stone surround and the carved head with the constant jet. The pale grey tile was just as good as blue at catching sunrays and throwing beads of light across the water.

The owners were due to arrive from Paris and cleaning the place from top to bottom was hard work. The dust in this valley had the red tinge of the Colorado Provençal, which was once again off-limits due to the risk of forest fire. After several hours there was a needling pain in my neck and my T-shirt was sticking to my back. When the phone intruded on 'Suicide Blonde' I didn't get there in time, but ten minutes later, when I'd finally stripped off for my swim, it rang again. I grabbed a towel as I ran to answer.

'Clémentine?' It was him, Ludo. 'You sound surprised.'

'How did you find me here?' Turned out he knew some-one at the agency and had told them he needed to get a message to me.

'What's the message?'

He laughed as if I were a child. 'I thought you might like

some company.' The idea of being alone with him left me too stunned to reply. 'You did say you were lonely. But if not, no problem,' he said, an edge creeping in. Ludo didn't seem like the kind of person you said no to, and it's not as if I wanted to.

'Sorry. I mean, sure, but I'm almost done here.' Bringing other people onto clients' property was strictly forbidden after a run of thefts and one place being wrecked when a caretaker threw a party. If anyone found out, this could cost my mother her livelihood.

'So where is the house, exactly?' He interrupted my attempt to give directions. 'I'm calling from the bar next to the church.'

That was three minutes away, four max.

I was standing in the hallway topless, towel discarded, my chest heaving. After hanging up, I ran around, changing direction every few seconds as I tried to remember if my clothes were in the bathroom or by the pool. I checked my face in the nearest mirror and a stab of pure excitement got me as I pictured myself opening the door to him like this. Wasn't I going to give him what he'd come for?

Maybe I was wrong. Thinking of the other men I'd been with, I still wasn't sure he'd looked at me that way. Men and women could just be friends, whatever anyone said. The fact that it was Ludo, of all people, and my mother's reputation – about which I had no doubt – made me throw on my cut-offs and T shirt as he pulled up outside. I pressed the button to open the tall iron gates so he could park the pickup next to our Renault 5. Both he and the vehicle smelled of grapes on the turn, different to yesterday.

He strode in without asking. 'Not bad, I suppose,' he said, looking around. 'I knew the previous owners. Used to play tennis with the son in Lourmarin. That's going back a while.'

'It belongs to some Parisians. They've had a lot of work done.'

He turned to me intently. 'Aren't people unimaginative?' I felt bad on behalf of the owners and their lovely pool. 'I mean, if you lived a cushy life in Paris, is this what you'd want for your free time? I'd want to go somewhere nobody's ever heard of, like a jungle or a desert. Test myself, not have it easy.'

Ludo wasn't like the other men I knew. He wanted conversation. He was interested in what I had to say. Swallowing my instinct to admit I'd never thought about it, or simply to agree, I pulled my shoulders back and took a breath in.

'Two things occur to me,' I said, with more conviction than I'd ever mustered in class. 'Firstly, it's easy for us to forget this is a *belle région* because we grew up here. It rains a lot in Paris and people live in tiny apartments.' Ludo went to interrupt, quite likely to out me as someone who had never set foot in Paris or knowingly met an actual Parisian. But he wasn't quick enough. 'Okay,' I conceded. 'Probably not these people.'

He was trying not to smile. 'And your second point?'

'It sounds like you think you have the right to judge others' dreams, and that only rich people get to have them.'

'Huh,' he said, pulling a face. 'Not hard to see whose daughter you are!'

My gut response was that he was right about that, if nothing else; that my mother was right all along with her tirades about the ruling class. Maybe our neighbours really were a bunch of grasping, entitled pricks.

Ludo and I were glaring at each other. It was weirdly arousing.

'Well!' he said, 'I think we should change the subject, don't you? Luckily I picked up some cold beer at the bar.' He flipped the tops off the Kronenbourgs against the edge of an expensive-looking mosaic patio table. 'No harm done!'

he said, running a finger through the red dust on the bright ceramic pieces. He held out his beer. '*Santé!*'

'I haven't got to the terrace yet.' I was a cleaner, but I couldn't bear for him to think I was useless at it.

'Not sure I believe you.' He pointed to the towel I'd brought with me, the English edition of *Perfume* (I'd read the French translation every year since I was fifteen) and my bra on one of the loungers. The decent black one, not the old one I was wearing yesterday. 'Looks to me like you were settling in for a rest. Perk of the job, eh?' I coloured up, but there was more to it than embarrassment. Ludo could make trouble for me and my mother if he felt like it. 'Only teasing! I'd do just the same.'

Except that Ludo didn't have to steal a taste of the good life. His family had a stone *mas* with a beautiful terrace, a pool of their own. He would inherit a winery one day. The only perk available to me was no novelty to him.

'If you were planning a swim, don't let me stop you.'

I set my bottle of beer down after only a couple of swigs. As I rarely drank, the effect was strong and my inhibitions began to crumble straight away. There was no doubt whatsoever that he was looking at my chest, my nipples standing out against the thin white cotton. I smiled to myself as I whipped my T-shirt off. I certainly wasn't cold.

Ludo gave a low whistle when he saw me all but naked, but not in a vulgar way. This is what I'd been missing with my boyfriends: they liked nice tits and legs but mostly they wanted a pretty girl to screw – it didn't have to be me. With Ludo, I felt like nobody had ever looked at me before.

I walked to the edge of the pool and dived in, gulping to absorb the impact, my body tingling in the knowledge that when I sliced through the surface, nothing would ever be the same again. I swam a few lengths, Ludo's eyes following me, before discovering how difficult it is to towel yourself dry in front of someone you desire without every move feeling as provocative as a stripper's.

He smiled at me. 'You're nothing like I expected.'

I didn't recognise myself either, but I liked who I was around him. 'Neither are you,' I said. Still he didn't reach for me and my newfound confidence began to fade. Maybe he saw a silly, immature girl throwing herself at him. The things I'd missed out on in childhood were making it hard for me to grow up. All the time I'd spent watching other women and I still didn't understand how they did it.

I ran my finger down his forearm, disgusted with myself as I imagined what I was willing to do with him – on his lap, on my back, on my knees. It felt so urgent to find out if he wanted me.

'Don't take this badly, Clémentine. *Tu es une fille superbe.* Truly you are. But look at us here in these strangers' dream home like hundreds of others . . . ' I folded inwardly, grateful and mortified that he'd bother with such an inventive excuse. 'We can do better than this. And anyway, what's the hurry?' He leaned to kiss me lightly on the mouth. 'We have all summer, don't we?'

Chapter 8

There had been no further interest in my sales vacancy. Every time the door opened I looked up in case it was the woman whose name I hadn't asked and who wasn't the right person anyway. I took a photo of the magazine cover displayed on a *kiosque de presse* to send to my daughter now it was finally on sale. The news stands on the way home would have done just as well, but my instincts often led me to the river.

I reached a favourite little square next to the École des Beaux-Arts. I always pictured it in springtime, covered with pink blossom set off by bright blue sky, but in the autumn dusk that image couldn't compete with the scene of deserted stone benches in the shape of open books, large curled leaves and a newspaper blowing around. Where two streets met, something in the window of an antique shop shone in the glow of the street light. I went over to find a wooden box with a worn silk lining containing three ribbed glass bottles with silver stoppers. A travelling perfume case.

I didn't expect the door to be unlocked. Seeing nobody, I rang the bell to no reply and stepped inside, wanting to hold on to the rush of excitement and anticipation, if only for a second or two. The temptation to touch the flacons too great, I was about to give up when a man appeared from the shadows. He seemed as surprised as I was.

'*Bonjour, madame.* Sorry I wasn't here when you came in.'

'Not at all. I should have waited. I haven't touched anything.'

'Oh, I wasn't suggesting . . . '

'I know you weren't.'

Now he was out front I could see him properly. Early forties, at a guess. Average height, collar-length dark hair with a slight wave. Soulful green eyes. I waited for him to ask if he could help me.

'You must excuse me. I know nothing about running an antique shop. This was my father's business. My late father's.' I waited for him to continue. 'You're the first person through that door all day. I can't imagine why he bothered opening on a Monday.'

You open on a Monday to catch weekenders who are still in town. That's why I close on Tuesdays. I smiled distractedly without saying anything. He was standing quite close and I couldn't help noticing how good he smelled. It usually took more than hair wax and a faint hint of peppermint to activate my sensors like this. I hadn't experienced that around a man in a long time.

No, I told myself. *No.*

'But you must be interested in antiques,' he said, and seeing the puzzled look on my face, he added, 'since you're here. You probably know more than I do.'

It was easier to smile than to contradict either of these misconceptions. 'I was passing when I saw the travelling perfumery case.'

He went to the display. 'Do you mean this? I'm ashamed to say I'd never noticed what it is. I only get to see it from behind.'

Perhaps he was right about his lack of suitability for the job. A shopkeeper who doesn't know what's in his own window? When he picked up the box and blew dust off the wood, I sneezed hard three times.

'Sorry, I wasn't thinking! You have a sensitive nose.'

'You could say that.'

He motioned to me to step forward. Gently, I lifted one of the bottles from its recess in the washed-out violet silk. The colour underneath was astonishingly vibrant, as if the passage of time was a joke we'd all fallen for. I pulled out the stopper and raised the bottle to my nostrils.

I could imagine all kinds of transporting elixirs but I didn't need props for that. The reality was musty and dank, the glass clouded, the bottles neither pretty nor of good quality, and it didn't take an expert to see that. The lids had been crudely engraved with initials too swirly to decipher. The second and final bottles were no more promising in olfactory terms. The reluctant *antiquaire* watched my reactions, his own typical of those with a weak or underdeveloped sense of smell, and there are a lot of them. He shook his head as if this were another failing on his part.

'Don't worry, you wouldn't expect empty bottles to smell of much after all this time.' I pointed out the manufacturer's name on the inside of the lid: Georges Dutrac, Toulouse, 1913. It was a safe assumption that they were no longer in business.

'Frédéric Lagarde.'

'Where does it say that?'

'It doesn't. That's my name.'

I couldn't trust myself to say I've always loved the name Frédéric. '*Enchantée*,' I replied, 'Clémentine.'

His hand was smooth, his face visibly not, this late in the day. The top button of his checked shirt was undone. People talk about reading the signals, but I couldn't make sense of my own. There was a spark of some kind.

A phone rang, clearly a mobile, but that didn't stop Frédéric picking up the landline and looking foolish before rushing off to the back room. I took one of the bottles out of the case just to see that gorgeous violet again, and to touch the virgin silk, which was much softer than the rest. At one end there was a pocket and I couldn't resist seeing if there was anything inside. Before I could register more than fragile paper, folded with traces of handwriting, Frédéric was heading back, looking straight at me.

'Are you tempted?'

When I failed to answer that question, the flush at his neck matched mine. Saying I needed to be somewhere, I left in a hurry, not knowing what I'd shoved in my bag or why.

❧

There was no one home, which was, after all, the most likely state of affairs. I was glad Édouard wasn't here, but at the same time the emptiness of the apartment unsettled me. I should have put some music on but couldn't think of anything right for how I felt, in my head or my body. For weeks my moods had been erratic, my thoughts hopping around, making it impossible to focus. But one thing was clear, and not only because my hands kept shaking: I hadn't been eating properly. In fact, I could not recall the last full meal I sat down to and when I accidentally put on a pair of jeans my daughter left behind, I could almost do them up.

An image hurtled towards me of my mother the summer she broke her arm and gave up on everything. That was all for nothing if I let the same happen to me.

And anyway, I love food. The scent of basil wafted around as I pounded it with garlic and pine nuts, adding a glug of olive oil. Always a good peppery one from down south, because I could permit myself that harmless taste of the past. There were olive trees lining the driveway to the vineyard next door; probably still are. It hadn't been easy to stay away, especially when friends from Paris own the kind of houses I used to look after, some uncomfortably close to where I grew up. *The children prefer the beach*, I used to say to Édouard. *Aren't we going away with your* (dreadful) *family again?*

And now winter was coming, when all I craved was light.

I'd cooked the whole packet of fresh tagliatelle on autopilot. Steam flowed from the ribbons as I extracted a generous portion from the tangled heap. The pesto crept over them in the bowl, dark and lustrous, the first forkful devoured before it reached the table. Caffeine and adrenaline had been my only sustenance all day, unless you count ugly perfume bottles and beautiful green eyes.

The papers I'd taken from Frédéric's shop were still in my bag. Since I had every intention of returning them, there was no harm in taking a look. First I cleared the table and spread out a clean tea towel, then put on a pair of disposable gloves – whatever this was, it came from an antique shop and deserved respect. The envelope was addressed by name only, to Mademoiselle Hortense Guerindot and must have been hand delivered.

I knew before I unfolded the single sheet folded into quarters that its contents would affect me, just as the air tingles before I unscrew the cap on a rare ingredient for the first time.

The letter was dated 13 February 1915.

Hortense, mon amour,
   This will be short as no words can convey the pain of leaving you. But no sadness or fear can equal

my joy when you gave yourself to me, in body and in heart. Mine belong to you for all eternity, God willing in this life, which has revealed itself to be sweeter than I ever imagined. Think of me every day as I will be thinking of you. If you love me half as much, I will be the luckiest of men.

Until we meet again,
Auguste

The *tendresse* of these strangers' story from over a hundred years ago hurt in my ribs. I breathed through it, telling myself it would be worse if I had never felt that way.

Chapter 9

That gorgeous young woman was back and the customer who passed her in the doorway turned for a second look before heading down the street.

'*Bonjour, madame!*' She didn't need to add, 'Do you remember me?'

I looked pointedly at the door, where the sales vacancy sign was back on display, seemingly invisible to anyone but Cam Anh Ngoc Lannier, as she introduced herself, adding, 'My parents couldn't agree on it, but you can call me Suzanne.'

'I think I'd better.' I broke off, concerned that I'd offended her, but Suzanne chose to take it as a sign that she was getting somewhere.

'And you are?'

'Clémentine Dujardin.'

'Ah! So Arôme de Clémentine . . . You don't just work here.'

'That's right, I'm the owner. I've had the shop almost ten years.' I relaxed into the details I tell customers all the time. They don't expect to meet the person behind the product, especially in the perfume world, with all its glamour and secrecy. If they're disappointed that the alchemist is a small middle-aged woman, they don't let it show.

My premises used to be a tiny old-fashioned bar, and I'd kept the original counter and a few stools. Suzanne wrapped a high-heeled foot around the leg of one and made herself comfortable, sending me back to my side as if we were about to do a tutored sampling. But Suzanne was not a customer and I simply couldn't imagine her standing where I was.

'So, about this job,' she said, swivelling to take in the shop floor and the fragrance on promotion, Numéro S. An accord of fig and cedar with warm, orangey top notes, a memory of summer that hints of something satisfying to follow, it sold well at this time of year. My idiosyncratic naming scheme was a talking point; based on the labels I gave the fragances in development, it defied all convention with its lack of poetic imagination, starting with Z and slowly working backwards. The packaging designer persuaded me to stick with it and call the range Alphanumérique, a good move, as customers never tire of telling me that letters are not numbers. They may not find their initial but they always attach some meaning to the one they choose. By then, my job is done. It's what they find in the perfume that matters.

'Did you bring your CV this time?'

'I don't have one as such.' As if that didn't say plenty.

'Do you have experience with perfume?'

She laughed with the lightness of someone unused to worrying what impression they make. 'Apart from wearing it? No.' This drew my attention to what else she was wearing, all of it black: skin-tight coated jeans, another see-through blouse and an intricate lace bra, which revealed more than it concealed. The straps stood out from her skin under tension.

If I were to employ her it wouldn't, couldn't, be for this.

'Any retail experience?'

'Depends what you mean. I used to work in a private art gallery in rue Mazarine.'

'That's not what I mean. This couldn't be more different. My brand is high-end but not exorbitant for what it is – a fifty-millilitre bottle of a fragrance worn every day will last up to six months. I want it to be a special experience for them, so it's very important to choose the right salesperson. If I had time, I'd serve everyone myself.'

In the right frame of mind, I'd still want to.

'Why did your last *vendeuse* leave?'

'She got pregnant and the sensory overload was too much. Summer was coming so I left it, but now I need to get back to my bespoke work and running the business. I was turning down commissions in September.'

Since the magazine interview, I hadn't completed a single new project, or come close. And not for lack of trying.

'But you shouldn't suppress the creative impulse like that,' Suzanne said. 'Or other areas of your life will suffer!'

That was certainly true of my business bank account.

'I can start tomorrow. You'd be back to it straight away.'

'I'm sorry, I need someone with experience. In between customers this job involves lots of time on your own without much to do. I doubt it's what you're looking for.'

I bent down to reach into the cupboard under the cash register, hoping a generous handful of samples would send her on her way with no hard feelings – everyone's a potential customer. Suzanne leaned across the counter at a right angle, her face suddenly level with mine. 'I *love* being bored,' she said. 'You're bound to get more customers than an art gallery. What else can I tell you? I'm thirty-two. I'm legal, if that's what's bothering you. My mother's Vietnamese but I was born here, at La Pitié-Salpetrière, my dad too. Here, let me show you my *carte d'identité*.'

She was making me feel like the police but it would be insulting not to look.

'That's a coincidence. You have the same birthday as my daughter. She turned twenty-three this year.'

'*C'est pas vrai!* You must have been so young!' Her astonishment seemed genuine.

'I was the age she is now, actually.' Again I stopped short. This was not a social occasion and I wasn't very good at those.

'Me, I have no kids, no *mec* . . .' Suzanne paused for me to reflect on how supremely astonishing this was, although I know better than to think that every woman wants a man. 'I'm quick, proactive, creative. Ask me about any of your products. Go on!'

I made no effort to hide my irritation. She would drive me mad in less than twenty-four hours. But if this is what it took to bring the excruciating encounter to an end, I had no choice.

'Tell me about Numéro V,' I said, my weariness not an act.

Suzanne headed to the right section without hesitation, sprayed some V on a sampling strip. It's a fruity *chypre* and she must have learned the ingredients from my website, but there was something about the way she brought it to life, holding the strip out to an imaginary customer. It was a painful reminder of what I'd lost, but she made me realise I wanted it back.

'You could have picked any of them.'

'I'm sure.' She could see doubt on my face; I saw hope in hers. 'This all feels a bit hasty. That was impressive, but I should probably wait to see if a more qualified person applies. And by the way, there's no such thing as *héliotrope noir*, either a plant or a fragrance. Am I right?' Suzanne nodded. 'Inventing things is generally considered a risky strategy for a jobseeker.' Her flinty expression gave way to a little smile.

'If you can't be predictable, at least be interesting,' she said. 'It generally works for me.' Now I couldn't help but smile at her boldness. 'Let me come in tomorrow, on trial, for free. If it doesn't work out, I promise not to bother you again.'

It no longer seemed such a smart idea to let her walk away.

'There won't be enough to do. Come on Friday and we'll see how it goes. You'll be paid, but you must understand I'm not committing myself.'

'*Merci*,' she said, shiny-eyed. '*Merci*, Clémentine. *Vous ne regretterez pas.*'

❧

I craved Martha's company. The worse things were, the more we ended up laughing, but her daughter Joëlle was home from the States for a few days before starting a semester in Rome and my troubles had staying power. I considered taking up an evening pursuit that didn't involve socialising – literary events, foreign films, art exhibitions on late-opening nights – but despite endless possibilities on the doorstep I couldn't be bothered with any of them.

Solitude wasn't always the problem.

As I put the groceries away, Édouard paced around the apartment, appearing in the kitchen several times, giving me shifty looks before walking out. I went back over the events of the other night, but he had no way of knowing I'd found out about his 'exclusive' tendencies. Tonight, when I was tired and didn't care where he went, he showed no sign of going anywhere.

The scene was repeated about five times before I cracked. 'Is there something up?'

He came to a halt, the only sign of movement in his Adam's apple. 'I'm about to be on TV.'

'What? Do you mean tonight?'

'At the end of the news.' He looked at the clock. 'In about five minutes, to be precise.' He nodded slowly, two deep furrows between his eyebrows, as he watched me join the dots. There were dangerous dogs less ferocious than the business correspondent on that channel.

'You watch it,' he said, 'I don't need to. The situation has escalated so much it makes no difference which bit they run with.'

Édouard looked as if he was about to vomit and the feeling was contagious. 'I get the impression you'd rather I didn't.'

Édouard had remained true to form by not keeping me in the loop and so had I by not enquiring.

'You have to. We're not going to be able to pretend this hasn't happened.'

By the time I'd fiddled with four remote controls, the business segment had already started. At first I thought they'd opened with a development in the wine-labelling scandal, but the presenter was working up to a parallel with Édouard's company. One of the national supermarket chains was threatening to drop them – a spokesperson delivering a well-rehearsed sound bite about cross-border opportunity bringing cross-border responsibility.

When the camera switched to Édouard, he couldn't decide between a grave expression and a calm trustworthy smile, and the resulting grimace was anything but reassuring. He looked old – pinched and shadowy – and the nerves he struggled to conceal lent a hardness to his voice as he evaded every question with a statement. 'We have not broken any law. The company in question is a third-party packaging supplier, not part of our group.' The presenter's eyes brightened – he at least was enjoying this immensely. 'But are you not keeping an operation suspected of safety breaches in business, as their biggest client?'

'There is no evidence of damage to human health.'

'Ah, I was referring to environmental concerns, but how interesting that you should be the one to raise possible risks to human health. Local residents will take comfort in seeing their worries finally recognised. These are scenes earlier today on the streets of Djarnobsk.' The camera cut to images of protesters with placards, ending with one held by a frail toddler in a pushchair that said 'YOU MAKE ME SICK'. The most memorable image from the interview didn't include Édouard's face, but I had a horrible feeling they'd be side by side in tomorrow's media.

The weather forecaster warned of a band of low pressure in the Atlantic but it wasn't talk of a storm making me shudder as I turned the TV off, continuing to stare at the black screen. Édouard was in the doorway. He hadn't been able to resist watching.

It was his cue to withdraw but instead he came to sit in the chair to my left. Months had passed since we'd spent any time together in this room. 'Forget what I am to you,' he said, as if that was no big deal. 'I need to know what people see when they see that.'

'Seriously?' He didn't withdraw his request. 'It makes no difference whose eyes I try to see it with. That can't be the official line, surely? Didn't the director of communications brief you?'

'She did, but it all happened so fast. They called, she agreed without consulting me, they sent a car ... That little bastard Corentin was gagging to do it. Can you believe he teased me for sending for a fresh shirt? *Sweating, are we?* When I got on set, all I could see was his smirky face, as if the interviewer's wasn't bad enough. My mind went blank whenever he asked me anything. I couldn't remember the comms stuff. All that came to me was what the lawyers had told us, and once I got on the wrong track, I couldn't turn it around.'

'But even so, couldn't you have said one thing to acknowledge those people's concerns? That poor mother looked so desperate.'

Édouard's face had shown no trace of empathy when the camera returned to him after the clip. 'It's probably nothing to do with us. There are other factories nearby. If there's really something going on it could be any of them. The locals have latched on to this one because of the connection with foreign money. The pay-out potential.'

'Well,' I said, as I got up. 'At least you didn't say that.'

Chapter 10

Hearing Suzanne rhapsodise about Numéro V had stirred something. I kept telling myself I was a *maestra,* the voice in my head kind and funny, nothing like the usual one. It *is* special to have a talent seen as mysterious and rare. It's also a permanent headache, a kind of madness. Even in this creative dry spell, I was never off-duty, processing everything that came at me. I can smell *glass.* After the look on Martha's face years ago, I'd never tried to explain this to anyone else.

The moment Suzanne left work, I wanted to escape too, even though by stepping outside I was swapping a controlled environment for one where there's no avoiding the fumes and smoke, the stench of piss and drains, any more than the aroma of bread, coffee, plants and yes, perfume.

It was a glorious day. All around me, people were loosening their scarves and taking off their coats. The café terraces bubbled with laughter and high spirits, everything upside down. I feasted on the improbably blue sky, invisible from the shop as the street's too narrow. The colour made me think of an intense violet I'd seen.

I wondered if the travelling perfume case was still in the

window. There was also the matter of returning the old letter, because until I did, I was a shoplifter whether or not Frédéric knew it was missing. This wouldn't be easy, given my obvious low opinion of the goods and the intimate nature of the correspondence, but Frédéric was so not with it that I'd find a way. If the case was still there, I could slip it back in the pocket when he wasn't looking. But I hoped Frédéric was out sunning himself like everyone else. The gloom in that shop would make anyone depressed.

The case was gone, leaving its rectangular shape in the dust on the plinth. Even the space had a fine covering. I could see better uses for these premises – it was a prime Left Bank location, close to the river and the Pont des Arts. Footfall is heavy all year along the *quais*, apart from high summer, when most small shops close anyway. With a lease that must be costing a fortune and an owner without a clue, the days of this antique shop were numbered, and I had a feeling Frédéric knew it.

One of those yellow 2CVs used for tours of the city sped past, crammed with adults squealing like kids at a birthday party. 'Smile!' one of them yelled at me, holding up his phone. I love hearing what visitors make of Paris, how it affects them, the false impressions I don't contradict. If a customer mentions Venice or Barcelona in the same breath, Paris has failed in its conquest. But when Paris touches a heart it's as transporting as the right perfume, which can light up a special occasion or an ordinary day; a place to revisit at will.

Ignoring the bell, I opened the door and came face to face with Frédéric.

'I wasn't expecting to see you again, Céline. Catherine. No, wait . . . ' he held a hand up. 'Caroline!'

As a shopkeeper, you can't go far wrong with *madame*. 'It's

Clémentine,' I said, coldly. I'd been thinking about his eyes and the smell of him and he didn't even remember my name. I resolved never to walk down this street again.

Putain, he smelled divine.

'Clémentine, *bien sûr!*' He shook his head. 'Forgive me, I'm a bit, a bit ...' His hands swivelled as if the missing word was out there waiting to be caught. 'It's for the best that I'm hiding away in here all the time.'

'It might do you good to make the most of this lovely weather – it's like spring out there.' My skin was prickling with heat and embarrassment at having returned without a reason I could admit to, and I couldn't take off my coat without looking as if I planned to stay. There was a nasty dampness in the creases of my elbows but my lips were dry and uncomfortable.

'There's too much to do. And I have to be here in case a customer comes.' He noticed my doubtful expression. 'You, for example. You came back.'

I did, and what a mistake. 'I was curious to see if anyone had taken the perfume box. And you've sold it, so that's great!' My forced sing-song tone felt familiar, dating back to Bastien's prolonged phase, around age six, of keeping shop for teddies and throwing elaborate parties for Apolline's dolls with a miniature porcelain tea set.

Apparently a lot of antiques dealers are gay.

Frédéric was not really an antiques dealer.

I was having a lot of random and illogical thoughts.

'I would have had to get rid of it anyway, once we'd both decided how hideous it was.'

Neither of us had said so, but we both laughed, Frédéric in a way that suggested the topic was closed. How could I put things right now? The letter was part of its history, the best thing about it. I snuck a look at him when I could be sure he wouldn't notice. His shirt collar was slightly frayed, as were the cuffs. The effect was endearing and very confusing.

'Well, as long as the new owner is pleased with it. I'm sure you have lots of fine pieces,' I said, with more optimism than certainty. The larger items loomed like unidentifiable hulks in the half-light. The rest of the showroom must get no sun at all.

'The problem is, I wouldn't know.'

'If the plan is to sell up – I mean, since antiques aren't your thing – you could get someone in to value the stock and make an offer on the whole lot.' We knew a dealer, a friend of Jacques and Gabrielle, who did clearance.

Frédéric looked me straight in the eye. 'There's a lot of history here, and a year left on the lease. It's too late to get anything back. I might try to make a go of it.'

My head filled with questions I couldn't ask. Where did he live? How could he drop his usual occupation, whatever that was? Didn't he need to make a living? I didn't get the impression he was from Paris, although nothing as tangible as a regional accent led me to think this. He had none of the self-assurance that usually goes with money, whether or not the owner knows what they're talking about. Often it was enough to bluff it.

Once again, I turned away and covered my nose before being rocked by an enormous sneeze, only to discover I'd been leaning against a piano, which now had a shiny patch the size of my bottom. My blue wool coat was covered in the dust of months, if not years.

'I'm so sorry.' Frédéric went to brush it off before abruptly pulling back. 'Are you allergic to dust?'

I breathed in deeply and set myself off again. 'Frankly, with the place like this it's not about being allergic. It's not surprising you don't know what's here. All this stuff piled up – you

do realise someone could sue you if that fell on their head?'
My industry was so weighed down with regulations that it
had driven some people out. I pointed at a heavy footstool
clinging to the side of a tall glass-fronted dresser by two
legs – the more obvious question would have been how it was
staying put. 'The public are very litigious these days,' I said,
more softly. 'I'm telling you for your own good. Anyway, I
must go, or I'll start sneezing again.'

'You're right, it is in a real state. Next time you come,
I promise it'll be spotless. And I'll be sure to remember
your name.'

Chapter 11

Provence, 1992

I could have cleaned the house in Cucuron in half the time, but after I'd been over every surface twice there was no delaying the drive back up the gorge any longer. I kept telling myself the Combe was less terrifying on the way home – at least going uphill I didn't feel I was about to lose control on a bend and plunge into the dry riverbed. After double-checking that I'd locked up, I looked at my hands gripping the steering wheel and a thought struck me with the power of a great line in a book: I was going to ditch my fear of almost everything right here and drive off without it.

As soon as I left Lourmarin it was clear that I'd mistimed my return. We never used to get many foreigners in the area but it had changed since that Englishman's book. It was his *Year in Provence*, but they all wanted July and August. On the plus side, I was no longer the slowest driver or the most nervous, and I began to unwind.

Next time I looked in the mirror, the small car that had been behind me from the start had been replaced by Ludo's pickup and he was gesturing frantically. Ignoring him, I kept my eyes on the road until he sounded the horn and indicated left as we approached a narrow lane before the big right-hand bend. I pulled off and he drew up a centimetre from my bumper, grinning as he got out. He leaned against the Renault and I squared up to him, hands on hips.

'What was that about? I'm trying to concentrate on staying alive.'

'You're doing fine, unlike those idiot tourists. Didn't mean to annoy you, I just thought . . . ' He came a little closer, and when I didn't object, a little closer still. 'I thought it would be fun to go for a drive together. Maybe I can change your mind about this road. I like it.'

Of course he liked it.

'How, when we have two vehicles?'

'Leave your car up there and we'll come back for it later,' he said, indicating a spot up ahead where the road widened. 'The owners of this place aren't around.'

To hear him, you'd think Ludo knew everyone in France and their business too.

'I really don't get what you're suggesting.' He cocked an eyebrow and I blushed deeply. He must have been trying so hard not to laugh.

'It's lovely up in the cedar forest at this time of day. We'll have it to ourselves. Definitely best to take my truck, though – that road's full of potholes.'

The cedar forest covered the long low mountain. I hadn't been up there in years, the side trails too steep and rocky for ordinary walkers.

'It must be off-limits, surely, like the Colorado. Risk of wildfire.'

Ludo caught my chin in his hand and bent down to kiss me. 'You're not afraid of fire, Clémentine.'

I laughed, not sure what I felt. He was crazy, but so gorgeous he could get away with anything. We passed the 'entry forbidden' signs unchallenged and there was only one other vehicle parked before the tarmac ran out. Ludo noted my tennis shoes with approval and grabbed a small rucksack from behind the seats. 'Just some water,' he said. 'It's still hot.'

There was plenty of shade, the sunlight filtering through the dense leaves of the cedars, hitting the forest floor in ruler-straight rays. Away from the traffic and other people, we'd stepped into another world.

A surge in my chest marked the countdown to what must surely be about to happen, laced with panic about doing it outdoors. As Ludo led me through the trees to the edge of the outcrop to look at the view to the south, every sensation fuelled my excitement: twigs snapping beneath my feet, the leafy smell, the sun beating down on my skin. When he started talking again, I longed to tell him to shut up. The view wasn't going anywhere but I'd waited all my life to want a man the way I wanted him.

'It's so clear. Is that the sea, *tu crois*?' There were no seams in the vivid blue, a couple of eaglets coasting on a current, taunting us when we could only stand and watch. Not that I cared. My life, the one I chose, was about to begin.

'Yep, all the way to Marseille. And look, you can even see the iron cross on the Sainte-Victoire today.'

To our left, the mountain was a huge wave suspended against the sky. Ludo was used to mixing with outsiders and I didn't mind him treating me like one – it wouldn't have surprised me if he'd mentioned Cézanne. There was something entrancing about being the focus of his attention that made everything feel new.

'Let's go,' he said suddenly. He took me by the hand as we made our way back through the trees to where some kids had built a hut the shape of a wigwam from fallen branches, like my friends and I used to when we were small. I'd loved the make-believe of a neat and cosy house, brothers and sisters, a pet cat.

We went around the back out of sight and Ludo pulled a blanket from the backpack. He stretched his arms wide and was about to spread it on the ground when he came to a stop in mid-air. 'What is it?' he said.

I pointed at the checked wool without speaking. Ludo had a reputation – the kind that seemed to be okay for men – but did he really carry a blanket around on the off-chance?

'Ah, I see how this looks. It wasn't by chance that I ended up behind you on your way home.' He wouldn't let me interrupt. 'That house you were at this afternoon must have been so dirty – *how* long were you there?'

A heavy feeling came over me, which I knew well. Maybe it wasn't just Ludo I didn't understand, but people in general. I asked him why he hadn't come to the house when he'd made the effort to drive down, and his answer took me back to the afternoon by the stone pool. 'It belongs to strangers. This,' he drew a big circle in the air around us, 'this belongs to nobody. I've been thinking a lot about what you said, not taking the place for granted.'

I smiled, not because my words had made an impression but because he still thought he had to win me over.

'You're a very pretty girl, you know.'

'I do know.' That wasn't difficult, compared to everything else.

We pulled each other down onto the blanket where it had fallen and began to kiss, desire leaping around my body in bursts. He pushed up my T-shirt and had undone my bra before I'd noticed his hand at my back. He kissed my neck, caressing my breasts – it felt so good I could hardly stand it. 'I liked it, that you let me see you that day. I've been thinking of you constantly since I saw you swimming.'

Ludo undid his fly. It was too crude to say but I'd been thinking about what I had in my hand now, an urgent thread of pulse against my palm. He tipped his head back and moaned softly, but before I got too far he said, 'No, you first.' He laid me flat and kissed and licked the length of my body before sliding his tongue between my legs, finding the spot straight away. I gasped loudly and he made me come in what felt like seconds but was probably minutes. I wanted hours. When he said, *Was that good?* it wasn't a real question and nor was him muttering something about whether I was taking the pill, considering he was already inside me. I understood now why he'd wanted to warm me up and would have lied rather than have him stop. He lasted much longer than me, his body such a perfect fit that it felt strange when he pulled away to lie next to me. I smoothed out the ridges in the blanket and moved a stone that was digging into the back of my knee.

Ludo was out of breath, with a dopey, happy look. 'There's nothing like doing it *en plein air*,' he said, stroking my face and pushing my hair behind my shoulder. His ego was big enough without me revealing I'd never done it outside *or* with a man who knew what he was doing and made me feel like I did too.

'Don't,' I said, when he went to light a cigarette. 'It smells good here.' I wanted to bottle it. Beneath the juices of our spent bodies was the tang of pine needles, the spice of cedarwood and baked earth that hadn't felt rain in months. It was threatening the *vignerons'* harvests.

'I can tell you don't normally do this. Without getting to know each other first, I mean.'

I looked away, convinced I'd committed some embarrassing beginner's error; after all, it was the first time I'd ever really lost myself to it.

'But you do.'

'This is about the two of us. I want you to know this means something to me.'

I was mystified by his high opinion and blinked back tears. 'It's not as if we're strangers.' I said. 'When I was little, I got it into my head that your dad was my dad too and that's why we couldn't all get along.'

Strange that the slap Maman gave me when I asked, *Is that man my papa?* didn't immediately cure me of the idea. It was one of my earliest memories.

Ludo spluttered so hard he had to sit up and have a drink. 'Jesus,' he said, 'there's absolutely no way!' So preposterous he didn't consider it for an instant. My humiliation and a pang of sadness for Maman disappeared when he pulled me close again. 'It's not our problem what our parents did or didn't do. What happens from now on is up to us.'

Every time we parted, he said something to keep me in anticipation. I wondered if he even knew he was doing it.

Chapter 12

When you want something badly enough, you don't always spot the flaws in your plan. I thought Skyping Apolline would be the perfect opportunity to get Bastien in the same room as his father and me, a little family reunion with our attention directed to the southern hemisphere. When Bastien pointed out that the two of them could talk any time, I don't think he even noticed my stupidity, but he certainly recognised it as a ploy.

That left Édouard and me hovering in the kitchen waiting for the call. Recent events were making it very hard for me to be around him. I reminded myself that if we'd never been together there would *be* no Apolline and Bastien, a scenario presumably as unimaginable to Édouard as it was to me, considering how he dotes on our daughter.

'She's late.' It was two minutes past nine in the morning, just gone five in the afternoon in Brisbane. We'd tried various ways of accommodating the eight-hour time difference, none ideal. 'Maybe the wifi's not good at the hostel. Let's give it a while longer.'

Édouard began to prowl around, his polished half brogues

thudding on the floorboards. Just as well our downstairs neighbours worked twelve-hour days. It brought back the horrible night of his TV appearance and I tried to grit my teeth without letting it show. 'Does she know I have a ten o'clock meeting?'

It surprised me that he'd be so keen to get there. I crossed my fingers that Apolline hadn't heard about the TV fiasco. Mathieu had just flown out to join her and after so long apart, they were unlikely to be following the news back home.

'Édouard, could you wait a bit longer before driving us both insane? She's on holiday now.' As soon as the ringtone struck up, the tension eased a little. Édouard was smiling before her face appeared, making him look like a different person, which in turn made it easier to sit close to him so we could both be seen. On the other side of the world, Apolline and Mathieu didn't have to try, glowing with excitement. Mathieu had soon shaken his jetlag. Brisbane was far hotter than Sydney. 'I wouldn't have lasted three months up here, *c'est infernal!*' I'm used to seeing my younger self in Apolline, a likeness that's often remarked on, but when she swept her hair up, suddenly it was my mother I saw. 'We can see you're suffering!' I said. 'Be careful not to burn. You know how dangerous it is.'

'I know, Maman, *too much sun is very ageing.*' Apolline trotted this out like some mantra of mine when I didn't recall ever having said it, and it stung.

'Actually, I was thinking of skin cancer.' I looked away, wishing I hadn't sounded so sharp, when Mathieu tactfully intervened, grabbing an orange plastic bottle and waving it in front of the screen. 'Don't worry, Clémentine. Everyone takes that seriously here.'

Édouard got them chatting about reef trips, kite-surfing, a possible trip into the outback. 'I hope you know how lucky you are.'

'*Oui*, Papa, we know.' Apolline is an expert at playing him, and he has no idea. 'We'll never forget it.' This was as much a reference to Édouard's largesse as the trip itself, maintaining his principles and their dignity with the fiction of a loan. Apolline had persuaded him it would be a shame to spend her limited travel time behind a bar or cleaning dorms. If Bastien asked for money to travel, Édouard would tell him to get a job on a farm or a building site to pay his way. But then, Bastien never would ask.

'So how are things at home?'

Édouard took a deep breath and for a second I thought he was about to tell them.

'Oh, *fine*,' I rushed back into the frame. 'Nothing special to report. I'm recruiting a new assistant and there's someone who seems promising. It'll be a big help to get that sorted out.'

'It's so quiet now, with just the two of us,' Édouard chipped in. 'We miss you.' He included Mathieu, having pre-approved him as a son-in-law, should the matter arise. Mathieu was from a solid middle-class family, self-made and respectable. He was a fine broad-shouldered young man who liked sports and pretty girls. For Édouard it wouldn't be a bonus that they were smitten with each other. Love could prejudice long-term decisions. And so could doing without.

'I suppose it must be weird, with all of us gone.' Apolline's smile had vanished too. We shouldn't have raised her to be so polite. I had no idea Édouard felt like that. What made me think only I could hear the silence? And the way he said, *The two of us,* as if that was a meaningful concept or we'd ever been capable of easing each other's sorrows. I wasn't used to thinking of us as a sad story.

'Have you seen Bastien?'

The muscles in my face were burning with the effort it

took to conceal just about everything. 'Yes, he came round the other day and we were both home.'

'How was that, Papa?'

Now it was Édouard's turn to fake it, and Apolline and Mathieu's quick exchange of surprise did not pass me by. She looked pleased, though – clearly she hadn't spoken to her brother all that recently. 'It's great that you've turned the page. I used to think you'd never work things out.'

❧

Despite her excessive keenness, I wasn't really expecting Suzanne to turn up. Part of the reason for stalling was the possibility that she'd find something else or think better of it. Our encounters to date had an implausible feel, both in the moment and even more so afterwards, as if I'd dreamed them up out of sheer boredom. I had employed many *vendeuses* and done that job myself, long before Arôme de Clémentine. Suzanne's spontaneous instinct for it was almost an insult to the years I'd put in, proving that diplomas weren't everything. In any case, selling the fragrances is very different to creating them.

When I got my first job in Paris, on a premium-brand counter in one of the department stores on boulevard Haussmann, nobody cared if I was interested in the merchandise, and I soon worked out it was best to stick to the sales patter and not let on. It wasn't easy being on my feet all day, having to be helpful and friendly no matter what the customer was like. Some were so demanding and unpleasant that I pitied them for being in a foul mood when purchasing luxury goods. The flash of diamonds and a ladder of credit cards from someone like that no longer bothered me the way it did when I was living in a tiny room in a Saint-Denis tower block where the Stade de France now stands.

The customers were mostly women, but I liked the novelty of selling to men, their sense of smell generally less acute and the purchases rarely for their own use – most male fragrance is bought by women. For men there was often a motive beyond the joy of giving: sometimes I could see it in their eyes; sometimes they felt the need to confide the missed anniversary, nights 'working late' and all kinds of unspecified misdeeds.

Let's just say that I had long been intimate with the smell of a guilty conscience.

I first noticed Édouard a week before he approached the counter where I was always quick to offer assistance as a respite from my colleagues' endless gossip. That first time Édouard consulted the store guide (he needed a watch battery), headed up the escalators without a backward glance – until he did exactly that, caught my eye and disappeared. It sounds like the start of a cheesy romance.

There was little chance of seeing him on his way out, as the down escalators faced the back of the store. It wasn't so much his appearance that struck me as the way he looked at me, almost in astonishment. I wondered if he'd mistaken me for someone he knew. Imagining the lives of customers was the best part of the job but, rather unfairly, I didn't like anyone looking at me.

It's amazing how much you can absorb in seconds. I noticed how upright he was, though I couldn't tell how tall. And when he came to the counter the next week, he was undoubtedly good-looking, in a classic way: fair-haired, clean-shaven, with an angular face and inscrutable grey eyes, which seemed distant even as he approached. An air of sophistication at twenty-seven, which impressed me at twenty-two. I'd come to Paris for a taste of that, along with all my other reasons for leaving the south. And now I was looking to prove that one turbulent summer hadn't poisoned my future for ever.

Paris scared me, even after Marseille. It was beautiful and chaotic and so crowded. There were so many temptations and traps to fall into, not out of weakness this time, but mounting desperation. I knew nobody, and that was for the best, given the disastrous entanglements that had brought me here.

Despite my long hours I could barely afford to eat after paying the rent, and worry was keeping me awake. Two customers had offered *opportunities* I was determined to resist in my wish for a normal life, back when I believed there was any such thing. For a while, Édouard changed my view of the city and myself. When I told him the job was temporary it wasn't true, but we both believed it. When he pointed out that abandoning my studies didn't make me less intelligent, I believed that too. It's true he didn't make me feel much apart from safe and relieved, but that was fine by me. I liked stories about other people's lives; he said I'd make up for all the books he would never read.

Above all, Édouard was nothing like Ludo: rational and dependable, not sexy, not a bad influence. Life wasn't a wild adventure, it was a project, and projects could be managed. I wanted Édouard enough, not enough to want more; but when the time came I said *yes* to the question he should never have asked.

The memories wouldn't stop, and it was such a relief when Suzanne appeared that I hurtled across the shop and then came to an abrupt halt.

'Have I got the right day?'

'Absolutely. Let me show you where to put your things.' I led her into the back, where she noted the Nespresso machine and the instruction that coffee was to be consumed there, and there only. I had this one pegged as a rebel, so it was reassuring that she didn't find this strange. 'My workshop's a bit small, but I like it. This is where I see bespoke customers.

I can't be without my perfume organ, the tools of the trade, so I have one here and a bigger one at home. I consult with a lab on the technical side – there's a chemist there who's very in tune with what I do. The products are manufactured in small batches in Grasse.'

Suzanne stared at my desk, where everything was neatly lined up: paper smelling strips, measuring equipment, bottles of alcohol and three shelves of amber glass bottles. 'Those are the basics. There are about three thousand ingredients in common use, of which only about ten per cent are naturals. The rest are synthetics.'

'Really? I thought everyone wanted natural these days?'

'This comes up a lot. People often assume natural is better and synthetics are bad, but it's not that straightforward. Perfumery as we know it wouldn't exist without synthetic chemicals – the classic brands only came into being when they did. That was in the 1880s. Read up on it if you're interested – I've won lots of customers over with a bit of history.'

'I definitely will.' Suzanne was rapt, with an off-guard innocence that pulled in the opposite direction to her look and what I'd seen of her attitude. I'd hoped she might tone her outfit down for work but in the end I was glad she hadn't. She'd come up with a satisfying version of herself and committed to it, which was more than I could say at nearly fifteen years older.

She accepted my offer to make herself coffee and I couldn't settle to anything while I waited. There was stock to unpack, but I could get her to do that. Within minutes I heard her on the phone, speaking in murmurs, which made her sound very different. Only one moment gave any clue to the tone of the conversation, when she flared up and started speaking twice as loud and twice as fast. Then she burst out laughing and before long it was *ciao!* and *bisous* and all over. She came out into the shop rubbing her hands in anticipation, unruffled by the kind of exchange that would leave me brooding all day.

'Have a seat.' I took a stool behind the counter, pushing away reminders of the uncomfortable discussion about Suzanne's ID. She ran her hand over the marble, admiring her immaculate purple nails, the indestructible kind Apolline likes.

'It's great what you've done here. Very tasteful.'

'Thank you. The window design is new, from when I did a magazine feature back in the summer. It was looking a bit tired.'

'Must have been. I've walked up and down this street hundreds of times without noticing your place.'

The modest frontage had done the job well enough. 'I expect you have a good eye, from working in an art gallery.'

Her smile faded when I asked about the job. She flexed her fingers (could she actually *do* anything with those nails?), buying time. 'It was a small place. The owner was a dealer who was in business with an older couple, who were like the backers or something. He represented artists nobody else would touch, which was good, but it meant the stuff was hard to shift. Political, often, anti-establishment, and with everything that's happened in Paris ... I looked after the place day-to-day, handled the logistics for exhibitions, getting the artworks shipped in and out, that kind of thing. Sold maybe one piece a week, for thousands of euros, rarely to the person who would own it. We mostly dealt with brokers, a lot of Russian and Chinese. I speak a bit of both – Mandarin, that is. And English, fluently.'

'That would be an advantage for working here. And did I just hear you speaking Vietnamese?'

'Yes, but I doubt that'll be very useful. My mom was driving me nuts as usual. I've only just arrived and she wanted to know how it's going.'

It was hard to imagine Suzanne having a clingy mother. 'If you don't mind me saying, it surprises me that you want to move into high-street retail. This isn't any sales position, as you can tell, but it doesn't involve the responsibility you're used to. What's the gallery called again?'

We both knew she hadn't said. 'I left when it closed down and there've been pop-ups since: clothes, shoes, vinyl. I'm really interested in what you do and it's something I'd like to get into, but if you can't consider me without giving me the third degree, I won't waste any more of your time.'

Her defiant glare didn't hide the fact that she was almost in tears.

'I'm happy to give you a chance, just as we agreed.' By the time we moved on to the practicalities, we'd switched to the informal *tu* and I didn't even know who started it. Two very chic women had been hesitating on the opposite side of the street for long enough to tell me they were likely to come in.

'Take your cue from the customer,' I said. 'Start with the minimum, never impose. Some are hugely knowledgeable. Some enjoy talking about what the perfumes convey for them, others appreciate a bit of guidance. And don't be discouraged if they take some time to decide – that makes sense with this, and you'd be surprised how often they come back. But most important of all – remember this is not something people buy every day.'

The women came in and started spraying too many products around. Customers enjoying themselves is good for business, but I know not to read too much into it. Sometimes people who look broke splash out, others buy nothing after quizzing me about every fragrance at length and seeming enthralled. 'Over to you, Suzanne,' I said.

Chapter 13

It was only the third time I'd been to Lagarde et Fils and my visits were starting to feel like a habit. I'd resolved not to go back, but so few people set foot in the shop that I didn't like to think of Frédéric's efforts to smarten the place up being for nothing. If he'd got around to it.

Frédéric had become an antidote to Édouard. There was something likeable about his lack of front. I'd never met a man like that.

He was standing on a dining table with his back to me, pointing an exceptionally noisy vacuum cleaner into a corner of the ceiling. His shirt had come untucked on one side. Recalling his smell made me feel pleasantly light-headed, like the drink that should be the last of the night. Other than this, I had no sense of his body and, I was disappointed to realise, no great curiosity on that score.

It was the first time I'd really seen him smile and a long time since anyone had looked this happy to see me. 'What do you think? I'm not there yet, but it's progress.'

There was clear floor space now he'd rearranged the contents of the shop, and at last, some room to move. Smaller pieces were neatly displayed on shelves and dressers. The air was still musty but cut with beeswax from some bunched-up cloths.

'What a transformation!'

'That's good to hear. My back is killing me and you know how it is with the sneezing once you get started. Thank you, by the way.'

'For what?'

'For making me realise I had to do something.'

I winced. 'Actually, that's one of the reasons I came by.' One of them. 'To apologise. I had no right to lecture you like that. I don't even know you.'

Coming here made me feel better. I felt my mind and my body relax the moment I arrived, the slight frisson enjoyable rather than threatening. It was a while since I'd met a man who showed signs of more than tolerating me, and even the possibility that Frédéric might find me attractive came as a shock.

'Of course you know me. You're my best customer!'

Who had never bought anything. Since I didn't care for antiques and Édouard actively disliked old stuff, there was little prospect of me becoming a real customer. It wasn't fair to Frédéric and it would probably be best to leave and not come back.

'You know what you're talking about,' he said. 'Your shop looks fantastic.'

I held my breath too long and it was as if he could hear the thoughts running through my head: that he'd been following me, watching me, that he knew where I lived.

'I was walking past the other day when I saw you behind the counter,' he said, dismayed. 'It was the big perfume bottles in the window. I'd never have noticed them before.'

He was relieved to see me smile.

I didn't know if he'd read it, and I wasn't about to ask, but anyone searching for Arôme de Clémentine now would be directed to Delphine's feature. Suzanne was in favour of displaying it in the shop but so far I had resisted. 'Thank you,' I said. 'Good to know it has the desired effect.'

Frédéric cast his eyes around the showroom and heaved a big sigh. 'There's no comparison with this. My father made a go of this business for thirty years before he fell ill and it started to fall apart. You mustn't judge it on what you've seen. The difference is, people want what you're selling.'

Perhaps I could give him something worthwhile before leaving.

'Sit down for a moment, because this is more important than that,' I said, pointing to the vacuum cleaner. We could both have sat on the button-back leather sofa but I chose a chair. 'You need to understand: you'll never sell anything if you don't believe it's worth having. Think about why people buy anything they don't need to stay alive.' Frédéric looked at me blankly. 'Okay then, what was the last thing you bought?' I asked.

'A tin-opener from Monop' on the rue de Rennes. My father only had one of those old-fashioned ones with a prong that could stab you in the hand.'

Not the greatest example. 'So that's something you needed, to be able to eat. What about the last thing you bought because you wanted it?'

'I've always hated shopping.' There was a heaviness to the way he'd sunk into the sofa, as if he intended to spend the rest of the day there.

'Sorry, I've been training a new sales assistant who finds this interesting. I appreciate that not everyone would.'

'It's not that. I'm finding it hard to take anything in at the moment.' My expression seemed to clinch something. 'The last year has been hell, even before my father died. No,' he said, refusing sympathy before I could offer it, 'you don't want to hear. If someone tried to tell me this story, I'd be looking for an excuse before they got halfway.'

Inside my handbag, Auguste and Hortense lay folded together for the rest of time. I didn't come here looking for stories but now I couldn't seem to walk away without one.

'What's your favourite piece in the shop?'

Without hesitation he led me to a framed seascape in which a sandy path clung to the edge of some simple white houses with shutters mostly ajar, a low parapet separating them from the water. I gave a big sigh.

'You like it?'

'Yes. It's so calming, and so bright at the same time. Where is it?'

'That's a mystery, and so is the name of the artist.'

'I don't think it's France, somehow.'

'Me neither.'

Wherever it was, we were in a different place now.

&

I'd developed an aversion to our apartment that I couldn't shake, wandering from room to room. I never dreamed that I would live somewhere like this back when the tiles blew off the roof and my mother and I had to stick our hands in the cistern to flush the toilet. Changing the furniture or redecorating wouldn't help. Our home was lovely; we were not. I felt such contempt for myself, knowing Esmeralda was about to arrive, her hour-long journey from the *banlieue* one she has been making for over twenty years to make life easier for people like us. We didn't need her any more, certainly not twice a week, but I couldn't let her go after all she'd done for me and the children, for as long as we'd lived here. Esmeralda

76

understood that it was possible to miss jammy knives on the counter, finding the fridge empty and paintbrushes marinating in cloudy jars of white spirit. She regularly told me this was not how people lived in Cape Verde. It's hard not to make those comparisons when your job is cleaning up other people's mess.

A man with a black beard had moved into the flat opposite. He'd been giving me funny looks when he saw me out on the balcony, sometimes in high winds and once in a slanting downpour. He called his girlfriend over and she was draping herself around him, her bare arms and legs making me think they'd started the day making love. I'd forgotten how that felt at any time of day. There was nothing between my fingers either as I mimicked smoking a cigarette in languorous Marlene Dietrich style, and when they looked at each other in confusion, I cackled like a madwoman.

They were annoying, but this was also why I liked it out here. This *carrefour* was alive, full-size people level with us, small ones on the street below. Pigeons swooping between the rooftops. Umbrellas distorting, blue rectangles glowing behind thin curtains. Small dogs taking a badly timed shit on the pavement, their well-dressed owners glancing around before continuing to the Luxembourg, where I'd recently seen a more civically minded couple attempt to pick up their *crottes de chien* with a large autumn leaf. A group of students heading for the law faculty made me wonder what Apolline and Mathieu were doing on a tropical Australian evening. I used to plait my daughter's hair out here in summer. The kids used to eat their after-school snack at the small round table, baguettes and squares of dark chocolate, glasses of milk.

I preferred who I was then to now.

I preferred the balcony me to who I was inside.

My perfume organ looked like any other kitchen cabinet.

Inside were two hundred or so little bottles with natural oils of plants from all over the world, aromas that science does better and those that only chemistry can capture, either because the source material doesn't lend itself to extraction – like leather – or its use is illegal, such as products of animal origin and endangered plant species. My catalogue of past creations still came to me but I could only hope for new inspiration, telling myself each new day could be the one the block shifted. When Tante Yvette lost her sense of smell last year, she told me she was glad the brain tumour would soon kill her. There was something almost comforting about missing Yvette the way I did, with no mixed feelings. She was the reason I couldn't give up, even when I felt like it. My response to external stimuli hadn't changed and I hadn't completely lost my imagination, but any ideas evaporated before I could make anything of them.

I closed my eyes and my head flooded with colour: deep yellows, dusty oranges and a blue so vivid it made me forget where I was. The rush resembled my usual one, a kind of precursor to scent. Recalling the painting from Frédéric's shop lifted me as if I was looking at the real thing.

My dabblings didn't amount to anything but I managed to lose myself for a while now Suzanne had a key to the shop. I still wasn't entirely sure about her. My previous sales assistants had been competent and dependable but lacking genuine enthusiasm, whereas Suzanne was reasonably reliable (I wasn't a stickler for timekeeping), delightful when she felt like it but sullen and offhand when she didn't. I tried not to leave her alone for too long, ostensibly because she was still getting used to a job so different to her old one. In reality, it was so I could intervene if things became uncomfortable with a customer.

This was not ideal, especially as I had so much paperwork

to catch up with. Sometimes I sat in the workshop making my 'Suzanne face', which was naturally nothing of the kind but a hand clapped over my mouth. But when she was on form, or with someone she liked (it varied more on this basis than her general mood), it was a captivating spectacle. We were getting more people through the door and considerably more men. It shamed me to think how close I came to discriminating against Suzanne's beauty; it would have been a big mistake, though most people probably didn't see beyond her appearance. There was a strong increase in sales across the range, many customers now leaving with two products after she persuaded me to offer a small discount on the second. All in all, Suzanne was good for business.

She looked up from behind the counter with a weary expression. 'All these people coming in all the time – I can't get used to it!'

I laughed before realising she wasn't joking. 'That's the idea. This isn't the kind of business that can survive on one sale a week.' I had a complex about Suzanne coming from a more cultured environment. 'And it *is* my shop.'

She shrugged. 'You're right. It's just some days get off to a bad start. I'm not a morning person.' I resisted the observation that this wasn't the most desirable trait in a shop assistant either. 'The boiler in my flat keeps breaking down and the landlord won't pay to get it fixed. Every time I complain he insists on coming round himself, but he doesn't have a clue. So for now it's either cold showers or wasting hours going to my mother's because she never lets me leave without cooking for me.' There was a curious mismatch between the description of Suzanne's place in the 13th and the designer bathroom and walk-in wardrobe I'd have imagined for her, with row upon row of shimmery black garments and perilous shoes. I gave her my plumber's number and suggested that she should discourage any more visits from the landlord, whose motives struck me as suspect. '—And then, when I finally got here, there was a strange woman in the doorway trying to stop me unlocking the shop.'

'Was she homeless?' That seemed unlikely, as the narrow pavement offered neither space nor shelter.

'I don't think so. She didn't have anything with her; she was just trying to get in my way. I've seen her a couple of times before, on the other side of the road. She stood there for ages between the butcher's and the ice-cream café, staring.'

I'd never noticed anyone like that. 'Did she say anything?'

'Nothing at all, even when I asked her to move.'

'Oh well, you know how it is. There are lots of strange people around.'

By now the two of us had swapped places and Suzanne broke off for a moment while the coffee machine operated – she was costing me a fortune in capsules. I was looking forward to some peace in my workshop when she launched into yet another drama. 'Not long after I'd opened, an obnoxious woman came in. At first she seemed normal enough but when I asked if she'd like any help – not being pushy, like you said – she snapped at me, saying she knew every perfume in this shop better than I ever would. I mean, the woman outside seemed harmless but this one was a real *connasse*!'

'What did she look like?' Apart from a few journalists and perfume bloggers, there aren't many who could claim that level of expertise.

'Large. Not attractive,' Suzanne said.

'American, do you think? Curly red hair?'

'Yes, didn't I say? She acted like she was famous or something. Then she stormed out and I still have no idea what it was about.'

'Okay, that was my friend Martha. She's not famous.' And

as Martha's energetic dating schedule proved, she was not unattractive.

Suzanne was not impressed by my taste in friends. 'What's her problem? I promise I didn't do anything.'

'Martha's not a morning person either. She was probably hoping for a chat with me and it may have touched a nerve, finding you here. I think she hoped I'd offer her the post. In fact, I know she did.'

After twelve years, Martha's contract at the language school hadn't been renewed. Whether it was ageism or her personality clash with the new male director was unclear. *Let me do it – how hard can it be?* she'd said. I had to explain that it's best to employ strangers in case things don't work out. Her answer was that I'd never had to fire anyone. *Yet.*

'I'll have a word with her. I'm sorry to hear she was rude to you. Between us, you know more about my fragrances than she ever will. Just don't tell her I said so.'

Chapter 14

Provence, 1992

Ludo didn't always say the right thing.

As he drove me to my car from the cedar forest, he tried to take back the comment that it was my decision whose company to keep, admitting that he didn't know what it was like for me. Nobody ever had. I'd have to pick my moment to make a stand, but with the state Maman was in lately, this really wasn't it.

As I set off to Ludo's party I pictured one of the confident and improved versions of myself strolling up the driveway to the Domaine de Bellechasse. Instead I made for the track that ran along the base of the mountain and climbed over the sturdy stone wall between our land and theirs. No wonder they were so keen to mark the boundary, Maman said, having as good as stolen it from us.

As I jumped down, I remembered that Ludo and I had agreed to forget about all that and it made me happy. My social life had dried up since returning from Marseille and I was buzzing with nerves and anticipation. Everything was happening so fast. I'd only just got used to being alone with Ludo and there would be workers from the vineyard and the local co-operative. 'Just a few drinks and some music in the old barn,' he'd said. 'Good for morale. You never know, the weather might break and we'll end up dancing in the rain.'

There wasn't much chance of that: a violent sunset made different patterns every way you looked, as if an artist had gone overboard. Silver veins imitated the lightning we were all longing for against an orange and purple backdrop. It didn't cool down until long after dark and never enough to get a good night's sleep.

When the wind was in the right direction, sound carried from the neighbouring properties on summer weekends, some a fair distance away in the hills. Music, voices, even fireworks. As a teenager I'd daydreamed about my adult persona gatecrashing one of these parties or wedding receptions. In a simple but glamorous dress, I'd have perfect hair and make-up, the kind of smile that brought attention and acceptance without too many awkward questions. I'd act like I belonged among these people from somewhere else. The one thing I never imagined was being invited.

This was not that kind of party, but it was a start. I wore a short denim skirt and a bright pink T-shirt, which would either compensate for my shyness or make me feel even more self-conscious. My job in the hotel bar had taught me that the harder you had to try, the less you could afford to let it show. The music got louder and 'Losing My Religion' felt like a positive sign. I'd got good at acting cheerful and outgoing while hearing that song a thousand times, and now I had to do it when I wasn't getting paid. I summoned my courage, turned the corner and screamed.

A wild boar the size of a motorbike lay dead inside the open doors of the barn, a bullet hole in its flank. One more step and I'd have been on top of it. Baby boars were cute but I'd never seen an adult male up close and had no idea they were this big and covered in bristles, not fur. Suddenly aware of the laughter coming from inside, I looked away from the boar at the faces watching me. Ludo got up and came over, brushing straw off his shorts. 'Cut it out,' he told the others. 'She's had a shock.'

'Yeah,' one of the men cuffed the big guy next to him. 'She didn't scream as loud as this girl here.'

'Take no notice of them,' Ludo said, knocking the animal softly with the side of his foot. 'If you'd come the normal way you'd have seen it. Justin here shot it late last night and we haven't had a chance to move the carcase.' Beaming, Justin made a pistol with his hand and went 'Pow!' Ludo gave him a pitying look. 'So, for those who don't know her, this is Clémentine from next door. Someone get her a beer.'

They introduced themselves but only one name stuck. Most of them were at least mid-twenties like Ludo, muscular with deep tans but otherwise nothing like him with their bad haircuts, earrings and dodgy moustaches. Ludo would have been the kingpin even if he wasn't the boss's son. He would be anywhere.

'Something's off with the guest list, Ludo. Eight *mecs* and only three *meufs*.'

'Bring your own woman next time, Serge. Not my problem that you can't hold on to one.' I recognised the girl with the bleached hair from one of the market stalls. She was straddling a rat-faced man who was groping her in front of everyone. 'Get out back, you two, and spare us the porno.' Ludo said. 'Our young friend's going to be wondering what kind of people we are.'

He put his arm around me like I was his little sister, there to ruin the party for everybody. As I pulled away, laughing it off, I caught the only other girl, Racha, staring at me. About my age, she was scarily beautiful, with thick black hair almost to her elbows. Her kohled eyes ordered me to back off as unmistakably as if she'd shouted it out loud. I looked away, my face burning. Was it really so stupid of me to have thought Ludo and I were together? When he went back to the empty space next to her, I didn't know any more. She whispered something to him, laid a hand on his chest and looked up at me. Ludo motioned to me to sit down opposite. It was a game where nobody had any intention of telling me the rules.

The music got louder still as more and more people arrived. By now it was pitch dark, with only the curved blade of a new moon. For the first time, I started to see the appeal of drinking the way my mother drank, blotting my humiliation and disappointment with one beer after another, pretending to listen to stories that led nowhere, watching the others dance.

Trying not to watch Ludo and Racha kissing, which was driving me wild.

I went outside for some fresh air, although it was still so hot the cicadas were joining in with the sound of the crickets. I looked up at the stars, millions of tiny flecks, and the Plough, the black sky I had loved here for as long as I could remember. This was supposed to remind people how small we are, how quickly everything passes, how little anything matters – but I just couldn't settle for that.

'There are places you can't see the stars,' Justin said, creeping up on me.

'Why would anyone want to live there?' I was giggly and unsteady, tilting my head back so far I nearly fell over.

'Whoa! I think you'd better slow down.' He tried to kiss me but I screwed my face up and said, 'Sorry, I'm with someone.'

When he left, I leaned against the wall of the barn trying to sober up enough to find my way home across the rough ground. A glowing cigarette tip came out of the bushes. 'So, *Clémentine*,' Racha said, as if we were continuing a conversation. 'Who is it you're with?'

Sober, I wouldn't have dared to say it was none of her business.

'As long as you're sure about that. I saw you staring at me and Ludo in there. Were you enjoying it?'

'No,' I said, which was both the truth and a lie.

To my surprise, her frown disappeared. 'If you live next door, how come it's taken you so long to show up? I've been here a month and Ludo throws these parties most weekends.'

I knew this because of my mother complaining about the noise, although we both knew she didn't give a shit about that. Now Racha had decided to be friendly there was a very different look in her eyes, as if she was as intrigued by me as I was by her, but I couldn't shake my first impression that she was trouble. My instincts were telling me to cut the conversation short and make a run for it while I could.

They didn't stand a chance.

Amid the smell of booze, fags and dope from the barn and piss from the bushes, there was a strong woody scent on Racha that I'd never come across. A pendant lay in the dip of her collarbone on a gold chain so thin it was almost invisible. She picked it up and held it out to me. 'My name means gazelle in Arabic. Are you *berbère?*'

'No, what makes you say that?'

'Something about your eyes. Never mind, my mistake.'

I'd never imagined myself anything but a *française de souche*. From here, right here, rooted in the earth we stood on.

I could hear she was from Marseille, just not the one I knew. Racha lived in the *quartiers nord,* no-go areas for anyone who had a choice. She told me she was related to the Bellechasses' longtime housekeeper, Zohra, and that she'd come here for the summer after 'getting mixed up in something'.

'Don't look so worried,' she said. 'I'm not going to tell you.'

'I wasn't going to ask.'

'Good. Because someone like you wouldn't understand anyway.' She wasn't wrong about my ignorance – how could I know? But if she thought I was like Ludo because we were neighbours, she'd be in for a shock when she saw my house in daylight.

Then she changed the subject entirely. 'You spend years reading books and writing about them. Where does that lead?' It would have been easier to answer if she'd been provoking me, but she wasn't any more. For years I'd held out against my mother's contempt for education; now Racha was making me question it.

'I don't know, teaching other people to do the same?' Maman didn't read, but since books kept me quiet as a child, she'd been considerably keener on that than my other hobby of macerating every plant and flower I could get my hands on and trying to make 'perfume' out of it. 'I know that must sound strange.'

'To someone like me?'

'You're the one saying that, not me. Ask Ludo if you think I'm looking down on you. I'm not sure I'll be going back anyway. This is probably it for me: minimum wage, seasonal unemployment. But the views are lovely.'

Happy now? I think she was. Her eyes widened and she gave me a wicked smile, grinding her cigarette butt into the dirt underfoot. She took both my hands in hers, raising them up against the barn wall, taking advantage of my astonishment. A jolt ran the length of me.

'Over here, *les gars*, the girls are getting it on!' said one of the guys, coming out of the bushes. Racha gave him the finger, her eyes clinging to me.

'Don't let's fight, you and me. Sounds like we're both stuck here for a while. We'll figure something out.' She let her body fall into mine for no longer than it took to kiss me on both cheeks and say *à la prochaine*. Until next time. I was counting the seconds before I walked away.

Chapter 15

After wasting most of the morning chasing missing payments, I walked two circuits of the Luxembourg trying to clear my head as clouds gathered over the Senate building. It was all so frustrating when I'd been craving the freedom to get back behind the scenes and create. I had come to rely too much on the reward of customers enjoying my perfumes, and the fact they would still exist if I never made another one gave me no comfort. Was my career, my refuge, really on the way down as well as everything else? The thought jabbed at me with every step.

I'd been various degrees of unhappy for so long that it passed for normality. The pressures of work and the regular spikes of conflict between Édouard and Bastien had relegated my feelings to lowest priority. If you've put up with something for a long time, the easiest course is to put up with it some more.

There had been nothing easy about it.

Later, on her third attempt to give me my change, the lady in the *boulangerie* touched my hand and asked if I was all right. By the time I got home, the baguette was flattened around the middle.

Édouard noticed me out on the balcony. Hard not to, when it was this breezy and the doors to the kitchen were open. 'You'll get cold,' he said, to my back. We had barely exchanged ten words in a week.

'I don't care.' And I really didn't, despite my teeth chattering. People drank and cut and drugged themselves not to feel how I felt. I'd have swapped Paris for the Arctic. 'Go ahead and close it if you want to.'

'You know I can't do that.'

I turned to Édouard, startled by this flare of tenderness in the dark.

And then I got it: the balcony doors had no handles on the outside. That's all he meant. The last time I'd locked myself out, Bastien had soon come to the rescue after the boy he'd brought home kept pointing at the windows until he cottoned on and let me in, making fun of me.

I surrendered to full-on sobbing, something I could not have done indoors. It was horrible and miserable and the most incredible relief. Édouard went to fetch a blanket from the sofa, which he draped round my shoulders in lieu of an embrace. It was a concession that he hadn't insisted I come in. He sat down beside me, each of us staring outward as if we were on separate islands with no concern for the other's whereabouts.

'It's freezing out here,' he said. 'What's the matter?'

I understood him less than ever. He didn't seem in a rush to go anywhere. He hadn't said any more about his work, and I hadn't asked. Édouard hadn't just forgotten how to answer questions, he'd asked one that could not be answered with 'yes' or 'no'.

'I . . . feel . . . awful.'

'I can see that. Can I, do you—?' He spotted that we had an audience from across the street and stood up to shield me, cursing 'those people and their triangular balconies'. In fact, the bearded man and the young woman were behind the double-glazed windows, as any sensible person would be at this time of year. Édouard frowned at me like a discrepancy on a spreadsheet. 'Do you need to talk to someone?'

God, not this again. There was a limit to how many times I could pretend to spill everything while keeping the interesting bits to myself. I'd recently spotted the therapist I gave up on a year ago in a café with some of her friends, laughing and messing around, in contrast to her grave professional demeanour. It had upset me that she came in two such different versions when I could only manage one.

'We need to talk to each other. That's what couples are supposed to do,' I said. There was a stunned pause – I was as surprised as Édouard by what I'd said. 'You ask what's wrong, but not as if you want to know. I have no idea how you feel most of the time. What's it been like for you, being with me all these years?'

I wasn't shivering any more, I was quaking. Édouard shook his head and nothing could have shocked me more than the sadness in his eyes. 'We're not like other couples, Clémentine. I thought you wanted it that way.'

❧

I knew the street code to Martha's building but had to slip through the door to her staircase as a neighbour was leaving. Since she lost the day job we hadn't seen each other alone for a while. Martha liked coming to my place but only if Édouard wasn't around, and I needed a change of scene. She says visiting me reminds her of the years she lived in a posh apartment with Jean-François and the twins, the subtext loud and clear. In the lobby of her building a smoky cat I hadn't met before was winding around my legs, purring so loudly it made me laugh. Bending down to stroke him, I wondered if I could make do with some*thing* to love. 'I have to go now, Zéphyre,' I said, looking at his name tag.

There was no lift and I stopped to get myself together before pushing the tinny bell, although the long walk and the cold night air had done me good already. Martha's neighbours were making goulash, or possibly something with chorizo. My stomach was protesting at missing yet another meal.

'Strange time to call!' Martha said, wrapping her arms around me. 'I've only just got in. All these private lessons are killing me, but I have to eat.'

'How's Joëlle?'

'Very excited! She arrived in Rome this afternoon. We did FaceTime with Chloé. To me it's strange only seeing one, but they've had three years of not being together all the time. I guess moms are always the last to move on. Anyway, thanks for asking. I thought you'd come to tell me off for being such a bitch to your salesgirl.'

'I'd forgotten about that. But I'm curious to know what happened, now you mention it.'

Without asking, Martha poured me an inadvisably large glass of red wine, which I accepted. She pushed a huge bag of tortilla chips and a squeezy bottle of salsa in my direction. 'Something to soak it up.'

'Suzanne's still acclimatising. She can be a bit unpredict-able.' Just in time, I realised that confiding in Martha about the circumstances in which I'd hired Suzanne wouldn't be very tactful.

'In fairness to your sexy sidekick, she was charm person-ified. The way she looked at me set something off. Envy, I expect. God, Clem, if I'd known you were after someone like that I never would have put myself forward.'

'Very striking, isn't she? Apart from the obvious—' Martha

opened her mouth. 'Not that,' I said firmly, before she could say anything to annoy me. 'Appearances aside, she's very self-assured. You would have to be, to cope with the attention. She's really into the merchandise and an excellent saleswoman.'

Martha tipped her head from side to side. 'Okay, I get it. She's right for the job and I'm glad. Please tell her I said sorry. Wait, did you even tell her you know me?'

'Of course! I take it you're not planning to avoid the shop for ever. Honestly, you would have been bored in half an hour. And can you imagine me as your boss? You're always telling *me* what to do.' Although I often ignored her counsel. Martha has never quite grasped how different we are.

'True enough! Anyway, how are things? Did you get credit for good behaviour at Gabrielle's party?'

That felt like a long time ago. 'I didn't stay long enough to drink too much or cause a scene, so I suppose that's a yes. Although, can you believe Édouard asked me about that man who was looking at us?' Now I was being tactful – there was no doubt he'd been admiring me before Martha moved in on him.

'Truly, your husband misses nothing. What did he say?'

'Just wanted to know who he was. I said I didn't know and pointed out it was you he hooked up with. That was rather indiscreet of me, sorry.'

Martha grinned, and then winced, pulling a hardback book from behind her cushion. 'Édouard's opinion of me doesn't have a long way to fall. Anyways, that man was of no interest to him, I'm sure. A second cousin of Gabrielle's from Alsace. Nice enough guy, very average fuck. You can tell him that, if you like.'

I found it hard to know how to react to the lowdown on Martha's sexual adventures. I'd have preferred to hear less about them but didn't know how to say that either. Since the divorce she'd been making up for lost time and I was happy for her. She managed not to be bitter about her ex being in the market for a partner ten years younger when she had to look ten years in the other direction. It was only a few months since she'd met the latest love of her life, Lars, a Swede from fencing club. Unlike the *alsacien*, Lars had been *phenomenal* in bed. He hadn't lasted any longer than the rest.

'Don't you ever get tired of all this?'

Martha's eyes narrowed. 'Nope, still not, since the last time you asked. Honey, I put in the years with Jean-François and it felt like an eternity. Even my girls keep telling me to have some fun – you're the only one who gives me a hard time about it.'

Martha was always telling me to do the same, and if sex was really all I wanted, *I* wouldn't be the one having a hard time.

'Do you ever think about when it'll be over?' I said. What a cruel and pointless question. Who knows how long anything will last? Life would be intolerable if we did. Martha still regarded me as in captivity, whereas she'd been released when her husband left her.

'Are we talking about when no man will go near me? Because I like to think that's still a way off. You're going to get such a shock when you turn fifty and realise you're not dead from the neck down.'

'Sorry, that wasn't a reflection on you, Martha. It's just that now Bastien's gone and it's only me and Édouard, nothing feels right. I know what you're about to say, but I don't just mean with him. Seeing Suzanne rave about my work makes me feel I've lost my touch – that's one of the reasons the magazine interview felt so unnatural, like faking. I miss Bastien so much there must be something wrong with me. You didn't go to pieces like this when Chloé and Joëlle left.'

'I always thought they'd go to the States for college. And

being in the middle of a horrific divorce didn't give me much chance to dwell on it, if you recall. It was such a catfight I was glad they were out of the way. And I'll say it again, I would not have made it through that time without you.'

I didn't like coming here. Every time I looked around Martha's shabby little flat, a lifetime of belongings strewn and stacked all over the place, the insistent sound of a tap dripping, it reminded me of her strength and my lack of it. Martha hadn't had a choice.

'Would you ever have left Jean-François, do you think?'

'Wow, you really are cutting to the chase tonight.' She took her time. 'I like to think so. What's all this about? Are you finally going to do it?'

'I've found out Édouard uses sex clubs. Escorts, that kind of thing. I don't know how it works, but I found a card with an appointment on the back. In his handwriting.'

Martha grimaced. 'Gosh, is this what it takes to push you over the edge?'

'I can't explain why it upsets me so much. I've known for ages he sees other women – you know that. But to find out he pays for it ... I'd made my peace with the idea of a girlfriend in some nice place, someone he cared for.'

Martha put her hand over mine and squeezed it. 'Oh, did you really think that? Because if I'm honest, that would surprise me more.' I'd pictured it so often, the woman younger than me, of course, seductive but classy, regardless of her taste in perfume. Martha was right. It didn't stack up at all. 'Does he know you know?'

'Do you think I was going to mention it? Since then there's been the TV disaster. Did you see it?'

'I read about it. Sorry.'

'Earlier tonight I broke down and he just stood there. He thinks it's all about Bastien leaving but it's not. It's everything.'

'Bastien would have left sooner or later. That's what kids do.'

'I know that! But this isn't just the natural way of things. I can't stop thinking we've failed him. If only I'd really stood up to his father all those years. He probably thinks I'm as bad as Édouard for colluding with it.'

Martha heaved herself into an upright position on the sofa and waggled her finger at me. 'No,' she said. 'No fucking way. I've watched that boy grow up and I'll be damned if I sit here listening to you say that. You stuck up for Bastien. You made him feel it was okay to be himself. That's what those rows were about, don't you remember?'

I'd finished my wine and poured us both some more. To hell with it. 'The rows were dreadful but I almost miss them. Now there's nothing left to say, or if there is, we can't find a way. I was harsh with Édouard about the TV interview but I was appalled – not about him losing the plot, I can relate to that – but because he tried to justify the things he'd said. It was like, right, you're this heartless person when the mask slips. I've spent twenty-five years with a stranger and I feel totally empty. I tried talking to him this evening—'

'You did *what*?'

'Exactly. After he suggested I go back into therapy. His reaction to seeing me in distress is: *Who can I delegate this irritating problem to?* He can't help it, that's how his mind works.'

There was a lengthy silence. Martha gazed intently at the floor as if she'd forgotten I was there. 'Want to know what I think? Don't say yes unless you do.'

I agreed.

'For twenty years I was married to an absolute jerk. Jean-François was immature, a womaniser and a lousy father, but there was nothing clever or complex about him. Even trading me in was a cliché – part of me always knew he would.' This called to mind Martha's less-than-rosy predictions about my marriage. 'But Édouard is different. He has you in a vice you can't even see. It's completely part of the plan that you can't imagine leaving him. Haven't you noticed half of Paris is divorced? Think of all the couples we know who stayed together until retirement then realised they couldn't face being together all day, every day. That is twenty years away and this is how you feel after a couple of months – does that seem like a good sign to you?'

'It's a major life change when the children leave home. Everyone says so. I'll get used to it.'

'Christ, I really hope you don't. This sex club thing isn't just upsetting you because it's sleazy. It's forced you to realise he doesn't have anything serious with anyone else. Hoping your husband will leave you so you don't have to end it is the marital equivalent of suicide by cop. Plenty of women would settle for what you have, but if you want more, you're the one who has to do something because he likes things just fine as they are.'

As my sadness converted into anger, I had to get out before it turned into words.

'You may hate me right now,' Martha called down the stairs. 'But one person's bitch is another's best friend.'

Chapter 16

Frédéric was hunched over a large leather-bound book. Now we greeted each other with the *bise* like friends, both drawing back further than necessary afterwards (unless it was just me). I wanted to bottle those fleeting seconds, imagined burying my face against him to breathe in every atom, deeply. A man could really only come to one conclusion, but it wouldn't be the right one. The Iso E Super in his laundry detergent is a molecule commonly associated with sex and the bedroom, but I was only getting clean sheets.

Frédéric didn't look as if he'd been eating *or* sleeping, the skin under his eyes dark and fragile. Maybe I was looking for a diversion from worrying about Bastien; someone I could see, even only once a week. If Frédéric were to ask why I kept coming back, one half of the truth – *To return something I stole the first time* – was less embarrassing than the other – *It's not what you think, or at least I don't think so, but actually I don't know why I want to come here. I just do.*

He didn't ask, pointing to a chair at right angles to his.

'So you've decided it is worth opening on a Monday?'

There's something particularly lovely about a real smile from a sad person.

'Yes, but we won't be sitting here next week. Earlier today I sold this table and six chairs for more than I used to make in a month!' Frédéric grinned and I felt my heart lurch. I ran my hand across the mahogany tabletop, polished to a shine.

'*Bravo, génial!* If you don't mind me asking—'

'Four thousand euros! I said the first number that came into my head. It could have been anything – they didn't try to knock me down.'

Social graces will never be my forte but I've picked up a few during my Paris years. 'That wasn't what I was going to ask.'

'It's okay – we're both shopkeepers. So what was it?'

My intended question suddenly seemed far more inquisitive, but I couldn't think of an alternative. 'What did you do before this?'

Just in time, I stopped him from absent-mindedly scratching the table with a Bic he'd been twisting in his hand since I arrived. 'I managed a plumbing supplies factory near Lyon.' He gave a loud sigh. 'You see why I'm struggling with your world.' My world? I tried to unfrown myself. 'Perfume, antiques, art: things created to be pleasing rather than—'

'—practical,' I jumped in. 'So you've really decided to change paths?'

Frédéric pushed his chair back and put his feet up on another, fortunately not part of the dining set he'd sold. He leaned back and stared at the ceiling. 'I didn't decide anything,' he said, unwilling to meet my eye. 'The factory closed earlier this year when they moved the operations to Asia. People there work for a fraction of the money and think it's a good wage. My wife had left me the day before I found out. I wasn't expecting this,' he looked around the shop, 'on top of everything else. But I figured, what else am I going to do? Maybe – I know it sounds ridiculous – it's some sort of sign.'

'I'm sure your father would be pleased. Was he Lagarde *Fils*?'

'Yes, the original Lagarde was my grandfather. As for what my father would think of me taking over, I can't say. We hadn't been in touch for some time.'

My chest tightened, a reflex kicking in. I'd been estranged from my mother for half my life when she died. Yvette had begged me to see her one last time but I was never sure if it counted; Maman wasn't herself and nor, apparently, was I. She talked about her daughter as if I weren't there: *A good girl who went bad.* It was the nicest thing she'd ever said about me. *Poor Clémentine has no family except for one aunt*, my mother-in-law told a friend the day before Édouard and I married. She would have loved to know Yvette was in fact my half-aunt, my mother's much older half-sister. *Have you ever heard of anyone who has nobody but one aunt?*

'I'm so sorry, Frédéric. What a terrible time you've had.'

'Still, today's not so bad, what with that big sale then finding this.' He returned to the heavy bound ledger. 'It's a mystery how it ended up under the stairs.'

The smell of worn leather and old paper floated up from the browning pages – I could also detect the blue-black ink. The antique love letter was still in my bag, now in a robust outer envelope to keep it safe.

'Is it the inventory?' I got up to take a look.

'No, that's a separate book. My father never made it into the twenty-first century, computers or any of that – he loved fountain pens. This is more like a history of the artefacts, the provenance, how he came by them. Little anecdotes.'

'What elegant handwriting! This is a work of art in its own right. I bet there are some wonderful stories.' As we bent over the pages, side by side, I saw a single tear land to my right, sending a few words swimming with colour. I dabbed it with the tip of my scarf before it could spread, watching the moisture climb the fabric, giving Frédéric the chance to compose himself. 'The words are still alive,' he said, wrapping his hand in the scarf, touching mine for an instant. I hoped he wasn't about to start scrubbing at the paper. I missed the pressure on the back of my neck when he let go.

As I said, an instant.

'Of course, there may not be any truth in it. He may have made it all up to keep himself entertained. Even for a quiet man like my father, this is a solitary occupation.'

'Is there anything in there about the painting?' I couldn't bring myself to mention the perfume box.

'No,' he said, back to normal now. 'I went all the way through, searching.' Like the simple fact of me being here, taking up position in front of the canvas felt like a comforting habit.

Its extraordinary luminosity struck me even more this time. Here we were, in Paris in advancing autumn, when colour is a gift, the air often heavy with mist, the streets turning to windows in the rain. But this picture radiated heat, languor, mystery.

'Any more ideas where it might be?'

'Guesses. Maybe Andalucia, or somewhere in North Africa. With no people, there's not much to go on.'

The brushwork was remarkably precise. The components of the oil paints – linseed, ochre, ground stones – bloomed as strongly in my nose as the bougainvillea trailing down the side of a house, no need for a scented variety.

'There's an incredible sense of tranquillity to it.'

'And of heat, proper heat. Imagine that sun on your face.'

Had he noticed the absence of shadows, as I did in that moment? The thought that this might not be a real place or by an especially talented artist didn't disappoint me. I followed his finger as he pointed here and there, speculating. There was a new fluidity to his movements which put him in the scene, walking towards someone, smiling. I couldn't place myself there but nor was I here, all I could feel of my body was a rigid sandal post between my toes.

I looked down at my black leather boots.

'I don't know that much about art but this picture is like a well-composed perfume.' They sometimes broke the rules too. 'It draws you in every time and holds your interest,' I said. 'Look how we lose ourselves – somehow it's never the same place twice. Even when you look away, it lingers.' I felt my cheeks redden, grateful that here in the real world it was too dark to be obvious. Innocent on the surface, even the idea of finishing what I was saying had a charge: *I can't stop thinking about this picture. Everything it conjures, and one of them is you.*

'I don't know anything about art *or* perfume, but that's a nice explanation. What's the name of your perfume?'

'Well, there are ten on sale in the shop and I make others to order.'

'No, the one you wear. I really like it.'

I laughed. 'Believe it or not, I don't wear perfume.'

He made a tiny, barely audible inhalation. There was a shift, as if something unretractable had already been spoken.

'I can tell you need to leave,' Frédéric said. 'You were looking at your watch.' He was looking at my wedding ring, and there was no explaining that.

❧

The bathroom filled with verbena-scented steam. I wiped the mirror with the sleeve of my towelling robe and the woman there was almost smiling. Not bad at a glance, even with her hair scraped back. A sigh escaped me as I slid into the tub; for once I'd got the temperature just right. I'd had a burning ovulation pain on the left all day, my body faithful to its familiar rhythms, this one reliably causing a spike in my libido. It didn't let me forget its demands, if only for the weekly re-set I could give it. Not that it didn't feel good – it was pleasurable as routine chores go. But I couldn't touch myself the way my body longed to be touched. I could not be my own lover, nor could I picture the one I wanted. The water made me work harder, made it take longer, but the greater the frustration, the greater the release. I could scream with it. Sometimes at the crucial moment, the connection failed, but not tonight. The best part was surrendering my body to the water afterwards, feeling it surround me. Almost as if someone was holding me.

Chapter 17

It was the first time I'd left Suzanne in charge of the shop all day. When I asked how it went, she did a celebratory shimmy. 'Look at the takings.'

'Wow! That must be a record for a Thursday outside December.'

'That magazine article, between the people who come in having seen it and those who see it in the window—'

'Okay, I admit you were right about that.' She'd persuaded me in the end and it was gratifying that some good had come of the ordeal. How sad that Édouard wouldn't care. I wouldn't bother telling him.

Suzanne had only displayed the front cover in the window – supplied by the publisher, nothing as amateurish as one ripped off the magazine – and the double-page spread inside. After asking me who'd designed the storefront, she'd persuaded them to supply the line '*Le parfum, c'est l'émotion*' in white lettering for the window and made sure to have it added when I wasn't around. The occasional doubts about my sales assistant hadn't extended to her making furtive and unauthorised decisions about the business, but on the evidence it wasn't such a bad thing.

Seen back to front from inside, the quote didn't grate quite so much. 'I felt so foolish when I came out with that. Maybe it's not such a cliché after all.'

Suzanne roared with laughter. 'Are you serious? People love clichés – that's how they come about, *non*? Anyway, it's absolutely true what you say about perfume and emotion. You can see it in people's faces. I can see in yours that this is your passion. It turns you into a different person.' Whenever Suzanne embarked on a topic I was torn between wanting her take and the unsettling suspicion that I might prefer not to hear it. Unless I intervened, she'd tell me anyway. 'You often look a bit down the rest of the time. You've reached the age where . . . ' Suzanne held her hands up to her flawless face but instantly abandoned any hope of conveying the ravages before her. She shrugged on seeing my expression. '*Mais c'est normal!* We're all going to die one day.'

That was over the line. 'Suzanne, your perspective can be very enlightening but frankly, I'm only forty-six and you're pushing it.'

'Anger is an emotion,' she said, gleefully. It came to me, the reason I enjoyed the banter when it wasn't quite this personal. Suzanne had no filter, like Bastien when he was growing up. His attempts to provoke Édouard were often entertaining, except when they really succeeded. The left-wing politics. The innuendo at the dinner table. His love of philosophical debate, which Édouard absolutely cannot stand. 'But if you'll hear me out,' said Suzanne. 'You come to life when you talk about your work. Actually, you don't even have to say anything. It's like you're thinking about your lover.'

At that, I really couldn't look her in the eye. Not because she thought I might have one, but because the idea no longer seemed so far-fetched. I'd had a few opportunities over the years, once getting as far as the door of a hotel room in Grasse before losing my nerve. It had been a point of principle not to behave like Édouard. One of us had to show some respect for the show we were putting on.

'Any interesting customers?' I ventured a return to safer territory – perhaps. I couldn't ask outright if Suzanne had offended or taken against anyone who'd come in, but lately it concerned me less, thinking of the rude and neglectful service I sometimes received elsewhere. There was bound to be the odd casualty. Some customers loved to take offence, and while Suzanne didn't go out of her way to provoke confrontation, she was happy to go the distance with anyone so inclined.

'The big sale was a tiny old man from Taiwan with this huge lump of muscle for a bodyguard. I could tell from how he was standing that he was carrying a gun.'

'Eight-fifty in one transaction? That *is* a record.'

'He took a liking to me, asking where I'm from and all that.' Brave man. Suzanne's standard reply to this – not unreasonably – was, *The 13th arrondissement.* 'Anyway, when he said he had lots of female relatives to buy gifts for and could I help him decide, I said why not take one of each and let them fight it out? I was being cheeky, but he took all ten.'

'You're incredible! I hope he doesn't get into trouble trying to take that much perfume on a plane.'

'Not our problem.' Suzanne's expression changed. 'That reminds me. That woman was back – the one who tried to block the door the other day.'

I'd still not seen this person. 'Just take care of the customers. There's nothing we can do about what happens on the street. As you say, not our problem.'

We paused, watching the window cleaner chase suds across the glass in flamboyant arcs as if peeling an orange in one strip. 'Look at that technique,' Suzanne said, with a little growl. 'Makes you wonder what else he might be good at.'

'Suzanne, stop drooling! That's Diouc. He'll be in for his money in a minute.' Diouc was certainly good-looking and had a lovely smile, but I wasn't used to thinking of him that way. After he'd gone back outside, I couldn't resist a tease.

'I can't believe you asked him where he's from. It would have served you right if he'd said Seine-Saint-Denis. For example,' I added quickly. Suzanne would be surprised to learn that I used to live there.

'But he didn't, did he?' Diouc took pride in telling her he was from Mali. 'Hard to believe anyone who works as a window cleaner has money to send home.'

'He works three jobs and I've never heard him complain.'

'The things people have to do to get by.' Suzanne was disarmingly upfront about her sexual appetite and had opinions on everything, but I'd never seen her in contemplative mode.

'While we're selling luxuries? Don't think I'm unaware.'

'Pfft! what people do with their money is up to them. In the gallery clients would spend fifteen thousand on some hideous piece of crap they would never even look at. Sometimes they paid and couldn't be bothered to get it shipped.'

Diouc was busy packing up his kit.

'I must go and set up for my bespoke at eleven. You can have a proper lunch break today.' Suzanne nodded but she still looked serious.

'I didn't finish the story about that odd woman. She came in yesterday and stood in the middle of the shop, staring at the merchandise, not touching anything. When I spoke, she ignored me, so I just left her to it. But it freaked me out. Luckily there were no customers or it would have been very awkward.'

I made the thoughtful sigh that usually precedes something worth saying. 'Hopefully that'll be the end of it.'

'That's what worries me – I don't think it will. As she left, she said, *I've found you, Clémentine.*'

❧

As if I wasn't nervous enough about my first bespoke consultation in months. Meeting a new client was usually one of the best parts of the job: the expectation, the possibilities. The challenge of creating something unique, which could give pleasure for years – some have been coming to me since before I opened the shop, returning for refills or to commission something for the new season or a personal landmark. It mirrored my social life in that there were now more divorces than weddings; the newly single generally seemed elated, but it wasn't likely that I would see those who were devastated.

I'd responded to Suzanne's revelation as if the woman was a troubled stranger. After all, even the name of my shop could set someone off if they had history with a Clémentine. (I hadn't said this because Suzanne would have been on to me right away.) I kept trying to focus on my client, Dolores, who'd recently moved to Paris with her husband on his final diplomatic posting pre-retirement. Reluctantly, it appeared. She explained at great length that she hadn't wanted to leave Washington DC and her two grandchildren in the States. The bespoke perfume was a gift from her elder daughter, whom I remembered from her visit to the shop earlier in the year, and the brief, as Consuela told me then, was a perfume to make her mother fall in love with Paris. I hadn't foreseen what I'd be up against. Dolores made it clear she wasn't listening when I started running through the safety precautions.

It didn't help that we were both having to do it in our second language and she had the advantage. I had never spoken English day in, day out, but Dolores was fluent, with a heavy accent both Hispanic and American and a mournful note perfectly suited to her mood, or if I was really unlucky, her personality. 'I don't understand why people love Paris so much. Everyone tells me what I'm supposed to feel. I just don't.'

I replied that some places take a while to reveal themselves and it was the same with fragrances, some going for instant seduction, the finest acquiring new and unexpected layers as time goes on. We could even find inspiration in this when designing hers. With Dolores staring at me as if I was spouting nonsense, it started to sound that way. 'It's like the length on a wine,' I said, still casting around for an image. Her complete lack of enthusiasm made me realise how much I was usually fuelled by the client's ideas and excitement, which I channelled to help them decide exactly what they wanted. It's so rare that you can have that to order. A bespoke perfume is worn often, not like a couture dress – they must want to live with it. For it to be a success, they need to love the boost it gives them, delight in how it makes them feel.

Dolores and I had established nothing except her wish not to be here. I tossed my notebook and pen down on the desk. 'We're both wasting our time. You can have a refund.'

She inhaled her indignation, as if I'd told her to fuck off, although that was basically the gist. 'Is this how you speak to clients?'

'Not at all. But I've never had to create a perfume for someone who's not interested. It can't be done. You'd be better off treating yourself to something that *will* please you.'

'But Consuela must have paid a lot of money for this.'

'She did indeed. You could probably get an Hermès scarf for what I charge. Maybe you could fall in love with that.'

For a second I thought Dolores was going to hit me, and I deserved it. Instead she dissolved into hysterics. I couldn't help joining in, and before long we both had tears streaming down our cheeks. Once we'd mopped our streaky faces and it was clear I'd failed to drive her away, I resolved to behave in a more professional manner. The cathartic episode had freed Dolores to find some pay-off in the experience: not in perfume, but in annihilating Paris, Parisians, tourists, beggars and *leaves falling off trees in autumn*. She turned her nose up at nine out of ten ingredients (on average – we sampled more), ruling out practically any harmonious combination, but left beaming, clutching an envelope of tester strips.

I leaned on the wall outside the workshop, so drained I could hardly stand up. I'd been so convinced the odd stranger would be waiting in the shop that it was an anticlimax to find nobody there but Suzanne, who glowered at me before flouncing out for lunch. On her return I pleaded a headache, truthfully, saying I was taking the rest of the day off. At the river I walked westward this time, counting off the bridges and wishing I'd remembered to change into more practical shoes. The cobbles hurt my feet as if I was barefoot. It was tempting to sit down, but if I stopped moving I'd be more vulnerable to the shock.

My hands clawed at the lining of my coat pockets.

Had I known all along it was Racha? Certainly not the first time Suzanne mentioned her – it really could have been anyone at that point. But the Ludo lookalike at Gabrielle's party had destroyed the illusion of distance between my life now and my life before, and one did not obliterate the other. It had suited me not to press Suzanne for details of the woman's appearance or to speculate about her reasons for loitering outside my shop. Some things it does not pay to think about.

But I had never seriously entertained the idea that it could be Racha. When someone has been out of your life for over twenty-five years, you never expect to see them again, to be forced to look back and see them in a different light. I didn't have to lay eyes on Racha now to know how painful this would be. Her strange behaviour made me fear what the years had done to her. I never thought it was possible to feel greater regret over what *I'd* done to her. But it was, and I did, and I was going to have to face it.

When Édouard first took me to the Jura to meet his family, I overheard his sister saying, *He's still in love with the girl before.* It was a perverse comfort to know we both felt the same way.

You tell yourself you've moved on because how could you not, after so long? The evidence gathers in years, in your face: who and what you live for; who and what you destroy.

Ludo used to be the dangerous one, before I was driven to it. I had to wonder whose turn it was now.

Chapter 18

Provence, 1992

'Clémentine, there's a Marc asking for you on the phone!' My mother yelled from the kitchen, as it would be too much effort to make it to the bottom of the stairs. She was hardly ever up before me. My bed sheet was on the floor next to my clothes, which stank of booze, straw and smoke. I pulled them on and stuck my head out of my bedroom door. 'Who?'

'Marc from Marseille. Do you think he wants you back?'

I ran downstairs, hangover lurching around my insides, and snatched the receiver. There was no Marc who'd be calling me, from Marseille or anywhere else.

'*Ici Clémentine.*'

'*C'est moi,*' said Ludo. 'Thought I'd better stay incognito with things as they are. I knew your mother wouldn't recognise my voice.'

I kicked the door to and felt the house judder. 'Leave her out of this, *Marc*. You've got a nerve calling *with things as they are*. What do you want?'

'You didn't say goodbye last night.'

The overpowering feelings Ludo set off in me came in several varieties, all good in some way. I'd learned very early to tamp my emotions down. 'Are you serious? What were you playing at, inviting me in the first place?'

'*Calme-toi!* We can't discuss this on the phone. Meet me up at the track.'

'Give me one reason why I'd do that.'

'Because you want to.'

As I slammed the phone down, I snarled like my grand-dad's old dog we used to suspect was rabid. I would go, but I would not calm down. Within moments of going outside I was sweating, heat coming from the ground as well as the air – the sun was directly overhead and it was barely morning at all. Peace had been restored *dans la nature* with only the sound of cicadas – not even a tractor, as it was Sunday. Nothing marked the boundary between our land and the public path apart from a faded tin sign saying 'Private Property – No Hunting', as if anyone would bother trespassing. Ludo was waiting in the shade and his expression caught me off guard, as if I'd been about to sing the words of one song to the tune of another. He held up his hands before I could begin. 'Whatever you're going to say, you're right, and I'm sorry. You're young and it was too soon – you didn't know what to expect.'

'What, after you'd said *this really meant something*?' The sarcasm dripped deliciously off my tongue. 'It's not as if it only happened once.' We'd met up several times between the forest and the party. 'Is it some kind of sick game you play with your girlfriend? And then you send her out to rub it in. Bet you both had a great time laughing at me.'

Talking about Racha brought her so vividly to mind that I looked around, as if she might step out of the trees. She'd said some weird things, for sure, as upfront as Ludo was desperate to appear mysterious. At first I mistook my sudden gnawing for hunger, having missed breakfast, but even though we'd only spoken for a quarter of an hour, I missed her. I stifled a laugh. Ludo wasn't as clever as he or I thought. 'Was it supposed to help you choose, seeing us together? Because it looked to me as if you'd already made up your mind.' A nasty sensation crawled across my skin, recalling the torment of watching them, having to pretend I wasn't, and to myself that I didn't want to.

Ludo looked thoughtful, but he couldn't quite manage sincere. 'It would be hard to choose between you girls. You're very different.'

'But to be clear, you're happy to fuck either of us.'

He winced. 'No need to be crude. Especially when I was about to say that you're so sweet and Racha's so tough. She's seen things you and I couldn't even imagine. But in your own ways, you're both very exciting.' Ludo didn't know what was making me smile. I was used to being ignored, insulted and looked down on, but I was starting to realise it gave me the upper hand. Nobody had a clue who they were dealing with. 'I knew I could count on you not to be too bourgeois about this, Clémentine. It's summer! We are young! How old are you?'

'Twenty.' I startled myself with the truth.

'Well then! You won't be twenty for ever. Just think how you'll look back on this summer when you're forty-five or . . .'

Maman was precisely that age and I'd seen a lot of her lately, as she couldn't get dressed without help. She said she used to have breasts like mine: not large, but full and round and firm. What had happened to her face was my fault too, apparently; nothing to do with the drink or the fags. 'Thanks,' I said. 'I get the idea.'

'Let's go to my place, start over. Or pick up where we left off, however you want to look at it. If you didn't like me, you wouldn't be so cross, eh?' He made a silly *forgive me* face and I couldn't help myself – he could be incredibly annoying, but the sex . . . 'I've got the old lodge on the far side of the *domaine*. It'll just be us, I promise.'

I watched a large ant carrying a leaf make a detour round my foot. 'I can't. I have to get to the market. There's no food in the house.' Going late was not purely a matter of laziness. The stallholders dropped their prices towards the end, or sometimes gave away fruit and veg past its best. Ludo looked around. 'How about here then?'

'Are you mad? Anyone could walk by.' I was starting to think Ludo had something against doing it indoors.

'Oh, come on. It's Sunday lunchtime – nobody's going to be out walking in this heat. Let's go behind those trees. Imagine what Racha would say.'

Something flickered at the idea that she and I wanted the same thing.

'So you're not going to make me wait then.' Ludo already had a hard-on, covering my hand with his. Just metres from the track, he bent me over, one arm tight around my waist, working me with his fingers at the same time. It was sweaty, uncomfortable, the pleasure intolerable. I dropped to the ground, eyes tight shut as it reverberated. I didn't need to see his face.

❧

Maman had gone back to drinking during the day. By the time she got out of bed she was more interested in red wine than coffee or *tartines*. She ate next to nothing, said she didn't need to. 'I'm not doing anything, am I?' I'd learned to be patient when she was like this, thinking the world had it in for her. 'You broke your arm. It was an accident,' I said, for the hundredth time. It was pointless trying to make her feel better. She wasn't even a happy drunk. 'It'll mend.'

And it would, eventually. But our visit to the hospital in Avignon had brought bad news: her arm wasn't healing right. They needed to operate and that meant the last month in plaster counted for nothing. 'What if it stays as it is?' I asked. The nurse looked at me as if I was evil, but my mother looked at her almost hopefully before turning to the doctor. 'Out of the question, I'm afraid,' he said. 'You would never recover full use of the limb. It's bad luck, but one of those times you have to take the long view.'

Anyone could see what he thought of us. For some people, there is only the short view. I could have recited what this meant for my mother like a shopping list: losing her job, worsening depression and heavy drinking pulling her into a hole that was very hard to climb out of, even with two functioning arms.

At home, I waited for the raging and cursing like when I was little and used to hover around, scared to leave her, scared to make things worse, like the time I asked if she'd feel better if my papa came back. *But how can you not know?* was the question that ended my innocence.

I was older before I realised that *We're damned, my girl* was not a typical family saying and now she was only saying it about herself it sounded wrong. She was freeing me to walk away. For once she wasn't blaming the Bellechasses, the mayor or the government for her problems. Or the church. 'Mary Magdalene was a bigger slut than me, and she made it into the Bible,' she once yelled across the village square at the brave priest who'd made several attempts to offer spiritual guidance. 'Bet you just want your cock sucked like all the rest.' Maman's outbursts often reached me on the grapevine, but I was with her that time, aged around thirteen, and she'd laughed at my tears of mortification. Even though I was an adult now, she still called me the *Holy Virgin* sometimes, though she knew I was neither.

With the news about her arm, the balance shifted. I was no longer a millstone but someone with the ability, finally, to help make things better. 'I'll get fired when you go back to Marseille,' she said flatly. 'You'll never be twenty again and you've wasted your summer for nothing.'

I didn't stop to think, or even to register the rareness of my mother taking me into consideration. 'I haven't wasted anything, and I'm not going back.' I did want to be a good daughter – I always had – but there was more to it. One of the many things she hadn't noticed was that I was having the time of my life.

Chapter 19

'Madame says you know each other,' Suzanne said, from behind the counter. The woman with her back to me was leaning heavily on a crutch. I couldn't breathe in the seconds it took her to turn around.

'*Te voilà*,' Racha said, her voice the same as ever. Two words was all it took, but it was the sight of her that nearly made me pass out. I showed her through to the workshop, but once we were alone she seemed in no hurry to say anything. It was obvious right away that she was now shorter than me, bowed by a pronounced limp. Her hair was dyed a dark reddish brown with grey roots. In the face of a woman much older than we were, it wasn't the creases and shadows that shocked me but the eyes I used to stare into so close up they resembled nothing. They were Racha *tout simplement* and they hadn't changed at all.

After the consultation with Dolores, I'd left the desk strewn with notes, equipment and ingredients, some of the bottles still uncapped. It had never looked such a mess. Racha's eyes swept around the small space, coming to land on two pairs of heels lined up underneath a bench where clients wouldn't see them. She hesitated before taking off her long down jacket – not the brightly coloured ultra-light type that people were wearing in Paris before winter set in, but a heavy one with matted fake fur round the hood. It swamped her and she looked fragile without it.

She turned her attention to me, raising her eyebrows as she looked me up and down. With my clothes on, I don't look so very different to back then, but I doubted either of us wore much in our memories. 'Time's been kind to one of us,' she said. 'Don't deny that you're shocked. You're going to hear what the last twenty-five years have been like for me, *ma belle*, but you get the general idea.'

Her gesture was like a hideous parody of Suzanne's delight in her perfection, but I could tell Racha was who she'd always been; it was me I wasn't sure about. It's rare to be held to account for the mistakes of youth decades later. Sometimes people with history meet again and feel nothing, but I couldn't, not without reliving the times we made each other laugh and cry and far more that hurt to recall.

'Don't pity me! I haven't come here for that.'

I sighed. Playing games was something I'd grown out of – Édouard and I didn't needlessly antagonise each other. 'What have you come for?'

'Never thought you'd see me again, did you?'

'No, I didn't.'

'Never wanted to?'

I snatched a breath behind my hand, not wanting to be the one who broke eye contact. Now I was back in her grip, Racha wasn't going to let me go.

'There hasn't been a day I haven't thought of you.' This was true, if you included the thoughts I'd held beneath the waterline. Tried and failed to drown.

'That's very touching,' she said, 'but it's not what I asked.'

119

'Correct.' My reply reminded me of Édouard's chilling TV performance. 'I never wanted or expected you to reappear in my life.'

Racha's smile was bitter but not without amusement. 'No wonder you're not pleased to see me.'

'What do you expect, turning up at my shop like this? Not just today ... those other times you came here, acting unhinged. If you wanted to see me, now you have. If you're not happy with the welcome ...'

Racha got to her feet, pulling herself up against the crutch and reached for her coat, snatching it from me when I held it out for her. 'Listen,' I said, 'I didn't mean—' I didn't know what I meant.

'Oh, did you think you were driving me away? I'm tougher than that. You have no idea how tough I've had to be.'

She gave me no choice but to follow her back to the shop as if I were the interloper here, in my own life.

As if? I was.

Racha made sure Suzanne was watching. 'I didn't come here for an apology,' she said. 'I'm way past believing fine words do any good.' She looked around again and wrinkled her nose. 'Any more than this fancy stuff. It changes nothing.'

❧

Édouard was leaving for five days in New York, to be chastised by the parent company no longer so pleased with their latest European acquisition. I felt none of the usual lightness in anticipation of sleeping in my own bed and being able to just *be*, but I could absorb the impact of Racha's arrival without having to act naturally. It hadn't fully hit me, but I could feel it coming.

'Are you all right? You're looking very pale,' Édouard said. There was concern in his voice but not surprise; if our recent dealings had established anything it was that I was definitely not all right, each day less than the one before. My eyeballs were the dead grey of overboiled eggs and some new upright bunches of lines had appeared at my temples, bouquets without blooms.

'I've been sleeping badly. Last night hardly at all.' I'd lain awake until gone three, rigid with anxiety, willing my body to release its weight into the mattress.

'Leave the new girl to it and get some rest.' I'd eventually mentioned Suzanne in passing. Even the most strained small talk has to be about something.

'Good idea.' Much as I wanted to believe there was no chance of seeing Racha again if I stayed away, instinct told me our unsettling encounter wouldn't be the end of it. Despite her promise, she hadn't told me anything, not even where she lived. The thought that Racha might have been in Paris all along made my skin prickle – it was difficult to imagine any of us continuing to exist away from the south, although that's precisely what I'd done. Tearing up your own roots is a form of violence.

I didn't have the excuse of being young and stupid any more.

'Where are you staying?' Édouard and I had little contact when he travelled unless there was some delay to his return.

'Some place on the Upper West Side. Can't remember the name.'

He may not have opted for his favourite hotel but he was in for a five-star roasting and he knew it.

'You'll get through this,' I said, aware that this was only true in as far as it was unlikely to involve death. Édouard looked so dejected that I pitied him. This wasn't what he had in mind, after all the years spent getting where he'd wanted to be. The absence of love doesn't necessarily equal hatred, or even indifference. Sometimes, like now, there was a strange prickly bond. It didn't give me hope for us as a couple, but there was a glimmer for each of us, a vestigial sign that we were still human beneath our many flaws.

Édouard gave a weak smile. Men like my husband are paid to make everything look good and go right, and to be the head that rolls when it doesn't. A notification flashed up on his phone and he reached for his overcoat and suitcase. 'Car in three minutes,' he said. 'I should go down.' Poor Édouard didn't even get to share his woes with the cabbie – they were both public knowledge and confidential. 'Look after yourself, Clémentine. You'll feel better when you can spread your little bottles all over the kitchen.' I tried to smile, telling myself not to feel patronised when he was trying to be decent. 'And you can have that son of yours over to visit,' he added.

Not twenty seconds ago, I'd thought we might celebrate our temporary release from each other with a commiserating hug. Instead, I turned away with a barely audible '*bon voyage*', going onto the balcony in time to see his Uber leave for Charles de Gaulle. It would take far longer than the RER but since his TV appearance and the press coverage that followed, Édouard spent every hour on damage limitation, the signs increasingly suggesting that the damage was primarily to him and his hitherto illustrious career.

Édouard wasn't to know how I'd been feeling about my own work, but I sought comfort where he had predicted, in my perfume organ. I removed every bottle, bundling them onto the kitchen table in random handfuls. A few fell on the floor, rolling around, and one disappeared under the sideboard. When the shelves were empty I set to cleaning the cabinet with plain water, inside and out. Waiting for it to dry, I reordered the contents alphabetically by section, breathing from the base of my lungs to energise my body or calm my mind or something. Once Dolores decided what it was she wanted, I would have to come up with her perfume some-how. Unlike everything else, there was a solution to this – I had records of every fragrance I'd ever made and could cheat if I had to, but it wouldn't come to that.

Whoever and whatever I lost, I would have this – Yvette was right when she forced me into the garden of her house in Grasse, making me see it was spring outside the shutters. I had no inkling that she was teaching me my trade. The ingredient she began with was *super bleue* lavender, grown at altitude in the Alpes de Haute-Provence, a plant exceptionally intense in both colour and note, a harmless high. 'If that doesn't make you want to live,' she said, 'nothing will.' Yvette would have been a good mother.

As my head filled with the scent, my worries fell into order, Édouard going to the bottom of the pile as his parting words rose to the top. Whatever Racha wanted would have to take second place to *my son*. Our only contact since he and Édouard had met at home by accident was the text exchange:

Ça va?

Ça va.

I'd invite Bastien over, not because his father had suggested it or even because I was still missing him as if someone had snatched my newborn baby. Even if he didn't come, I needed to know he was okay. I picked up the phone to try.

Ça va?

Shit, I'd done it again, instead of asking a question that needed a proper reply. I slammed the phone down and picked it up, expecting to find that I'd cracked the screen.

He'd already replied. *Not great.*

Dinner at home? Papa in NY this week.

It's not that bad!

I left it for now, but with a smile.

Next I would reclaim my space. It was always strange to

walk into what was supposed to be the marital bedroom. At this time of year, Édouard rarely opened the shutters – it was dark when he left for work and dark when he got home. In these conditions, my nose goes into overdrive – I'd make an excellent sniffer dog. I detected the leather of some shoes he doesn't wear very often, a younger design; the wool of a perfectly cut dark grey Italian suit, with the faintest tinge of dry-cleaning fluid. Particles of a different cologne to his usual hung in the air. Like my products, it had a short formula, the seductive citrus spicy accord comprised of only a handful of ingredients. I glanced around for the bottle, suspecting Terre d'Hermès, but of course he'd taken it with him. A seminal undertone in the room told me that despite his *relations extra-conjugales*, I wasn't the only one falling back on solitary pleasures.

Time to air the place out. The section of balcony belonging to the bedroom was unloved, joined to the rest but separated by plant pots. The view was of the side street leading to boulevard Raspail and the traffic noise was more noticeable. A few degrees, a change of perspective, the ripples of another distant memory about to break the surface.

This was the only home we'd ever owned. I stood out here the day we moved in, five-year-old Apolline running around shrieking with excitement, Bastien squirming in my arms, a year old but not yet walking. It wasn't the street view that I recalled but looking into the room and catching Édouard's eye, holding it for once. Something passed between us, a kind of *we've really done it now*. I felt a forlorn hope that we could make something of it. The main ingredient was missing, but there were others, after all. Two we'd made together.

It could be said that our marriage had worked, on its own odd and unspoken terms. It must have, for me to still be here. Turning to strip Édouard's bed sheets, I found a white envelope propped against the pillows, unsealed and unad-dressed. Evidently he knew I moved back in the second he went away.

The expanse of blank space added impact to the single handwritten line:

You're right, we should talk properly. It's not that I don't want to. I don't know how.

I sat down hard, staring at the page, and something inside me twisted. Édouard and I had more in common than I'd realised.

Chapter 20

'If that woman bothers you again, let me handle it,' Suzanne said. 'I was about to get rid of her yesterday when you walked back in.' Her protectiveness was touching, despite the tone. 'None of that would have happened if you'd gone home like you said. And after that Dolores in the morning too . . . Don't look at me like I'm some sort of prima donna!' I tried not to look however I was looking. 'You've never had to serve customers with that racket going on at the back.'

I'd completely blown it with Suzanne where professional boundaries were concerned. It made no difference hiring strangers in the end; working closely alongside someone, you learn too much about their opinions, moods and habits, and even without a crisis, it was hard to hide my own.

'Assume I could walk in at any moment,' I said, although I didn't mean it to sound so creepy. 'And anyway, you're my *vendeuse*, not my bodyguard. Treat anyone who comes here as a customer.' She gave me the foxy smile I'd seen a few times. 'A *customer*, Suzanne, not who you're thinking about. One you're nice to.' I sat down behind the counter, rubbing my back through my coat. Sleeping in my own bed hadn't brought me comfort or peace. 'Racha wasn't going to give up without speaking to me – it would have happened sooner or later.'

'If you knew who she was all along, why didn't you say?'

'I didn't, until you said she'd mentioned me by name. You weren't very forthcoming with the details, and I hadn't seen her in an extremely long time.'

'I assumed she was a nutcase. She doesn't seem like someone you'd know. What was I supposed to do – offer her an appointment?'

When Suzanne moved away from the counter I had a burst of panic thinking she was about to walk out on me. 'You haven't done anything wrong and I'm sorry you had to get involved. She'll be back, but you have my word we'll take it elsewhere. If I'm not here, call me straight away and get her to wait at the café.' I didn't think to say a different café to my usual, and it would sound bad if I changed it now. 'You can take Friday afternoon off, if a long weekend would make up for the stress?' Suzanne didn't work Saturdays because of a film project with friends, which was ideal for me because I didn't like spending Saturdays at home.

'Thanks, it would.' She perked up. 'I thought you said it would be boring working here. So, who is she, then?'

Suzanne never wasted time disguising intrusive questions. 'A friend from a very different period of my life. I suppose "former friend" would be more accurate. Things ended badly between us.'

'Sounds more like a break-up.'

It was nothing like any break-up I'd ever heard of. 'Haven't you ever had a friendship end painfully?'

'I've had all kinds of things end painfully.'

As I walked towards the river I had a premonition that the antique shop had disappeared and Frédéric with it, so when I turned the corner and saw the lights on I had to stop and pull myself together. He was with a customer, and although it would have been more tactful to wait until the man left, I was curious to see Frédéric around other people. I slipped in with a quick greeting to show I didn't intend to interrupt and made for the back of the showroom to look at the painting. The two men were still visible and within earshot, but only just. The stranger was older and faintly familiar, although I wasn't sure if I'd seen him or just knew the type, exuding wealth and refinement. This was a very different Frédéric. He was clean-shaven and smartly dressed, and as he still hadn't had his hair cut, it was starting to look rather arty and suited him. Most surprisingly of all, he was holding forth about the short-case clock near the desk like a pro. When the man suddenly announced he had to leave, Frédéric didn't appear too disappointed and they parted with smiles and a handshake.

Frédéric seemed to sense the swell of pride I felt, as if he meant something to me. After the second *bise*, he rested his chin against the top of my head and sighed deeply. On realising that he'd wrapped his arms around me, I tensed up and he released me with muttered apologies. I brushed them aside but it was as intimate as if he'd kissed me. Almost more.

'Things are going well then? With the shop, that is. You have a nice way with customers.'

Frédéric ran the back of his hand across his forehead and took his jacket off, hanging it over a balloon-back chair. 'I wasn't really expecting Michel to buy anything, although he may at some point. He was a friend of my father's – I vaguely remember him from when I was growing up – but we didn't really speak at the funeral. He's very interested in clocks, but that wasn't the hard part. That was not letting on how things stood between me and my father, although it seems Papa was pretty good at that himself.' Mindful of Suzanne's nosiness and the natural response to clam up, I waited, but eventually took his silence as an invitation to ask. He could change the subject if he wanted to. 'When my dad died, we hadn't seen or spoken to each other in five years. I know what you must be thinking.'

A red umbrella in the street drew my eye. I looked away for the time it took several vehicles to pass. No one ever knows what anyone's thinking.

'I'm used to disapproval, from colleagues, friends, even my ex. People find it unnatural. Wrong.'

'No,' I shook my head. 'It's sad. It's not how it's supposed to be. And judging others is the only way some people can live with themselves. Do you still have your mother?'

His shoulders dropped. 'I never had my mother. She died in labour. It was just me and dad. You might think he'd hold it against me – they hadn't been together very long and they were really in love. But if he did, it never showed.'

'Oh, Frédéric, that's desperately sad, for both of you.' Now I wanted to hug him, I couldn't risk it. There was resignation as he continued, in a quieter voice. 'Yes, but nobody was to blame. That was part of the problem. Dad never sued the hospital, said that sometimes tragedies just happen and you have to carry on the best you can. Later I could see how exhausting it must have been to earn a living and look after me – nothing could bring her back. But I needed someone to be angry with. Livid. I was a little shit as a teenager, baiting him, rebelling, desperate for him to lash out.'

'Plenty of teenagers are difficult without what you'd been through.' Maybe I'd tell him about Bastien one day. 'Your dad must have understood. He sounds like a lovely man.'

Frédéric dabbed at his eyes with the cuff of his shirt. 'If my ex could see me now she'd be amazed – I'm useless at communicating, apparently.'

'You're not, and anyway, it's not easy.' Maybe that's why I ended up with Édouard, safe from conversations in a language neither of us speak.

'Sorry, I don't know why I said that. I'm glad Agathe's not here.'

'But you stayed in contact with your dad for years after leaving home. That counts.'

'True, only to fall out for no good reason. He was trying to tell me how to live my life and siding with Agathe against me. I should just have told him to back off. It all goes back to my childhood, like everyone says.' Frédéric looked at me and groaned into his hands. 'I wish we hadn't got on to this. It's pathetic. Here I am, forty-two years old and still not over never having a mother.'

'No!'

'No, what?'

'It's not pathetic. Nothing you've said surprises me. It's not the same, but I grew up without a father. Never even knew who he was and I don't think my mother did either. Eventually I had to accept that I'd never find out.'

'That must have been very hard.'

'It was, especially as we made that absence so much worse for each other. It was as if she was my half-mother, me her half-daughter, when there's no such thing. As a child, I longed for this ideal person who would have made everything all right.'

Frédéric nodded. 'That makes sense. Imaginary parents don't have faults.'

'My mother filled it with anger towards men, though she couldn't stay away from them, and me if I wasn't careful. She wasn't as noble as your dad in that respect, and I wasn't as brave as you. I didn't dare act up. For a long time I didn't dare do anything. Anyway, all I wanted to say was—'

'It's okay, I understand.'

'Exactly that – I understand.'

'Thank you, Clémentine.' Frédéric stood up and put his jacket back on. 'Unbelievable,' he said, as I followed him to the front of the shop.

'What is?'

'How you get up every day without a clue what might happen, even if you think you do. I spent all morning swotting up on early-nineteenth-century Swiss wall clocks and we end up talking about this.'

I was light-headed, as if I'd stood up too quickly. Maybe I did speak that language after all. 'It is a very pretty clock. I'd love to hear your spiel, if you can remember it.'

I didn't so much see the spark of connection in his green eyes as feel it, and smiled to hide a sudden urge to cry. The clock chimed a single note on the half hour. 'You know what?' Frédéric said. 'It's gone right out of my head.'

Chapter 21

Provence, 1992

'It was an open–top car, vintage, with four people dressed in 1920s style. They did this synchronised wave, like they were in a movie. You should have seen them!' The sun was setting and although it was over in seconds, I'd been replaying the scene endlessly in my head.

'I have seen them. Several times, over the years.'

'Do you know who they are?'

Ludo hesitated. 'I wouldn't go that far, but I have an idea.'

'Are they from Paris?'

He laughed. 'Oh, Clémentine, it's going to be such a let-down when you finally get there. But as it happens, they are, or thereabouts. They're just ordinary people who like playing bohemians,' he said. 'It must have made their day, seeing the wonder on your pretty little face.'

I felt myself blushing, but I was pleased, after worrying that Ludo had begun to tire of me. 'How do you know all this?'

'They come down every summer. One of the men is related to the people with the château near the Sainte-Victoire.'

'He's a Picasso?'

'Not *that* château! There's another big house at the far end of the mountain – it's the back of beyond. I could take you, if you like.' I must have looked dubious. 'Think of all the years I've spent going to markets in the area, drinking in bars,' he said. 'There are at least five places they think of me as a local. I know the caretaker. Bet you anything the owners will be gone like the holidaymakers after the *quinze août*. All sorts of things go on in that property if someone's willing to cross the old man's palm. Showing you around won't cost me more than a few drinks.' He saw my reluctance. 'What's the problem? You go into strangers' houses every day, touching their things, the beds they fuck in.'

I hated Ludo talking about my job like that. There was no comparison with what he was proposing and it depressed me that while I did what I had to, he could pick and choose his amusements. Even the family business was like a hobby to him. But he was talking fast and his eyes were shining, all because of me. 'Come on, *tu vas adorer*! It's an empty house – nobody's going to get hurt.'

We agreed to meet at his place and I was looking forward to the drive down the gorge with Ludo at the wheel. It summed up what it was like with him: out of control, swinging between danger and feeling intensely alive. There were voices from inside his cottage: Ludo and a woman with a deep, unusual laugh. Racha. And it was her voice calling me as I turned to walk away. 'Clémentine, where are you going? We've been waiting for you.'

Ludo appeared in the doorway, holding the keys high above her head. '*On y va?*'

Racha ducked back inside. Her hair was loosely plaited with wisps escaping. 'There's something wrong with you,' I told Ludo under my breath. 'Surely you don't think I'd go anywhere with the two of you?'

Ludo threw a glance behind him but there was no sign of Racha. 'Listen to me before you stalk off. Racha's only hope is to get away from that place, and even here she doesn't have it that great. She's got no car, no way of getting around. You have to understand, she's never seen anything—'

'—except that shithole she comes from.' Racha leaned out of the door, swinging on the frame, a shadow hiding the view down her vest top. It was hard to tell if she was amused or insulted.

I had never seen Ludo on the back foot. 'I didn't say that.'

'No,' she grinned now. 'I did. Let's get on with it, if you're so keen to show us poor unfortunates how the other half live. You don't mind me coming, do you, Clémentine?'

The mother's a drunk who's banged half the neighbourhood. The girl's been dragged up. They're permanently broke and the house is falling down.

She must have heard about us.

I'd have agreed for the hopeful look in her eyes, a feeling that something, anything, bound us. We had to squash up in the front of the pickup, Racha in the middle and me on the far side. The road was quiet and Ludo couldn't resist trying to impress us. Racha and I started out with our legs touching, mine in shorts, hers covered by a filmy gypsy skirt. It had a long belt with metal tags that jingled as Ludo threw the truck around the bends, whooping as we begged him to slow down. By the time we reached the bottom of the pass, Racha and I were clinging to each other and when we hit the straight road into Lourmarin, we looked at each other and our still-joined hands before letting go.

We waited outside the bar when Ludo fetched the keys. 'Why don't we drive off and leave him?' she said.

'Then we wouldn't get to see the house. I don't even know where it is.' I didn't ask what we would do instead. 'I'm glad you came with us,' I blurted.

'So am I. It's not too bad being Ludo's charity project.'

If this was true, she wouldn't have joked about it. Racha worked at the co-operative, not for the Bellechasses. She earned her keep, but they'd arranged it all, and some people saw kindness as a debt to be repaid. 'You don't think he's taking advantage of you?'

'You're the naïve one here! Nobody takes advantage of me – that's how I get into trouble. Ludo's not making me do anything. He's not really my type, but he's got something.' She eyed me meaningfully. 'Not that you need me to tell you.'

My breath caught in my throat and I wound the window down, sticking my head out. Racha laid her hand against the back of my ribcage and I let it stay there, trying to record how it felt, inside and outside.

'How hard must your heart be beating for me to feel it like this,' she said.

I turned back just as Ludo reappeared. We'd forgotten him even though we were talking about him. 'Sorry, *les filles*. God, that man goes on. He insisted I join him for a beer and I couldn't refuse in case he changed his mind. I've got the keys – we just need to return them before the bar closes.' Neither of us responded. 'So, are we all friends now?'

'Don't worry about that,' Racha said. 'Just drive like a normal person, please. Remember, we already know you've got a big dick.'

'You really did have a nice chat,' he said, smirking. She elbowed him.

As we passed the Château de Vauvenargues, Ludo explained to Racha that it used to belong to Picasso. 'You do know who he was?' Her eyes swooped to me and I made a swirly motion on my lap, out of his view. It could have meant writing, or it could have meant nothing.

'The artist,' she said, cool as anything.

'How much further is it?' I no longer recognised anything except the iron cross I'd pretended to be able to see from the cedar forest. There was no way it would be visible from there. The mountain itself looked a completely different shape from this end.

Ludo took a right onto an even smaller road leading to a huge stone house. He jumped out and started fiddling with the gates, cursing. 'We'll need to look at the car first, before it gets dark. There's no electricity in the garage.'

The wooden doors dragged against the gravel and it took all three of us to open them. '*Aïe!*'

'What now?' said Ludo. It was a long time since we'd set off, and none of us had eaten.

'I've got a splinter in my thumb,' I said. 'I'll never find it in this light.'

Racha grabbed my hand and shoved it towards my mouth. 'Sometimes you can suck splinters out, no need to see.' Before I could protest, she redirected it to her own mouth. I'd hardly registered the warm, weird sensation before she was done, spat on the ground and asked if it was gone. Ludo gave a low whistle. 'You two! Who needs vintage cars?'

I gasped like a little kid when he took off the canvas cover. 'That's it! It's even more glamorous close up. Did he tell you the story, Racha?'

She nodded. 'Nothing round here surprises me. You're all Parisians as far as I'm concerned.' It hurt that she would try to take the shine off.

Ludo ran his hands over the powder-blue paintwork as if the car was a woman he was about to seduce. 'It's a Delage de Villars from 1933, according to my old mate. Concourse condition. Want to get in?'

Racha took the wheel because she didn't have a licence yet. Serge was teaching her to drive. 'Hurry up, if you want to go in the house too. I've had enough messing around with locks and I forgot to bring a torch.'

In the first room we entered there was a grand piano covered in framed photos. 'It's them!' I pushed it under Racha's nose. 'That's exactly how they were dressed.' They'd been snapped at a party in this room, only the four of them in focus, posing in character. You would never think the 1990s had arrived. Ludo figured out the old-fashioned gramophone and crackly jazz filled the room. 'What fascinates you so much about these people?' Racha asked me.

I shrugged, looking at the brunette in the picture, so elegant and self-assured. It wasn't that they were well connected or wealthy – I knew from my studies that arty types were broke more often than not. 'Their refusal to settle for *une vie banale*. They don't just dream of this – they do it.'

When Ludo asked if we wanted to see upstairs, the voice in my head told me to say no, that it was getting late. Racha and I hadn't even had anything to drink. But she said, 'Sure,' leading us up the curved staircase. I hung back to look at portraits of the family, realising with a jolt that the people who'd experienced that decadent era dressed in tweed and silk must all be dead by now. Ludo and Racha worked their way along the landing, opening doors and exclaiming.

'Look at this! You could fit my entire flat in here.' The master bedroom had wooden panels and a dressing table with a curved mirror and built-in lights. In the middle was a huge four-poster bed. 'Do you think all four of them sleep here?'

Racha couldn't have said anything worse. We were both facing Ludo, whose comment that it was romantic didn't get around the awkward fact there were three of us. He looked from me to Racha and back again. 'Sorry, I didn't think this through.'

'Let's just leave,' I said, finally. They ignored me. Ludo gave a little shudder and his expression cleared, as if something had fallen into place. 'Come here,' he said. We hesitated, unsure which of us he was talking to. 'Both of you.'

He kissed Racha, longer and harder than that night in the barn. As she began to respond, her hands travelled across his back as he stroked the side of her body. I stood, transfixed, flooded with arousal as if it were mine. When her eyes snapped open to look at me over his shoulder, I sighed so loudly that it reminded him I was there. Racha melted onto the bed, taking off her top and idly touching her breasts, so different to mine, as Ludo started over with me. I closed my eyes but could still see her; all I could think of was her mouth, her hands, how her body would feel to touch. Panic rose in my chest and throat. As I ran for the door, nothing had ever felt more urgent than getting out of that house, if I had to walk all the way home in the dark. Nothing Ludo said could have changed my mind.

But then she said, 'Don't go.'

Chapter 22

Halfway through my second attempt at a first consultation with Dolores, I began to shiver. 'You're cold? So am I, all the time. The weather here is so dreary, the chill in the air, leaves falling from the trees . . . '

Not this again. Perhaps I'd imagined the thaw between us last time. Any subject could unleash a fresh wave of complaints. 'Actually, after the hot summer, the leaves have lasted much longer than usual.' I'd made myself notice. 'We *parfumeurs* often find inspiration in the changing seasons.'

It must have been hard for Dolores, following her husband around the world on his postings and having to send their children to boarding school. More than ever, it was beyond me how families could endure that separation. She wouldn't have had much say in this, which might explain why she now enjoyed making people like me jump through hoops.

Dolores no longer cared for the ingredients she'd previously liked or any of the sample accords I'd prepared. I explained that it took several passes and tweaks to perfect a bespoke fragrance, but even when I separated out the main notes, nothing pleased her.

'Am I right that you're wearing La Panthère by Cartier?'

'I'm not here to have you copy something I already own!'

'Of course not. Just tell me what you like about it.'

'The bottle.'

I did my best at an encouraging face. 'It is an incredible bottle. When you wear it, how does it make you feel?'

'Sad.' (It wasn't an easy expression to keep up). 'It's warm, sweet. Somehow it reminds me of my grandmother's baking and her cherry orchard.'

Nostalgia can go either way. 'I expect you'd rather evoke a place with happy memories.'

'Who wouldn't? But anything that reminds me of my country is too painful. Why are we talking about this? I keep telling you Consuela wants this to be my Paris perfume. She'll be disappointed if that's not what I get.'

'I understand. But we need to put in the groundwork. It's going to take patience.' A *lot* of patience.

Dolores's guard dropped in front of me. 'Time is something I have – it's not as if I've got anything else to do. But Paris is not a happy place for me.'

'Have you been here long enough to be sure?'

'Maybe not. I wasn't expecting this to be so complicated.'

'Me neither. But I've just realised what the problem is: we're working from your daughter's vision, not yours. My suggestion would be to stick with Paris and see how that goes. Forget *falling in love*. You can't do that on demand.'

꙳

Dolores went home with instructions to note down anything she found positive or beautiful about Paris. I'd never given a client homework, but she showed a flicker of interest when I mentioned doing the same with things that lifted my spirits. Admittedly I had ulterior motives planting that idea in her mind.

'She's changed her tune,' Suzanne said. 'You working miracles back there?'

'Far from it. We're back to square one.'

Suzanne hadn't grown out of the adolescent eye-roll, probably because it was such an arresting sight on her. 'It's real work, isn't it, what you do with these clients? I thought it was just indulging people and giving them a variation on one of the existing products with their name on it.'

Dolores had exhausted my daily supply of forbearance and diplomacy. 'I'm upset you could think that when you seem to have such an affinity with what I do. Yes, it is work. Some people think anything's a waste of time if it doesn't save lives or make a fortune. What on earth did you say to the artists in your last job?'

Suzanne dismissed this. 'They all thought they were extraordinary geniuses. They weren't interested in my opinion, but if they'd asked, I'd have given it to them straight. People find honesty so difficult, but if you ask me, it's worse to be fake. Imagine what it would be like if everyone said what they really thought all the time?'

I laughed. 'It would be a disaster! Society doesn't work like that. Nothing works like that. I think you underestimate how much you can get away with, Suzanne.'

Having stuck by my decision not to mention the way she dressed, it was the first time I'd risked any kind of personal comment.

'Believe me, I don't always say what's on my mind. Here's an idea – for the next twenty-four hours let's both say what we really think.'

I shook my head. 'Ah, *non*. I've seen you with some of my

141

customers. I haven't spent more than ten years building this business for you to destroy it in one day. It's ridiculous, in any case. Nobody speaks all their private thoughts out loud. A lot of people would end up in jail.'

That got a loud tut. 'I don't mean you walk down the street reciting them. Just that you express yourself frankly with the people you naturally come into contact with, including me. Tell the truth when you would usually avoid it. Does that really seem such a big deal to you?'

What it seemed to me was unfeasible. What about courtesy, discretion? What if being blunt would hurt someone's feelings? (Not that this overly concerned Suzanne.) I wasn't sure I could cope with knowing what anyone really thought of me.

And yet I accepted the challenge. What choice did I have? The deciding factor was that Édouard was safely out of range in America.

We were interrupted by a clattering as Diouc arrived to clean the windows. 'What timing!' Suzanne said. 'Let me show you how it's done.' She opened the door, swung half her body out into the street and whatever she said to him, I'd never seen a man look so delighted. Diouc had never smiled at me like that.

'That seemed to go well.'

'Ask me tomorrow morning!'

'If there was ever a moment you didn't need me around, this is it. His money's in the usual place.'

'Before you go – your girlfriend was in again, while you were with Dolores. She wants to know if you're free tonight.' Suzanne handed me a mobile number written on the back of my business card and I took it, my face burning. 'So you like women too? *C'est cool*,' Suzanne said. 'It's not as if I hadn't noticed.'

I rushed past Diouc, almost knocking him over, but as

always everything I wanted to escape went with me. The last time I'd felt on balance was in early summer, before Apolline left for Australia, before my perfumer's block set in and the conflict between Édouard and Bastien reached breaking point. I kept thinking Édouard was going to collapse with the stress and had a recurring dream in which he was lying on the floor, only able to communicate with his eyes. I had a mobile in my hand but chose not to use it. My subconscious didn't give a very good account of me.

I was regretting this pact with Suzanne already.

If Édouard wasn't on the other side of the Atlantic, I'd have to respond to the note he'd left right now, a conversation we'd avoided for decades. I would have to be honest, and I honestly didn't know what I would say.

And just as well it wasn't Monday, because things had begun to get a little intense with Frédéric, and the ambiguity was part of the attraction.

This was going to be impossible if I couldn't be honest with myself.

For a moment I considered marching back to the shop to give Suzanne a taste of the straight talking she was so fond of, to tell her all the normally unspeakable reasons it wasn't working out having her around.

The thought of you and Diouc drives me out of my mind. I'm afraid nobody will want me that way again.

I envy you, because you like being who you are.

Thanks to Racha and her big mouth, you know something I've never told anyone – and then you have the nerve to tell me you'd guessed.

A funny look from a passer-by made me realise a strangulated noise had come from me. If one more thing, large or small, went wrong, I would crack. I crossed the Pont des Arts and went down to the riverside, rotating the card with

Racha's number inside my pocket. Much as I wanted to ignore her demand to see me tonight or pretend to be busy, there would be no peace until I'd found out what she wanted. And now I couldn't lie.

I spent a moment contemplating some huge black-and-white photos of Spanish dancers displayed high on the walls of the *quai*. A young man paused his bike ride to snap one in which the superbly honed naked backsides of dozens of men had been arranged to look like ocean waves. Sexy, if you liked that. If only I could say I didn't.

Even so, the only man I'd physically craved or been satisfied by was that prick Ludo. The chances of anyone living up to what he'd unleashed that day in the forest were pretty slim, but Racha had – and more, much more. You never forget desire like that. Love like that. And in shutting them out, I had left for dead parts of myself that now clamoured to live.

I sat on a low wall bordering a flower bed and examined the tiny flowers of a tall purple plant. The cobbles were strewn with curly orange leaves and I forced myself to absorb the colour, knowing that soon Paris would be wearing her grey winter coat most days.

To re-engage with Racha was to risk everything. My life had only functioned because she and Ludo weren't in it. I should have known the length of my leash by now; what frightened me was that it wasn't tied to anything. I played with phrases, which were sincere enough. *Sorry, I don't think it's a good idea. Maybe it's best to leave things as they are, after all this time.* What was I going to do, wish her all the best?

The image of Racha's worn lace-up shoes came to me. I'd spent more time staring at them than meeting her eye.

'*Âllo, c'est toi?*'

'*C'est Clémentine.*'

'I know, I have everyone else's number. And now I have yours.'

I had to stop hearing menacing undertones in everything she said. Maybe Racha didn't have bad intentions. Maybe – I was really tormenting myself now – meeting up could leave us in a better place.

'Sorry I wasn't free when you came back. I hope Suzanne took care of you.'

Racha laughed like she used to, with relish. She always loved to tease me. Without her in front of me, the old and new Rachas merged and, again, it threw me. 'Anyone would think I was one of your posh customers!'

'How may I be of assistance?' It came out wrong and I sounded like a cold-hearted bitch. Racha hesitated. 'I didn't fancy hanging around in some café not knowing how long you'd be, so I thought we could meet at your place. *Ce soir, ça marche?*'

No way was Racha coming to my apartment, this evening or any other. The solution came out of nowhere: Apolline and Mathieu's tiny flat was empty. They'd refused to let Bastien stay while they were away – fair enough, given his smoking habit (various substances) and inability to turn off appliances. I was supposed to be keeping an eye on it but hadn't been for weeks. It wasn't ideal, but nor was seeing Racha in a public place.

She asked me to repeat the address and Métro station, and then read it all back to me. I didn't ask where she was coming from, but she clearly didn't know Paris well. We agreed on eight o'clock. My habitual anxiety about receiving guests was triggered even without Édouard monitoring my every move. The afternoon dragged and it was only after hours of time-wasting at home, going out onto the balcony and back in, that I could focus on the preparations. For a start, I'd have to offer Racha something to eat and drink and let her smoke if she wanted to. Apolline and Mathieu would be furious if they knew, but I'd switched to dealing with whichever problem was most pressing.

They'd jumped at the chance of a cheap sublet from a friend who was spending a year at Princeton. Édouard had never acknowledged the existence of the 13th before they moved to the Butte-aux-Cailles and I still didn't know the area well. I went an hour early to turn on the heating and realised I'd given Racha the wrong directions from Métro Place d'Italie – a dead giveaway, not that this flat would pass as that of a middle-aged couple. I pictured Racha labouring in the wrong direction, in that coat, with that crutch, searching for street names she wouldn't find, and returned to the station, looking for the right way out.

Chapter 23

Racha couldn't conceal her surprise when I greeted her as any other friend. 'Like old times,' she said, watching for my reaction. We hadn't lasted long on *bisou bisou* terms back then.

'You told Suzanne about us,' I said, since she'd been so quick to bring up the past. 'It's a shame you felt the need to do that.'

'What are you talking about? I said we knew each other a long time ago but she seemed to know that already.'

'Oh,' I said. 'She was sounding me out and I fell for it.'

'She thinks a lot of you. Anyone can see that.' I took Racha's coat, pretending I hadn't heard. She looked at the Netflix home screen on the TV, which had been there since I arrived. I'd wanted a distraction but was too distracted to pick anything.

'Amazing, isn't it, all these wonderful films and programmes about people like you. We don't get a look-in unless it's terrorism, drugs, gangs. You'd think we didn't exist if people didn't hate us so much. It's getting worse all the time. See this?' She pointed to a dark stain on her coat, which I'd been holding at arm's length without noticing. 'Some bastard in the street just spat at me and called me a *sale arabe*.'

If I'd been there, I would have ripped his throat out.

'That's appalling. Things have changed since the attacks – Paris has suffered so much. Some people have softened, pulled together, obviously some idiots have gone the other way. I'm so sorry.'

'None of us should have to apologise for anyone else,' she said. I chased away a vision of Bastien's sweet face the first time it happened: the split lip, the black eye. He was only fifteen, walking down the street with another boy, not hurting anyone.

I'd thought Racha and I might find ourselves short of things to say at first.

'If you still drink, I expect you could do with one now.' Alcohol was one of the things Racha had never tasted before the summer we met. I'd chosen a perfectly drinkable €4 red from the Carrefour City on the corner. Two bottles, in case it was needed. Racha held out her glass to touch mine but my response was half-hearted. I had not invited her. The horrible experience she'd had on the way here only emphasised that there was nothing to celebrate. Racha attacked the small bowls of olives and crisps as if she hadn't eaten all day. 'That's better,' she said.

Her eyes roved over me, pausing where they used to. I was wearing black jeans and a plain grey jumper, minimal make-up. '*C'est dingue* – you haven't changed.'

But I had, and there was nothing crazy about it. If I pinched the skin of my forearm even slightly, it cross-hatched like the bark of a tree. My neck had a newly delicate texture and my bare thighs were a different matter to what she could see. Saying someone hasn't changed demands a reply in kind, but I couldn't do it.

148

'Not your place then,' she said, most of the apartment visible from the sofa. The decor was a cross between IKEA and Tiger Copenhagen, functional and kitsch, cherry red and lime green. I explained about my negligence as Apolline's caretaker. 'If I'm not careful, that's going to be the only plant surviving.' On the mantelpiece was a large neon cactus, which I'd decided to plug in, having run out of time to move it to the bedroom. 'Any other children?' Racha asked.

'A son, Bastien, nineteen last month. He's just started art school.'

'I have an eighteen-year-old son, Tariq. He's just started a year's jail sentence for trafficking.' My hand flew to my mouth before I could stop it. 'Where?' I asked, as if that mattered.

'Les Baumettes. I never left Marseille again. Our lives have gone like this, yours and mine.' She brought her index fingers together from a distance and lifted them up before sending them apart again. It almost worked as an image of us, almost: the time touching too short, our separation too long. Nothing could convey it.

'That's terrible, Racha. For you. I'm not judging. I know we can't control our children's choices.' That was a loaded word in our household and I immediately wanted to take it back, in view of what I'd repeated to Édouard since Bastien was about ten, when it became clear it wasn't a phase that he was going to grow out of. A lot of things look like choices to those who can't imagine not having one.

Racha was tracing patterns in the fake suede of the sofa. Under the layers of scarves and cardigans she'd removed, her clavicle stood out, her hands and wrists bony and frail. I was looking at somebody consumed by long-term anxiety. 'Is he innocent?'

She whacked the arm of my chair so hard that the wine glasses jumped on the low table. 'No, he's not innocent! He's a stupid, naïve kid who never stood a chance. He wanted men to look up to, to pay attention to him.' She pointed at herself. 'Imagine me being all you had.'

'Was it always just the two of you?'

'Since he was eleven, although God knows how I stuck it that long. I never wanted to get married.' She gave me a quick sideways look. 'To think I got rid of my husband fearing he'd be a bad influence. The lawyer was hopeless and Tariq was guilty the moment they heard his name. They're four to a cell in that filthy place, packed in like animals. If he makes it to the age of twenty-one without reoffending, he can apply to have his record erased, but he'll be part of something far worse by the time he gets out.'

'I don't know what to say.'

Racha shifted her weight, listing to one side before righting herself. Her body spelled pain; her face, anger. 'I don't suppose you do. After you and Ludo, I was back where I started. The Bellechasses dumped me back home like a mangled piece of garbage. In case you ever wondered what happened to me.'

She struck her right hip and to my horror, she reached for my hand and placed it there. No doubt who the accused was now. 'Six pelvic fractures. Compacted femur. It's never been right since and it's getting worse with age.'

'Racha,' my voice broke up. 'Don't.'

'You can't bear to *hear* it?'

'Whether you believe me or not, I'm sorrier than you could imagine. But we were twenty years old, not much older than our boys. I was completely out of my depth, but we all were. I would never behave the way I did then.'

Racha gave a single snort. 'Don't insult me with the *changed person* routine.'

Maybe it's delusional to think we can ever escape the

150

people we used to be, comforting ourselves with fantasies of reinvention.

'Since we did meet again – which is what you wanted – I have the chance to tell you it was an accident. It wasn't you I meant to hurt, Racha. Ludo and I were fighting over you, surely you realised that?' Three's a bad number. At first it was addictive and thrilling. But when it went wrong, one of us had to go.

Racha's mouth tightened and then she gave a bitter laugh. 'You really think I remember the details after what I went through? Leave him out of it. This is about you and me. It always was.'

'How can I leave him out? You think I wanted it to end that way? I regret it, deeply. You can't know.'

'Strange regret, to show no concern, to make no effort to track me down in twenty-five years.' Her eyes widened. 'Did you think you'd killed me?'

On any other day I would have agreed to this, the only explanation that could make me less of a monster. 'No, but that's all I knew. My mother kicked me out immediately. I always told you she'd freak if she found out about me and Ludo. The Bellechasses wanted both of us off the scene.'

As Racha went to speak she suddenly wrinkled her nose. 'What's that burning smell?'

I jumped up. The oven was so useless that I'd despaired of it getting hot enough to cook the chicken satays. Adrenaline normally heightened my sense of smell to unbearable acuteness. Racha followed, peering over my shoulder. 'Shame,' she said. 'Those would have been tasty.'

I pulled the tray from the oven with my bare hand and dropped the whole lot on the floor, shrieking. Racha pushed me to the sink and held my hand under the cold tap on full blast even when I tried to get away. 'Let go! It hurts worse than the burn.'

She stroked the nape of my neck, telling me to breathe. 'What were you thinking? It was obvious from the minute I arrived what a state you were in.'

I sank onto a kitchen stool, hand wrapped in a wet towel that was soaking my jeans. 'How can I not be? You decided to turn up in my life, not the other way around. Seeing you reminds me of us, how we used to be. It makes me sad and angry and ashamed, and before you say anything, I know I don't have the right. You were always so strong and now you're . . .'

'Pitiful.'

There's no knowing what word I might have come out with. 'I hate seeing how you've suffered. But I can't change what happened, Racha. I don't understand why you'd want anything to do with me ever again.'

'Oh, *mon amour*, I can see it's going to be just as complicated this time.' She dropped a kiss on my forehead and touched my lower lip with her finger, my body only flinching when my brain kicked in. 'What do I want? Should you be afraid?' she said. I'd made a point of not saying *frightened*. 'Even I don't know the answers yet. But this time, it'll be me who decides when it's over.'

Chapter 24

Édouard texted from New York to ask how I was. His unpredictable behaviour was getting to me. I opted for, *Good, you?* but by then hours had passed and he didn't reply. It was the first time he'd gone away for more than one night since Bastien moved out and I'd been so looking forward to lying on the sofa, watching films he would hate or reading in the bath for ages. Somehow I enjoyed these things more when I knew he wasn't coming home.

His wrenching little note was still on my mind as I walked to work. It was a good idea to see Bastien in his absence but I resented Édouard suggesting it. I wanted to scream that it was too late, that our son was grown up now and the damage was done. I also wanted very much to believe this wasn't true.

Around eleven, Gabrielle turned up at the shop. It made me nervous when friends came in. I'd have to try channelling the me Suzanne saw, so passionate she could be thinking of her lover.

'Mmm, that works so well on you.' Gabrielle was wearing my Numéro T, her favourite – I gave her a bottle for her birthday but noticed with satisfaction that she was already wearing it at the party. Hours after the ephemeral citrus notes had evaporated, the jasmine and iris root lingered on her skin in one of my best drydowns.

I made myself release her, as it's not done to luxuriate in another adult's scent unless you *are* their lover.

Gabrielle purchased gifts for a colleague and her mother-in-law – easy, because we know what they like – but that couldn't be the reason she was here on a workday. As our husbands worked together, I assumed it was somehow connected to Édouard's fall from grace. When Suzanne appeared and Gabrielle realised I could get away, she asked if we could speak privately. The memory of my backroom reunion with Racha too fresh, I suggested Café Madame and we walked there in silence. Gabrielle stirred her espresso repeatedly despite not having added sugar.

'This is very awkward, Clémentine, but I would never forgive myself if I didn't tell you and something bad happened.'

'What are you talking about?'

'Mireille went to a concert at the Bataclan with her boyfriend last night and they saw your son begging by the canal. She said it looked like he was sleeping rough.'

I burst out laughing and Gabrielle looked horrified. 'It can't have been him,' I said firmly. 'He's at art school now. We're renting him a studio – it's nothing special, but ...' Bastien had insisted on taking a dive in the 10th for the lowest rent possible, since he intended to pay us back, or so he said. I'd seen nicer *chambres de bonne*, although it was bigger than a garret nine metres square.

'Well, that's what I thought, but Mireille's convinced it was him.' They had worked together on a mural project in Belleville a year ago, but thousands of young men resembled Bastien on one of his more restrained days, and a fair few on the others, especially in certain *quartiers*. 'He's always changing his look. When I last saw him, he'd dyed his hair pale blue.' His natural colour is darker than mine; he bears no resemblance whatsoever to Édouard.

Gabrielle went to stir her coffee again before noticing it was all gone. 'Mireille mentioned the blue hair. I'm sorry, Clémentine, I hate interfering and I know you must have other things on your mind. She begged me not to.'

I tried to summon my resigned-but-okay face. In truth, I was glad the charade was over – it's not as if I hadn't been wondering what Bastien was up to. Édouard could look after himself. 'Thank you. You did the right thing,' I said, fighting my recollection of Gabrielle and Jacques' son smirking when he asked after ours. Too bad if we were a topic at their table – I didn't have the luxury of being offended. 'Things were tricky in the run-up to Bastien leaving home and we've been giving him some space. Possibly too much,' I said, forcing a smile. I was tempted to tell her the whole story, that everything was falling apart, especially me, but Martha would be very hurt if she found out I'd confided in someone who, however kind, was a lot less likely to understand.

'It must be a huge change for you and Édouard, with both children gone. I'm not looking forward to that, although I don't think Mireille will be in any rush to leave.'

Something about the way Gabrielle said 'toi et Édouard' irked me, as if it was a given that there was something precarious about our marriage. She had to rush off to a meeting and when we parted, her scent made me nostalgic for the moment she'd arrived, before this latest blow. Could nothing stay the same?

I caught her hand as she got up to leave. 'Thank you again. I know this wasn't easy. Hopefully it'll be ... ' A case of mistaken identity? A prank? A carefully considered lifestyle choice? Gabrielle left me with a compassionate smile, her long, chic earrings swaying. I texted Bastien saying I needed to see him urgently. The time for treading carefully was over.

❧

When Bastien raised no objection, I announced that I would come to the studio with takeaway from Lucky Temple. Make everything easy except for the conversation. Regardless of how it went, we'd get to eat Kung Pao chicken, and prawn soup with coconut and lemongrass. Most of my favourite foods are chosen as much for smell as taste, and that is heavenly. I got off at Jacques Bonsergent because it's less hectic than the Gare de l'Est, but between the Métro and the studio I was approached by several people asking for money. A young woman followed me for at least fifty metres, intent on telling me her misfortunes, and finally gave up at the point where she switched from calling me *madame* to *vieille pute*.

I didn't tell Gabrielle that Bastien's place was a short walk from where her daughter had seen him, in a side street off the Quai de Valmy. If for some unfathomable reason he was begging, he was practically doing it on his own doorstep. If we'd been talking about anyone else, the idea would have been absurd.

The studio took me aback with its unlived-in feel. Bastien had brought enough belongings to fill the boot and back seat of my car, but either they were crammed into the wardrobe and chest of drawers or he'd sold them all. Seeing him in a room of his own that wasn't covered in posters, drawings and photos was the equivalent of him returning home to a forest canopy hanging from the ceiling. I found myself welling up, which would annoy him, but I was past caring. Given the choice between an overprotective mother and one who showed no love, I know which I'd have preferred.

He hadn't shaved for a week and he no longer had blue hair.

'I've missed you.' Honesty doesn't work as a twenty-four-hour project. Once you've got the hang of it, you can't stop. That Suzanne, I could kill her sometimes.

'I miss you too, Maman,' Bastien said, simply and without embarrassment, like a little boy. 'Are you lonely?'

I assumed he meant while Édouard was away. Or maybe not. The answer was the same either way. We unpacked the food containers with the vacuum-sealed tops that are hard to undo but effective – it was still steaming. When I got the lid off the noodle soup, we both savoured the aroma and smiled. 'Like your Numéro S,' he said, 'or is it R?'

'Right first time. But they both contain a lot of ingredients that I hope are not in this soup.' I suspended the glass noodles high on chopsticks as the colourless broth scented the air. 'You can taste it before you taste it,' was something Bastien had been saying for years, whereas it drove Édouard mad that I could never just get on and eat. He also hated that it was Bastien, not Apolline, with the real appreciation for my work. It makes no difference how often I tell him that like chefs and fashion designers, many of the best perfumers are men.

'So,' I said, mindful that my attempts to sound casual come across as loaded, according to Martha. Apparently the look on my face doesn't help, so I waded in strategically when Bastien got up to fetch some cutlery. It was a family tradition to pretend we could manage with chopsticks then switch to forks and spoons before the food went cold. 'I thought you'd have put your mark on the place by now.'

We balanced the plates on our laps. The table was covered in paints, brushes and half-finished projects but that was the only sign an art student lived here. 'Putting stuff on the walls isn't allowed, although I don't get why you'd be bothered when I'm not.'

I helped myself to a big piece of chicken, avoiding the slithery mushrooms Bastien was popping like grapes. 'I don't know, it doesn't feel very cosy. In fact, it's chilly. Does that radiator work?' I reached out but the sight of my burnt fingertips made me think better of it. Bastien was watching me with a bemused expression – nothing new about that – and I was suddenly keenly aware he wasn't a child any more.

'What's up, Maman? Is this some sort of mission to persuade me to move back home?'

'No, what makes you say that?' The thought had genuinely not occurred to me, just as I had never registered that the four of us would never live together as a family again. It was over, all that. *Fini*. But wherever I am in the cycle of people being added and taken away, my children will always be my children.

'Why was it so urgent to see me tonight? Surely not to comment on my decor?'

'It didn't have to be tonight. It's just we've hardly heard from you since that day you came home and Papa was there.' He went to interrupt but I continued,. 'I understand you don't want me bugging you but surely replying to one text a week isn't too much to ask.' Now he looked shamefaced. Like this ugly, depressing room, it didn't feel right, getting on his case. 'Your problem's not with me, is it?' This was disloyal and unfair, and parents aren't supposed to run each other down, but the rules of decency operate on the assumption that everyone deserves it. What about when people are treacherous, bigoted, unfeeling?

'True,' my son said. 'It's not you.'

'You may be surprised to hear it was Papa's idea for me to see you this week.'

'Not like you to take orders from him.' Bastien couldn't look at me while taking that tone. The observation jarred;

it certainly felt to me as if I lived within parameters set by Édouard. *You can be yourself as long as you don't annoy or embarrass me. You must not question anything I do. You can consider your business a success, as long as you never forget the venture was originally underwritten by me.* None of this had been articulated but I'd heard it loud and clear. Our children had watched it play out. Survived it, but *surviving is not thriving* and the proof of that was right in front of me.

'I'm here because I want to be,' I said. 'Your father wrote me a letter, which he's never done before. It's hit him, you leaving home. He regrets the way things were between you.'

Bastien was running his index finger around the food containers, licking the sauce off. He could do it just as well without looking. 'Has he said he regrets it?'

Admittedly, Édouard hadn't said as much. The flicker in Bastien's eye was contagious. I included the ceiling in my look around the room, trying to roll the tears back in. 'Do you have friends over?' It was hard to imagine any fun taking place here that didn't involve the bed. I recalled our excruciating discussions about protection when Bastien was in high school and disconcertingly open about discovering sex. He'd caused me far more worry on that score than his sister.

'No, I go to theirs. They live closer.'

'There's nothing to stop you coming home between classes, bringing people back like you used to. Nobody's there during the day.'

Bastien pressed his lips together. *My mother,* he'd tell them. *She's so exhausting.*

'Nothing to stop me? Is that really what you think?' He kept picking up his phone, putting it down and checking it out of the corner of his eye. 'Believe me, it's better for all of us this way. I mean, Papa's writing you letters! Next thing you know he'll be speaking to you.'

I breathed in sharply but there were two notes to it and the second sounded like a sob.

'Sorry,' he said. 'You don't deserve that.'

When I exhaled, it was with the hint of a laugh. 'What are we like?' I said in English, another throwback to his teenage years. No wonder he needed to lose us. The constant phone-checking told me he had other plans, which was as it should be. 'I must be going,' I said, and he gave me a puzzled look. Maybe he just thought I was losing my mind. 'Okay, there was a reason I wanted to see you, but I didn't want it to ruin the evening. Gabrielle, you know, Jacques Delacombe's wife—'

'I know exactly who she is.'

'Their daughter Mireille thinks she saw you begging by the canal last night. She says you had a dog.' I looked around, trying to make light of it but we both know I'd have smelled a dog instantly. Now the food smells had cleared, it was a fight between oil paint, the ashtray and the overflowing bin.

'*Et alors?*'

'*And*? Is that all you have to say?' Bastien shrugged and the cluster of anger in my windpipe shrank. Stay calm, I told myself. I hadn't come to make things worse. 'Mireille wasn't wrong, then. It was you she saw.'

'It was me.' He let out a sigh so deep I could feel his breath on my face. 'Give my congratulations to the brilliant young detective.'

I let this sink in. 'Can I ask why, when we're paying for this place you chose? You said you wanted somewhere to be yourself, but you don't seem yourself at all.'

'Well, it's not easy, is it?' He looked at me intently and I felt the layers of pretence and appearances and falsity start to peel away.

'No,' I said. 'It really isn't. It feels lonely here. Is that what

160

this is about? You're an adult and you have the right to make your own decisions, but you can still talk to me. I'm your mother, Bastien. I'm not going to apologise for caring if you're happy.'

He smiled and squeezed my shoulder as he got up. 'If it makes you feel better, I haven't been sleeping on the streets. One of the guys I was with last night was getting beaten up near the Gare du Nord last week and I managed to scare them off.' He grinned at my reaction, not being of the build usually associated with breaking up fights. 'Since then I've been hanging out with them. At first I just wanted to see how he was doing. He might have broken ribs, but like he says, what can you do?'

'Who are they?'

'It's not going to be anyone you know! I think they're from Kazakhstan or somewhere like that, their French isn't too hot. They've customised this balcony on a vacant office building by the canal, put cardboard between the railings. They have duvets and pillows and stuff.'

'And a dog.'

'A really cool dog. It's hard to explain, but I prefer spending time with them than other students. They seem more real.'

'Have you been giving them money?'

'No! But they do make more when I'm with them.'

I was so wary of saying the wrong thing that my lips felt as if they were cracking. 'Be careful, Bastien.'

'Is it what I'm doing that bothers you, or the fact the *famille* Delacombe know about it?'

I'd forgotten the last conversation I had that wasn't a nightmare. 'Don't make me the bad guy. Whether you like it or not – and I *know* you didn't ask for it, we've been through that often enough – your father is in the public eye and you've had every advantage going. I get that you enjoy their company, but you have nothing in common with these people. You're romanticising their hardships as if they're some kind of adventure holiday. There's something a bit distasteful about it.'

I thought I'd offended him, but it was worse than that.

'You may think they're losers,' he said. 'But they're worth a hundred of us.'

Chapter 25

Provence, 1992

As summer wore on, Racha and I let Ludo think he was in charge. That mattered to him and we didn't care. He was full of his parents' plans to convert some outbuildings into a guesthouse. Not just any guesthouse but one that would outdo all the others in the area, just as Ludo himself was used to outshining everybody. But even when he was boring on about the project, he gave the impression that he didn't take anything seriously. He asked endless questions about the hotel where I worked, but I knew nothing about the management and Marseille didn't attract many tourists. I served drinks to businessmen, thugs and the overdressed women who accompanied both. This required the ability to smile, serve the right drinks and put up with dull stories and lewd remarks. A man once asked in front of his friends how much I wanted to sleep with him; I stunned the whole table with the answer, *Ten million francs.*

Whenever the city came up in conversation, Racha went quiet. I wasn't going to ask why, but when Ludo did one day, she said she missed the sea. He did one of his exaggerated double takes, drawing back like something was about to bite him on the face. 'Miss the sea? I thought you lot stayed put *chez vous*.' Ludo's knowledge of where Racha came from was no better than mine, limited to the view from the autoroute and sensational news coverage she had told us not to believe. Racha offered no alternative version, saying she'd learned the hard way to keep her mouth shut.

She sent a lethal scowl in Ludo's direction. 'And I thought *you lot* spent your time inbreeding here in the middle of nowhere. *Je suis marseillaise* – where are you from, *gros con*?'

The insults weren't aimed at me. When Ludo got on her nerves she didn't always keep her mouth shut, but it was precisely because he considered her so different that she could get away with things I couldn't. He planted a light kiss on her mouth. 'Forgive me, *ma belle*. Isn't she gorgeous, Clémentine?'

I wouldn't have been part of the odd trio we'd formed if I didn't think so.

'Yes,' I said, nudging him out of the way. Racha was glowing, her anger more real than he realised. I kissed her as he had, but she pulled me onto her lap and as she started to stroke my hair things began to hot up, and for once it wasn't for his benefit. The feel of her tongue in my mouth made me wet and I could scent her excitement. When she slid her hand up my top I suddenly caught sight of Ludo as if he'd just walked in on us. The coldness in his eyes made me pull away and she immediately knew to stop.

'*Oui, j'adore la mer*,' she said, as if nothing had happened. 'We didn't go often but I like that by the water's edge, the view is the same for everyone.'

Ludo nodded silently. I'd had the same thought many times, standing against the railings on the hotel terrace between clearing tables, looking out at the turquoise, the islands, the rocks. Making sure he wouldn't see, my fingers reached for Racha's. I had never felt so close to anyone, and more than I had ever wanted a fuck, I wanted to make love with her. The two of us, alone. We'd done a lot of things – but nothing that felt like that.

Longing for her didn't make Ludo go away.

'Let's go then. To the sea,' he said, with a big smile. 'What? Anyone would think I'd suggested a trip to Paris.' He winked at me but I ignored him, looking at my watch. 'We'd be back really late. I have to work tomorrow.'

'We all have to work tomorrow. At least you get your poolside naps. Wait here, both of you. I'll be quick.'

'Where are you going?' Racha called after him.

'To fetch my mother's car. The pickup won't do for this trip.'

If he hurried, he'd be less than ten minutes. Racha and I looked at each other. I was beside myself with frustration but it was impossible to rewind to where we were before. 'We don't have to go with him,' I said.

She laughed. 'He's doing this for me!'

When I'd asked Racha what Serge expected in return for teaching her to drive, she'd shaken her head sadly and told me people could simply be kind. If I carried on thinking like my mother, I'd end up being like her. 'You're right,' I said.

'Don't stir up trouble, Clémentine,' she said, eyes trained on the big house before they flashed back to me. 'With Ludo, about, you know, him and us. He comes out with some stupid stuff, but his family helped me out as a favour to Zohra. I had nowhere to go this summer. Do you understand?'

We both scanned for him. 'He must have got talking to his dad. Come here a minute.' I crossed to her side of the table and, still sitting, she laced her hands behind my hips and pressed her face against my body. I writhed like an animal that can't tell the difference between pleasure and pain. 'For Christ's sake, Racha, why can't we just—?'

She placed a forefinger on my lips. '*C'est comme ça*. It just is. Come on, you really like it with Ludo. You should see your face when he gets you off.' She closed her eyes and breathed heavily.

'All right, you've made your point!'

'Do the two of you still get together?' she asked.

I hadn't noticed that he never wanted just me any more. Our first time together seemed so distant. To think I'd been shocked that he kept a blanket in his truck. I didn't know what it would take to shock me now. The shame, the elation, my desire for him; they'd all shrunk to toys next to everything Racha made me feel.

I shook my head, withdrawing. 'Do you – see him alone?' It was unfair to make her say it.

'Yes, but he still wants both of us, I promise you.'

'Indeed I do, and I'm a lucky man to have you both,' Ludo said, appearing at the opposite end of the cottage to where we'd been keeping watch. He'd had to leave the car where the track met the driveway to his parents' house because there wasn't room for a second vehicle up here. I had an uneasy feeling, knowing he could have been listening out of sight. 'Okay, Racha, you've seen our place, now it's time to show us yours.'

She lowered her eyes. We'd wasted so much time that our only hope of catching the sunset was to take the autoroute. Ludo gunned it in his mother's new little BMW – neither Racha nor I had ever been in a car that didn't rattle or smell of anything except expensive handbags. Since he'd pointedly asked her to join him in the front, running my fingers over the soft leather of the back seats distracted me from a sense of dread I couldn't identify; I was very afraid of something.

While Ludo occasionally glanced back at me, Racha didn't dare, although I could tell from the way she was fidgeting that she wanted to.

When we passed the *cité* Racha was from, her right hand dropped down the side of the seat and this time she was the one reaching for me. I stroked it with my foot to avoid attracting Ludo's attention. I'd known it all along, but wherever life took us, Racha's idea of home and escape would never be the same as mine. Ludo stared at the huge huddle of tower blocks and boxes on the hillside but none of us said a word as we sped past.

By the time we approached the centre of Marseille the silence was more than I could stand. A ferry was leaving port. 'I've always wanted to go there – everyone says it's lovely.' Ludo was sure to have been to Corsica and have stories to tell. Instead, Racha stiffened and he sniggered in disbelief. I turned back to see *Algeria Ferries* on the side of the ship, staring at the words as if they could tell me whether to apologise or make a joke of my mistake. Racha had got upset the time I asked if she'd been there.

'How come we don't have any music on?' she said, fiddling with the knobs on the dashboard until Nirvana came blaring out at an unbearable volume. Ludo joined in, rolling the window down and yelling *Hello, hello, hello . . .* Racha's hair was tied back but mine flew in all directions as the stench of the sea flooded in, mixed with fumes.

'Are we going to stop for a walk?' We'd already reached the far side of town, clinging to the Corniche Kennedy as the sun spilled its last rays out across the water. I pointed out the hotel, where the manager was still expecting me back in September. The time before I knew Ludo and Racha seemed as unreal as anything I'd ever planned to do next. In fact, I couldn't think what those plans had been.

It was not a perfect evening, with low grey clouds and a wind whipping up. Ludo grabbed Racha by the arm and flung his other hand at the view, noticing only then that this didn't leave any for the steering wheel. 'Happy to be back?'

'Yes,' she said. 'Thanks for bringing us.' It must be strange for her, coming here but not going home. She looked back as if she'd heard my thoughts and we both smiled. Often Racha seemed much older than me, but right now, in the soft, orangey light, she looked so young it scared me. 'Although actually, you're taking us somewhere I've never been.'

'How do you know that until we get there?' Ludo asked.

He thought he knew it all, but there were a lot of things he didn't get because he'd never had to. Some people hadn't heard of Picasso. Not everyone's parents could take them on outings to beauty spots. If Ludo told his father he wanted to move to Paris or America or to go to university after all, it would happen – there was nothing keeping him down. Racha and I could have the occasional taste of his world, like now in this flashy car, but for me each was more bitter than the last.

'Nearly there now.' We drove through eastern parts of the city that I'd never seen either, though I'd worked out he was following signs to the Calanques.

'At this time of day, really?'

It was tempting to tell him I'd seen the sheer cliffs and fjords of this coastline from a luxury yacht before I came home for the summer, when the owner asked me and two other girls from the hotel to waitress at a party on board. Ludo closed the window as a red light halted our progress through an area with groups of Arab men hanging around on street corners. He thought they were staring at the car but they were just as likely to be wondering what Racha was doing with us. There wasn't anywhere the three of us wouldn't offend somebody.

Twisting steeply now, the road was almost vertical and barely one car wide. Most drivers would take it very gently, but that wasn't Ludo's way. Every hairpin bend left my stomach on the one before, heat rising in my throat. Racha looked back at me nervously. '*Ça va, toi?*'

I pressed my hand over my mouth and shook my head.

'You're making her feel sick with your showing off. Stop right now!'

'Where do you suggest I stop?'

'If you don't, I'll puke in your mum's car myself, if I have to stick my fingers down my throat.' Bursting out laughing made me breathe. I leaned back and as the nausea subsided, an inky calm flowed into the space behind my eyes. One more bend and Ludo pulled off the road with a wheelspin and shower of pebbles. 'This is the top in any case. Go on then, enjoy the view.'

Racha opened the door and put her arm around me but only until we moved away from the car to look back the way we'd come. It was hard to believe we were still so close to the city, spread out in front of us like a sparkly shawl. '*C'est magnifique!*' she said, and to me, in not much more than a whisper, 'We'll come back one day without him.'

Ludo stomped off the other way, towards the inlet. Even in the last of the light, the sea's contrasting turquoise and *bleu marine* made my heart swerve. 'The plan was to drive you down there,' he said, shooting me a dirty look as I joined him. 'It's not allowed in summer, but I would have.'

If it wasn't forbidden, it wasn't fun.

And watching Racha blow him in the front seats wasn't my idea of fun that night. I could have closed my eyes instead of getting out and slamming the car door but nobody teaches you the etiquette for such situations. The wind was cold and it seemed a long time before Ludo came over to where I was shivering in the darkness, contemplating the city lights. He'd mellowed because sex did that, but when he kissed me, I could smell her on him. It was a message. A taunt.

'It's something special, what we have.' He wasn't talking about the view. 'Most people wouldn't understand.'

I understood in that moment that Ludo had nothing over me. Ratting me out to the agency would make him look uptight or sleazy, neither of which he would want. As he'd always said, many of those second homes were now rented to outsiders who could get up to whatever they liked, so what was the big deal?

'You saw how tense Racha was when we passed her place. Things need to settle down before she can go back.'

'Are you threatening me?'

'Who said anything about you?' He tilted his head, and with it, one eyebrow. He always said I was a clever girl.

I was not the target. I was the ammunition.

Racha came over, hugging her arms over her chest. 'What's going on? Shouldn't we be getting back?'

'I was just asking Clémentine if she'd prefer to drive, as she didn't enjoy the ride up.' The smile left Racha's face as she glanced at me – this road was ten times worse than the Combe. 'Or if not, maybe you'd like the practice? Serge would be impressed. I feel extremely tired all of a sudden. One of you is going to have to.'

'Give me the keys!' I grabbed them with such violence that it almost ripped his finger off. That'd teach him. Downhill is really not that hard. Once you commit to it, you have to keep going. All the way, until you reach the lowest point.

Chapter 26

The evening at my daughter's apartment had left many marks. Racha's threatening tone when we parted was more pitiful than alarming and yet, after all she'd been through, I half hoped she would find a way to hurt me. The skin from the burst blisters was discoloured and my fingers stank, the dried shreds catching on my clothes. At my cry of pain, Racha had forgotten everything, her concern instinctive. There was another context to the incident, the truth of the matter: that she couldn't help caring about me. There was no burying a history like ours. We'd be living with those *live for the moment* actions for ever.

And then there was what I'd formally agreed to for ever, without realising what a very long time that is.

'Oh,' Édouard said, parking his suitcase in the hallway. 'I thought you'd be at work.'

It should be natural enough to tell your spouse you stayed behind to greet them but Édouard didn't look as if he needed any more surprises. He was pale and drawn, and unless I was imagining it, there was more grey in his hair than five days ago.

'Rough trip?' I held up his favourite coffee and he nodded, taking a seat at the table and flattening his hand across his face from jaw to ear. Until I put the cup in front of him, he made no attempt to communicate.

'I'm going down for this,' he said, with such gravity that I thought he meant prison.

'In what sense?' I kept my voice level.

'Naturally the group wants to distance itself. The share price has dropped through the floor. These Americans: sometimes they're unbelievably blunt and sometimes they just can't seem to come out with it, going on about *adjustments to leadership style* as if we don't all know exactly what that means.' He drew a finger across his neck and looked at me wild-eyed.

'If only I'd been able to rope Kerglaven in at the very beginning, when I tried. He could have converted this to a win—'

Édouard must have been desperate, to be discussing this with me. He'd never credited me with any understanding of his business in the past, but this was crazy talk and anyone with half a brain and a shred of conscience would know that.

'Sorry, Édouard, I don't see how, when people are getting sick from toxic emissions and grass won't grow in their town any more.'

'We're not the ones doing that.'

'No, but it always comes back to you keeping those who do in business.'

'There is no definitive evidence of a risk to health,' he said, unaware how closely I'd been following the story since the interview. There was no evidence because health studies take years. Air-quality analyses don't.

I clapped my hands in front of his face. 'I can't believe you still don't get this! Stop talking like a machine and stop obsessing about Olivier Kerglaven! He couldn't help you now if he wanted to. This isn't about putting a positive spin on a pile of shit – it's about cleaning up your act.'

'I'm not a machine,' he said, hurt. 'That's what I was trying to tell you in my letter.'

Funny that we both thought of it that way, when it was only a line. My outburst now felt cruel and mistimed. 'I found it,' I said, quietly. He looked at me expectantly but my face must have said it all. We'd spent twenty-five years not talking and now he wanted to, I just couldn't. There was no point.

'Don't worry about that now,' I said. 'You're tired and you have enough on your plate.'

'Your fingers! What happened?'

'It looks worse than it is. I did it on the oven.'

'Does that mean Bastien came over?'

Since Édouard had been acting as if Bastien didn't exist for two months, I resolved to take any reference to him as a positive. For once, talking about our son was the easier option, but the prospect still exhausted me. I'd achieved nothing while Édouard was away apart from rushing around between crisis zones. There was no question of raising the visit from Gabrielle, or the begging by the canal. (However Bastien wanted to present it, if it's your cute face boosting the takings, you're part of the operation.) 'He didn't come here, I went to the studio.' Édouard nodded, his mouth pulling a little at the side, whether from emotion or lack of sleep I couldn't tell. He'd never seen the studio and it would upset him if he did. 'We got takeaway from Lucky Temple. He's working hard – we couldn't eat at the table because he's got so many projects on the go.'

'C'est bien, ça.' If only Bastien could hear this murmur of acceptance. I'd kept the last sketch he made of Édouard, four years ago, though he'd made dozens of the rest of us. His rare ability to capture likeness had emerged precociously, although I'd wondered if the warmth in his father's expression owed more to wishful thinking. At sixteen he'd joined an adult life-drawing class, one of his earliest efforts a portrait of a muscular man, penis lolling against his thigh. It shocked me too, but at least I knew my reasons: for its sensitivity, its knowingness, its truth to life. In a disastrous attempt to appear mature and bolster her brother's confidence, Apolline had shown the picture to my in-laws and the family line had never wavered: *This should be discouraged.* It made no difference that it was soon followed by a sensual and languorous drawing of a woman. Bastien had understood there was more to *this* than that.

'I'm hoping he'll switch to a flat-share – it's too much of a leap living alone at his age.' To disguise the tremor in my voice I pretended to notice something out on the balcony, although the small round table had blown over in high winds several days ago. God knows how, as it was so heavy I needed Édouard's help to get it upright. As we took the weight, it turned out the glass top was broken down the middle. It started to slide towards the gap beneath the railings. We dropped the table, jumping clear, each of us grabbing one half before the pieces disappeared. We stood looking at each other, holding our strangely shaped daggers. I peered over the Virginia creeper to see two people who'd just walked by six floors below and wondered what I would do if I knew this day was my last on earth.

Chapter 27

This time I was going through with it. I was here with a purpose, even if it was the same as the last four or five times. I couldn't refuse to talk to my husband about a letter he wrote because I complained we didn't talk. But nor could I do it while in possession of a letter that was not mine. Thinking of Frédéric wasn't the consolation it used to be and this long-forgotten piece of correspondence, so passionate and genuine, had the potential to make something worse than a thief of me.

I'd really missed Martha since she'd been called to her mother's bedside in the States. Often I imagined her response to what I couldn't face telling her, although if she knew about Frédéric I suspected how it would go. She'd make sugges-tive comments inspired by Lars the expert swordsman and Gabrielle's cousin, Mr Average Fuck. Or if I persuaded her to be serious, she'd probably say that two strange (her verdict on me) and lonely people enjoying a nice chat – or many – was no big deal when the spouse of one of them (me again) had an escort habit.

No doubt about it, I was afraid of what my closest friend might say. She already thought my life was a mess. Nothing really described what was going on between me and Frédéric. We'd become attached. It felt like more than friendship, but I wasn't sure how much more. There had been moments that had shaken and touched me, but we'd been alone every time and none of the usual things had happened. I couldn't stand the transformation in his eyes when he saw me, or the way it made me feel. One thing alone was clear: that this couldn't go on.

It tore me up to think how Mondays would feel when I stopped coming here. Or the six long days in between. Frédéric was smiling at me and I wished he wouldn't.

'Is something wrong? You seem stressed.'

'Oh, I've got a few things on my mind.' Before I knew it, I'd taken off my coat and he reached for it as usual, hanging it on the mahogany stand with the elaborate brass hooks. One day it would head off to grace some grand *vestibule* who knows where. Nothing lasts, in the end. It sounds so sad and yet we'd all be much happier if we remembered that.

Frédéric was waiting for me to say more. Or do something. He'd probably be relieved if I stopped wasting his time. Return the letter, apologise and be on your way, I told myself. It was not a complicated mission. Embarrassing, yes; hard to explain, but what did that matter? I could still walk this way on a Sunday when the shops were closed.

'Sit down, Clémentine. I've got just the thing.'

Today Frédéric didn't need to turn the place upside down. 'Here we are. I haven't had home baking in a long time.' It was a box from the *pâtisserie* around the corner, which someone had reused, adding their own narrow satin ribbon, frayed at the ends. Inside were two rows of plump golden madeleines.

'You haven't even had one yet!'

'Madeleines aren't my favourite. Maybe you'll like

them – apparently they have orange-flower water or something in them, she said.' As I bit into my madeleine, he was sniffing his. 'Just eat it! Even I can only smell the butter and sugar, and a tiny hint in the flavour. It's mostly the idea people like.'

'As usual I can't smell much, but I must admit, they're good!'

There was a pause, like that day in front of the painting. Him liking my own non-existent perfume.

'Who's bringing you cake?' If I wasn't the only one hanging around with no intention of buying a *belle époque* dresser I'd feel better about not coming back. Or worse. One of the two.

'An old lady called Blanche who used to have a shop nearby. The first time she came in I got the wrong idea when she said she was my father's *amoureuse*. I laughed, which was a bit rude.'

'Good for them. Love isn't just for the young.'

'It wasn't only that. She seemed a bit muddled, almost as if she expected to still find him here. But once she started talking, she knew a lot more about his life than I did. She just wanted to meet me, that's all. And to tell me she misses him.'

'That's so sweet. Does it help to know he had someone?'

'It does. But if I can speak freely ... ' He didn't wait for the go-ahead, which pleased me. 'It makes me so angry with myself that I can hardly bear it. I miss him too. I was so determined to punish him for not being on my side, when that's all he'd ever done. He could have married again and had more children – I made sure he didn't. When I was a little boy he didn't have the energy and in my teens I shoved my grief in his face every day, on top of his. The women he met couldn't cope with it.' Frédéric didn't look angry now. He looked as sad as anyone can be who's not weeping buckets. 'Sorry, this isn't a good day to be around me, cakes or no cakes.' He looked at my coat hanging there, and so did I. But he was offering me a get-out, not asking me to leave.

'Is it okay if I have another?' I took the slightly wonky one. 'You couldn't let any of this show when Blanche was here. My guess is your father didn't see it that way at all. What happened to your family was heartbreaking. Nobody could blame you for being angry at what you'd lost.'

Frédéric raised his hand as if about to disagree, before breathing out heavily and sitting back again. 'That much is true. But Blanche said he often talked about me. That made me think she was a bit loopy too, as if she didn't know we'd fallen out. But she did. Now it's too late, it feels unforgiveable that I turned my back on him. I've been pacing around for two hours not knowing what to do with myself. I didn't speak to my own father for the last five years of his life. What kind of person does that?'

My throat was dry and the sweet taste in my mouth all wrong. 'I'm going to fetch some water,' I said, as if it was my place. Vacillation felt like a physical state in those few moments. If I stayed any longer, it would be much harder to go through with my plan to walk away. I returned with half a bottle of Vittel and two cut-glass goblets, as I couldn't find any normal glasses.

'We are both that person, Frédéric. I was estranged from my mother for twenty years and when I finally saw her, she didn't know me. I'm ashamed of how this must sound to you, but I let everyone think I had no mother when I did. My husband didn't even know until she died five years ago. I can't listen to you beating yourself up and not say that I know what it's like. Sometimes the only option is to cut the ties. The longer it goes on, the harder it is to turn back.'

Frédéric looked at me without blinking. 'Thank you,' he said eventually. 'I'm taken aback that you've told me all this.'

'So am I.'

'Twenty years is a long time. You must have had your reasons.'

'I did, but none of them were as important as they seemed when everything came to a head between the two of us. It can take a long time to see that. How about you?'

'The same. I resented my father's meddling. My wife and I were going through a bad patch – it was hard for me when she chose to confide in him, although I suppose it made sense in a way.'

'Marriage problems are bad enough without other people interfering.'

'If it had been about anything else, he wouldn't have. Agathe wanted children, I knew that all along. The thought of something going wrong terrified me because of what happened to my mother but I hoped I'd be okay when the time was right. But it never was. I kept persuading her to wait, saying we needed a bigger place, more money coming in. That worked for a while – she's younger than me. But after a few years, she got so upset that we started trying. The stupid part is that I would have loved to be a father and my dad couldn't bear me to miss out on that. They both suggested I go to a *psy*, but I couldn't face having the whole miserable story dragged out of me. Instead, Agathe and I started to have ... problems.'

To my horror, we were both staring at his crotch and I had to stifle a nervous impulse to laugh. He went on to say she'd found someone new and there was something about the way he said this.

He wasn't thinking about not doing it with her.

'Do you and your husband have children?'

Frédéric was probing, now I'd given him a way in. I'd never mentioned Édouard before. He may have thought I was a widow.

'Two, grown up. That all seems a very long time ago. It *is* wonderful,' I said. 'I can't imagine my life without them.' For a start, it was unlikely I'd still be with Édouard. 'But nobody tells you how hard it can be, especially with baggage you're desperate not to pass on.' I was only now thinking what I should have realised all along. 'Luckily our daughter gravitated to her father. We get on well but she's never needed me the way most girls need a mother. Maybe she sensed there were things I couldn't give her; sometimes you just know. For example, my impressions of customers often turn out to be right: whether they're in a good place or trying to get over something.'

'And do your powers of intuition work in other people's shops?'

'I'm not sure they work anywhere *except* shops.'

Suddenly there was no doubt about the way he was looking at me. I took an audible breath in, which could mean all sorts of things.

'So I don't need to tell you . . . ' He leaned towards me and touched the side of my face, one finger straying to the far corner of my mouth. His scent flooded me; I knew how he would taste. I screwed my eyes shut and every outward part of me closed down. On the inside I howled.

He got up and was facing away from me as I put my coat on.

'Frédéric, you must be wondering about the purpose of my visits,' I said. 'I should have given you this a long time ago.' Reaching into my bag, I handed him the envelope.

'Are you a bailiff or from the tax office?' he said, forced humour a poor disguise for hurt.

As he unfolded the antique letter, his eyes moved along the lines and returned to the top. I watched for the dip in his Adam's apple, and it came. 'I don't understand what this has to do with me.'

It all came out, how I'd found it in the perfume case, panicked and pocketed it. How sorry I was that I hadn't returned it sooner, though I'd been meaning to all along.

Frédéric held it out to me. 'As you can see, I wouldn't have missed it. You can keep it if you like. Then your visits won't have been for nothing.'

Like mine, his voice had gone cold. Without the misappropriated letter, I'd have found some other reason, but I couldn't say that now. I was an unfulfilled, middle-aged woman living on fantasies I couldn't identify and the memory of anyone wanting me.

Here was the proof that I couldn't deal with it in reality, and I was going to have to live with that. The world wouldn't end if nobody ever loved or touched me again. *I* would not end. There need be no witnesses to the aches in my bones, the loosening of my flesh, the changing shape and texture of the parts of me, including the one that would never fully recover from this.

'The perfume case must have belonged to Hortense. The letter should stay with it. I'm so sorry, Frédéric. For everything.'

'Do you think they ever saw each other again?' he called after me.

My favourite square was locked, and too close anyway. When I reached the river, rain was sheeting down but I made no attempt to take shelter, tilting my head to the sky in a place where I couldn't see the stars.

Chapter 28

Provence, 1992

The sirens had stopped but the blue lights were still flashing. Behind the dustbins where Racha and I were hiding, she was still shaking, my arms tight around her. Since the Calanques, Ludo had been raising the bar with every escapade, and tonight the whole gang was along for a party at a disused rest area on the autoroute. It was a great place for it, until Serge managed to set fire to the edge of the adjoining field. He'd put it out, but not quickly enough. The air smelled of grassy smoke.

Ludo's charisma was working on the police from the nearest town. He had a gift for bending other people's perceptions to his own, making all kinds of things seem normal that weren't, and right now I was pleased he was so good at it.

'It's okay,' I told Racha, 'he's sorting it out. One of them's laughing now.' I didn't get why it was taking so long. An officer started walking in our direction and Racha gave a terrified whimper. I clapped my hand over her mouth as he stopped, frowned, then went back to his colleagues. I was scared too, but the way Racha was behaving, you'd think we were in mortal danger. Her eyes looked weird, like she wasn't really here and she couldn't seem to register any attempts to reassure her. We'd shared a joint but that didn't explain it. 'What is it? Have you taken pills or something? If you have, I'm going to ask them for help, I don't care what they do to me.' I shifted, my legs aching from crouching, and she grabbed me, thinking I was about to stand up.

'It's not that. It's the guns.'

'They haven't touched their guns and they're not going to. This is nothing – we're just a bunch of idiots getting a telling-off. They didn't even call the fire brigade, and as for you and me – they don't know we're here.' Racha went limp in my arms and began to sob. 'What are you so afraid of? This isn't about tonight, is it?' She shook her head as the police car took off and Ludo called out it was time to go. When we got back to her place, I went with her to the door while Ludo dropped Serge at the end of the lane. We only had two minutes, and I knew what she was going to say. 'Come back tomorrow. By yourself.' She looked for an answer in my face, could seem to see my heart pitch with joy and fear. '*Merci*,' she said, and when the headlights reappeared, I quickly wiped her tears from my cheeks.

≈

They'd let her have the room above the co-operative rent-free. Racha still wasn't used to the quiet of the countryside. She missed being surrounded by people, although it was clear there were some she didn't want to see again. The village was a long way on foot or by bike and mostly uphill. Serge and the manager's wife brought her food, and Racha was trying not to touch her wages, saving for the future.

When I pulled up outside, she raced down to open the

garage, where there was just room for my Renault alongside the truck full of empty fruit cartons. We were part of a sum that didn't add up, whichever way you looked at it. People knew about her and Ludo, and they probably had an idea about Ludo and me. Nobody would be too surprised that a young man like him had more than one *petite amie* to choose from. But the three of us together was a secret, and it wasn't in Ludo's nature to consider himself expendable. I closed my eyes for a moment before getting out of the car, trying to still the worries whirling inside me. Why should I hide? Why did we need him?

What if it wasn't the same without him?

'It's about time we had a *soirée filles*, don't you think?' Racha said, but only after the car was safely out of view. She couldn't make up her mind – sometimes we were women, now we were girls again. I was glad. Girls were allowed to be unsure of themselves; women knew what they were doing. Racha led me up some stairs at the back. Her room was large and ugly, saved by the gold evening light. It wasn't finished as a place to stay, with breeze-block walls and a few pieces of second-hand furniture. 'Bit of a comedown, after those places you look after.'

She knew I had never been happier to be anywhere.

'Wow, you've really got a postcard view!'

Racha stood next to me, so close that our shoulders touched as we took in the hilltop villages, half in shadow, and the long, low mountain the shape of a hippo.

'Where's your house – about there?' Her grasp of the landscape was surprisingly poor.

'Further along, but you can't see it. Behind that hill with the white villa. That's the garden I take care of. The owners wouldn't mind me showing you sometime – they're very proud of it. But I can't invite you to my place.'

She grinned, not even trying to be sexy. Today she was somewhere between the scared little girl of last night and the lippy, self-assured character Ludo and I were used to. 'I don't care what it's like, you know.'

I sighed. 'It's not that. Firstly, Ludo lives next door – think about it. Also, I'm staying out of the way because my mother's got a new *mec*. Not a boyfriend – someone who turns up to screw her. I don't even know how they can, with her arm like that. Sometimes I hear them and it sounds like wild boars in the vines at night.' Racha thought I was trying to be funny but it made me feel sick. 'He doesn't talk to her or even stay for a beer.'

'Nice!'

'She has no taste in men. None have been *nice* but even so, this one's a bastard. I can see it if she can't.'

Racha's eyes narrowed. 'Do they bother you?'

'Not this one. He asked me how old I was. I said twenty-one and that was that.'

'Uh? What's the point of adding one year?'

'I've been doing it for ages. It's a kind of superstition, I suppose.'

Racha nodded and went to fetch a big packet of Flodor. We took huge handfuls of the crisps but they made me thirsty and there was no sign of anything to drink. 'Apart from that, what's she like?'

'Like you haven't heard.' People called Maman things I couldn't repeat. It wasn't right.

Racha swatted at something near my head. 'I'm not interested in anyone else's opinion.'

'You wouldn't like her, nobody does. And she doesn't like anyone.'

'But she's your maman. She must love *you*.' Racha said, as if that was all there was to it. The thought that my mother

185

loved me had never crossed my mind. If it was true, it made everything so much worse. 'Come on, what would she make of *me* though?' Racha struck a pose, with a hand behind her head. She was trying too hard to cheer me up but I was grateful that she bothered at all.

'No idea. I've never taken friends home.'

Racha's expression changed. 'She'd think I was a *sale arabe*, wouldn't she?'

Even the tips of my fingers went red. I wanted some water so badly. That was exactly what my mother would say, if not something worse. 'Probably, if you must know. There are reasons I don't want you to meet. My mother drinks. She also hates the government, the rich, the church, intellectuals, the entire human race. She *detests* the Bellechasses. *Bref*, if she insulted you it wouldn't mean there's anything special about you.' I stood up, feeling heavy. This wasn't at all how I thought it would be. 'Know what I like about Marseille? The fact nobody knows anything about me or my mother. Here nobody can see me for who I am.'

Racha pulled me back down with the same gesture as last night. 'I see you. And I know that's not how you see me.'

'What difference does it make?' What you could *see* gave only the tiniest clue to anyone. 'I'll never know you unless you tell me why you're here. Just like you could never really know me without the things I just told you. It's not fair that Ludo knows when I'm the one who cares about you.'

Racha breathed in, her eyes searching mine. 'Ludo only thinks he knows. Zohra told his family a story that made them willing to help a blameless, unfortunate girl. If I tell you, it'll be the whole story and you won't like it.'

'I want the whole story.'

'By the time I was eighteen, I realised I didn't want what was expected of me. I fancied girls, for one thing, but above all I didn't want to end up like my mother and all the women I knew, keeping house and looking after other people. I started to hang around with guys my age from my building. They couldn't get rid of me and eventually they stopped trying. It got me a reputation – funny really, considering I didn't sleep with any of them, but who cares about the facts when a girl won't conform? It was hard on my parents – all they wanted was a quiet, respectable life. They were always saying I was the first in our family to be born French, as if I had something to prove, but I've never felt like any of the things I'm supposed to be.'

She stopped. 'You miss your family, don't you?' I said, and she nodded.

'*Anyway,* the guys started planning something in the city and they finally found a use for me. It was a raid on a jewellery store they'd had their eye on. They wanted me to pose as a customer, wearing a long, smooth wig – it's amazing, with the right clothes and make-up I can pass for a *française* or *italienne*. I would pretend my boyfriend was going to buy me a present and I needed to drop him a hint. The plan was to go at the end of the day when the *vendeuse* and the manager were emptying the window and the safe was open. They promised there'd be no violence – I'd deal with the shop assistant, which would be less frightening for her than a man, one of them would handle the manager, and the others would get what we'd come for.' Again, she paused for breath. 'I was so nervous – I'd never done anything like that and I hadn't seen the place. A few days before, I decided to do my own recce. Nobody had mentioned the woman and the manager being a couple, but I could see that right away, and thought it would complicate things. She saw me looking in the window and smiled, made a sign that I could come in – I saw my reflection in the glass, my own face, no disguise, and suddenly it felt completely wrong to do this to another woman. I was supposed to restrain her, keep her quiet. It couldn't be anything but terrifying and she seemed so nice.

'I just left. Close to home, I pretended to feel dizzy in front of a woman who was a real gossip, knowing it would get back to the rest of the group. I stayed in bed pretending to be ill for two days, thinking I was too important to the plan for them to go ahead without me. But on the day I saw four of them crossing the car park at the agreed time, when there were only supposed to be three.'

'Shit,' I said. 'What did you do?'

'I snitched on them.'

Strange that this detail shocked me. 'In time to stop it?'

'Yes. They got them all outside the shop. It said in the newspaper the couple's four-year-old daughter was with them that afternoon.'

'So why the fear of guns, when you weren't even there?'

I could see she'd been dreading the question. 'The police shot Samir, the one who wasn't supposed to be involved. Maybe he freaked out and they thought he was armed. The others were, but there's no way they'd have given him a gun – he wasn't very sharp in the head but he was incredibly strong. They must have changed tactics when they had to do it without me.' Her eyes filled with tears. 'Samir was a softie – we'd known each other since we were small. It was like he'd been born in the wrong world. If I hadn't pulled out, he'd still be alive.'

'It's horrible what happened to him, but if it wasn't for you that entire family could have been wiped out. Can they charge you with anything, or is it that you're scared of testifying?'

She shook her head with a short, bitter laugh. 'The police don't know who tipped them off. I used a phone box nobody goes near because it's like a *pissoir* and I wore the gloves I'd been given for the job. The others can't be sure they got caught because of me. Once he knew the plan Samir could have blabbed about it; he wasn't good with secrets. But when I panicked and told my parents, they said we couldn't take any chances – they have three younger kids to think about. Maman arranged it all with Zohra and my uncle drove me here in the middle of the night.'

'So where does everyone think you are?'

'They were told I'd gone to Algeria to get married. At least my parents knew *that* wouldn't work.' I closed my eyes but that only intensified the scenes in my head. Instead of Algeria, she was here with me, in a place she wouldn't have known existed if it weren't for what she'd just told me. 'If you want to leave, I understand,' she said. 'Even if you hadn't asked, I'd decided things couldn't go any further without telling you.' This time her laugh felt genuine. 'I feel so much lighter. Now you know. The rest is up to you.'

But it wasn't, not at all. I loved her before and I still loved her. I wanted *to go further*; for her I would go anywhere. Her hand was cold and shaky when I laced our fingers together. 'I don't want to leave. But from now on I want it to just be the two of us, and I think you do too.'

She didn't say yes or no. Racha put her lips to mine and ran her tongue along my teeth. She'd added something to the perfume oil I picked up on her the night we met. Maybe jasmine. The third ingredient was her skin. Usually when we were together there was the smell of booze, fags and Ludo. Our blood, sometimes.

'We taste of salt.' Racha licked her lips and we both giggled. 'You've gone shy,' she said. 'Me too.' She slid her little finger into my mouth, and I bit it softly. 'You know,' she said, 'that first time at the château, I didn't think you would.'

189

'I can't believe I did. None of this would have happened without Ludo.'

'You're wrong. I was about to kiss you when he came out of the bar.' My heart thumped, like it did then in the truck, to think it could just have been the two of us all along. 'I thought, Bet she's beautiful naked, and you are.' She set to undressing me and threw my clothes into the corner one after the other. The first thing I'd noticed was that she wasn't wearing anything under her long sleeveless dress – anything at all, as I pushed it past her black-haired nakedness and it joined mine on the floor. We lay back on the bed, bodies damp, kisses feeding the swell of wanting between my legs. 'It's as if you've never touched me before,' I said, as she started to move lower, her long fingers stroking my skin. 'I haven't, not the way I want to,' she said. She'd reached my breast, circling my nipple with her tongue. This much we knew and it wasn't enough.

Ludo had always been in the middle, never letting it go too far between us girls. I saw now that everything had been about his gratification, him directing that *nobody comes unless Ludo's in on the act.* He didn't want to risk it and I didn't get why we'd gone along with it. Unless we'd both been holding out for now.

Tonight it was Racha telling me not to be scared.

She scooted down and I was holding off from the brush of her hair against my thigh. She reached for my hand, met my eye as I moaned at her to take it slower. I made myself breathe, take my time, my body giving, taking, sinking, right until it peeled off the bed then practically folded in two. My orgasm surged through me, out of me, and yet every cell clung to it.

I wanted to kiss her but recoiled from tasting myself all over her face. She grabbed a bottle of water from under the bed, tipped it into her hand and mouth without making contact and ran to spit it out of the window. I drank some of the stale, lukewarm water and lay back, my chest heaving, eyes closed until she returned to my side.

I licked her neck; she twisted against me. 'Touch me,' she said. 'Because you're all I think about when I do it.'

'I don't know how.'

'I promise you do. We like the same things.' She lay back, opening herself to me with a smile just short of a laugh. I nuzzled the hair in her armpit, moving onto the familiar shape of her nipple, wider and darker than mine, responding to its bumps and contours in my mouth. I dipped my fingers into her, and out, and between and around; of course I knew. I rocked my thumb against her where I would want it and she was gone, grabbing at herself, pushing on her belly. When I swapped it for my tongue there was nothing but sensation transmitting between us, building, until her body convulsed in the seconds between *Stop!* and *Don't stop!* And when I did, it wasn't over, her ribcage rising and falling as she pulled me up to feel her heart bumping my ear.

Everything merged between me and my love. Nothing separating my heart, my mind, my body. *C'était le comble du bonheur.* Peak happiness. Once in a lifetime, often.

Chapter 29

Dolores had made several unscheduled visits to the shop. The homework I'd given her had branched into perfume research and she was proving a useful source of intel on what other brands were doing; I couldn't spend five minutes at a perfume counter without drawing attention to myself.

'I love those sticks you pull from a hole,' she said. Suzanne and I exchanged amused looks. It surprised me that she'd taken to Dolores. Sometimes I thought Suzanne would stand a better chance of coming up with her fragrance. 'You know,' Dolores said, 'where there's a different perfume in each drawer.'

'Okay, I know what you mean.' Many big brands do that now. It's tactile and fun, but not messy. It plays on the mystery of the unseen, but people don't have to spend all day stinking of something they can't stand. 'Those displays are great,' I said, 'but they cost a fortune and we don't have the space.' The one I was thinking of was set into a polished wooden sideboard that could last a hundred years but would probably be gone in a fraction of that time.

'So now you've tried all my perfumes—'

'Several times!'

'—as well as all these others, are you any clearer what you like?'

'I like Habit Rouge. My husband used to wear it when we first met. It's still good, but it doesn't smell like it used to.'

Customers frequently make this observation.

'A lot can change: the formula, your skin chemistry, even your sense of smell. What do you still like about it?' Dolores looked like a kid stumped by a question in class. 'Don't worry, there's no right answer. It might be an ingredient you can pick up on, the style, the way it makes you feel . . . '

'Is there something flowery? No, that can't be right. It's for men.'

'Lots of masculine fragrances contain floral notes. Orange blossom, in this case.' It was pure luck that she'd picked one I'm familiar with. Édouard wore Habit Rouge for a while in his thirties before concluding, long after me, that it didn't suit him.

'My name means "orange petal".' Dolores and I both turned to Suzanne in surprise. 'My Vietnamese name. Cam Anh.'

'How lovely! You should have mentioned that when you were trying to persuade me to hire you.'

'Didn't need to, did I?' Suzanne gave me one of her *anything I want, I get* smiles.

Dolores looked at me. 'You needed persuading, Clémentine? This makes me the only one without a nice orangey name.'

We both knew what Dolores means, and we weren't going there.

The arrival of a customer gave me an excuse to steer Dolores into the workshop. 'You seem to be enjoying this more now.' Perhaps that was pushing it. I'd taken such a strong dislike to her a few weeks ago that I wanted to confess and apologise. In the time it had taken me to get nowhere with her, I would normally have completed her tailor-made. When my bespoke clients left with their perfume I liked guessing if I'd ever see them again. Now I was wondering if I could continue doing this at all.

'You're right. It's given me something to do. I know you didn't tell me to visit perfume shops, but it goes well with the other assignment. So do cafés. You notice much more on foot, but it's very tiring.'

'Is Paris starting to grow on you?' I awaited her reply as if it was some reflection on me, absurdly. There's no guarantee anyone will love Paris, even less that it will love them back. It can be a bit cold that way.

Dolores pulled a leather notebook from her bag. It didn't seem to have occurred to her that this wasn't how I normally operated. Despite the time it was taking, it was good to come at it from a fresh angle.

'I decided to make notes starting from my apartment, but if I was only supposed to include positives, you're going to be cross. I haven't separated them out.'

'Tell me what you have and we'll see if it's any help.'

'There's a stunning view from my roof terrace – we didn't choose it. The apartment belongs to the embassy.' I tried to visualise what she might see from the rooftops of the 16th. My river walks sometimes took me that far and we have friends in the area, but I'd never had a high vantage point. 'I like looking down the river at the landmarks, even if I don't know what most of them are.'

'You must have a great close-up of the Eiffel Tower from there,' I said, going for the obvious, although at a work reception of Édouard's a foreign guest once confused it with the Arc de Triomphe. We were all looking right at it and nobody dared to correct him.

'Ah, the Eiffel Tower is next on my list, after the screechy birds on the roof. I don't like it. That's not a good sign.'

'So what? I can't stand the Pyramide du Louvre.'

'But what about the Eiffel Tower?' she insisted.

I had premonitions of an interminable afternoon debating the appeal of tourist attractions. 'I do love it, since you ask. Especially at night, all lit up. Sometimes I turn that corner by the Invalides and it makes me feel like a little child.'

Dolores wilted. 'This is hopeless. Look at you, all happy and emotional. Nothing on my list makes me feel like that.'

'My feelings about Paris are irrelevant. What else do you have?'

'There's a waiter in a café near Odéon who reminds me of a man I knew when I was pregnant with Consuela. It was Javier's first overseas posting, in Singapore. Torsten worked at the German Embassy and the two of them used to play tennis. The moment Javier turned away, Torsten would gaze at me. I have never felt so beautiful before or since. I had erotic fantasies about him – for years – and seeing this man makes me feel like it was yesterday. I can't look him in the eye! But that's not really about Paris, is it? I was twenty-six then and now I'm nearly sixty. It feels like I'm talking about some other woman's life.'

I couldn't conceal my excitement. 'But you're feeling it here and now, Dolores. Want proof that you are still the same woman? Nobody else could have told me that story.'

'Do you really think so? You're a lot younger than me. Is that how you feel?'

I didn't have a choice with Racha around, holding my head, forcing me to look.

'I can't believe you didn't think there was anything powerful in your notes. That's very sensual.' Now I've finally seen Dolores lit up, I bet Torsten has never forgotten her. 'Does this feel like inspiration?'

195

'We both know the answer to that!'

'Keep talking,' I said. 'I'm going to start playing with some ingredients, but I'll still be listening.'

'There's a horrible smell of drains and dog shit everywhere.'

I screwed up my nose. 'It's better than it used to be. Give me a good one to cancel that out.'

'Does it matter that most of these don't have a smell?'

My job is to help people gain confidence in their own senses. That's why I don't tell them about mine. 'Not at all. We're still working on the story.'

'I love the sculptures. Especially the marbles in the Musée Rodin. They're so perfect. I think of my little grandchildren coming here and looking at these same statues when they're grown up, and everyone who's seen them in the past. But when I found out about Rodin's relationship with the mother of his child, I wished I hadn't.'

Who but them could ever have known how it was?

'It wouldn't be a very joyful world if you had to consider the personal lives of everyone who creates beautiful things. I do know Rodin wrote Rose a very poignant letter at the end of their lives – they died the same year. I saw it in an exhibition. And your views about this clearly haven't stopped you being moved by his work.' *Iris, Messenger of the Gods* had made a big impression on me in my twenties, so powerful, female and sexual. Some still can't deal with what it represents a hundred years later.

'Oh, it moves me. I stood in front of *The Kiss* with tears pouring down my face. This young couple asked me if I was all right – the girl gave me a tissue because I couldn't find mine. I ruined their romantic moment!' Laughing to herself, Dolores took off her glasses and rubbed her eyes, leaving grey crescents of mascara smudge. She looked at me without putting them back on. I didn't know how much she could see, but suddenly I saw something very different in her.

'Can I tell you something?' She didn't ask permission for the story about Torsten. I sat up. 'Since our three children were small, my husband has taken a mistress in every posting, as far as I know.' I skipped a breath. Women don't always *know very far*. Or want to. 'I went along with it for years. Decades. Things were better between Javier and me when he had someone else. I could always tell when it had ended or gone wrong. I never understood why I wasn't enough for him, but the anger . . . Not his,' she said, seeing my concern. 'Mine. The rage, of being forced to send our children away to school so I could be with him, support this career that he had chosen, when he didn't even want me. And that's why we're here in Paris.'

'I'm sorry, I don't follow.'

'Earlier this year I went to visit our son and his girlfriend in California. Javier must have misunderstood my plans because when I returned, he had a woman half my age in our house, in our bed. I opened the front door and she was walking across the hallway in a tiny robe, nothing underneath, about to take two cups of coffee upstairs. It was the middle of the afternoon. She didn't spill a drop when she saw me. She didn't try to cover herself or look the slightest bit ashamed. It would have been something if she'd even said hello.'

'What did she say?'

'Nothing. She looked through me as if I didn't exist and carried on upstairs. I heard laughter from the bedroom and then Javier came out onto the landing – he must have thought she was joking. When he saw me, he looked right through me as well.'

'Unbelievable! What did you do?'

'I picked up my bags and got a taxi to one of the best

hotels in DC. I went to the ATM and gave a fifty to every employee who crossed my path. I even considered paying for a handsome man to come to my room, but I couldn't face someone pretending to desire me. Deciding I'd had enough of Javier's crap was so thrilling I couldn't sleep in that huge bed. I remember the feel of the linen sheets – they were so soft. The next day I went back and told him, *This ends here or I'm leaving you.*'

I was listening but my brain was busy on another plane.

'And it did end between him and that woman, whoever she was. But so did everything else, unofficially. That's how we've *ended up* in Paris, after he applied for a move without telling me. I've made a bad situation into an unbearable one. By confronting him I've destroyed my self-respect, in my eyes and his. Our children don't know. They missed us as much as I missed them when they were growing up and they'd be devastated to think it was all for nothing. My relationship with all of them is much closer than I deserve. So now you see why it's so hard when my daughters keep asking if I'm loving Paris.'

'You were right. This isn't about Paris.'

'But Paris would understand?'

I smiled. 'You're starting to get the hang of it. Will you leave him?'

'I don't know. What would you do?' She reached for the simple accord I'd put together while she was talking and inhaled deeply. I wasn't sure if her sigh was contentment or relief but it was far from her usual demeanour. Suddenly she held up her hand. 'This is it,' she said. 'At last something's going to be about me.'

It would take a lot more work to round it out, to achieve the harmony where the ingredients speak to each other and every phase plays its part. Now I understood who I was making it for, I couldn't wait. The breakthrough had both of us beaming.

'This is just the starting point, Dolores.'

And it was, for her. For me, it was good to be back.

Chapter 30

Since Édouard's return from New York, I'd exchanged more words with the concierge about a missing parcel than with him. 'How is monsieur?' Madame Chabas asked as she finally remembered where she'd put it. I'd never understood why she liked him so much more than me. I wouldn't have said either of us was particularly *sympa*.

We don't see much of him! She saw plenty of his dawn starts and nocturnal comings and goings. Madame Chabas knew everything about everyone, especially the things they wouldn't want her to.

'Such a lot of work for you at this time of year,' I said, pointing at the multicoloured pile of leaves by her feet. Bizarre, considering the courtyard only had a few small shrubs in planters. 'Our patio table blew over in that wind last week.' Just in time, I stopped myself from mentioning the broken table-top that could have sliced the jugular of an unsuspecting passer-by. There would be house rules against that kind of thing. Madame Chabas looked up from her broom. She was fascinated by the view from the upper floors; in fact, she normally delivered parcels to our door, angling for an excuse to come in and survey the *carrefour* from high up. It was a shame we'd never hit it off – she had to deal with some very self-entitled residents but whatever her origins, they couldn't be much lowlier than mine.

'Ah yes, monsieur told me about the table.'

Fantastic. Édouard talked to her more than to me.

'A section of guttering blew off *sixième gauche*,' she said. None of us had names. We were sixth floor, right. I feigned interest. Our neighbours of several years had seemed pleasant enough until the man made a homophobic comment when he found himself alone in the lift with Bastien. I had cut them dead ever since.

'I was sorry to hear about the people opposite who've been bothering you. So indiscreet.' Édouard really must have been annoyed with them and she must be wondering what on earth they found so interesting about us and our balcony antics. 'According to Madame Daubrades from over the road, the man with the big beard is a film director, Italian. *La petite* is nobody.' She shrugged, scoop over.

With a delicate blend of insouciance and self-deprecation, I couldn't resist asking Madame Chabas what she'd tell anyone about us. She went up considerably in my estimation by not making any claims to professional confidentiality.

'No more than they already know,' she said. 'Seeing as you've both been in the media recently.'

I could imagine.

He's in charge of the food company getting all that flak. Not quite so full of himself since the disaster on TV.

She's got some fancy perfume shop. But you'd barely recognise her from the pictures in that glossy magazine.

The two of them live separate lives.

Then I remembered: not many people know that last part.

❧

Édouard was finally spending an evening at home. It was work, not fun that had been keeping him out. The air in our apartment, the clothes in the laundry basket and draped over the bedroom chair reeked of stress, not sex. I could tell from how long he spent in the shower, which cologne he wore, the only constant that it was never one of mine. I didn't have to lay eyes on him, let alone for us to talk, to know he had never been wound so tight. This troubled me in ways I didn't fully understand, as if his anxiety had somehow wormed its way under my skin.

But even so. He'd chosen to write me that note in the midst of this crisis and we couldn't avoid the subject much longer. I'd missed the moment when he raised it that red-eyed morning, and I had to get it back.

I placed the note on the kitchen counter where he would see it whether he opted for water or wine. He poured himself a glass of the Cinsault I'd opened and picked up the piece of paper without appearing to recognise his own words. Édouard's handwriting is elegant, controlled and very regular, but here it was smaller than usual, shaky, as if he'd dashed it off. Even now, the onus was on me to broach the subject, as his helpless expression reiterated the message that he didn't know how. 'You wrote to me.'

'I tried.'

I tried not to think of Auguste's letter to Hortense. I tried not to think of Frédéric turning away from me, though I failed at this every day.

'You knew I didn't go in for romantic gestures when we married,' Édouard said. 'You're not that kind of woman. That's why I thought it would work.'

I am not any *kind* of woman.

It choked me to hear him speak of our marriage like a mediocre business proposal everyone later thought better of. Particularly as I had no right to be hurt.

'Romance is not the issue, Édouard. This is about communication. The fact we have nothing to do with each other, nothing to say.'

A muscle was fluttering next to his left eye. This must be very uncomfortable for Édouard. Not setting the agenda. Wasting time on something he fundamentally considered a waste of time. 'For God's sake, which is it, Clémentine? You complain we don't talk and when I try to find out what it is you want, you turn around and tell me there's nothing to say. I don't understand you. I never have.'

'Have you tried? It's hard to see how. There's no ... no emotional intimacy between us.'

Édouard spluttered. A voice in my head called me what I'd been for so many years. *Hypocrite.* 'That's rich, really it is,' he said. 'You should look at yourself before heaping reproaches on me. And deal with facts before worrying about *emotional intimacy.*'

'Did that business about my mother really matter so much to you?'

'It was strange, to say the least, to find out after twenty years that your mother had been alive all along, when you'd gone out of your way to give the opposite impression. I suppose I was in the wrong there, not interrogating you about something you obviously didn't want to talk about?'

'I never told you she was dead.' I heard a younger Bastien in my tone: petulant, combative.

'No, you didn't, not even when it happened. I doubt you ever would have, given the option.'

I remembered every detail of the Saturday morning when I no longer had any option. Édouard handed me the special delivery from the lawyer's office in Avignon after Madame Chabas brought it to our door. He was wearing a green jumper. The sunlight made an isosceles triangle on the kitchen table. His face said, *What's all this?*

I was lucky Édouard hadn't given up on me years ago, if luck is what it was. 'You're right. Emotions, intimacy, we're better off without them. Forget I said anything.'

It had taken me a long time and several people to realise what I was missing by living like this. The fact was, I was never going to find it here.

'No,' Édouard waved his finger at me. 'It doesn't work like that. You can't bring this up then backtrack.'

His stomach growled so loudly it sounded hollow. 'My God, when did you last eat?'

'This morning, probably. Or maybe last night. It's not exactly my top priority at the moment.'

I gave him a pot of olives from the fridge and he went to watch the news. The ongoing protests by the *gilets jaunes* meant that the company hadn't held the spotlight for long. 'I'll throw something together quickly before you pass out.'

As I sliced some peppers and onions to make a bowl of noodles, my hands were shaking. Was there any point talking now? I'd only thought of breaking up, not the possibility of things being different. Édouard hadn't seemed particularly surprised or upset back when he found out about my mother. He'd never expressed much curiosity about my past, before or since. His ultra-Catholic, ultra-conservative family was such a pain that it was one less hassle that I didn't have one. For them, divorce was still shameful, mistakes things you lived with. Édouard faced their disapproval himself over his refusal to hunt. He'd shown an interest in the value of the land (ironically high, after all those years of scraping by, but heavily mortgaged) and the clause prohibiting its sale to the Bellechasses only reinforced his *Jean de Florette*-inspired preconceptions of grudge-bearing Provençal peasants. It had all quickly faded into the background as Apolline was taking her *bac* that year and things were beginning to ramp up as Bastien hit puberty.

Looking back, it was hard to see when would have been the moment to say enough is enough.

Édouard came back into the kitchen unbidden and went to take his usual seat at the table before noticing that I'd laid two places at the far end next to my perfume organ. We never sat there.

He devoured several forkfuls of noodles and downed a large glass of water before saying anything. 'I know you're having a hard time. That's what I was trying to say that evening out on the balcony. But is it really all my fault?' He brought his fist down on the table but without raising his voice. 'I've worked so hard for so long, and I've been paid more than I deserve. But it's only now, when it's basically all over, that I can see it wasn't worth it.'

This was quite the reversal. Earlier in the year, Édouard and Bastien had an ugly row over the remote chances of Bastien ever earning his living as an artist. When Bastien had quoted his philosophy teacher on a study concluding that beyond a certain level, more money doesn't bring more happiness, Édouard had lost his cool, slamming both philosophy and happiness as delusions. He liked things that could be counted. I must score highly on something, but I doubted it was anything to be proud of.

'You can't dismiss your entire career like that! You've been incredibly successful. It's meant a lot to you.'

'Because it's all I know. You said it yourself, before I went to New York. I'm a machine. My gut reaction on hearing about those protesters was that they were a problem to get rid of. But it's worse than that, isn't it? *Je suis un salaud.* People I've never met think so. You're my wife and you think so!'

I found myself wavering. Surely you can't be a bastard if

the possibility bothers you. Édouard had never been one to doubt or reproach himself; both our positions had shifted and it was hard to tell if we were moving closer together or further apart.

'You've never cared what people think of you,' I said. Édouard gave me a look of pity and sadness, my feelings reflected on his face. I had never actively wanted to hurt him. And now I wanted not to. 'Sorry, I don't think you're a bastard.'

After all that, he didn't seem to hear. 'I looked at the departures board at JFK, all those places – São Paulo, Abu Dhabi, Moscow – and it was all I could do to board the right flight. That's how much I wanted not to return to this life.'

I scratched my head and stared at the floor as I absorbed this. Édouard was as unhappy as me, just not because of me. I didn't feature that prominently.

'Think what that says about me and the children,' I said. 'The nearly twenty-five years we've been together.' Because the fact was that we were still together when few marriages last this long.

'The children are gone, Clémentine. Isn't that what's getting you down? Apolline will come back from Australia and start her job, and later she'll get married and—'

This was the cue for Martha's line. 'But that's what they're supposed to do, grow up and have their own lives! Apolline would be horrified to hear you talk as if you're losing her. You've been a good father to her and she adores you. Allow yourself that.'

Édouard got up to fetch more wine. 'Thank you,' he said to my back. 'You didn't have to say that.'

We both knew what was coming next; it was time to stop manoeuvring around it.

'Your note touched me – somehow I haven't got round to

saying so. It was a big surprise. But you'd ruined the effect before I even saw it, calling Bastien *my son* in that horrible tone. He's *our* son. Your son. There's nothing I can say that I haven't said a thousand times.'

'You blame me for him moving out.'

I shook my head, studying the level in the glass as I poured myself a drink. 'That's not true. I blame you for how it happened. He may have decided to do it anyway, just as he could have chosen to leave Paris altogether. I'd have missed him and worried about him wherever he went. But I wouldn't have felt relieved for him. It tears me up that he feels so rejected by his own family that he'd rather be by himself in that dump.'

'By me, you mean.'

If I couldn't find the courage to be honest now, I never would. 'Yes, Édouard, by you. Bastien isn't the son you dreamed of, but he has the right not to be like you. He doesn't *want* to be like you, but that's not the issue. We don't get a say, any more than we get to choose who we are. Even in the rare moments you soften, you make being him seem like an affliction. Bastien has a lot of growing up to do but he's happy with who he is. He doesn't owe you an apology.'

Édouard's mouth twisted and I wished we could both break down and cry. I hated lecturing him on his short-comings. I'd created some sublime perfumes but I hadn't been a loving wife or wonderful homemaker. I hadn't been a devoted mother and nobody but Martha would call me a good friend, and that's only because she is.

Actually, Gabrielle might. Again I wondered if I should tell Édouard about Bastien and the Kazakhs. Naturally I *should* tell him, just as she'd felt obliged to tell me. But Édouard would snap. Worse was the possibility he wouldn't care.

'You probably won't believe me, but I miss him.'

'Whether or not I believe it isn't the problem. Bastien

wouldn't. What is it you miss – taking out your frustrations on him? You should take up kick-boxing. It wasn't just that you can't handle your son liking men or wearing fake fur and floppy hats. You had more than eighteen years to give him some sign that he was enough for you.'

'You can be so hard, Clémentine, though you're fragile with it. You say kind things about me and Apolline but it always circles back to what a bad father I am to Bastien. What do you think it was like, being blanked in my own home that morning? It was humiliating.'

For once I was not fragile. All this honesty was giving me a buzz. Call it hard, call it sick, that's how it was. 'Don't, Édouard. I'd feel for you if you'd said it made you sad. But "humiliating" is about your ego. It's only come to this because you wouldn't give any ground when the son you got wasn't the one you wanted.'

'*Tu me tortures!* You think I wanted it like this? You could always connect with him in a way that I couldn't. The worse things got, the more mistakes I made. It's difficult to keep loving someone who's turned away from you. It's too painful.'

As my gaze returned to the knot in the floorboards, I knew Édouard was trying to meet my eye. Now he was talking, really talking, I could hardly bear to listen.

'You have no idea how sad it made me that day. When I got out of the lift, I had tears in my eyes. Ask Madame Chabas if you don't believe me. You want to know what she said?'

'No, strangely I don't give a shit what the concierge said.' God help her if I found out she had hateful views about our son.

Édouard told me anyway. She said it must be hard for him to be alone with madame.

If I was hard, I could be strong. The progress we'd made was more important than the sting of him repeating such a nasty comment. He must have needed me to know. Maybe the two of us had just spent years in the place most couples end up if they haven't bailed out sooner.

More likely, as Édouard said before, we are not like other couples.

We both said, *It's my fault* at the same time. I didn't know if that meant we shared the blame or took half each.

Chapter 31

Racha and Dolores had been driven to action over their failing marriages. Maybe mine was difficult or lacking rather than unbearable. So much so that other people could see it.

I favoured the theory that Édouard was feeling vulnerable about work over the possibility of our relationship showing unexpected signs of life. But I did feel hope: a little shoot, a tiny spark, even as everything was dying around me. I was taking some time away from the shop to think about Dolores' fragrance, my head swirling with the molecules that would make it captivating and unique.

Autumn was holding its own on this bitterly cold day, with an icy, pale blue sky, the rays of light through the trees too weak to hit the ground. In contravention of the rules, there was a crowd on the lawn at the Observatoire end of the Luxembourg, and as I drew closer, a serious fashion shoot came into focus. Despite the temperature – everyone except the joggers was dressed in thick winter coats – two models about Apolline's age were wearing strappy ballgowns trimmed with feathers, one in black, one in white. I joined the onlookers as the girls were photographed staring at each other with a blankness I had never witnessed in real life, their cheekbones matching the angularity of their collarbones. Between shots they stood shivering as a woman in ten-centimetre platform boots wobbled around barking orders. 'They are too thin,' a stranger with a German accent said to me. 'You French were supposed to be taking a stand against size zero,' she added, resuming her run before I had the chance to agree or say it was nothing to do with me. I was getting enough punishment for things I had done, *danke*.

After the initial buzz, the spectacle had dampened my mood. My phone rang as I moved off and seeing Racha's name took me aback, as if I'd forgotten she was back in the ten minutes since I'd last thought about her. 'I need somewhere to stay, urgently,' she said, no please, no greeting – a throwback to when we would do anything for each other. She sounded much younger on the phone without the unwelcome reminders of the years in between. 'What's happened? Are you all right?'

'I've been staying with a cousin in Bondy,' she said, clearing up that mystery. An area I'd never heard of until France won the World Cup again this summer. 'The last working lift in her building broke down yesterday. I got as far as the seventh floor and she had to get a neighbour to carry me the last four.'

'Oh, Racha.' I stopped myself. She never wanted pity.

'When's your daughter back? I could stay there, as it's empty, and do all the things you haven't been doing. Water the plants, get it properly cleaned up.'

'There's no lift.'

'The flat's on the first floor, Clémentine. Believe me, I notice.'

Questions sprang up in my mind but that's where they stayed. How long for? What are you really doing here? How does asking favours tie in with the vague threats you've made? But the way Racha put it, she'd be doing us a favour. I could fall in with her wishes or give her yet another thing to hold against me.

'Apolline and Mathieu are coming home next month,' I said, nothing more precise. I didn't want to lie. I didn't want to panic either, but that was not so easy. 'But surely the lifts at your cousin's will be fixed now it's urgent?'

Racha laughed, but I could hear her relief. 'You're priceless! This isn't your posh building on a street so lovely you won't tell me where it is.' She hadn't asked, but it was true I didn't want her to know. 'It could take ages.'

'I see.'

'Cosy little place they've got there. I'd take good care of it, you know.' Her voice faltered. 'It's sad that you don't trust me. You never used to think you were better than me. I never really considered you a *française*, and now look at you.'

I puffed out hard – so what if she could hear? 'That's completely unfair. We both know I'm not better than you.' Lacking the will for an argument, I stuck to the fundamentals. 'I can't give you an answer straight away because it's not my flat. You're in difficulty, so I'll ask Apolline, but I can't promise anything.'

'Thank you. It would really help me out. She won't say no. I saw the pictures of her and her boyfriend at the flat. Lovely young couple. Your daughter's stunning. It's like looking at you back then.' I couldn't think what to say to that. 'You're lucky, to have her as a reminder. There's no record of me anywhere how I used to be.'

There was, but I couldn't say so.

'Okay, I'll text them. But it may be tomorrow before I can let you know.'

It was out of my hands and I was glad. I couldn't have

refused to pass on the request. The part of me that hoped Apolline and Mathieu would refuse was ashamed.

I headed to a quieter area of the gardens and sat on a metal chair opposite a maple with brilliant yellow leaves too magnificent to fall off and get trampled on. Now and again someone would slow to take a picture. An older American couple made me get up to take photos of them on a phone, then stand there – 'Oh, wait, just a moment longer!' – while they inspected them. 'Very nice,' I said, in my best *now get lost* tone. 'Enjoy your stay.' So what if I was a rude Parisian now and then? People love having their preconceptions confirmed.

Some day off this was turning out to be.

Old friend needs place to stay urgently. Can she use yours?

I was trying to sound laid-back. Édouard's dislike of house guests would spare me any tricky questions about why this friend couldn't stay with us. Apolline replied straight away.

Anyone I know?

No, friend from before.

Nobody you've mentioned then.

My daughter's way of saying she knew next to nothing of my life before I met her father. *Is she a good person?* she added, as if she'd pressed send too soon. I was no longer confident of the answer but luckily Apolline couldn't see me crossing my fingers.

When she asked how long for, I said a week, optimistically. Maybe a comfortable end to her stay here would help Racha feel ready to go home. Surely she must want to visit her son. Édouard was right about me being harsh; at some point, a wall had gone up around my feelings without me noticing. Things did touch me – Racha's anguish over Tariq, acutely – but I couldn't seem to let it show.

My phone went quiet as I imagined the conversation between Apolline and Mathieu. He was unlikely to object, having stayed with us so often he's practically part of the family, not an honour people are queuing up for.

OK, came the reply. *Counting on you to explain everything.*

Racha wasn't expecting an answer yet and I was tempted to leave it. I would have to drop everything to go and change the sheets and clean up after the burnt food incident. But then I thought of her imprisoned in an eleventh-floor tower block while I was free to do as I pleased, and saw the situation for what it was. Nobody can give you anything if you don't hold out your hand. Not even a chance.

Chapter 32

Racha had insisted on making couscous to thank me. An everyday dish for her, to me it brought back the times she and Zohra had made pans of tender lamb in Ludo's kitchen, as they continued the debate about how they were related, whose sister had married whose brother from which village, who was here and who'd stayed *là-bas*. Which recipe was best.

When I told Édouard of my dinner plans with a friend, I didn't say who and he didn't ask. It would help to avoid any more difficult conversations before we saw Bastien, now they'd agreed to meet. Was it a sign of Édouard feeling better that he'd seen one of his *exclusives* last night? I pictured her as the long-haired model who advertised the screechy oriental perfume that woke me up when he came through the door at one in the morning.

Once I reached Apolline's neighbourhood I passed several bars and would have had more chance of guessing what those strangers were discussing than what my evening held in store. With time to spare, I stopped to look at the left-wing graffiti I'd always walked past and stared for too long at a stencilled portrait of a woman with cropped hair, topless apart from an unbuttoned black waistcoat. The *quartier* was run down compared to the 6th, with many vacant shops and restaurants. Without the liberal attitudes, it would feel more provincial town than capital city.

Racha had never lived anywhere like it. She enjoyed telling me how she'd arrived on the back of one scooter with her luggage on another, courtesy of some kids on her cousin's estate. 'Wasn't that terrifying? Please tell me you didn't go on the *Périph'*?'

She laughed. 'You think they care that it's not allowed? They come up here all the time to work.' I didn't ask what kind of work and her shrug was half defiant, half apologetic. 'Anyway, I got here safe and sound. It's fantastic having everything I need around the corner.'

'I'm glad you like it.' Racha looked so at home in Apolline's apron, navigating the poky kitchen as if she'd lived here for years. Her face had lost the grimace, showing signs of the softness that had always been there under the surface. 'I slept well for the first time since Tariq was arrested,' she said. 'I'm taking the day off worrying about him. And my hip isn't giving me so much trouble now I have a comfortable bed. This is very kind of you and your family.'

I didn't want credit for my daughter's generosity. 'I forgot to get any wine,' Racha said, 'but I couldn't have carried anything else.'

'There's a bottle left over from the other night.'

She handed me the corkscrew. 'You never liked drinking.'

'It has its uses. I've been known to overdo it. My husband gets annoyed with me.'

'He's an important man. Édouard, isn't it? Must take a lot of discipline to get where he is.'

I had never mentioned Édouard by name. Racha was ladling the food into bowls, waiting to see if I would take the bait. The *ras el hanout* was making my mouth water but I would not eat with her until she'd answered the question I should have asked that first day. My chest was running with perspiration. 'How did you find me, Racha? And how do you know who my husband is?' The pieces of me don't join up in the usual way. Dujardin is a name I chose after my favourite actor and because the garden associations were perfect for a perfumer. Noting my change of tone, she gestured to me to take a seat but it felt more like a trap than an invitation.

'Congratulations!' she said. 'You've both done very well for yourselves. Especially you.'

My glass remained untouched and I ignored the food steaming in front of me. 'If you were really grateful, you'd answer my question.'

She sighed. 'This summer I took a part-time job in a beauty salon, cleaning after hours. It was an upmarket place in town – a facial cost twice what I earned per shift and the bus took for ever, but I needed something normal to focus on. I took a few liberties, like you used to with the holiday homes.'

My cheeks reddened even more. We'd worked our way round my route, sometimes with Ludo in tow, mostly not. I affected keen interest to steer Racha back to her story.

'When I'd finished work, I'd soak my feet and relax in the massage chairs before getting the 25 home. That made it the best job I'd ever had – I forgot everything, imagining what it might be like if every single part of my life wasn't giving me grief. It got me the sack when the boss found out, but I digress.'

'It was the magazine article.'

'That's right. More info than I could have wished for when I wasn't even looking. Seems like fate, wouldn't you say?'

We used to talk about that, spar over it, going round in circles. Fate's what you're given, destiny what you make of it. For some there's not much difference. Such abstractions didn't interest me any more. 'The journalist had no right to mention my husband. He's not involved in the business.'

Racha couldn't have cared less about the details. 'Imagine my shock, after all these years!'

'Hmm,' I said. 'Bit like you turning up at my shop.'

She conceded that. 'At first I couldn't believe it was you – it didn't sound anything like the life you'd have wanted. I know you were fascinated by Parisians but didn't you hate how the rich look down on *petites merdes* like us, buying their way to anything they want—'

'I couldn't have afforded that attitude, Racha. The fact is, they paid my wages.' The fact is, I made it my mission to become one of them. Somehow I never mentioned that.

'How's the lamb? As good as you remember?'

'Delicious.' My appetite had vanished and the couple of forkfuls I'd managed sat heavily in my stomach.

Racha was studying me with an unsettling smile. 'So you've really been with a man all this time? Of everything in that article, nothing surprised me more.'

'Are we really going to talk about this?'

'It's the reason we're here, whether we talk about it or not.'

If I was going to talk, I would leave nothing out. 'My aunt in Grasse took me in when my mother sent me packing. After a while she gave me an ultimatum.' I came to a stop.

'Well? What was it?'

'I fell apart as soon as I got there. What happened with my mother was painful enough but I thought the guilt over you would kill me if I didn't do it first. I refused to see a doctor. Yvette kept saying I'd start to feel better, but I didn't want to. Eventually she said I couldn't stay unless I got help or looked for *something to live for*. She taught me perfumery and said she could see me making a go of it. That's when I came here.'

I was prepared for Racha to dismiss my hell-in-the-head,

when I know she went through both kinds. She couldn't conceal her reaction and it wasn't that. It didn't tally with anything she'd told herself about me, but that was okay. We have to tell ourselves all kinds of stories to live with lost loves and disappointed hopes. Not all of them are true.

'Édouard and I were both on the rebound, not that he knew that about me. He'd been dumped by a woman he was crazy about. Paris was hard until I met him – we were both in a hurry to move on and I was far too young. I didn't even know what marriage looked like. It wasn't until Apolline came along – also too soon – that I realised what a huge mistake we'd made, settling for each other. And I'm starting to think he felt the same way.

'It's disgusting to be sitting here in my daughter's flat saying that. I love my children. I know this looks like a perfect life and I'm grateful, but it's never felt like I belong in it. I want for nothing, except the only thing I want.'

Racha tipped her head to one side. 'Not so perfect after all.'

The *perfect life* is one of the biggest myths going.

'When I had nothing, I thought money only mattered to people who don't have enough. That's not true. Money's like a fire blanket that can smother unhappiness with little consolations, things that aren't for sale, peace of mind. Do you remember the trouble I had getting the electricity reconnected that summer? Every day I think what it would be like to lose it all. Part of me will always be broke.' I watched the loose fist against my heart unravel.

Racha snorted. 'I know plenty of people dealing with the real thing who'd happily change places, if you're about to tell me you'd give it all up to be loved.'

'I'm not saying that. But that article is not my life, and nor are these notions you have. It's as if that's all you can see when you look at me.'

219

Racha nodded. 'Why have you stayed with him, if it doesn't make you happy?'

The shame is now in staying.

'You could say Édouard and I have made it work by making no effort to make it work. His job is his life.' I hesitated, knowing the account I was giving was no longer up to date. 'They say you have to sacrifice everything to get to that level and that's exactly what he's done. I was busy with the children and the business. It was easier to look the other way than look too closely at what was going on.'

'Are you saying he found time to cheat on you?'

'For years.' She was getting too much out of me already. I decided to keep the details to myself.

'And you,' she asked. 'Has there been anyone else?'

Racha's indiscretion didn't bother me, in view of the answer. 'No men, no women, certainly no *trios*. What happened between you and me was a one-off. Is that what you wanted to know?'

More than anything there was pity in the way she looked at me. 'Some one-off, that lasted for months, left me half dead and you wishing you were.' I got up to clear the table and make fresh mint tea, tensing my arms to stop my hands trembling. 'But as for the rest,' she continued. 'I wasn't expecting you to come out with it. You're more confident than you used to be, more direct. It suits you.' Her eyes were shining as I put the cups down. She found it attractive. She was pleased I'd never been with another woman. At twenty we followed our desires and were accountable to nobody, not even Ludo in the end. Racha was smart enough to work out that what I'd said then still held true – the best sex I'd ever had was with her.

'And you?'

'When I was young and stuck at home girlfriends could stay for hours when everyone else was out. Eventually there was pressure to marry and after putting my family through so much, I went along with it even though I wasn't anyone's idea of a good Muslim wife. I had a kid. We got divorced. After that nobody cared and I never had to go near a man again. I may not have much, but I'm free.'

And I was not.

The charged atmosphere was a sign to leave. I'd been determined to keep my distance, but now, tired and slightly drunk, I hadn't felt this relaxed in a long time. 'I know that look,' she said. 'Tell me it doesn't turn you on, thinking about those times. You talk about your husband's sacrifices, but what about yours? Is that really it, then – too bad about the rest of your life?'

'You'd get on well with my friend Martha. She can be brutal too.' Dishing up the truth with no dressing.

Marriage was to me what Édouard's career had been to him: the place we hid from each other and ourselves. He'd screwed me infrequently and dispassionately for as long as it suited him, but the last person to love and make love to me was right here, taunting me with it.

And she was right. I couldn't suppress my longing for something other than emptiness inside of me. Connected to a human; I can't be more specific than that.

With excuses about appointments in the morning, I thanked her for the meal. At the touch of a screen, my ride home was heading down the Avenue des Gobelins.

'I've hurt you with what I said,' she said remorselessly, the way a callous child might comment on an insect going around in circles when they've just pulled half its legs off. 'But never as much as you hurt me.'

'You could have read that article and left it at that. If you came here to punish me, you can see there's no need.'

'I came because I couldn't take any more. I thought, I'm

221

going to get away like I always intended, if only for a little while. See what life looks like somewhere else. Call on those who owe me.'

'You'd have done well to start with Ludo in that case.'

'I did.'

'What? You've seen him?'

'No, but we spoke.'

A cold prickling spread over my scalp. 'What did you want from him?'

'I'm not sure – we never got to that, he was so desperate to get rid of me. He immediately offered me money never to contact him again. He was whispering so his new wife wouldn't hear. They're selling the vineyard. I almost felt sorry for him.'

'And did you take it?'

She held her hands up, palms raised. 'What kind of a question is that?' It had shot out, after all my talk of *little consolations* to someone who *didn't have much*. Racha watched me squirm with shame. 'And yet I don't hear the one you should be asking.' What did she want from me? If this recent exchange with Ludo was anything to go by, I wasn't sure she knew herself. Luckily the repeated notifications from my phone gave me an excuse to rush away. By the time I got downstairs the Uber was about to leave without me. I hurled myself into the back seat. There was a banging in my chest and my hands refused to lie still. It was hard to imagine how I could compensate Racha for the pain of knowing me, but now I'd given her a roof, there was no showing her the door.

Chapter 33

Provence, 1992

September felt more like the end than the start of something this year. I told my boss at the hotel that I wasn't coming back. I dropped out of university and my favourite *prof* asked if I was sure. I'd worked my way through the reading list anyway while Ludo and Racha were busy with the harvest: Flaubert and Jane Austen, Duras and Camus. *The Great Gatsby* hadn't lived up to expectations.

Racha and I rarely spoke of Ludo; why would we, when we had each other? It was late enough by the time we met up each day. I started by rubbing her aching neck and shoulders. Serge said her biceps were bigger than his from lifting crates of fruit and bottles. Since he'd fallen out with Ludo there had been no more parties at the barn. Racha pushed Serge for an explanation I'd already guessed: he had refused to keep tabs on us, just as I'd decided to stop sneaking around, wasting precious minutes I could be with her. We were twenty years old, not fifteen.

Despite my hope that Ludo had given up on us, part of

me had known I'd get this phone call. Ludo wasn't used to losing. 'We should get together, Clémentine, just the two of us. It used to be so good.' I hadn't heard his seductive voice for a while and it made me sad to think of the early days, before everything got so messed up. When I was so naïve. It seemed like years ago.

'Things have changed, Ludo. I don't think it's a good idea.'

'No? We have a lot to talk about. I was going to suggest we meet at the track, just for a walk this time.' I got that he was trying to remind me of our last rendezvous up there but I wasn't the jealous one feeling left out any more.

'Sorry,' I said, not sure what for, or if it was true.

'Okay then, let's go out with Racha tomorrow evening. And before you say you can't, it's Sunday – what else would you be doing?'

'I can't speak for her.'

'Racha knows when to say yes,' he said. 'We'll set off from mine at seven and pick her up on the way. I have an idea of somewhere we can go.'

This was both reassuring and not. Good that he wasn't expecting sex; not even Ludo would risk a three-way outdoors. Not so good, given the track record of our outings together.

There was something stiff and odd about the way Ludo and Racha greeted each other. She sat in the middle of the pickup, and whether she was leaning into me or pulling away from Ludo I couldn't be sure.

He drove into the car park of the new golf club, where his vehicle stood out among the smart cars belonging to people having dinner, not that he gave it a thought. Ludo told Racha the romantic myth of Laure and Petrarch and the source of the River Sorgue nearby. I'd once been there on a school trip. Racha gave us the look that said, *You people and your*

224

glorious culture. We walked along the narrow irrigation canal, the khaki-coloured water swarming with tiny flies, the path overhung with thick reeds that scratched at our arms.

'Why not take us to the right place if you wanted to tell that story? This is horrible.'

'Haven't you ever been along here? You'll soon see the connection.'

As we trudged along behind him, Racha and I communicated in looks and gestures. 'Let's go,' I mouthed, jerking my head back where we'd come from. We could hitch a ride from the main road. When Racha didn't respond, I turned around to find Ludo staring at us in a challenge to confront him or back out.

'Come on, girls! Not like you to be so uptight.'

Racha took the next step forward into a section lined by woods on both sides. Ludo looked back with a big smile as we unexpectedly turned a sharp corner and came to a halt beside a steep embankment studded with trees. I shivered at the sight of the huge brick arches of the aqueduct. Having only seen it from the road, I hadn't known the canal went over it, bridging the rapids we could hear far below. 'Here's the river, and the source is up there,' he said. 'Didn't you ever come here to do kayaking, Clémentine? This was one of my favourite spots as a kid. When I got older, all the fun happened up here.'

The aqueduct was no more than a hundred metres long. The path crossed the bridge on the right bank of the canal as a narrow concrete strip covered in graffiti. At regular intervals were the rusty traces of a handrail that was no longer there.

It was the most sinister place I had ever been.

'There's an amazing view of the mountains and the river,' he said, pointing in both directions. 'From halfway across. Who's coming?'

It always took me by surprise how early it got dark in September. We wouldn't see much if we did go with him.

Racha cackled. 'No thanks, I think I'll stay here.'

'So that's it, then,' he said to her. 'You really won't do anything with me any more?' It was a bad moment for him to catch my eye.

I weighed in quickly. 'She's given her answer.'

'And I can guess yours.'

My fear converted to fuel. 'Sure, I'll do it.'

'You will not!' Racha said.

'Oh, forget it, both of you,' he said. Ludo set out, soon abandoning his tiny mocking steps to saunter along like someone on a wide flat beach. Halfway across, he stopped just like he said, looking up- and downriver. Then he covered his eyes with both hands and because it was him, we knew he wasn't bluffing.

I turned my back on him immediately. 'What did he mean by that?'

'By what?' said Racha.

'When he said you won't do anything with him any more?'

'What do you think he meant?'

'You've stopped sleeping with him?'

Racha shook her head. 'I can't believe this. After you said you wanted it to just be us.' She looked away but somehow I could still see the sadness in her eyes. 'We fell in love but you think I'm still doing it with him. What does that say about either of us?'

On the far side Ludo faced us, immobile. 'Sorry, Racha. I've not been seeing clearly. All I know is, we can't go on like this.' I went to kiss her, half expecting her to rebuff me, but she did the opposite.

Ludo could have done the return on two hands for all we knew. Insulted by our lack of interest, he dismissed Racha's compliments about his nerves of steel. 'Let's get out of here,' he said.

'Where to?' I asked.

'Hers, mine, wherever you like. You two are a distracting sight for a man on a ledge. I want to see what I've been missing. I promise to stay out of it.'

I was overcome with revulsion at the thought. 'You don't have a choice,' I said. 'Because it's never going to happen.'

'Bit late to say that, don't you think?'

'The show's over, Ludo. This is private.'

He looked at me with pure hatred. 'You've ruined everything. You have no idea how you've ruined *her*.'

'Nobody's ruined me,' Racha cut in. I'd never seen her angry with him without pretending to find it funny. 'And I know how much you like the idea, Ludo, but you haven't saved me.'

'You'll soon see what you're worth back home, now your trip to *Algeria* is over.'

'Who says it's over? Want to know what they say about me at work? That I'm worth two of any man. They won't fire me on your say-so. It was good of your parents to set me up with a job, but I don't owe you anything.'

Ludo took a moment to think. 'It's nice that the older generation have more sense of loyalty. I'm thinking of your friend, Zohra. Especially as she has no husband or children to take care of her. Nowhere to go, you might say.'

Racha muttered something in Arabic. 'You are better than that. Zohra loves you like a son. Your mother adores her – she wouldn't be capable.'

'You don't know my mother very well,' Ludo said. 'Or Clémentine's, I'm guessing.'

I growled so loudly that a bird flapped out of a tree, squawking. 'What does this have to do with any of them?

It makes no difference – Racha and I are leaving soon. Not for Marseille. We're going to Paris.' It came out of nowhere and threw us all, but Racha managed not to show it. I tried to recall the poignant things Ludo had said, about how we'd never be twenty again, that we'd look back on these days for ever. Instead I heard myself say, 'Summer's over.'

When Ludo went to speak, I was hoping for some echo of my wistful observation. There had to be a way to end this that didn't feel so sleazy and horrible.

'Shame,' he said. 'Still, maybe my father's right.'

I sighed. 'What does your father say?'

'*You've had your fun with those two little —, son.*' Where Ludo missed a word out, my mind supplied several. Darkness had fallen hard, the moon clouded over. 'I couldn't resist telling him you used to think he was your dad. He thought it was hilarious.' Something ignited in my chest. 'Although he says he did do your mother when they were young. Before everybody else did.'

'Don't you dare talk like that about my mother!'

'If you're interested, several theories were doing the rounds about *l'identité de ton papa*. One that it was your brute of a grandfather, and the other was a *bougnoule* who was hanging around the area at the time.' He looked at Racha. 'That's right, one of yours.' As she lunged at him, he took a step back and the heel of his boot overshot the bank of the canal. I pulled him upright on a reflex, only to realise from the surge of adrenaline that I could physically have killed him for the disgusting things he'd said. I released the handful of denim jacket but not before giving him a good shake.

'No offence, Racha!' he said. 'You're a hard worker and a fast learner. The things you'll do . . . To think I was your first. And you were mine, when it comes to an exotic piece of *cul*.'

As I swung back to punch him, he grabbed my other shoulder. I spun round, my arm striking the wrong body. Something white exploded in my head as I screamed Racha's name. She disappeared down the embankment. There was no sound but the water: rushing, rushing.

Ludo's fingers lined up across my mouth. 'Not another peep from you, okay?' he said. He wouldn't let go until I nodded. I broke away to try to look for Racha but I couldn't make anything out in the darkness. 'Are you *trying* to go the same way?' he said, pulling me back up onto the path.

'We have to do something!'

'Then stop wasting time. We can't get to her down there – we'll have to go back the way we came.'

Once we were on the straight, we ran. Just before the clubhouse, I doubled up and was violently sick into the reeds. Ludo spat on his fingers and rubbed at my face. 'It's the shock. Take a few deep breaths and pull yourself together. I'm going inside to use the phone.'

When he came back he handed me a fifty-franc note. 'You're lucky I'm giving you the chance to stay out of this. Get in the taxi I've called and go straight to bed when you get home. I'm going to deal with this and you're going to say nothing. To anyone. Ever.'

And we said nothing to each other until the headlights of the taxi swooped over us as it turned in and came to a stop, engine idling.

'But what about Racha? I have to know.'

He masked my distress from the driver by pretending to kiss me, his face contorting as our lips almost touched. 'I'll make sure you hear,' he said, quietly. 'How else are you going to live with it?'

❧

When voices broke through the haze of sleep, I didn't know where I was at first. The edge of the rug in the living room had made a groove across my cheek. With a small movement, the pounding in my temple was soothed by the cool stone floor. I was panting in terror at a bad dream, or so I believed.

Rolling over to ease the kink in my spine, I found my mother standing over me. She'd slept in yesterday's clothes but her expression was unusually focused. 'There's someone outside for you.'

I scrabbled to my feet, my eyelids so swollen it felt like I was wearing someone else's face. The blue sky and searing sunlight were wrong too, but if I had imagined it all, Ludo – *Ludovic Bellechasse* – would not be standing outside our house in front of my mother. She leaned against the wall, arms crossed, as Ludo looked from me to her and back. I wanted to shake him again in my desperation to know. Instead I stood completely still, saying nothing.

All of us were wearing the same clothes as yesterday. He'd been up all night.

'I took care of everything while you were sleeping.' He tipped his head towards the open window. So what if he'd seen me sprawled on the floor?

'Please, tell me if she's all right.' My voice came out as a croak. 'You said you would.'

'Obviously she's not all right, but it could be worse – for you and her,' he said, not *for all of us*. 'She's gone home for the sea view. That's all you need to know.'

Now I took a step towards him. 'No, it's not! You have to tell me everything!' There were at least three hospitals in Marseille and I couldn't remember her last name, only that she'd said it was a common one.

'I don't have to do anything. Remember, I'm not the one

230

who did this. You can't help her. Go to Paris like you've always dreamed – you were going to do it anyway. Get out of here, *right now*. And keep your mouth shut like I told you.'

'And that goes for you too,' he told Maman when she went to speak. He looked at the house and across our overgrown fields towards the boundary of his vineyard. 'It's shameful how you've let this place go. Maybe you should both consider a change of scene.'

'*Never*,' said Maman, in a savage tone. 'Now get off my land. *Right now*.' She kicked a fallen terracotta roof tile so hard it shattered against a metal water trough. Blood seeped around the edges of her big toenail but she didn't seem to notice. As he left, Ludo mouthed a single word that couldn't be anything but *ruined*.

'Stop staring at me like that,' I told my mother.

She raised her eyebrows. 'I'd heard rumours about you and the Arab girl,' she smiled nastily, 'but you've outdone yourself. Good idea, was it, getting mixed up with him? You kept me awake half the night with your blubbing and pacing around. I let you get on with it.'

But she's your maman. She must love you.

Without realising, I'd been waiting all my life for proof that would never come. In the home where I trained myself to feel nothing, I'd cried for someone I loved and my mother had left me to it.

'You do take after me in something after all – we're both sluts.'

'If you want to yell at me and call me names, you can do it later.'

I wanted to lie down and be alone. Try to stop the battle raging inside my head.

'Don't you turn your back on me! I only ever asked one thing of you: to stay away from that family. You could have got involved with anyone else. I suppose you did it to spite me.'

'It's beyond you to believe anything's about me, isn't it? I'd never spoken to Ludo until this summer, when I came back because of you. You didn't *ask* me to save your job but I did, because that's the way it's always been – me looking out for you. That was a shitty way to raise a child.' It wasn't twenty years' worth of tears I was holding back, it was twenty years of anger bursting through. 'You've never been a mother to me – I even had to do that job for you.'

I was shouting too. She looked at me with something that could be mistaken for respect, but I knew better.

'Bravo! Because you've probably cost me my job after all. They're not sure they want me back. Could you not let me be better at one thing? Even when you were little, you were so ashamed of being my daughter. Nothing was going to change that, no matter how much you pestered me about your father. You used to hang back in the street as if you didn't know me—'

'And that's a surprise? You brought me up to think the worst of everyone, but what do you think they thought of us? How was I supposed to grow up normal, cut off from everyone? Nobody cared about me apart from Yvette, and I hardly ever saw her.'

'I wondered how long it would take for Sainte Yvette to come up.'

My mother was right. This wasn't about Yvette. 'I'm an adult. I make my own mistakes because God knows I've suffered enough for yours. Yes, it's gone very wrong with Ludo, but why the hell do you care? If you had a good reason to hate the Bellechasses you would have told me. I've known for years that there's more to this than a dispute over a few hectares. Pierre Bellechasse isn't my father, and if we had to avoid everyone you've ever fucked we'd have to leave the area.'

232

The left-handed slap she gave me was deeply satisfying. I had earned it.

'But you're not grown up enough to drop the *who's my daddy?* stuff.'

I didn't say I'd been taunted over it just last night.

'I blame Yvette for planting all these *prétensions bohémiennes* in your head, all those novels and stinking perfumes and English magazines. Were you really so desperate for a rich father that you'd settle for one who didn't want to know you?'

No. That wasn't it at all.

'You made me swear years ago it was nobody you knew of and I didn't lie. I would never have had that man's child.'

'But there was something between you.'

Her face hardened and she looked around for her fags, balancing one between her lips as she took the first drag. 'Pierre Bellechasse was my *first love*. I was seventeen and he was twenty-one. He wanted to keep us a secret and it made me feel special. It made sense because our families were negotiating over the land your grandfather needed to sell to keep this place. We used to meet at the cottage where your boyfriend lives. I was so crazy about Pierre, you can't imagine.' She hesitated at the sight of my wretched face. 'I don't know, maybe you can. When he invited some friends over one night, I was happy and thought it meant he was serious about me. In reality he was bored. The four of them took turns with me. They treated me like a whore but it didn't feel that way until afterwards.' Maman shuddered. 'I actually remember laughing, flirting, acting impressed. They didn't force me. I didn't say no. I would have done anything for Pierre and he never looked at me again after that night.' She blew a plume of smoke into the air. 'So, there you have it.'

It explained everything and nothing. '*C'est dégueulasse!* Why didn't you tell me?' She hadn't spared me much.

'Would it have made any difference?'

I pressed my hands against my head and the questions coming at me, distorting and contradicting each other. Would I have rejected Ludo out of loyalty to my mother? Was it right for either of us to be judged on what our parents had done?

'I told you enough, if you'd listened. Imagine how it disgusts me to see you do the same, and with that girl too. You could say *like father, like son*, but the two of us are no better.'

'It's not the same *at all!* Whatever you've heard, you know nothing. What happened to you was not your fault. You should have sold up as soon as you had the chance, got away from him.'

'Why should I be the one to leave? This is my home.'

'And these are our lives, *putain!* You never thought about what it cost us to stay?'

'Oh, that's exactly what Yvette said – always worrying about us. In fairness, she could have made me go if she'd been in a hurry for her fifty per cent. I should have let her have what she wanted, in return for me clinging on so hard to this place.'

'And what was that?'

'You. I think you were about ten the first time she suggested it.'

I stared at Maman, convinced I must have misunderstood. She took a large breath, as if she was trying to suck the words back in. 'Yvette was always talking about everything she could give you, as if I'd let her swoop in and take you off my hands once I'd done the hard bit. Only until I got myself together, she said, and well, we're still waiting for that . . . '

The scent of Yvette's garden on my summer visits came back to me; the rest of those memories recast as things I'd lost. I had never wanted to come home.

234

'You never wanted me,' I said it flatly, the way Maman used to tell me. 'Yvette was trying to help us. Why didn't you let her?'

'Nobody takes what belongs to me.'

'The saddest part is you have nothing.' I turned to go inside.

'That's right, do as he says and get out of here!'

'What did you say?'

'You heard. Isn't that what you want? I'm sick of being your problem. Go, find your lover, live your big dreams. Just don't ever come back.'

Chapter 34

Suzanne was beaming and bouncing around the moment she spotted me in the street. Coming to work was a different experience these days.

'I have exciting news!'

'I'd never have guessed.' She'd landed an amazing new job. That had to be it. I'd try to be pleased for her.

'As you know, sales of Numéro Q and N are up—'

'*Up?* I've just been looking at the figures. It's incredible!' I'd never conceived my fragrances as masculine or feminine, but Suzanne had branded Q and N as *androgynes* and word had got out. Women were buying them as gifts and there was a big increase in male customers. Numéro Q had just been included in a Christmas gift feature in one of the weekend papers.

'You know Guillaume? He's been in several times.'

I couldn't keep up with the men who came in to talk to Suzanne. 'No, but never mind.'

'He freelances for one of those men's beauty mags – you know the ones.'

'Cover with bare torso, stubble, half a jar of hair product?'

Suzanne grinned. 'You have an eye for all kinds.'

'Anyway, the news?' I had work to do and not the sort I like.

'Guillaume's doing a series on creative Parisians and wants to feature me! Photos of the shop and everything. Can you believe it?'

I felt a rush of pride, like the day Frédéric talked about the clock. '*C'est super*! Congratulations!'

'There's a *but* though, I can see.'

Her endless reading of my face could be tiresome. 'At the risk of sounding . . . ' I couldn't think how to put it. But this was Suzanne – I should just come out with it. 'I get why the magazine would love anything about you and it'd probably be good for business, but these are my perfumes. I hope you haven't misled him.'

You know when you've said the wrong thing.

'You are joking? It's your name on them, not mine. My entire sales pitch is about how you create them – you've heard it dozens of times. I made sure Guillaume saw the piece about you.'

'Okay, thanks. What's it about, then?'

We each took a stool on the shop side of the counter. 'I shouldn't have mentioned it on work time,' she said, since I was wielding the rule book, 'but we got talking about my short films. He's already interviewed an indie movie producer and now he's interested in my work, especially as I do a lot of it myself and they have feminist themes. Men's magazines are trying to look like they take that seriously since MeToo.'

We pulled perfectly synchronised *that'll be the day* faces.

'So what exactly do you do?'

'It varies each time but I write, direct, produce, film – I even act in the latest one.'

'Wow, Suzanne, I had no idea! I had the impression it was

more of a hobby. This is why you need a CV. So how does the shop come into it?'

'The series highlights how creative people are forced to do other jobs because the pay is so bad. Working here is what I do, and it happens to be part of a creative vision that you've turned into a successful business. *Jolie histoire, non?*'

'That really does make a good story. Let me know when you need to have the photos done. We should celebrate, but the accountant's after me for these numbers.'

'You take care of that,' she said. 'I've got perfume to sell.'

❧

Late in the afternoon, Apolline's face popped up in front of the spreadsheet I'd been poring over. She was smiling on the icon but not on the screen.

'Are you okay? Isn't it the middle of the night there?'

'It's two in the morning. You're still at work though – am I disturbing you?'

'Not at all. What's up?' She never called from Australia without arranging it first.

'Mathieu and some guys from the hostel have gone on a bush trip for a few days. I didn't want to go and now I can't sleep and I wish I was home.'

'Here in Paris?' I asked, idiotically. Where else would she mean?

'Yes. How's your friend getting on in the flat?'

'Great. I went to see her yesterday evening.' I breathed through the tightness in my throat. Video is not the friend of anyone trying to mask discomfort. 'She's loving it and said to thank you both.'

'Who is this person, Maman? You're being really cagey.'

'No, I'm not,' I said, all light and fake. 'Her name's Racha. We knew each other well when we were young.'

238

'She's Muslim?' The question made me stiffen. Apolline seemed surprised, nothing more, but the fact she asked proved Racha's point about names.

'*Marseillaise, d'origine algérienne.* She needed a break from family problems down south and her plans here fell through.'

'Amazing!' I wasn't the only one overcompensating.

'Why can't you sleep – is it too hot?'

My daughter looked down, shaking her head, and then straight into my eyes. 'I wanted to talk to you before but I couldn't with Papa and Mathieu around, and there's no privacy in a place like this.'

'Why, what's the matter? You can call me any time.' She sounded apprehensive and I just felt it – Apolline had never been this way with me.

'I've just spent two weeks thinking I was pregnant. Don't worry, I'm not. I missed a few pills and in the end I was lucky. But it was a nightmare. I kept thinking how it would mess things up when I have everything organised in Paris.'

'You didn't tell Mathieu?'

Tears rolled down her face. 'I couldn't bring myself. It's ruined our time here. He picked up on me being irritable – it must have been a relief when I didn't go with them. I'd got used to doing my own thing in Sydney and it's too much, being together twenty-four-seven. I miss you and Papa, and Bastien. I miss my friends, even the ones I made at the firm. When we get back to Paris, we won't be together all the time, but we rushed into taking the apartment and I'm worried he might be planning to propose before we leave Australia. I'm only twenty-three – I haven't lived enough to know what I want.'

I looked away, knowing I couldn't for long, but it was better to make her wait than risk saying something stupid. Intimate mother-daughter chat is yet another of the things

I'd never experienced from the other side. But Apolline had me, and it was the best I could do.

'Poor you, that must have been incredibly stressful. Give things time to settle down – it's bound to take a while. Remember, nothing's wrong, although this shows you can never be too careful. You still have a few weeks of your trip and so much to look forward to when you're back.' She was nodding. Maybe I was capable of saying the right thing sometimes. 'I'd love to be in Australia. The days are so short now, and it's been raining a lot. Make the most of that lovely sun and heat. Do nothing for a change.'

Apolline is her father's daughter, incapable of switching off. Once she started work at the law firm that wouldn't be an option, but I didn't say so.

'What about when Mathieu comes back? What if I'm right? When does anyone know what they want?'

'Try not to worry about that. Not many people know what they want at your age. It's very hard to imagine the rest of your life then. I doubt Mathieu is thinking about marriage when you're both about to get started on your careers, but if he does raise it, you'll have to tell him you're not ready.'

'But then he'll dump me,' she wailed. 'You only ever hear about women saying yes. I don't want to lose him, Maman – I love him.'

'From what I've seen of the two of you – quite a lot – I'd be surprised if he did that. At your age everything feels so urgent, when really you have as long as it takes to decide what you want. And that will change as you go.'

It tore me up to see her crying at a kitchen table on the other side of the world. 'Wish I was there to give you a hug,' I said. 'Was that any help at all?'

She reached behind her for some kitchen roll and blew her nose loudly, nodding at the same time. 'Definitely. Thank you.' Apolline looked at me intently. 'But how come you knew, when Papa asked you to marry him? You were even younger than I am.'

'True.' My bright expression and matching tone of voice felt like a badly misjudged outfit. It's hard to be honest with your children without burdening them and, anyway, there's a limit to what anyone can learn from someone else's experience.

'I didn't know. I wouldn't change anything, of course.' It wasn't just impossible, it was unthinkable, looking at her. 'But I was far too young.' I'm not sure the children realise how quickly Édouard and I got married – we're not the kind of couple who goes in for romantic reminiscence. 'The fact is, nobody ever knows what the future holds.'

'But you've stayed together,' she said, hesitantly. 'I spent the whole of high school thinking you were about to get divorced. Sorry. Maybe I shouldn't be saying this.'

In the little screen in the corner, I saw my crooked smile-shrug. 'It's okay, go on.' I braced myself to hear she wished we had got divorced.

'Especially when things got so bad between Papa and Bastien. I know this sounds ridiculous, but one of the reasons I moved back home for my master's was because everything was falling apart between all of you. I know how to calm them both down, and it took the heat off Bastien, me being around.'

I'd come up with so many other reasons: the law faculty being close by, the home comforts, us being cool about Mathieu staying almost permanently – the only time I've ever had to intercede with Édouard on her behalf.

'That makes me sad, but it's good that you can express it. It wasn't your responsibility to hold the family together. I'm so sorry.'

'No, Maman, don't be. It would have been far worse if you'd split up. So many of my friends have been messed up by finding out everything about their childhood was a lie.'

The average Parisian marriage lasts thirteen years. That's not just Google, it's personal observation. 'Apolline, it happens to a lot of couples and it doesn't necessarily mean anything of the sort.' She couldn't stop yawning. 'It's very late there and I need to speak to Suzanne before we close up. Do you think you'll be able to sleep now?'

'Yes.'

'Let's talk again soon. Call me day or night, yours or mine.'

She laughed. *Merci, Maman. Je t'aime.*

Suzanne was looking out through the rain coursing down the shop window. I thought back to her first day, and how clearly I could hear her speaking Vietnamese to her mother. 'Look at them,' she said, without turning around. 'Half don't even have umbrellas.' There was a pothole in front of the shoe shop next door, which soaked pedestrians every time a car went over it. Suzanne and I knew not to walk that way when it was raining. 'Not good for business.'

'Unless you're a dry cleaner.'

We'd closed for the day but opted to wait it out. I can't bear the Métro in rush hour, especially on a night like this: wet leather, saturated fabric and bad tempers, the busking and *Excusez-moi de vous déranger* tales from people swallowing their pride for a few coins in a dented paper cup.

Suzanne kicked off her boots with a contented sigh and one came to land on its side next to my foot. No red sole today but still a work of art, a silver helix suspended in the Perspex heel. There was something endearing about her in black socks.

'Tough afternoon?' she asked.

I blinked, not sure if I was nodding or shaking my head. Whichever it was, the muscles in my neck and shoulders didn't like it. 'I've just had a very intense conversation with my daughter. It's the middle of the night where she is, but she's feeling a bit fragile. Hope it didn't disturb you out here.'

'Your daughter with the same birthday as me?'

I smiled. 'That's right, Apolline. She was asking me when you're supposed to know what you want from life.'

Suzanne's eyes narrowed. Just as she could never hide being bored, it was obvious when a topic ignited her interest. I got it now: everything she saw and heard was potential material. 'That *is* intense. What did you say?'

'It's not like there's an answer, is there? When I practically admitted getting married too young, she told me she'd spent her teenage years expecting me and her father to split up. It's one of those conversations that seems to change everything – looking back, going forward. I feel dazed. We've never talked like that.'

'You're not close?'

Not to anyone would have been my first thought until recently.

'No, although we get on well. Apolline's always been focused and self-reliant, done what's expected of her. I didn't take enough notice of her when she was growing up because her brother demanded so much attention. And after all the time I spent mediating between him and his father, he feels nothing but contempt for both of us.' I threw my hands up, as if this was something you could laugh off. 'Of course, it's easy to see where you went wrong when it's too late.'

To my astonishment, Suzanne pulled me into a hug. Without the killer heels, she was only as tall as me. I'd kept my distance from previous employees and never got the impression they liked me all that much. 'Your children are lucky to have you. You think your daughter would call from Australia if she didn't think so?'

'That's a lovely thing to say. How about you, if it's not too personal? Have you worked out what you want?'

Suzanne laughed softly. Unlike Apolline, she'd lived enough to understand the difficulty of the question. 'Depends if you mean *want* as in *dream of*, or what you might realistically get.'

'Interesting distinction!'

'Well, I'd love financial backing for my film work: access to studios, the best equipment, to be able to take on bigger projects. To make my passion my life, the way you have.' She probably took my awkward silence for modesty. At least I was starting to find my way back. 'In reality – although I can't see this happening either – I'd like my own home. Nobody to answer to, no landlord, husband, kids. It's the weirdest idea to me, hitching yourself to one person when there are so many gorgeous people out there. When I'm sick of my lovers, I drop them. It's good to have variety!' Clearly Diouc had joined a wide circle, which, as she'd previously intimated, included men and women.

'You make that sound very tempting.' I looked at the street, then at my watch. 'It's eased off. If we don't go now we could be here all night.'

Suzanne zipped up her boots and belted her black trench with the chrome studs. The second she stepped outside, a head would turn – I'd seen it many times. '*Bon weekend*,' I said, 'and good luck with your filming.' I adjusted the lighting for winter closing hours, leaving the window display glowing against the darkness of the shop. We were both on the pavement when she asked, 'Aren't you going to tell me how long it took you to work that stuff out?'

'Not yet,' I said, 'but I will.'

Chapter 35

Édouard's relief when I confirmed we had no social events at the weekend was short-lived when I reminded him Bastien was coming to dinner. Although it stretched my imagination to the limit, you were supposed to visualise success. When I said, 'I'm so happy we're doing this,' Édouard looked at me as if I'd segued to something entirely unrelated.

I'd chosen a meal we all like: lamb cutlets with ratatouille. The glass of wine I'd had to appear relaxed had left me wired and muzzy, and when a sharp knife slipped out of my hand, I leapt back to stop it impaling my foot, swearing.

'What *is* the matter with you, Clémentine?' Édouard retrieved the utensil, which had touched down three times before coming to land in a corner of the kitchen, spattering tomato sauce everywhere. It wasn't a sharp knife but a wooden spoon, which I stared at as if I'd never seen one before. Édouard was mocking my nerves to deflect from his own. In the absence of shared interests or pursuits, there were few neutral subjects of conversation between him and Bastien. When Édouard went to the bathroom, I snuck out onto the balcony to clear my head but also to hide his favourite cheese, planning to use the same excuse to retrieve it later. To me it smells like vomit.

Édouard wasn't wrong. I couldn't have been more uptight if we'd been about to host the Président de la République and his wife. That could be fun, actually, a night of the odd couples. Bastien was late, despite me asking him to come half an hour earlier than I'd told Édouard to expect him. I'd resisted saying *Don't dress outrageously* or *Don't wind Papa up* – the whole point was for us to show up as ourselves and find a way to get along. If there could be peace treaties between warring nations, how hard could it be? None of us was a monster or a psychopath.

I was definitely getting better at seeing the positive.

The buzzer startled me. I hoped it was a case of Bastien forgetting his keys rather than a statement – this time he knew his father was home. When he rang a second time, for longer, all I could hear was irritation. I sprinted along the hallway.

If only it was my impression that mattered. With a radiant and implausibly innocent smile, Bastien looked stunning, lots of eyeliner complimenting the long thick lashes that always made people ask if he was a girl, even as a bald baby dressed in blue. He was wearing a shell–pink cashmere beanie, which I prayed he would remove before Édouard appeared, despite knowing they're part of the look and worn all day, inside and out.

As I hugged my son, I stroked the hat. He took it off as if some reflex had been activated and put it in the pocket of a classic dark wool overcoat nobody could take issue with. At what would have been the ideal moment for Édouard to materialise, Bastien looked over his shoulder into the stairwell at the sound of someone out of breath. 'You'd soon get fit doing that every day,' he said. Just those seconds of interaction told me that Bastien and this other *beau gosse* were lovers, or about to be, the chemistry between them threatening to set the doormat alight.

A look of alarm from me has never worried Bastien and it didn't now. 'This is my friend, Rocco.' With his overcoat folded over his arm Rocco looked like a wholesome young American from the Kennedy era in horn-rimmed glasses, button-down shirt and V-neck sweater. 'I figured it couldn't make things worse,' Bastien added in a stage whisper.

'You're very kind, *madame*,' Rocco said, or something – he was halfway along the hall and all we could do was follow. As Rocco drew level with the door of Édouard's study, Édouard came face to face with him and did a double take, as if Bastien had recreated himself in acceptable form and half a head taller at that. I stood by as Rocco introduced himself, pumping Édouard's hand. We funnelled into the kitchen, where I responded to Édouard's perplexed expression with a shrug, hoping Bastien was right. If Rocco was intended as a distraction, he'd proven his worth already. Édouard and Bastien had avoided greeting each other, although some eloquent glances had been traded, to the effect of *What the hell is going on?* and *What are you going to do about it?*

Like everyone visiting our home for the first time, Rocco made for the balcony doors then sensibly opted for, *It must be lovely in summer,* rather than, *What is that piece of cheese doing there?* Bastien wore a look of joy so inconsistent with the occasion that I guessed he was under the influence of something.

My only option was to carry on regardless. Édouard had poured himself an enormous glass of red on autopilot without inviting us to join him. When I raised my eyebrows, more in encouragement than disapproval, he returned the glass hastily to the marble worktop, where the splashes sat brightly like blood. Bastien hesitated so long when I asked if he was going to take his coat off that I suspected they weren't planning to stay, but then he loosened his scarf and unfastened the buttons to reveal a battered leather jacket over a Lycra top with a lace panel across the clavicle and skin-tight grey jeans that made the last pair I saw him in look intact. Ignoring Rocco's adoring gaze, Bastien struck a pose aimed at his father, mouth slightly parted like the models I'd seen down the road in the Jardin du Luxembourg, with an added shot of provocation. Édouard's lip curled with such contempt I thought he was going to spit at him.

'I know what you're thinking,' Bastien said, addressing him for the first time. 'But we're going on somewhere else after this.'

There was a long silence, Édouard turning pink with the strain of trying not to erupt.

'You've known what I think for a long time. So why don't you forget this charade and go wherever it is right now.'

'Édouard!'

Rocco stepped in. '*Monsieur*, the club doesn't open until eleven. We haven't eaten for hours and the food smells delicious.' He looked a bit young, but I was starting to think Rocco must have some diplomatic training. He accepted a gin and tonic and the rest of us watched him peer into every corner of the room, enthusing over a Louise Bourgeois exhibition poster from 1996, a small acrylic painting of the Île de Ré and a lovely sketch Bastien did of his sister just before she left for Sydney. 'What a fabulous apartment! Unusual for Paris, this big kitchen/dining area. *Calme, lumineux, beaux volumes.* Two-bed or three?'

I'd changed my mind: he must be an estate agent, and one who can see light in darkness. We could all use that skill around here. My heart lifted at the hours of neutral chat promised by his company, even if I did have to feign an interest in exposed beams or moving house.

'Thank you,' I said. 'Three bedrooms. This is where the children grew up.'

'One hundred and forty square metres, *plus cave*,' said Édouard. 'Not bad, although it would be nice to have higher ceilings.' His mention of the cellar reminded me that I could always go down for a bottle and take the seven flights of stairs *ve-ry* slowly on the way back.

'If you're staying for dinner, go and put a shirt on. If your friend here can dress like a man, so can you.'

Bastien and I both took huge, livid breaths. He looked at me to intervene, to assume the role I was determined to quit. It occurred to me that the ordeal I was inflicting on us all was pointless unless Édouard and I stayed together; as things stood it was inconceivable that the two of them would have anything to do with each other if not. In the end, it was Rocco touching Bastien gently on the arm and nodding that persuaded him to get changed. As he no longer kept clothes at home, he headed for our – which was to say, Édouard's – bedroom.

'I assume you're not following the same path as Bastien?'

Rocco was as nonplussed as me by this almost-question. 'Who?'

'Our son,' Édouard said, and then, very quickly. 'Art school.'

'He's at art school? *Trop cool!*'

Édouard gave a pained smile – he'd had a lot of practice – and Rocco launched into a detailed account of his international commerce studies at the Sorbonne, where Édouard had done a similar degree. He was transformed by this revelation, full of questions about what Rocco planned to do next. Édouard had occasionally been invited to give lectures and hand out prizes. The only thing worse than those interminable ceremonies must be knowing he wouldn't be asked again, unless they were after a lecture on resilience in the face of professional meltdown.

Bastien reappeared in a skinny navy-and-white plaid shirt of his sister's, sufficiently androgynous to appease his father. The food wasn't quite ready but I called, '*À table*!' before Édouard could find anything else to object to – the lamb wouldn't take long, as we all wanted it pink. I took a handful of *herbes de Provence*, decent ones, not that green supermarket dust, and crushed them between my fingers before rubbing them on to the meat while the oil heated in the griddle pan. I was back at the beautiful garden the owners paid me to water when they were away, earning as much in that half hour on my way home as I did all afternoon. When flashes of the times I took Racha crowded in, I forced my attention back to the others.

Édouard was also revisiting his youth, telling Rocco about when he arrived in Paris aged twenty. 'I was intending to do a PhD in the USA when I met Bastien's mother,' he said, making me sound like a historical footnote even as I was standing just metres away, searing his meat.

'Really?' I said. 'You never once mentioned that.'

Anyone could hear my anger at Édouard's failure to acknowledge that Bastien had done as he asked, if only by deigning to look at him. I asked Bastien to pour some red wine so he wasn't left feeling like an intruder. It was a pleasant surprise to see Édouard hitting it off with Rocco but not at all helpful to the cause.

'What do your parents—' Édouard said, as I set the first plate down.

'—think of you being gay?' Bastien butted in, with a smile that turned from mischievous to toxic as his eyes swooped from his friend to his father. Poor Rocco must have been thinking no hook-up could be worth this bizarre invitation.

'They're fine with it. No problem at all,' he said apologetically.

'Please excuse my son,' said Édouard. 'He's well aware I wasn't about to ask anything of the sort, only to enquire what your parents do for a living.'

'Because my father *does* have a problem with it,' Bastien was off again, in a louder voice this time. 'A big problem, isn't that right, Papa? He can't look at me when I speak to him, not even when I've put on a shirt he likes.' Bastien pulled at the lapels and brought his fists together under his chin with a winsome pout.

Eyes down, Rocco was attacking his lamb and ratatouille as if it were his last meal on earth, rather than at our table, because I was certain he'd never set foot here again. When nobody spoke, he said, despite clearly recognising the unsalvageable nature of the situation, 'My mother's a dentist and my father works in insurance.'

'Papa's big in the food business – I don't think he got that far telling you about his CV, but I expect you've seen him in the news. The *hazardous material* sign the protestors made out of yoghurt pots and lids was genius!'

Rocco was staring at Édouard. 'That's you? I thought you seemed familiar!'

Édouard pushed his plate aside half finished. 'If we return to this subject, Bastien, it won't be in front of guests. *Bonne soirée,*' he said to Rocco. 'And all the best with your career. At least it looks like you're going to have one.' Was Édouard really about to walk out during dinner?

Rocco accorded me a look of solidarity. 'Sorry,' I mouthed.

'I must leave you. Thank you for the excellent meal,

madame.' Our guest was the only one who'd finished eating, but we hadn't set the bar very high when it came to table manners. Shameful as it was, I couldn't help wondering what it would be like to have him as a son, and for us to be *fine, no problem* parents.

In other words, not us.

Bastien began to panic. 'See you later at Up and Under?' Rocco forgot what a bunch of lunatics we were for the duration of a long, lingual kiss. I busied myself clearing the table until I heard the front door close. Édouard was out on the balcony, which accounted for the dramatic drop in temperature, head in his hands, which people don't normally do standing up. Something caught his eye. You'd think a film director with a girlfriend half his age would have better things to do on a Saturday night than stare at us on our balcony – in late November, for Christ's sake. Édouard shook his head slowly. I saw him register the cheese on the table, pick it up and hurl it across the street, yelling, 'Why don't you come on over, get a better view!'

I burst out laughing. It must have been stress or astonishment because Édouard never made me laugh, but he wasn't wrong about us making a spectacle of ourselves. 'Come inside, please. You're going to freeze out there.'

'Was that my Époisses?' It was too late to be regretting his choice of missile. Shame I'd never know how it went down with the intended recipients. Édouard is a decent squash player but I doubted his serve was that good. My guess was that it had landed in the middle of the road.

'I'm afraid so. But there's a delicious plum tart from Bon Marché and you haven't finished your meat. Shall I microwave it?' My tactics for distracting children from public tantrums were still serving me well. I kept my back to the kitchen, hoping Bastien would make himself scarce, but he stayed at the table, one foot on another dining chair, scrolling on his phone.

On a plane they tell you to put your own life vest on first. But in this family it was too hard to tell where their pain ended and mine began.

Chapter 36

Back indoors Édouard was shivering. 'Apologise to your mother.'

'This is nothing to do with her, so don't try to make it.' Bastien didn't look up from his phone. Something in me snapped, but not violently. More like something old and perished that can't take the strain any longer.

'If that was true, you wouldn't be here,' I said. 'But you know what? This evening has made me realise how futile it is to care if the two of you get on. *You're* the ones who'd have to want that. Maybe it took something like this for me to accept it's a lost cause.' Sometimes giving up really is the only option.

'Clémentine, you're going to disturb the neighbours.'

I shook Édouard's hand off my shoulder. '*I'm* disturbing the neighbours? Hear me out!' He took a step back. 'I've put up with this for years. Ten, at least. And I'm sick of it. I am drained. Bastien, you have no idea how often your father reproached me for always siding with you, and for once, he was right – I always did.' In my peripheral vision, Édouard flinched. 'As far as I'm concerned, you could have eaten dinner in your lace top and your pink hat too if it had spared us that awful scene.'

Édouard looked baffled but that was too bad.

As Bastien picked up his glass, I noticed that his hands were shaking.

'You knew why I wanted you to come tonight and, given your attitude, I don't understand why you bothered. There's no denying you were provoked,' – I glared at Édouard – 'but that doesn't justify the way you went on to behave.'

I really had stepped down as peacekeeper.

'Did you *pay* that young man to come with you?' Édouard seemed to be speaking the thought as it struck him. 'You clearly don't know each other.'

Bastien pulled a louche face and Édouard bristled as if exposed to a nasty allergen. 'You should have seen us last night, Papa. Which is when we met, if you really want to know. There's this new place at the edge of the Marais—'

'I don't want to know.'

'If Rocco agreed to come in good faith, that's worse, Bastien,' I said. 'This is bad enough without dragging strangers into it. I must say, he handled it remarkably well. He'll go far.'

Bastien hissed at me. 'What's this, the *Mom and Dad United Front* show? You need to watch yourself now I'm gone, Maman. It creeps me out, hearing you talk like him. *He'll go far*, my ass. Maybe you are just like Papa and all you want is to brag about us to Madame Delacombe without hearing that I've been spotted in the gutter, where I belong.'

'What does Gabrielle have to do with this?' said Edouard. 'Where did she see you?'

'He's showing an interest – surely not? When you weren't ignoring my existence, you trashed everything about me, right down to what toys I played with.' If Bastien could remember that, he hadn't forgotten anything. I once came across Édouard crouching next to him in his sister's room, saying, *You are a* boy, *you hear me?* Blood pounded in my ears, just like then.

Bastien was reloading.

'Yes, really, when you think about it: how I dress, how I speak, who I sleep with. Even my drawing offends you.'

'Don't be so melodramatic. It's undignified.'

'Prove me wrong, then. Name one thing you gave me credit for.'

I sensed Édouard's mental cogs whirring in tandem with mine. Surely there had to be something. But we reached the same conclusion – not one example genuinely originated from Édouard. The occasional *bravo* for an above-average test grade wasn't going to cut it, and even then I had to put him up to it.

In fairness to Édouard, he could not have looked more miserable, desperate and all kinds of emotional states never previously associated with him. 'This isn't how we brought you up,' he said. 'Surely you see that?'

Silently I begged him not to make any claims for us as parents. Or even worse, to personal integrity. Bastien blinked hard several times. Whatever he was thinking made him sad. It wasn't the something I'd wanted, but there was definitely something happening here. Bastien squared up to his father, looking him right in the eye.

'A lot of things are much clearer, suddenly. So the big problem is not me being *homo*? You'd manage to overlook that if I looked *like a man* and wanted to be a good little executive in a smart suit? If only I wasn't such an embarrassment and disappointment to you. It should be enough that Apolline's doing everything you want. Some parents get no joy at all, you know.'

I willed Édouard to acknowledge the truth about this fresh rejection, but Bastien had handed him something he could seize on. 'Don't expect me to deny that you're an embarrassment. I think you came here tonight intent on making a scene. Whatever your grievances, do you think that helps?'

'There is some truth in that,' I told Bastien. 'Papa was being polite to Rocco and they found something to talk about. You didn't tell us you were bringing anyone, which wasn't very wise, no matter who they were.'

'You really thought I'd enjoy a cosy evening with the two of you?'

'If you'd stuck to the plan, at least you wouldn't have had to compete for attention,' said Édouard. 'First you disrupted the conversation like a badly brought-up child and when that didn't work, you resorted to cheap insults. I was trying to meet you halfway, but I can't win. If I'd ignored your friend or been hostile, you would have been furious. I made an effort because I thought he mattered to you, out of common courtesy and because of all this.' He drew a shaky circle in the air indicating the three of us. 'But *sympa* as he is, it turns out he's someone you just picked up in one of those sordid places, who doesn't even know your name!'

An unsettling nasal laugh issued from Bastien. 'Do they know your name in the places you go?'

Édouard's eyes bulged as if he'd been winded. I was less shocked than either of them expected, but still.

'So you already knew, Maman,' Bastien said. 'I'm glad, because it would have been horrible to hear it from me.'

At first, Édouard had turned very pale but now the colour rushed back into him. He groaned and inadvertently swiped his hair up at a strange angle. 'How dare you?' he asked Bastien, and then, as if only to himself, 'How?'

'You know what a small world it is – everyone knows

someone who knows someone . . . Personally, I have nothing to hide. But discretion doesn't run in the family, unfortunately for you. And you can't always count on it from the people who work in *sordid places*. They move around, the guys who work the door. It's fighting that turns them on – they don't care what kind of fuck people are after. Sorry, Maman.' I gave a *don't mind me* wave – when have they ever? 'Not saying *bonsoir* to them doesn't make you invisible. Some clients are much friendlier. Me, for example. We get talking. We make friends instead of enemies.'

'When I find out who this is, they'll be out of a job immediately.'

The Édouard we knew was back.

'You never will. He moved on from your place a couple of years ago, but clearly you haven't. And there you go again – Maman is right here and your only concern is your reputation – what's left of it.'

'That's enough, Bastien!' I said. It used to feel like rock bottom when things got physical between them and I had to wail that they were frightening me. 'It's a low tactic, stirring up trouble between your parents.'

'It's not as if you need any help from me.'

'Good, then we agree on something. Our private life is not your business. You shouldn't interfere in things you don't understand and I'm surprised you'd want to.' Didn't everybody hate the idea of their parents having sex? There was something disturbing and degenerate about all of this. Bastien gave me a look he usually kept for Édouard, and my heart blistered. There are mothers who don't or can't love their children or take care of them, and it was not true of me. I had tried.

And I wasn't ready to give up, after all.

'What right does he have to lecture me? You've spent years

defending me against a hypocrite who treats us both like shit. What is it about this family you thought was worth us enduring all this?'

While our daughter had been worrying if we were going to stay together, our son had been wondering why we bothered. I couldn't leave for her sake, and for his, I shouldn't have stayed. I wasn't strong enough to risk tearing myself in half and this was where it had got us.

'I don't know what to tell you,' was the truest thing I'd said in a long time. 'Can we talk about this another day, when we've all calmed down? We're exhausted, but you're young and it's Saturday night. Go, forget about us. You got his number, didn't you?'

❧

Édouard had left the room. All those shots fired, without a hello or goodbye. I found him sitting on the end of the bed, staring at himself in the mirror. '*Je suis un vrai salaud*,' he said, without moving. 'I don't say that out of self-pity, only because it's the truth.' I stood still, only a couple of steps into the room, hoping he didn't expect me to contradict him this time.

Eventually he did look to me. My patience, restraint and everything that had kept me from losing it or absconding for the past two hours had evaporated. Gone for good, quite possibly.

'Seriously, Édouard, is that the best you can do?'

'What a disaster. And you had such hopes.'

I had to laugh at that. I sat down next to him, leaving about one person's worth of space between us, though it should have been more. 'Where to begin?' he said. I knew where not to begin. You put your children first. Always. The bones in my feet were aching, a sign that I should go and collapse in private.

'It got off to a bad start, about the clothes,' he said.

'*It* didn't. You did.' I pressed the heel of my hand against my forehead. 'Leaving that aside, I accept that you tried. Bastien derailed it spectacularly, but when he has a chance to think things over, he'll realise that. It wasn't a total disaster.'

'It feels like one.'

We both knew he wasn't just talking about the dinner and went to speak at the same time. Funny how that kept happening, when we never did anything together.

'I didn't know you knew.'

'I can't bear him knowing—'

Édouard cringed. 'You really are a *salaud,*' I added, 'and what's more, you must think I'm stupid. When a couple don't have sex for five years—'

'Has it really been five years?'

'Yes. You probably notice it more when you're the one going without.'

'But you never seemed to enjoy it much. I didn't think you'd mind.'

I was done sparing men's feelings. 'You're right about one of those. But whether I enjoyed sex with you and whether I mind you using escorts are two separate issues.'

'Okay, five years is a long time, but I don't see how you could assume...'

Édouard was anxious to avoid my scrutiny but the room provided no allies or excuses. He didn't want to associate with himself at this moment, not at all.

'But since I was right, you don't get to be indignant. Of course I didn't think you'd given up sex in your forties. I used to think you had a long-term lover hidden away somewhere. It's sad, but I could just about live with the idea someone was making you happy.' This might be satisfying if I was squarely on the moral high ground, but the cold fact was that a man

I didn't love didn't desire me. Nothing had brought Édouard happiness, except Apolline. If it had, he might have left me if he'd found the time. His schedule and my weakness had kept us together.

'There's never been anyone serious. That's not what I wanted.'

We held extended eye contact for the first time in years. I remembered the way he looked at me as he went up that escalator. I wondered what kind of life I'd have now if I'd stayed longer behind that counter: a different husband, different children, a flat half the size in a not-so-great area. A gorgeous woman, or a string of women and men. Different children, or maybe none, a flat who cares where or how big. No Arôme de Clémentine, perhaps. The possibilities were there; too many. It didn't have to be Paris, didn't have to be this way.

Not then, and not any more.

'Tell me everything. I need to understand what was going on.'

'*Écoute,* Clémentine . . . '

'Listening is exactly what I'm doing.'

'You're not going to like it.'

I raised my eyebrows. 'You never know, it might ease your *I'm such a bastard* crisis to get it off your chest. I am asking, after all.' Édouard was not convinced. 'When did it start?'

'What, originally?'

'In the beginning. The first time.'

'After Bastien,' he mumbled.

'What do you mean, after Bastien? He's nineteen!'

'Fairly soon after he was born.' I did a comedy blink, screwing my eyes as tight shut as they would go, then opening them as wide. Every muscle in my face went rigid. My husband had been unfaithful to me for most of our marriage. The fact he continued to sleep with me until five years ago took on a very different complexion. 'Are you hurt by that?'

'Hurt? No, I think it's fabulous.'

First Racha, now him. There must be something about me that invited it.

'You complain we don't talk, but this is what you do. You lash out, and it's childish. You say you want closeness but the truth is you don't allow anyone near you. That wasn't a good strategy for marriage.'

'It's hard to be intimate with someone who can't have a row without sounding like they're quoting from *The Seven Habits of Highly Effective People*. And is cheating on you,' I threw in for good measure.

'I thought you'd want to talk about what happened tonight.'

'This is happening tonight.'

Édouard's eyes flitted around, coming to rest in odd places as if he was checking for dust on the skirting boards. It's funny how you only realise after a conversation that you were staring at something, like a picture, or a gold pendant lying on skin. The snapping sensation I'd had earlier, the feeling that something was broken: it wasn't me. It was the me who existed inside this marriage. 'That night on the balcony, when you were crying.' His expression came back to me, poorly lit, between despair and irritation. 'You said you had no idea how I felt about being married to you.'

Oh God, I did say that.

'I don't generally think like that. I mean, that's more of a women's thing, reflecting on relationships. But since then I've given it a lot of thought, especially when I was in New York. Everything felt so far away, and nothing further than you.' Earlier, I'd been the historical footnote, now it seemed everything was. 'You had a better idea of who you were marrying than I did. I was always clear what I was aiming for.'

'That's true.' Not that there'd been any guarantee he'd get that far.

'You can resent me for working all hours, for not seeing more of the children, even if it's not entirely fair. But it always felt as if you wanted it that way, as if we had, well, an understanding.'

'Reached telepathically?'

'There would have been more chance of that than by trying to talk to each other. I realised within months of the wedding that you were having second thoughts. Do you realise we've only once told each other *I love you*? Do you want to know why?'

'Because you didn't mean it?'

Édouard forced himself to look at me, his eyes threatening to spill over. 'No. Because you didn't.'

I forced myself not to look away. 'Why did you ask me to marry you?'

'Why did you say yes?'

I exhaled sharply. 'I was young; I didn't listen to Yvette telling me to wait. I was confident we'd have a stable life together.'

'A *stable life*? Forget talking now, there's a lot you should have told me at the time. You didn't think I had the right to know what you were running from?'

'No. It was in the past. It didn't concern you.'

'If that's how you feel,' he said, standing up, 'there really isn't anything left to say.'

'What's it like with the women you pay?'

Édouard shook his head slowly as he looked back at me. 'You're being perverse. I don't know what's got into you lately.'

'Tell me the truth, whatever that is.'

I pictured the parade of pretty faces and perfect bodies passing through his mind.

'Okay then, I'll tell you. It's good. There are no strings. It's a contract, but nothing like the one we have. They're strangers, but they don't pretend otherwise.'

Chapter 37

Wrapping orders took me back to my earliest days as an apprentice perfumer, when I would spend hours at the kitchen table designing labels for the concoctions I'd made for Maman. Now the elegant writing was the name of my own shop on the ribbon, springing into loops as I ran the scissor blade along it. I looked up when I heard the door and pushed the packages away.

'You can't keep turning up like this, Racha. I have work to do.'

'You're ashamed of me. I notice it every time that girl's here.'

'Suzanne's been very kind to you, considering.' Suzanne, Cam Anh, orange petal, who never ceased to surprise me. I'd been thinking a lot about the conversations with her and my daughter.

'You're much more friendly towards Suzanne,' Racha said. 'You were always such a sweet girl.'

I was not.

'There's no comparison. Suzanne works here. Do you see my other friends wandering in all the time? This isn't a hobby, whatever you may think. Knowing where I started out, I would have thought you'd get that.'

It sounded wrong without the snappy retort I'd expected. 'Could I sit down for a moment?' she asked. The stools were no good to her, so I fetched a chair from the workshop and wished I'd brought one for myself. Instead I went to fiddle with the brochures at the far end of the counter. We could see each other better from a distance.

'I've worked whenever I could. There aren't many jobs for someone like me. Oh, I'm not just talking about discrimination,' she said. 'There aren't many minimum-wage jobs that don't involve spending all day on your feet, and I can't.'

My eyes zoned past her to the street. There was no sign of anyone coming in, not even the postman. 'Any news of Tariq?' I hesitated to use his name as if I knew him, but between us there could be no unmentionable sons.

I saw her arm herself to reply, touched that I asked. 'A friend went to see him two days ago, a woman he's always liked. She sometimes used to watch him for me when he was little. We look out for each other.'

'How's he doing?'

'Very withdrawn, but he was calm and agreed to see her. She didn't want to say, but he didn't ask after me.'

'Is it too upsetting for you to visit?'

Racha bit hard on her lip. 'He got hysterical the only time I went, begging me to get him out. He may be an adult on paper but he has no education – he dropped out of school just like me. Tariq's good at heart, not a troublemaker. He always wanted to be a fireman; the youth worker tried so hard to keep him on track but he fell in with the wrong crowd. The guards terminated the visit and I worry that seeing me might set him off and make things worse for him inside.'

I went to her, put my hand on her shoulder and she reached

266

up for it. 'This is not the life I wanted,' she said, without looking at me. 'You remember that, don't you? Me, my ex, Tariq – none of us have ever proven anyone's low expectations wrong. My brother and sisters have managed to make something of themselves. I really think it would have been different if I'd managed to get away, start again like you did. Am I kidding myself?'

'Of course not.' I couldn't risk saying *It's never too late*, in case it was. I couldn't sympathise or commiserate or say anything that might sound like an attempt to exonerate myself. I would never know how much responsibility to take for Racha; as I'd said to Apolline, nobody can know what the future holds, what luck or misfortune might strike at any moment. What did it feel like, to fall?

'Once you would have told me what you were thinking,' she said.

She wouldn't have had to ask. Racha stroked the sleeve of my cardigan then slipped her hand under the front edge, smoothing my blouse against my ribs, weighing my breast against her wrist. *'Jamila.'* When she said it under her breath, I felt it under my skin. I used to think it was just a beautiful name until she told me it was the word for beautiful. My body sprang to life at her touch. Some things can never be unseen or undone; this I could never unlearn. 'I look at you and it doesn't seem possible,' she said.

'What?'

'That you still have feelings for me.'

I knew then that it was more than possible. Flushed, I felt the weird tension, half pleasurable, half not, that sometimes grips me when I'm about to cry, sneeze or (different context, not unrelated) come.

'How could I not be moved by your situation? If you thought I was that cruel, you wouldn't be here.' Racha gave me the lingering look she used to in front of other people and it still embarrassed me. 'You console me even when you're trying to push me away,' she said. 'You can't help it.'

'Every time you turn up it shocks me as much as when I first realised you were back. I don't know where I am with you.'

She got up. 'But you know who I am.' Two women were window-shopping, and one made for the door, then hesitated. 'See the way they look at me. You'll have to imagine me kissing you goodbye.'

❧

I wasn't sure of the form on contacting someone you've told to forget you exist. Bastien had never been afraid to push back at Édouard's disapproval, but he'd never pretended not to care. I sent one text, a second one hours later and then I gave in and called, as if that would make a difference. I had a bad feeling. When Bastien was twelve, one of his teachers said, *Poor boy, he's not going to have it easy.* I was torn between berating her and thanking her for trying to imagine how it was to be him, even if she was wrong.

She wasn't entirely wrong.

'Do you mind closing up again tonight? I'm worried about my son and I want to see if I can track him down.'

Suzanne had often heard me talk about Bastien but I saw a question forming. 'There's been a lot of conflict between him and his father.' She nodded. 'At the weekend I got them together and . . . '

'It didn't go well.'

I shook my head, trying to smile when my mouth was heading somewhere else.

'I'll close up. Do what you have to do.'

If only someone would tell me what that was.

❧

I couldn't turn up unannounced, but even if he told me to stay away, it would be something. Off it went, another message that would go unanswered. Bastien's exact words escaped me but not the gist: *What was it about this family you thought was worth all this?* Apolline's friends had suffered when they felt their childhood had been built on lies. Édouard and I were still together, but what other conclusion could there be? Parents like to think young people only care about themselves because it suits us to believe they don't notice our mistakes and misdemeanours. I couldn't risk Bastien sharing our tawdry secrets with his sister, especially now. Anything that made Apolline turn to me was something I had to protect. My dearest wish for both of our children was that they'd look at us and think, *No way am I living like that.*

It was too far to walk and a cab was out of the question in rush hour. I took the Métro at St-Germain-des-Prés, where it was standing room only and I had to dive for a germ-infested pole I could reach beneath the hands of taller passengers. As soon as the train left the station, a row broke out between two men. 'People like you have no right to push in front of me.'

'So what are you going to do about it?' I watched the hands above mine tense. A teenage girl looked at me, eyes wide with apprehension. A woman with a heavy Russian accent intervened. '*Arrêtez!*' she said, with the air of someone accustomed to being obeyed. 'Don't fight over nothing. Aren't there enough problems in the world? The two of you are not so different.'

The one who'd started it got off at Odéon, swearing to himself. Someone said, *Bravo, madame!* and a few people clapped. The girl was back on Instagram. At Gare de l'Est I got off, hoping to be spared any more drama. If anyone accosted me for money today, I'd just hand it over.

Outside Bastien's studio I called him again. I knew the entry code but as there was no concierge to interrogate – not that I would be inclined, associating them all with Madame Chabas – there was no point going inside without a key. Darkness is a leveller, and the narrow street seemed less depressing than usual. I couldn't hang around outside waiting for Bastien to show up, so I backtracked to the little café-bar on the corner to ponder my next move. Only when I was about to order did I notice that I was the only woman and that all the men were staring at me, not with hostility but as if I was an incongruous foreign object. 'What can I get you?' the barman asked, curious to see if I held my nerve. I could have asked for directions to the station I'd just come from and been out of there in seconds, but instead I heard myself order a whisky. I closed my eyes and summoned heather, peat and morning mists burning off in autumn sunshine, while trying not to actively breathe in. The finest whiskies have a nose as rich and complex as the best perfume – like the worst of both, this one smelled of alcohol with something generically unpleasant on top. He only charged me €3 for a double measure, which would barely have got me the Evian I'd intended to order in my own neighbourhood. I sighed and the barman shot me a different look. 'Bad day?'

'I've lost count.' I smiled at my drink, tapping my nails against the glass. It was like being in a second-rate film. Once the glass was empty he poured me a generous refill I hadn't asked for and when I protested he said, 'Given how it tastes, I do mostly give it away.' The stiff drink filled me with reckless courage and unfounded optimism. An idea came, which I initially dismissed, but we were only fifty metres from his place . . .

'I'm looking for someone.' The barman made a mock-rueful face. This bad film was his every day. 'Not like that!

My son, Bastien. He lives round the corner. Maybe you know him.'

He studied me. 'Looks a bit like you, pink hat, all eyelashes?'

'That's him.' My boy. A hazy rush of pride came over me, instead of the usual defensiveness and anxiety. What a waste of energy, as Bastien said, when I could just not give a shit. 'Don't suppose you've seen him around the last couple of days?'

The barman threw the question out to his regulars, who looked at me with a new respect. 'He sometimes comes in for cigarettes, but look at us,' he said of the handful of unremarkable men in their thirties and forties. 'This isn't going to be his kind of place, is it?'

Clearly they were not aware of Bastien's eclectic taste in company.

Minutes passed before the guy playing pinball finished his game, giving the machine a victorious thump. 'Boy with the big dog? Saw him by the canal yesterday.'

'Where exactly?' The canal was long. It had two banks. Even the short distance to the nearest point was a trek I didn't fancy. My glass was empty again and the whisky sloshed around in my empty stomach.

The man tried to explain but I couldn't concentrate. It was night-time and I couldn't seem to retain the directions he gave me. I wouldn't have rated my chances of finding Bastien even before getting drunk; in all likelihood, I'd have decided to leave it and go home. But my informant insisted on walking me to the water and pointing me the right way.

The banks of the canal were deserted. It had turned much colder and a keen north wind carried salty hints of Le Touquet. I didn't walk far before seeing the infamous boxed-off balcony, my approach measured in steps and palpitations; if

Édouard could see me now, he'd have me locked up. Voices came from behind the cardboard and, recalling what Bastien had said about the language barrier, I took heart from the fact that one of them was speaking French. A head popped up and I leapt back, my hip touching a 4x4 parked at the kerbside. But the smile was as warm as if the man was answering his front door to a friend.

'*Bonsoir, monsieur,* sorry to bother you, but I believe you know my son, Bastien?'

'Bastien!' he roared, inexplicably making the sign of the Cross.

'*Chien!*' The man walked two fingers along his forearm and from inside the enclosure came a decent impression of barking. For years Bastien had begged us for a dog but Édouard didn't believe animals belonged in cities. Given the smell implications, that was one battle I chose not to fight.

Another of the occupants, the French one, stood up. 'Welcome, *maman de Bastien!*' Despite several missing teeth and a faceful of wrinkles, he was flirting full on. 'Do join us!' His name was Léon.

And Léon had to be kidding. It was hard to see how anyone could get up there, let alone a large dog. The first man vaulted over and made a rung with his enormous hands; I felt myself rising as if in a lift and Léon helped me over the top. My first thought, too late: I was in a dark, secluded space that I couldn't leave unaided, with a bunch of strange men; the second, that I'd better stay on their good side. If they really were friends of Bastien's or he was useful to them, surely they wouldn't hurt me.

There were five of them surrounded by a mound of stained duvets, pillows and cheap plastic laundry bags. Even though we were effectively outdoors, the air reeked of dog, fart and smoke, with dominant notes of sweat and piss. Grabbing an old nasal spray from my bag, under cover of my hand, I snorted double the recommended dose up each nostril to drown the stench with menthol and apologised with an excuse about sinuses.

'Do you think my son will be back soon?' I asked Léon.

'That depends.' He made the gesture for money but was upset when I thought he was asking me for it.

My maternal presence set something off among the men, who began to show me pictures of their wives and children. It was so sad that they'd ended up living like this, far from home and the people they love. Their roof was the balcony above and there was barely space for all of them to lie down. I was handed a scalding cup of black tea and it didn't end there with the botanicals, because next it was a freshly rolled spliff. I took a deep drag to be polite, assuming the idea was to pass it round, but they insisted I have one to myself. I leaned back against something soft and it only took a few tokes to remember why I used to do this, although this stuff was far stronger. The edges disappeared from everything. It made me want to laugh – so I did – and to crash out and sleep for days, which I couldn't.

'Thank you for my son,' I said. It sounded wrong and I didn't know why, or what these people had done for Bastien. But he liked them, and I could see why. Before I knew it, I'd finished the joint. 'Sorry I can't stay. It was great, honestly.'

They leapt up and repeated the routine to return me to the street. I nearly fell over but managed to grab a lamp post. One of the men wanted to come with me but I said no and turned into a side street, where I leaned against a building, my body too heavy for my legs. The knobs of my spine scraped against the brick through my coat as I sank to the pavement. It was so comfortable. Instead of that pain, now there was a swirly empty feeling between my eyes. I felt good. I was happy. Wanted so much to lie down. I couldn't go home like this, couldn't stay here like this.

It was very cold.

My finger raced through names on my phone. I couldn't find the man with the beautiful green eyes, the one who smells so good I want to kiss him – what was his name again? I didn't know who half these people were. Martha, yes, I know Martha. Her name looked strange, like there was something wrong with it. She always says French people can't say *th*.

Ah, it was her voice. 'Clementine, what's up? Has something happened?'

Why did people keep asking me that? 'I don't think so, why?'

'Are you sure? You never call me in the States. I'm still in Sag Harbor. I'll be back in Paris on Sunday.'

'I'm completely stoned, *Mar-ta*. I need to sleep.'

'What the fuck? Where are you? Who are you with?'

She should chill out. It wasn't that bad.

'By the canal. I was looking for Bastien and the dog but they're not here.'

She wasn't talking to me any more. Maybe she'd gone away.

Then she was back. 'Is Édouard home?'

'Don't let him near me!' I shouted.

'God, you're so right. He'd hit the roof.' I couldn't stop laughing.

Martha was saying, *Let me think*, over and over, and, *This would have to happen when I'm not there.*

'Got it!' She made me jump and I hit my head against the wall. 'Do you have Apolline's keys in your bag?'

'Yeah.'

'Okay, listen carefully. When we're done talking, open Uber on your phone. It knows where you are, so all you have to do is press Apolline's address and accept. Five diamonds, isn't it?'

'Rue des cinq diamants.'

'You got it. I'll call you back in ten minutes to check if they picked you up. Stay exactly where you are. Don't talk to the driver, or anyone else.'

Through the car window, everything was so sparkly and beautiful. I toppled over in the back seat at Bastille. The driver told me to put my seatbelt on but I couldn't get the metal thing to go in the other bit. Martha called back. 'Nearly there,' I told her. 'I'm so hungry. I haven't had anything in hours except those two big whiskies.'

Merde. I'd told the driver I wasn't drunk. He was staring at me in the mirror.

'Jesus Christ,' said Martha. 'Don't eat anything now. Drink lots of water and lie on your side, okay? Not your back. Sleep it off, sweetie. I hope you don't have plans tomorrow. When I get back, you and I need to have a talk.'

Chapter 38

There was something wrong. The *bip* on the key ring got me in downstairs. It was definitely the right flat. Apolline wasn't here, but noise was coming from inside. The key was turning but the stupid door wouldn't open.

Aïe! My shoulder hurt.

'Clémentine, stop or you're going to break something! I'm trying to let you in.' More noises. What was *Racha* doing here, wearing Apolline's robe? She hugged me, but I didn't like the way she was looking me up and down. 'Who did this to you?'

'What?'

'Have you been mugged? Your hair, your clothes . . . you've lost an earring too.'

I knew this wasn't funny but it made me laugh. 'Of course not! I've been having a great time!'

She sniffed me and screwed her nose up. 'Have you been smoking something? That would explain a lot.'

Racha was in my way and I really had to pee. I pushed past her and got to the bathroom but it went everywhere, the seat, the floor, hot and wet down my leg. When she asked if it was okay to come in, I started to cry. 'I really stink now.'

'How like you to worry about that! Let's get you in the shower.'

'You too.'

'No, I've had one already. That's why I'm in my pyjamas.'

She pushed and pulled my clothes off. When she said, 'Arms up,' I couldn't do it.

'Let's just go to bed,' I said.

'You can lie down in a minute. You'll feel much better clean.'

True. The water poured over my face and woke me up a bit. The shower curtain kept sticking to me. The bathroom smelled of plastic strawberries.

'Forget your hair for now.' She gave me a big towel and a navy-blue bathrobe.

'I'm not wearing that, it belongs to Édouard.'

'Don't you mean Mathieu? If it bothers you, we can swap.' Racha took off Apolline's kimono and belted it around me. It was warm. It made me shiver.

'You can rest now.' In the bedroom she brought me water and stroked my forehead. 'You're so buttoned up these days. I wouldn't have thought it of you!'

'I didn't do it on purpose.'

'That seems to be your motto, *ma belle*. If you can tell me the secret to getting high without trying, I'll finally be able to make my fortune.'

Bla bla bla. 'Don't go.' I smoothed the duvet. It was so soft and fluffy. The bed smelled of her. My skin was tingling all over. Racha sat on the side.

'Lie down with me,' I said, but she shook her head.

'Kiss me, then.' She leaned down to kiss me on the head, like a little girl. Her lovely hair wound its way round my fingers. I remembered how it used to feel.

'Not like that,' I said. 'A real kiss.' I pulled her towards me.

'Let go of my hair!' Racha rubbed her head. First she

looked angry and then she didn't. She kissed me on the lips, then it was mouths and it wasn't food I wanted any more. I grabbed her hand and pushed it between my legs, under the silk, not on top.

'I can't,' she said. 'Not like this.'

❧

My eyes didn't want to open and my neck was a metal rod. I was in my daughter's bed, wearing a kimono I'd given her, nothing underneath. I looked over my shoulder with a start, half expecting to find someone next to me.

I tipped the glass of water on the nightstand down my throat, swallowing only twice. Very slowly, I attempted to stand up. I was no stranger to a *lendemain de fête*, but there hadn't even been a party. As my brain made a feeble attempt to summon last night, I had the strong feeling that I didn't really want to know.

Looking around the room did nothing to reassure me. The clothes I'd been wearing on my top half were neatly draped over a chair, replaced from the waist down by things of Apolline's. It was the first time anyone had laid clothes out for me. I put on some underwear, then the robe.

Bleach hit my nostrils before I reached the bathroom, along with a draught so cold I could see it – the window was half open. Fragments of memory returned uninvited: of me wriggling like a toddler being undressed. Laughing. Crying. Racha by the shower holding a towel by the edges, hair loose like when we were young, but not as long. Like then, I must have been naked and thought nothing of it.

The kimono slid off my shoulder to reveal a large shiny bruise, which explained the mystery pain. I steadied myself against the washbasin and groaned as it all began to come back. Racha and I had kissed. It was good. I'd wanted more, had practically begged her for it. I doused my face in icy water with my eyes open and repeated out loud, *Nothing happened.* I wouldn't be capable of forgetting.

I had turned up completely out of it. I came on to her and she'd refused me, even though her eyes said yes. My last-night self was a disgrace, and Racha got double credit for doing the decent thing twice over.

I slunk back to get dressed before going into the kitchen, listening for any sign of her presence. The only sound apart from the apology I was rehearsing in my head was the washing machine. At a pause in the cycle, a panel of black-and-cream lace flattened against the glass. I'd outdone myself in the humiliation stakes but at least I'd been wearing nice lingerie. There was a fresh baguette on the small table, butter left out of the fridge. I tore the bread up and crammed it in, tasting blood as the crust pierced the roof of my mouth. The coffee on the hotplate made me feel sick but I craved it anyway. Next to the machine was a small green Post-it that I could have missed. There were no mistakes in her spelling any more.

Don't beat yourself up, I know you. Leaving you in peace to think.

To think about what I'd done.

Chapter 39

The parcel marked 'Fragile' had no return address but with ink and handwriting that reminded me of the antique shop ledger, its origins weren't hard to guess. The package was simply addressed to '*Clémentine*' and contained a box and two envelopes. One of them I recognised; the other, cream vellum lined in dark green tissue paper, exuded the scent of unstruck matches and slight dampness.

Chère Clémentine

Sending the enclosed to your shop seems less intrusive than turning up, after the way we parted. (I'm not sure I understand what happened.) You are the rightful keeper of Auguste's letter to Hortense, given the trouble you had returning it, although I'm glad that was the case. As you saw, I didn't know to miss this letter, but there's no doubt I was happier without it and, despite everything, I like to think that you were happier when it was in your care.

I am enclosing something that will interest you professionally, and which I hope will compensate for the disappointment of your original visit.

Auguste was a better letter writer than me. He probably wasn't a plumbing supplier. And he was right about being a lucky man. I hope he made it home.

Frédéric

P.S. Having sealed and reopened this twice, I blame my father's fountain pen (did you recognise it?) for adding I miss you terribly.

I watched a few words swim, then held my scarf – not the same one, but similar – to blot my tears from above. The words? *You were happy.*

I wished people would stop writing to me.

Inside the suede box, wrapped in layers of tissue paper softened by age, was a perfume flacon, square and simple, the lapidary stopper quite the opposite, with dozens of facets. All that remained of the tiny metal label was the indentation in the glass, but I suspected this was a Baccarat design for La Rose Jacqueminot, the perfume that launched Coty's career when (the story goes) he smashed a bottle on the floor of a Paris department store which had refused to stock it. They soon changed their minds when the fragrance came into bloom, drawing a crowd.

If I was right, it was rare and valuable, but that didn't account for the crystal splinter it lodged in me. By the time Suzanne arrived to cover my afternoon appointments – it was busier now Christmas was approaching – the package was resealed and ready to be returned. I went to tie a ribbon round it out of habit and ended up slashing the length I'd cut from the reel into dozens of tiny pieces. Both letters remained on the counter, the old one in its protective double envelope, Frédéric's to me face down.

'What's all this?' Suzanne asked, touching my arm when I didn't look up. 'It's her again, isn't it?'

I shook my head, lips pressed tight. Hard as it was to face anyone in a moment of such exquisite heartache, it was better than being alone. 'No,' I said, when I could trust myself to speak. 'Racha's not to blame this time.'

'But you never used to be like this before she turned up.'

'Like what?' I wasn't being defensive; I wanted to know what this looked like from the outside.

Suzanne frowned, and she wasn't one to tread carefully. 'I don't know. *Déséquilibrée.*'

Unbalanced. I'd expected a stronger verdict.

'Before Racha came on the scene, I never brought my problems to work. Most of what's been happening lately, I had coming. The scores are being settled.'

It took a moment for this to sink in for both of us.

'You do realise I have no idea what you're talking about?' *Settling scores* wasn't a phrase that belonged to my world. 'If you're about to tell me the shop's a front for something illegal, keep it to yourself. I like this job and I really need the money.' Suzanne scooped the butchered stubs of ribbon into her hand but had to admit defeat with the ones on the floor. 'If this is really nothing to do with Racha, what's going on?' she asked, pointing at the parcel.

'It's a gift. With this I'm only doing the wrong thing if I accept it.'

'But look at you! If it's this hard to part with, why not say thanks and keep it? *C'est quoi, déjà?*'

'It's an antique perfume bottle.'

Suzanne could be gentle. 'What am I missing here? Don't you like it?'

Words failed me as the bottle's fleeting appearance in the weak autumn light came back to me. I couldn't live with it throwing rainbows around. 'It's exquisite, but accepting certain gifts says more than thank you.'

Suzanne closed her eyes in concentration. 'This perfume bottle is the equivalent of a love letter.' She waved her hands around like a medium inventing messages people would strive to make sense of. 'And by refusing it—'

'Is this a film scenario?'

She opened her eyes. 'I suppose it could be. But it's just what I'm seeing. Am I right?'

Somehow we'd never called time on the honesty project. 'Yes and no.'

Suzanne radiated triumph and curiosity.

'No, as in, there was an actual letter enclosed.' (This was complicated enough without bringing poor Auguste and Hortense into it. Now *that* was a love letter.) At least I'd distracted her from me refusing a gift like this.

'Ah, it's starting to make sense. Racha doesn't care that you're married' – uttered with Suzanne's habitual disdain for the institution – 'but she *is* pissed off that you've already got ... someone else. Why is she even surprised? You are a bit out of her league, *franchement*.'

'I've told you this is nothing to do with her, and you're out of line, *franchement*. Does anyone ever tell you to mind your own business? I don't ask you intrusive questions.'

What was it about my personal life that made everyone feel entitled to an opinion?

Suzanne looked abashed, briefly. 'Now and again. But they mostly like someone showing an interest. Would you rather I'd walked in and ignored the fact you're really upset?'

'No,' I said. 'Thank you. I do appreciate it.'

'And you can ask me anything you like.'

We'd come a long way from *If you can't hire me without giving me the third degree.*

I smiled. 'You're like my son with his insistence on talking about things that might be better left unsaid. Your secrets are your business, and I'm sure they're much more exciting than mine.'

'You think?'

It was satisfying that my miscasting had finally come to light. I'd had it with my poor performance in roles to which I wasn't suited.

'You know, it's not passion that stops people living, or love or even desire,' she said. 'It's regret and disappointment.'

I thought of all the books and films and songs that proved her wrong and those that proved her right. And all the lives somewhere in between.

'Enough of your clever talk, Suzanne. I've been around a lot longer than you. That's easy to say when you're free and don't have to answer to anyone.'

'You could try answering to yourself,' she said, quietly. Loud enough for me to hear. '*D'accord*. I'll shut up before you fire me.'

'If you weren't so good at the job, I'd have to consider it. Right, I've got half an hour before my client. Time to deal with this.'

'You forgot to write the address,' she said, when I reappeared wrapped up against the elements.

'No need, I'm delivering it in person. You're right, it is rather delicate.'

'Good, they'll see what a state you're in.'

If I walked slowly, I'd barely have time to hand it over before needing to leave for a genuine reason. Suzanne's questions had unleashed a stream of doubt that ran through my body; in the reflection of other shop windows I looked too small and ordinary to house such violent emotions. The fantasy of setting the parcel down carefully and taking a run at a wall was less extreme than it might have been, given that I had recently tried to break down a door. Why did things that other people engaged in so freely feel forbidden to me? Before I turned the final corner, I paused to decide what I would say to Frédéric but set off almost immediately. There was no preparing for this.

And there would be no words. Lagarde et Fils was locked and in darkness. The shop window was empty except for the framed seascape on an easel, lit by a street lamp. A place I could only imagine.

Chapter 40

This time Zéphyre the cat followed me all the way to Martha's door. I hoped she was ready to head out for the walk we had planned. The two calls between us the night of the canal were fifteen minutes apart, each lasting less than three minutes. I hardly remembered speaking to her at all.

Martha greeted me as always, with hugs and smiles, calling me *Darling Clementine* in a completely different American accent to her own. But as with Suzanne, there was a wariness about her, a sense that she no longer knew who she was dealing with.

'How's your mom?' Presumably I hadn't asked that night, which was not good at all.

'Oh, no worse than the previous three times I've been called to her deathbed. She does like to give us the runaround, remind us she's in charge until the final whistle blows. Given half a chance, my sister-in-law would move into the house before the wake's over.'

'It is a lovely house.' I went out there with Bastien and Apolline a couple of times when they were small. Martha and her Manhattanite friends used to joke about forming a women and kids' commune to escape from men and the pressures of the city. I wished they were serious (apart from the tedious quips about turning lesbian) and had wondered out loud if I could get a green card.

'Long Island was looking gorgeous. We had a couple of perfect fall days: bright colours, glittering ocean. Made such a change from grey and misty Paris. I started to think about moving back, you know. What's keeping me here? My work's dried up, my daughters are over there and loving it. I came to France for a year and stayed for thirty. Maybe it's run its course.' Martha smiled a little sadly. It was never her way to dwell on the hard parts. We'd both given our best years to Paris, for better and for worse, just not in the proportions anyone hopes for.

'If you leave, I will too.'

'Come on, don't get all mushy on me. Let's go get some fresh air.'

We set off in silence through the outermost streets of the 15th *arrondissement* towards the Parc André-Citroën, Martha lacing her arm through mine. The deserted park offered nothing to lift my spirits (I hadn't given up looking), bare trees accentuating the brutal concrete design. Inside my leather gloves, my fingertips throbbed with cold.

'Do you want to tell me what's been going on with you?'

I made a face. 'It's a disaster.'

'What is?'

'Everything.'

'That's not possible. I've only been gone two weeks. Start with the other night.'

I had to start with the evening Bastien came to dinner.

'Okay,' she said, when I'd finished. 'You weren't exaggerating.'

'I can't believe I've made the situation worse. So now

Bastien thinks his father would be fine with him being gay if he was preppy and ambitious, which of course—'

'—is total bullshit.'

She frowned at my hesitation.

'I don't know what to think any more. Édouard's said a few things lately . . . ' At that Martha rolled her eyes openly. 'Bastien had good reason to be upset. That's why I've been so worried that I can't get hold of him.'

'But I'm guessing you didn't get high with Bastien, because firstly, how weird would that be and secondly, you wouldn't have been hanging around the *dixième* on your own after dark.' (Less weird than discussing his father's taste in nightlife, I'd have said). 'If I have this right, you downed a couple of double whiskies on an empty stomach before getting off your face with a bunch of homeless guys in a place nobody would hear you scream. Do you have any idea how badly that could have ended? I'm surprised you still had your phone to call me.'

'God, Martha, don't be cruel. Do you think anyone chooses to live like that? They were sweet – they even showed me pictures of their families.'

'It's lucky you had Apolline's place to go to, because I doubt Édouard would have seen it that way.'

'Fuck him!' I did not keep my voice down. 'He's in no position to judge me.'

Martha did an air punch. 'At last you're seeing the light! I apologise for how bad this sounds, but that makes me happy.'

One *psy* thought she was on to something with her incessant allusions to *the secrets we keep from ourselves*. I knew them. I just didn't want to keep them any more.

'It's not all about Édouard. Someone I was involved with before I came to Paris has shown up recently and seeing her has sent everything flying.' It was a reflex to portray Racha as the villain, but I still didn't know what I could accuse her of.

'Involved with, how?' Martha asked.

'We were lovers,' I said, but it wasn't enough. 'She was everything to me. I've never had to describe it.' After all this time, Ludo was still an omittable extra. Fuck him too. 'Say something, please, Martha.' Surely this deserved more of a reaction from the woman always chastising me for my failure to indulge my desires. 'You don't seem very surprised.'

It rattled me that Martha wasn't making a joke of it. 'Some parts more than others. A lover you've never mentioned turning up after twenty-five years, sure, that's a surprise, but you've never told me much about when you were young. That it's a woman, less so. I've crossed the line many times on the subject of you and Édouard, but some things were for you to raise if you wanted to. And I got the distinct impression you didn't.'

'I am now.'

'I did suspect there was something going on between you and my cousin Andrea that time.'

'Nothing happened between me and Andrea!'

Martha laughed. 'You need to redefine "nothing". It was unbearable to be in a room with the two of you.'

My workshop had seen a number of intense encounters, including the afternoon Andrea came to collect the bespoke perfume I knew she couldn't pay for. When she suggested buying me a drink to say thank you, I knew she had more than that in mind. That was the year I opened the shop, by which point Édouard had been cheating on me for around eight years, it turned out. After Andrea left, I swiped every last bottle off the shelves in my workshop, so hard I almost dislocated my elbow. Only one broke: the most precious, a sublime absolute of Rosa Damascena. When I discovered she'd left her perfume on the shop counter, I poured it down the sink.

'Why didn't you say something when I went through that phase experimenting after Jean-François? It makes me cringe to think of all the crap I made you listen to.'

That had been difficult, Martha taking up women like another new hobby, which is how long it lasted. 'It wasn't the same thing, Martha. You were trying to explain things I can't explain to myself.'

And the thought of all those questions . . .

We marched along without speaking for a while. 'Not to make this any more about me,' she said, as if the conversation had never stalled, 'but I'm sad you didn't feel you could talk to me.'

I came to a stop, my bottom lip trembling. After a few steps, she looked back.

'You'd have put even more pressure on me to leave Édouard.'

She made a wry clicking sound. 'I admit I might have tried. You know, I had the strangest feeling things were about to come to a head between the two of you when you called me under the influence.'

'Even though you told me to go to Apolline's?'

Martha looked weary. 'It was an intuition. Does he know? Sounds like you've both been airing out the closets.'

I had the intense urge to slap her. 'You really don't get it! Édouard's cracking up, we all are. Even Apolline – she's coming home early from Australia, on her own. This is not the time to add my personal shit.'

'You should hear yourself – it's frightening. I'd never claim to understand you lot, but one thing I do get, finally. You will never leave Édouard. There'll always be some reason, some excuse to put it off. That's how life goes by. And from the way you talk about this woman, you ought to know that.'

We'd reached the north end of the park, near the river.

It wasn't the prettiest view but I longed for my bridges, my solitude. I wanted my anger to be because Martha was wrong, not because I was weak. But before I could announce my plan to walk home along the *quais,* I had to thank her for helping me that night, for caring enough to be this blunt with me, because lately it wasn't fun to be a friend of mine.

My mobile rang. 'It's Bastien.'

'You met my friends, Maman!' I wondered what was coming, but the events by the canal simply weren't that remarkable to them. 'Shame I didn't see you. So, could I come by and fetch Apolline's keys? I've had some issues with the neighbours and things need to cool down for a few days.'

'Can I call you back in two minutes? I'm just saying good-bye to Martha.'

She made an airy *it's fine* gesture but I needed to talk to him without an audience.

Bastien dropped the nonchalant act. 'Don't hang up on me, Maman. I can't go back. You're the one who wants to know I'm safe. There's no way Apolline would refuse in an emergency. I'm her little brother!'

'I'm sorry, it's not an option. A friend of mine is staying there. With their permission.' My eyes were darting around trying to avoid Martha's. 'If it's that bad, you'll just have to come home.'

It was Bastien who hung up on me.

'Go,' said Martha. 'No explanation required.'

Chapter 41

Lovely flowers but I'd have preferred the cash.

I read the text with a shiver of malaise. There was little choice of fresh flowers in November and although I'd made a point of not picking anything large or showy, a person could eat for a week on what they'd cost. Racha had never made any allusion to money changing hands between us.

The card I'd written to accompany the bouquet said, *'Thank you for taking care of me.'* I regretted being too embarrassed to write *'I'm sorry'* in front of the florist, who knows me.

Can I come by this evening?

Yes, thanks for giving me notice, she replied.

I refused to spend the next four hours speculating about her tone of voice. This time, through no fault of my own, I had a tricky message to impart – another task that could only decently be carried out face to face. I'd switched to a bigger handbag and was carrying the Baccarat perfume bottle everywhere. Its presence was bizarrely reassuring.

Halfway up the stairs to Apolline's apartment, I felt a sharp pain in my chest at the thought that Racha might be about to disappear from my life again. I couldn't see how she belonged and yet I couldn't imagine it without her. The talk of money might be a test, but I knew I couldn't buy my way out of this.

It only made the mission worse that I'd started to think of this as Racha's place. I stared sadly at Apolline and Mathieu's names under the bell, thinking of the call when Apolline told me they were breaking up. I was sure it was something I'd said that made her tell him about the pregnancy scare, along with the details I'd been too dense to pick up on. It turned out that he'd cheated on her too under this very roof while she was in Sydney.

You can be forgiven for mistakes when you're young, or so the theory goes.

I used to find Racha's good moods contagious, but the smile flickering on her face annoyed me now. What did she have to be so happy about? To my relief, she didn't offer anything stronger than mint tea. She always took the chair now, leaving me the sofa.

'You just missed your son,' she said, snatching my attention from the sugar crystals at the bottom of my glass. So that was why Bastien didn't answer all those times I tried to call him back. 'He came by without any warning.'

'I had no idea.'

She laughed. 'I can see that! He decided to check out your story about me staying here. You should have seen the look on his face when I opened the door.' He would have loved to see mine now. 'Relax, it's fine. We had a nice talk. He's lovely, Bastien, so outgoing and intelligent. I don't know why you haven't told me more about him, especially considering . . . '

She made me wild with hostility. 'If you mean because he's gay, well, now you know. There's far more to Bastien than that. I didn't mention it because I knew you'd make something of it.'

It was the second time in one day that I'd said something

like this to a friend. What was it Édouard had said about me not letting anyone get close to me? But Racha was not Martha, and we used to be as close as it gets.

'I don't know why you're getting so worked up. Bastien seems very comfortable with himself and it's clear how much he loves his maman. I've seen how talented he is. He did a drawing of me. Wait, I'll go and get it.' She must already have put it in a safe place.

'My God,' I said, taking it from her. 'It's as if he's known you his entire life.'

'Or mine,' she said. 'It shows my age but flatters me all the same.'

I looked at her and at the sheet torn from the small sketchpad Bastien carries everywhere. He'd captured her in a few dozen strokes: her defiance, her austere beauty and her fragility, the only part I didn't remember from the first time we met.

'Flattery is not his style, *je t'assure*. Quite the opposite. He only lasted an afternoon in Montmartre.' I was smiling in the last sketch Bastien made of me, months ago.

'You're not happy that he came here. Is it really so bad for me to meet your family?'

A screech of frustration escaped me. 'Things are complicated enough! This is a very stressful time for all four of us. By the sound of it Bastien's on the verge of getting kicked out of his studio; Apolline and Mathieu have split up; Édouard has huge problems at work – the whole country knows, so I can't imagine you don't—'

'And you've had me showing up and being a nuisance. You can say it.'

My face settled into a downward line. My jaw ached, my head too – it was tempting to pay another visit to my new friends by the canal. So what if it was dangerous and irresponsible? It was bliss to have a break from all this. 'You're not the only problem I have, Racha. Far from it.'

'Okay. I get it.'

'Sorry,' I said. 'Everything's coming out wrong, but you asked for that.'

'I thought you'd changed, but under the surface you're as scared as when we first met. I thought I was watching you become the real you.'

'If so, it didn't last,' I said. 'Did you say anything to Bastien? About us?'

'Of course not. Although if you ask me, he'd be fine with it.'

'You have no idea. You spent five minutes with my son.'

'Actually, he stayed for over an hour and we talked about all sorts of things. He's very open-minded and thoughtful. You must be so proud of him.' Racha must be thinking of Tariq but there was no trace of bitterness. She'd listened to my son when he needed someone. I had not.

'I *am* proud of him. It's just that recently we've all got too mixed up in each other's business. He knows too much about me and his father without adding to that.'

Racha's head straightened. 'Things with Édouard are worse than you've let on, aren't they?'

'Right now everything is worse.'

'To think that anyone envies you. With all you have, you still manage to be unhappy.'

'For pity's sake, Racha, I don't know anyone who envies me!' There was a tight feeling in my throat, but I couldn't keep the words in. 'Édouard and I haven't slept together in five years. He uses escorts, and apparently our son has known for longer than I have.' Racha's eyes opened wide. 'So no, I don't think it would help for Bastien to know you and I were involved. It's ancient history and best if it stays that way. If it hadn't ended as it did, we'd have forgotten each other long ago. It was a phase, Racha, a summer fling. It was nothing.'

Her head turned with the impact and there was the kind of silence that follows.

If we weren't in my daughter's flat, she'd probably have asked me to leave. But Racha would never have the power in any situation, whether she was right or wrong – my mother used to say the same about the two of us when I was growing up. I sickened myself and Racha knew it. She despised me for thinking you could change camp, though whether for succeeding or failing, I couldn't say. My hands were shaking and hers were tightly clasped, a picture of dignity.

'Now I know what you were thanking me for,' she said. 'That nothing happened between us the other night to contradict the story you're trying to tell yourself. Because it could have, if I'd let it. You were all over me. You tried to make me touch you.'

It wasn't in my interests to reveal that I could remember events in the bedroom much more clearly than the rest. 'I'm absolutely mortified and so sorry. I keep thinking I've hit the low point but that really was.'

'Ha! First time in years anyone's made a move on me and then you go and spoil it,' Racha said.

'You did the right thing, protecting me from doing anything rash. I've only ever known you to be good to me. I know you can't say the same.'

'So where did it come from? You insist that's all in the past, but there's no doubt in my mind that you wanted it.'

I couldn't think straight with her scrutinising me like this. 'I can't explain. You know people lose their inhibitions and do things they wouldn't when sober. I've just spent the afternoon with Martha. I called her before coming here that night. She was worried sick.'

'And you look it.'

'I put you in a very difficult position.'

'It was, for all kinds of reasons.' The moment in the shop. Her damp hair, smelling of synthetic strawberry shampoo.

We could never go back.

'You can't possibly have come here with hopes of rekindling our relationship,' I said. That would be totally unrealistic.'

'I didn't, but I'm not the one lying to myself. I feel sorry for you, Clémentine. You don't know what you want and if you did, you wouldn't go after it. You seem to have real trouble living with yourself. The thing with me and Ludo was not a one-off.'

'I'm telling you, it was.'

'Okay, the fact there was a guy involved. But when you tell me you've never been attracted to women since, I don't buy it. Not after the other night.'

I'd lost the right to say it didn't concern her.

'I never said that. I said there hadn't been any.' We stared at each other. 'Racha, it doesn't follow that if I started something with a woman again, it would be with you. Nothing about this is logical.'

Racha wore the look of someone proven right after considerable perseverance. 'For a start, anyone can see that Suzanne is more than an employee to you.'

I laughed at that. 'Suzanne pushes everyone's buttons, one way or the other. But you're right. She's become a good friend. We have something in common and she's been the only person I can talk to about you. It is possible to find someone attractive and not want to sleep with them.'

'Édouard doesn't know about any of this?'

'No, and I doubt he'd particularly care at this point.'

'Are you going to separate?'

Martha's words struck up in my head, as they had all the

way back along the river. Seven bridges: Mirabeau, Grenelle, Bir-Hakeim, Iéna, Alma, Invalides, Alexandre III – I was sick of them by then. I chose my words carefully. 'The last thing any of us needs now is more upheaval, including you. My priority has to be my family. Crazy as it seems, they're all turning to me in a crisis.'

'Even your bullying, cheating, bigoted husband? I had one of those and I sent him packing. Admittedly he was less of a catch.'

I stood up. 'You've gone too far. My husband is flawed and difficult, but, as you see, so am I. It's amazing that our marriage has lasted this long. Édouard paying high-class hookers is a more honest deal than he's ever had with me. Want to know something Suzanne and I often talk about?'

Racha nodded uncertainly.

'How rarely anyone tells the truth. We were doing a twenty-four-hour truth experiment the day you left your number demanding to see me. That's the only reason I didn't pretend to be busy. You and I should do the same now.'

Racha sighed at the prospect of my stupid game, just as I had when Suzanne laid down the challenge. 'Fine – makes no difference to me. What makes you think I lie to you?'

'Doing this makes you realise there's more to being honest than not lying. You've been here for weeks, asking favours, making threatening noises, raking up the past and insulting the life I lead now. If that was all, I would know where I stand. But you've also been kind: the other night, the time I burned myself, looking after this flat so well. And today you took the time to talk to my son – it was probably what he needed, someone who's not involved.'

'Where are you going with this?'

'When I asked, you said how you found me. I know you needed to get away, but you didn't need to come here for that. Apolline will be back in a few days. If you're ever going to come out with what you want from me, that's how long you've got.'

Chapter 42

Madame Chabas rapped on her window when she saw me crossing the courtyard, drenched. My umbrella had sprung a leak, although, on the upside, she wouldn't notice my nose was running. 'He says sorry for staring, *le barbu*. You know, the Italian from opposite. He asked Madame Daubrades to ask me to tell you.'

'Oh, you mean Luciano? That's all forgotten – we bumped into each other yesterday in the pharmacy and he introduced himself. Delightful man. Says we gave him the idea for a screenplay! I've asked him and his daughter over for an *apéro* on the balcony.' Madame Chabas opened her mouth but no sound came out. 'It's not the ideal time of year but we'll be glad of the company,' I added. '*Now it's just me and monsieur.*'

Some things are worth getting wet for.

When the lift doors opened, voices from inside the apartment made me check I hadn't got the wrong floor.

My son and his father were talking at a normal volume. Édouard laughed. I let myself in quietly, torn between wanting to see it and fear of breaking the spell. After putting my umbrella in the shower, there was nothing else for it. I had never felt such trepidation about walking into my own kitchen.

They were sitting at the table drinking beer. Édouard raised his eyebrows in a *can you believe it?* manner. Bastien was wearing the top that had caused so much trouble the night he and Rocco came over. I greeted him as normal and because I couldn't not, I kissed Édouard on both cheeks. My arrival had indeed brought the conversation to a halt. 'I should go and dry my hair,' I said, separating the ends, which were cold against my neck.

'Wait a second, there's something you should know,' Édouard said, checking in with Bastien.

'Sit down, Maman.'

'You're worrying me.'

'I've apologised to Bastien for my behaviour when he came to dinner. Among other things.'

It made no sense to cover my mouth when I was smiling yet make no effort to hide my tears. Bastien took my other hand. 'And I'm sorry for being a little shit and ruining the evening.'

Édouard was nodding. 'Everything about it was awful for you, Clémentine, and neither of us was thinking about that. I hope you can forgive us.'

I had never found myself in the middle of *this*. 'Of course I forgive you. It wasn't our finest hour but, well' – I looked around the table – 'here we are.'

'Speaking of the hour, I need to get going,' Édouard said. 'I came home to fetch my squash kit. I'm sure Jacques is only doing this to make me feel better.'

'Jacques asked to play you at squash? Why would he do that?'

'He probably thinks I need a legal excuse to hit something. But he won't need much persuasion to go for a drink instead.'

'What about the conference in Brussels? I thought you were getting the train this evening.'

'Corentin went instead. He's welcome to it.'

After all the day's walking and talking I asked Bastien to order a pizza and went to lie on the sofa. When he joined me in the living room, he was wearing a plain black T-shirt. 'I've really gone off that top,' he said. 'I only put it on to make Papa happy.'

We both laughed. 'What a day of surprises,' I said.

'You did say to come home.'

'Yes, I'm glad you did. I'm glad you met Racha too, even if it was because you didn't believe me.'

'Ah, you know about that. I thought you were lying to me for Apolline's sake. She's great, your friend Racha.'

'She was touched by your lovely portrait. Paris has been a bit of a shock, I think.'

'But she says you've been good to her.'

'Really? I could have done a lot more – I'm just not sure what. Did she tell you about her son?'

'Yes, I felt bad for them. But you can't change the world for Racha, just like you can't change it for me. When you can't take walking down the street in peace for granted, everything counts – right down to whether someone's willing to look you in the eye. Most of your stuck-up friends couldn't give a shit about anyone who's not like them. But you're different.'

'Well, I was wrong to make judgements about your friends from the canal. How are they doing?'

Bastien gave me an uneasy look. 'Not good. Did my land-lord call you?'

'No. Are these things connected?'

He cleared his throat. '*Bon*, I admit it wasn't the best idea for them all to come at the same time. Five of them took a shower in a row, it backed up and caused a big flood in the flat below. And I suppose we *were* making a lot of noise – the dog's not used to being indoors and he wouldn't stop barking. That was my fault – they were going to leave him chained up on the balcony.'

'Something tells me we won't be seeing the security deposit again.'

'Sorry. But I'll pay you back. I'm waiting tables a couple of evenings a week at a Brazilian place by the Porte Saint-Martin. I'm going to look for somewhere else to live.'

'Not by yourself this time, I hope?'

'No. You were right, it was depressing. They're gone, the Kazakhs. The owners of the building got them moved on. Still, I kicked my skunk habit thanks to them. That stuff of theirs was mental – I couldn't cope with it. You know what Léon said? *We didn't hear any complaints from your mother!*'

'Honestly, what a joker!' Bastien's smile faded quickly. I remembered these fleeting expressions from his childhood, laughing one moment, sad the next. 'I know you'll miss them, but this is a good day for us. To come home and find you talking to Papa ... I can't get over it. I really had given up hope after the dinner.'

'I said terrible things about our family that night. You'll pretend you've forgotten, but I haven't.'

'It's okay. Tough things needed to be said. I'm not sure you were wrong about any of it.'

'But you're *not* like Papa. *Papa's* not like Papa. He seems really different suddenly.'

'It's not sudden.' The more Édouard changed, the more I recognised him.

'He even apologised about the dog earlier.'

'Which dog are we talking about now?'

'The one he refused to let me have when I was a kid. And now I understand.' I looked at him blankly. 'Papa said that when he was little, he got very attached to the sheepdogs on the farm. He used to get upset whenever one of them died, and his brothers mocked him for it. So, when he was twelve, Granddad made him watch them shoot a hunting dog who'd been attacked by a wolf, to *make a man of him*. He still thinks about it when he has to do something he dreads.' Bastien's eyes were about to dissolve and I was heading the same way.

'He never told me. Poor Édouard, that's appalling.'

Bastien's phone beeped and he broke out in one of his radiant smiles on reading the message.

'I'm guessing that wasn't an update on the pizza?'

'*Merde*, I forgot to order it, sorry. I'll be back later – if you're sure it's okay to stay for a while.'

'Of course it's okay. And Bastien . . . ' He looked back at me from the hall. 'You've grown up a lot these last few months.'

'Thanks, Maman. So have you.'

Chapter 43

The shop looked so pretty, with a dusting of glitter on the suspended bottles in the window. I'd told Suzanne not to go overboard on the Christmas theme because of my doubts about perfume as a gift – people won't wear it unless they love it. After giving me a lecture on my lack of business sense, Suzanne had hit on the idea of selling testers of all ten fragrances in a gift box with a voucher valid for a full-size bottle online or in the shop. As usual I was sceptical and she was right. I'd had to order more after she managed to get it featured in *Stylist*.

The last time I'd woken up feeling this bright it was July and thirty degrees.

Suzanne had been to the hairdresser and the new colours in her fringe reminded me of a peacock's tail. She didn't seem to hear my compliment and when she looked up, her smudged make-up and sad eyes pinched my heart. 'Oh no! Has Martha been in again?'

'*No*,' she said, although I got the shadow of a smile with my rebuke. 'Some sleazeball touched me up on the Métro and *j'ai flippé*.'

'Ugh. Weren't you wearing a coat?'

She snarled. 'This is exactly the problem, *putain*! I can wear what I like. But according to this guy, I'm inviting men to grope my tits, dressing like this.'

'What a jerk. Suzanne, you do know I wasn't suggesting—'

'I know. It was rammed and boiling hot. I'd undone my coat, since you ask.'

'Anyway, you said you flipped?' She normally enjoyed flipping.

'I said, *And you're inviting this*, shoved my bag into his balls and got off at the next station.' She gave a loud sigh. 'I was on a downer even before this.'

'Oh?'

'They're not including me in *Creative Parisians* after all. It's not Guillaume's fault – it's an editorial decision.'

'On what grounds? Clearly they've got nothing against our products.'

'Not yours. Mine are too strong for a mainstream audience, apparently. Especially my new film. Uncomfortably realistic, more like.'

Suzanne had never shown me her work. 'What on earth is it about?'

'It's about a year in my life. After the gallery. The one you wouldn't find on my CV, if I had one. This is a fucked-up society, you know? Porno made by men is everywhere, violence against women is entertainment, but real women's lives? The things we have to put up with? We can't have that, *putain de merde*. Sorry, Clémentine. I've been making films for ten years and I'm sick of waiting for my big break. Maybe I'm just a loser.' She paused. 'A really hot loser.'

'I'm sorry, Suzanne. That's so disappointing. I have an idea though . . . ' I broke off on seeing Dolores about to cross the street. 'Why don't you go out for a break?' You had to be in the mood for Dolores. I didn't have hours to spare and this way I'd have to stay out in the shop.

'Is she okay?' Dolores said, as Suzanne left.

'She will be. Are you ready?' I said, bringing her perfume out. Dolores looked overcome and I tried to dispel my fear that she'd hate it and we'd have to start all over again. 'Clients normally name their own, but I've taken the liberty of calling it Numéro D. This has been a very special one to make.'

The one that nearly broke me.

'*Dios mio!*' Dolores was baring her wrist and neck as if for some kind of initiation ceremony. 'Does this mean it'll be on sale in the shop?'

'Absolutely not! It means you're the only person ever to have your own Arôme de Clémentine Alphanumérique fragrance. No one will know it exists – how's that for bespoke?'

My heart was thumping as she opened the box and stroked the label. I tried to stop twisting my hands as she uncapped it.

'Remember, the final version will smell slightly different.'

I pushed her hand back gently as she went to spray it too close to the skin. 'Let it fly before it lands.' We both went quiet as our other senses faded out – that's why people usually close their eyes to take in a lovely smell. What happens next, happens inside.

'It's even more gorgeous than I expected,' Dolores said. 'Those citrus notes are making my mouth water, and there's something green.'

'That's blackcurrant leaf.'

'And then ... ' – she sniffed at her wrist but it was there in the air surrounding us – 'it opens up like a huge bouquet –I'm getting the Bulgarian rose, and the orange blossom, of course, but it's not only flowers, is it? There's something warm about it – soft, almost. It's making me feel happy.'

She wasn't the only one. 'Cashmere,' I told her, smiling

to myself. Dolores felt the cold. 'And vanilla – that's what reminded you of your grandmother's baking. Just a hint, though. I chose one that's not too sweet. You don't want to smell like a *pâtisserie*.'

'Oh God,' she said. 'Do you remember the first time we met? I was so sour.'

'Would you believe me if I said no?'

'I didn't make this easy for you. It's extraordinary how you came up with this. Oh, it's doing something else now ...'

'The base notes will start to creep in behind the florals and make it last longer – in *eau de parfum* concentration that should be hours. The sandalwood has great synergy with the damask rose and there's a dash of pink pepper in there to keep it lively. This is your creation, Dolores, everything about it is inspired by you. We didn't go the usual route, but we got there in the end. It made me rethink the way I make perfume.'

I broke off to serve a few customers and Suzanne returned, make-up and composure restored. 'Wow, Dolores!' she said. 'You smell like a goddess!' Dolores was squealing as Suzanne nuzzled up to her neck. 'You've got to let us sell that.' Suzanne looked at me. 'Quite a change in style, Clémentine. Much more sensual and complex.'

'You can't have this one, but we'll definitely be adding a few more letters next year.'

Dolores purchased the fragrance Consuela liked and took a chance for her younger daughter. 'Bring it back if she doesn't like it; we can always use it as a tester.'

'I'm not going to be back any time soon,' Dolores said. 'I'm going to Washington for Christmas with my grandchildren and then for my sixtieth birthday I'm going to stay with my sister who lives in Brazil for at least a month. I said to myself: *Why do winter when you could have summer?*'

I might take that as my new motto.

'What about Javier?'

'I have no idea what his plans are.'

'We'll miss you,' said Suzanne.

Dolores hugged us both at the same time. 'I was determined not to make any friends here, but I seem to have failed. Turns out I do like Paris after all.'

Chapter 44

Édouard walked into the bedroom as I was fetching a dress from the wardrobe. Even though I was fully clothed, I hid behind it on its hanger.

I said, 'I'm just going.'

He said, 'I'll come back.'

Neither of us went anywhere.

'Pretty dress,' he said. 'I've always liked that on you.'

'Édouard, you don't need to do that.' I surveyed it at arm's length. 'And neither do I.' The dress was already back on the rail and I reached for a different one.

'What did I say?'

'It's fine. You reminded me the bra I have to wear with that digs into me. Even if I don't eat, I get stomach ache from holding my belly in. And all so I can spend the evening terrified I'm about to commit some social crime.'

His brow furrowed. 'Hearing that makes me wonder why we're going to the Kerglavens' party.'

'I have no idea why they invited us when he's been blanking you for months, even less why you'd want to go. But you put the invitation on the mantelpiece, so I assumed you thought you should.'

To tough it out. Showing his face so people couldn't talk behind his back.

'And I didn't think you'd want to miss it after Delphine's piece has done such amazing things for the business. Aren't you curious to see their new apartment? Jacques and Gabrielle have been – it's an old artist's studio, top of the building – huge windows . . . '

' . . . high ceilings?' We both smiled. 'Good things have come of Delphine's piece, it's true, but it was work for both of us, nothing more. *Suzanne* has been amazing for the business. So if it comes down to whether I want to see their apartment—'

'Let's give it a miss.'

'I should warn Bastien that he's not going to have the place to himself. It's too soon to inflict us on Rocco again.'

'Wait,' said Édouard. 'Put the dress on – whichever one you like. Let's go out anyway. Talk to each other.'

I took a breath in. There was a different note in his voice. It would have felt less exposing to strip off in front of him, not that he was expecting me to. 'Édouard, I'm very relieved that things are improving, but—'

'I don't mean a candlelit dinner. Won't you come for a walk with me, a drink?'

As he pulled a jumper over his open-necked shirt, I caught a waft of the cologne hanging in this room the day he'd left for New York. The day he left me the letter. It was the special edition Terre d'Hermès with vetiver. One tiny thing I'd almost got right, among the many I'd got wrong. Édouard was waiting for an answer. Inside I was collapsing with sadness at the realisation that I quite liked him. He could make someone a good husband with those looks, with that bruised but hopeful look in his eye.

'Sure, I'll come for a walk.'

I put on some biker boots I'd never worn with a dress. More eye make-up than normal. It wasn't an everyday event or a special occasion, in the usual sense. The hairdresser had done my *brushing* far too straight and severe, so I swung my head down, messed it up and sprayed it in – or rather, out – of place. Instead of searching for imperfections in the mirror, for the first time I saw a woman at home in her own skin.

'Nice look, Maman,' Bastien said, wishing us a good evening in his haste to get rid of us.

'*Tu es magnifique*,' Édouard said, in a low voice. ' Don't let anyone tell you otherwise.'

'They wouldn't dare,' I said, catching his eye.

'Which way?' he asked, at the door to the street.

'Towards the river.' We crossed rue de Vaugirard heading for Odéon before either of us spoke again. I realised too late that the route Édouard was taking would lead us up the rue de Seine past the Beaux-Arts, but I did nothing to stop it.

'It makes me nervous, having Bastien back at home,' he said, 'wondering if things are about to flare up. Maybe he feels the same.'

'I'm sure he does. We shouldn't expect too much. If he stays more than a few days, something's bound to crop up. The important thing to remember is you're not where you were before.'

It's hard, when you've spent a long time in one place, to remember that's not where you live any more.

'You could have given me some tips over the years,' he said. 'If I'd shown any interest.'

'You're giving me too much credit.'

I did my best to fix my gaze ahead as we approached the antique shop but my reluctance to stop had the opposite effect on Édouard.

'Look at this!' he said, skirting the little square to stand at the window of Lagarde et Fils. 'What incredible colours – it's like they're lit from inside. Makes you feel you're there.'

'So you're into art now?'

'Do you like it?'

'Hmm,' I said, blinking my eyes out of focus. 'I wouldn't want it on the wall.'

I didn't need the painting any more. I know that place exists.

When we reached the Seine, Édouard went to turn left along the Rive Gauche as I headed for the Pont des Arts. We came to a stop. 'Carry on the way you were going and I'll meet you over there,' he said, pointing across to the north end of the Pont du Carrousel. 'There's something I need to say and I want to get it straight in my head.'

As we each walked our own two sides of the rectangle, I wasn't just thinking about what Édouard had to say to me. I was thinking about what remained for me to say to other people.

We went down to the waterside. The lights on the bridge I'd just crossed threw flares on the river. Two young Asian couples were taking pictures of each other in wedding outfits with a tripod, then had the idea of swapping spouses in fits of giggles.

Édouard glanced at me, then straight ahead as we walked. 'I've spent my adult life ticking boxes: degrees, jobs, marriage, children, one promotion after another. And now everything's shifted, I've lost my bearings. I feel very unsure about the future. I don't know what you want either, but I do know it's not me.' His voice cracked and I felt the hot splash of tears down my face. 'You've been trying to tell me for months that we can't stay together,' he said, 'and before that, all those years of silence would have told me something, if I'd been listening.'

313

I took my glove off and reached for his cold hand, before sliding it back into his pocket.

'Everything you said that time was true,' I said. 'I did have second thoughts very early on. I should have been honest with you. I was never cut out for this.'

I would have had to raise Apolline alone. Bastien would never have existed.

'What are we going to tell the children?'

'Nothing they haven't guessed, Édouard. They may be sad but they won't be surprised, not even Apolline.'

'I thought I'd fetch her from the airport Friday afternoon. We'll need to give her time to get over the journey first.'

'Definitely. But won't you be at work?'

'There's a board meeting at ten, at which I'm going to resign. I'll be free by lunchtime. They've been itching to replace me with someone younger for a long time. Why cling on when I don't want to be there? I'm fifty-one – if I go now, there's time to do something worthwhile, something I enjoy. Or I hope so – none of us know how long we've got. Is that funny?' he said. 'It wasn't supposed to be.'

'No, I just like it that you've made a depressing thought sound optimistic – inspiring, even. You're right. Life is short.'

You can never hear *that* too often.

We had crossed the Pont de la Concorde and started back down the boulevard Saint-Germain. 'I have no intention of behaving the way Jean-François treated Martha,' he said. 'So don't worry about that.'

'I might have in the past, but not now.' I shook my head with a little smile.

'What?'

'I was just thinking how strange this is. It's nothing like you'd expect ending a long marriage to feel.'

He hesitated. 'No,' he said. 'We never did get the hang of it.'

'I didn't make up for all the books you never read,' I said, not sure if he'd remember.

'That's not your fault,' he answered immediately. 'I should have read more books.'

Chapter 45

The picture was gone and the shop was half empty, the door locked. I tried to recall my much-tested rationale for deciding when to give up and when to keep trying. Unfinished business had taken enough of a toll on me. It was worth one more attempt.

The doorbell sounded louder than before, jangly and intrusive. I left, then doubled back, the words Frédéric had written reverberating in my head. I couldn't leave it like that. I ran back to the door next to the shop and pounded it with my fists, pressing the bells to all of the flats above. Maybe the neighbours would know where to find him.

A window opened on the first floor and when Frédéric himself leaned out, I felt myself sway. His hair was wet, his expression hard to read, although surprise was in there somewhere.

'I hope he's worth it,' said a woman out with her dog. If she hadn't been watching, I'd have abandoned the parcel and run to the corner.

He reappeared to let me in and I walked up the stairs in

the wake of his scent. The way his T-shirt was blotted against his back where he hadn't dried it properly made my own skin prickle.

I should have run, *putain*.

'I thought I heard the bell downstairs when I was in the shower,' he said over his shoulder. 'Come in.'

I looked around what had clearly been an old man's place. 'It never occurred to me that you lived above the shop,' I said, weighing this knowledge for significance. The living room was sombre and sparsely furnished but with a pretty view of the square which, along with everything else, looked different from this angle.

Frédéric had bare feet. He patted his jaw on both sides and retrieved a towel tossed over the back of an armchair. There was something intimate but illusory about it all, like the aftermath of something that had never happened. 'Take a seat,' he said. 'I just need to finish shaving.'

I wanted to say, *Don't*. He came back fully dressed, down to socks and shoes. A till receipt marked his place three-quarters of the way through last year's Goncourt winner, which I had read. He saw me notice the book, and his eyes said, *Don't*. Frédéric and I didn't have the conversations you can have with other people. It was tempting to dispense with words altogether.

'I wasn't sure I'd see you again,' he said.

'Likewise. It looked like you'd gone away.'

'I went to Lyon to visit friends and they persuaded me to stay on for a while. I think they were concerned about me, after everything.'

'And now you're packing up the shop.'

'That's right. I took your advice and a dealer made a very fair offer for the lot. Had to face it – I'm no *antiquaire*.'

'I've been past a few times. It was good to see the painting again but . . .' I couldn't believe I'd evoked the moment I realised he wanted me.

'A Canadian woman bought it the other day on first sight. To be honest, I put it in the window so I wouldn't have to look at it.'

I nodded.

'Clémentine, I'm sorry about the last time you were here – in the shop, I mean. Clearly I misread things.'

'You were having an intense day,' I said. 'Emotions running high, and not just yours—'

'The only part I regret is upsetting you,' he interrupted.

I pulled the parcel out of my bag, hoping the sight of it would transmit whatever I should be saying.

'And then I made it worse with the gift,' he said. 'I just couldn't bear you thinking that's all it was, that I'd been working my way up to some awful, clumsy move when your visits were so important to me.'

'Frédéric, I didn't think that at all. And for what it's worth, it wasn't a clumsy move,' I smiled, embarrassed, and so did he and this was a much better kind of awkward, knowing we'd both thought about it. 'Your letter was beautiful and so is this.' I looked into those green eyes, which diverted to the box containing the perfume bottle. 'I did want to return the old letter, but that didn't keep me coming back – you did. There was no disappointment to make up for.' I slid the box across the table towards him. 'Quite the opposite.'

He looked at me questioningly.

'I must have given off mixed signals, based on how confused I felt. These last few months I've been blundering around my life like someone blindfolded.'

'You spent so long listening to me and you never said. Grief has made me very self-centred.'

'This was an escape from everything going on. My

children had left home, my marriage was on the rocks. I felt old, useless, disconnected from everything and everyone until I started coming here. I couldn't even make perfume any more. We were both lonely, both in a bad way – we helped each other through it, a random guy in a shop and a random woman off the street.'

'This almost deserves a place in the ledger.'

'Listening to you made me realise I couldn't see my future until I'd faced up to the past – I'd never met the right person to talk to about that. I've hurt people and they've hurt me. I haven't grieved my mother. Not just her death; the hole she left when she said she never wanted to see me again. I couldn't face the risk of her rejecting me.' I wept, unashamedly. The emotional turbine I'd been trapped in for so long was slowing, preparing to spit me out.

Frédéric put his arm around me and pulled me to him. It was the first time we'd touched without jumping clear of a flame. He let me cry. I didn't apologise. 'Are you okay?' he said.

'Yes. More than I've been in a long time.'

'Are things going better with your husband?'

'Yes. We're getting divorced.' His eyebrows shot up. 'It's been a long time coming. I think we'll get on better when we're not married. That will make it easier for the children. Have your friends persuaded you to go back to Lyon?'

'Yes, it looks like there might be a job for me there.'

Suzanne would be wondering where I'd got to. 'By the way, a perfumer friend from Grasse looked at this flacon the other day. We both think it might be one of Coty's original twelve and if so, it's worth a lot of money. The metal tag was missing but we found it in the box.'

'I still want you to have it.'

'Even if it makes me sad?'

'Why's that?'

'Because we're never going to see each other again.' He didn't contradict me. 'And to use your words, I'm going to *miss you terribly.*'

He didn't need to repeat it.

'The small items have already been collected. Sell the bottle, give it away, it's yours to do with as you wish, but don't refuse my gift, Clémentine. Is that really how you want us to say goodbye?'

I put it back in my bag and we stood up to embrace. His hair had dried. I buried my face against him to breathe in every atom, deeply. Life comes to a lot of wrong conclusions. It was a moment outside time, outside the ordinary, suspended between two realities. The moment known as now.

Chapter 46

'So this really *is* your place. It's the first time I've ever seen where you live, then or now.'

'Oh,' I said. 'I suppose it is.' Racha was wearing a dark green dress with a black belt. She'd put on make-up and her hair was coiled up. 'You look beautiful.'

'Thank you. I'm glad I made an effort. I just met your husband in the courtyard, with his rackets.'

'To speak to?'

'Yes. I forgot which staircase you'd said. He introduced himself. I already knew who he was. He was charming. No,' she corrected herself. '*Charming* sounds insincere. He was kind. Nothing like I imagined.'

'He knew you were coming.'

'You didn't *tell* him anything, did you?'

I knew she was teasing but I felt oddly ill at ease. '*Arrête*, Racha! No, I didn't. It's a bit of a long story.'

She ran her hand along the kitchen table. 'So this is where you work, like in the magazine,' she said, having already stuck her head into the living room. 'And here's the famous balcony.'

'It's not famous yet. Maybe one day,' I said. There was no knowing what Luciano and Suzanne might come up with. They'd talked out there for hours, bundled up in coats and scarves.

Racha turned her back to the view.

'I wanted to take it all from you. Him. This. Your business, if I could have worked out how.'

My arms flew across my body to stifle a shudder. 'What are you saying?'

'You asked why I came to find you, and didn't we agree to be completely honest?' She didn't offer me a chance to change my mind. 'At the start, hanging around your shop and upsetting Suzanne was just a game. I was working up to my big line, imagining the dread you'd feel when she told you, if you hadn't guessed. It was hard not to laugh.'

I turned away, reminding myself that I had invited her, invited this. Tormenting me wasn't incidental to her goals – it was one of them. What if only the malevolence had been real?

'You're shocked. I understand. It shocks me to hear myself say it.'

My anxiety dropped a notch. 'Carry on,' I said.

'When we finally met again, I decided you deserved any-thing I could inflict on you. You were—'

And then it spiked. '—unpleasant, callous, desperate to get rid of you,' I interrupted. 'Do you think any of this surprises me? I couldn't imagine you having any other motive than to hurt me. But you're not the only one who can put on an act, Racha. Seeing you shook me badly, just not the way you thought.'

Inside their rim of kohl, her eyes softened. Her mouth pulled. 'But I didn't know that then,' she said. 'I waited to see what you would do, now you're in a position to make nasty things go away; if you'd threatened me, reported me for harassment or tried to pay me off like Ludo did, I would have done my best to ruin your wonderful life. I could have written to your husband or blackmailed you, except that with you it was never about money. I could have got the boys from my cousin's estate to mug you in the street or mess up your shop.'

'But you didn't do any of those things.'

'No,' she said. 'And neither did you.'

The timer beeped on the cooker. I picked up an oven glove. Her eyes lit up. 'Is that what I think it is?'

'That's right,' I said, biting back the venomous comments on my tongue. 'And today they're not burnt.'

'Incredible timing, because the chicken satays are exactly when the plan started to fall apart. I hadn't anticipated how it would feel, seeing you. That we'd end up spending time together, talking about personal things, our children, our problems – it hadn't occurred to me that you would have any.'

'It's true, there's not a lot we haven't talked about.'

'I haven't told any lies, but there are things I should have said. I know the aqueduct was an accident, Clémentine – I always did. I haven't spent all these years believing it was your fault or plotting revenge. I've been too busy trying to get by. I was at the end of my tether when I saw you in that magazine,' she pressed her hands against her forehead. 'It felt good to have someone to lash out at. But it shouldn't have been you. Me turning up when I did was the last thing you needed.'

'You're wrong. You haven't lied. I have.'

'When?'

'The other day, when I told you what happened between us back then meant nothing to me. You didn't challenge it and the thought that you believed it has been eating away at me.'

'You know I didn't!'

'I've spent all my years in Paris trying to bury everything from back then and convince myself I'm not that person any more. It scarred me so much and yet everything has been measured against it. I had to look those things in the face, Racha, and I never would have, if you hadn't shown up. You didn't make me who I am, but there's something about you that doesn't leave me any option.' She stroked my hair and I tipped my head into her hand. 'I can't keep holding everyone at a distance. I can't keep thinking anyone who loves me must be wrong. I'm not twenty any more, but I want to feel some of those things again. After I've learned how to be alone.'

'What about Édouard?'

'It's over. There was always too much missing. We went for a walk one evening, and once we'd agreed, we went for a drink to discuss the practicalities.'

Racha laughed. '*Trop bizarre*, the way people do things here. Are you okay?'

'Yes. I really am.'

She looked at the kitchen clock. 'Sorry I can't stay longer but I need my sleep. I've got to be up very early.'

'Why, where are you going?

'Marseille, where else? On the first train. I've got a date with a *belle sénégalaise* next week.'

'That sounds good!'

'She's my orthopaedic surgeon. I'm having a ceramic hip replacement and a new metal femur. It should have been done years ago, but the technology's moved on. I'll be able to walk much better. I've cancelled twice and she called me herself the other day. She knows how scared I am but she said, *Madame Benassoun, if you don't show up this time, I'm going to come and fetch you myself.*'

'I'm so glad something can be done. How will you manage afterwards?'

'I'm going to stay with my youngest sister. I want to be on form for when Tariq gets out. He's been asking for me.'

I went to hug her. 'That's the best reason you could have to go home.'

'Maybe you could come and see me after the operation.'

'I will. It's about time I went back. And Racha,' I just had to come out with it. 'If we can do anything for Tariq ... Édouard knows a lot of lawyers. It was Bastien's idea.'

'Well, anything for our sons ...' Racha wound a long orange scarf around her neck three or four times. Her scent would fill the air long after she had left. She put her hands on my shoulders and looked at me with the tenderness of a mother, a sister, a lover, a friend. 'This is all I want from you. No more than this.'

We found you, Clémentine.

Acknowledgements

Real life goes on while novels are being written and published and I have so many people to thank for reasons personal, professional and often both.

I'm so grateful to Sarah and Kate Beal for the belief they have shown in my writing by publishing *Scent* and reissuing my debut novel, *Paris Mon Amour*. I love their vision and approach to independent publishing and it's a joy to be part of it. Thanks to designer Jamie Keenan for the beautiful cover, to my tireless publicist Fiona Brownlee, and to Kate Quarry and Laura Mcfarlane for their meticulous work on the text.

Four people have played an essential role in the book getting this far: my wonderful agent, Diana Beaumont; Kristin Celms, far away in Minnesota yet so close to everything I write; Voula Tsoflias, whose psychological insights transformed more than just this story, and Matt Bates, the best champion a writer could wish for.

Thanks to Andrew Wille for the game-changing idea of retyping the manuscript from scratch, and to Claire and Chris Atkins for giving me a place to work on my edits during the first lockdown.

Scent is set in two places close to my heart and I would never have written it without the help and hospitality of my French 'family' and friends. *Merci*, Gaëlle de Quelen in Marseille, Roselyne Morello in the Lubéron, Jean Guellec in Paris, Isabelle de Quelen and Armelle Haëntjens. Thanks to Wallis and Lisa Sauvée and Manuel Prothon for the younger generation's take on French life and to Helen Stanton for being my bridge to France in the previously unimaginable year I couldn't set foot there. I miss you all but we'll make up for it!

I am indebted to Emmanuelle Moeglin of the Experimental Perfume Club in London and Stéphanie de Bruijn in Paris for sharing their fragrance expertise and industry experience (the artistic licence is all mine). Many revealing conversations fed into this book, and for that I thank those who talked to me about Marseille's *quartiers nord* in the nineties, my therapist and my podiatrist for enabling me to see the world through different lenses, and those who opened up about very personal things and listened to me in return. My characters owe you and so do I.

The support and encouragement I've received from countless people over the years has been both touching and motivating, from members of the writing community, my extended family, my book group and friends from every stage and place in my life. The same is true of the readers, bloggers, reviewers, my Twitter followers and everyone who reads the Literary Sofa blog – this is my chance to say how much I appreciate it.

Love and thanks always to JC for support and understanding of the 'above and beyond' variety, and to our two fine sons, just for being themselves.